"Deidre Knight has cr.... ...g .... .. g...s, demons, and immortal warriors. Her heroine, Shay Angel, is both strong and sympathetic, a woman discovering powers she never knew she had. Legendary Spartan Ajax is handsome, seductive, and haunted—a hero to inspire delicious dreams. I can't wait for more!"
—Angela Knight, *New York Times* bestselling author

Praise for *Parallel Desire*

"Riveting."   —*Romantic Times*

"Twists, turns . . . and scintillating romance."
—ParaNormal Romance

"[A] wonderful book . . . [an] outstanding series."
—*Affaire de Coeur*

Praise for *Parallel Seduction*

"You can always count on Knight to take an intriguing plot and bend it like a pretzel. This fascinating series is extremely intricate with its competing time lines and complex character growth. There's never a dull moment in this terrific series!"   —*Romantic Times*

"Deep emotion, fast-paced action, characters who come alive, and a plot full of surprises . . . one of 2007's can't-miss reads!"   —Romance Reviews Today

continued . . .

Praise for *Parallel Heat*

"Powerfully sensual and mind-blowing ... a hot romance ... a great paranormal."
—Romance: B(u)y the Book

"Once again Knight explodes with another compelling page-turner that is a must-read for fans she hooked with her debut, *Parallel Attraction*.... One heck of a riveting, sensual ride." —The Best Reviews

"Deidre Knight once again hits all the right notes.... The realistic dialogue, fascinating characters, and flexible time all contribute to making this a riveting novel and a must-read." —Romance Reviews Today

"A story with an intelligent and complex spin ... a combination of fine characterizations, great pacing, action-packed plotting, and a truly imaginative take on the dizzying intricacies of alternate realities."—BookLoons

"A real page-turner ... the twists and turns keep coming until the last page." —Once Upon a Romance Reviews

"Knight's unique perspective and clever plotting make this story and this series something to savor!"
—*Romantic Times*

Praise for *Parallel Attraction*

"A fantastic and riveting new voice in paranormal fiction."
—Karen Marie Moning,
New York Times bestselling author

Red Fire

A GODS OF MIDNIGHT NOVEL

DEIDRE KNIGHT

A SIGNET ECLIPSE BOOK

SIGNET ECLIPSE
Published by New American Library, a division of
Penguin Group (USA) Inc., 375 Hudson Street,
New York, New York 10014, USA
Penguin Group (Canada), 90 Eglinton Avenue East, Suite 700, Toronto,
Ontario M4P 2Y3, Canada (a division of Pearson Penguin Canada Inc.)
Penguin Books Ltd., 80 Strand, London WC2R 0RL, England
Penguin Ireland, 25 St. Stephen's Green, Dublin 2,
Ireland (a division of Penguin Books Ltd.)
Penguin Group (Australia), 250 Camberwell Road, Camberwell, Victoria 3124,
Australia (a division of Pearson Australia Group Pty. Ltd.)
Penguin Books India Pvt. Ltd., 11 Community Centre, Panchsheel Park,
New Delhi - 110 017, India
Penguin Group (NZ), 67 Apollo Drive, Rosedale, North Shore 0632,
New Zealand (a division of Pearson New Zealand Ltd.)
Penguin Books (South Africa) (Pty.) Ltd., 24 Sturdee Avenue,
Rosebank, Johannesburg 2196, South Africa

Penguin Books Ltd., Registered Offices:
80 Strand, London WC2R 0RL, England

First published by Signet Eclipse, an imprint of New American Library,
a division of Penguin Group (USA) Inc.

First Printing, October 2008
10 9 8 7 6 5 4 3 2 1

PUBLISHER'S NOTE
This is a work of fiction. Names, characters, places, and incidents either are the
product of the author's imagination or are used fictitiously, and any resemblance
to actual persons, living or dead, business establishments, events, or locales is
entirely coincidental.

The publisher does not have any control over and does not assume any re-
sponsibility for author or third-party Web sites or their content.

*Dedicated to Anne Bohner and Claire Zion
for treating this book of my heart with such love
and care. Ladies, thank you for believing
in me and this series!*

Acknowledgments

As always, there are far too many people than I can possibly thank in this small space, and of course there is always the possibility that I might overlook someone. So apologies in advance if I do.

Big hugs and megathanks to so many friends, family, and colleagues, all of whom have done one or all of the following: nurtured me, answered questions, sent cyberhugs, prayed for my sanity, promised me a nap, read my pages, reread my pages, sent me funny voice notes, taught me about Greek culture, helped with research, made me smile and giggle, reminded me that chocolate isn't on my diet and that McDonald's is a curse word ... you get the picture. I have a fabulous network of people in my life, all of whom give to me and uplift me in their own unique manner.

In no particular order, my huge appreciation goes out to: Judson Knight, Tyler Knight, Riley Knight (go Knight family!), Angela Zoltners, Rae Monet, Steven Pressfield, Kim Acres, Brian Stark, Christina White, Louisa Edwards White, Pamela Harty, Shauna von Hanstein, Marty Barnes, Christina Dodd, Gena Showalter, Angela Knight, Maureen Wood, Jessica Andersen, and Cindy Miles.

Lots of gratitude and humble thanks to my amazing NAL team: Anne Bohner, Kara Welsh, Claire Zion, Liza Schwartz, and everyone else there who has given me such incredible support. Bless every one of you!

At the Knight Agency, I bow before every one of my wonderful friends and coworkers: Pamela Harty (agent extraordinaire!), Elaine Spencer, Nephele Tempest,

Jamie Pritchett—you make every day a joy and a pleasure. Thanks for all you do for me.

And thanks especially to Sue Grimshaw for her extremely gracious input on the manuscript. You are a gem!

Prologue

More than two thousand, five hundred years ago, there was a land where the bravest, most valiant warriors were hammered like bronze, forged into human weapons by years of rigorous training and sacrifice. These men were noble, heroic, stalwart—they would willingly give their lives for their homeland and face down even the most terrifying enemy. Their home, called Sparta, lay nestled in the rocky heart of ancient Greece; its people were private and plainspoken, their lives austere. The men of Sparta made a life of war, always eager for the next battle.

Then there arose a threat of epic proportions, a Persian force numbering in the hundreds of thousands. The Spartans' Greek neighbors to the north reported that this Persian war machine had trampled entire villages, left forests devastated, the land ravaged and scorched, and that their ranks numbered more than the stars in heaven. Unbeknownst to these mortal soldiers, a much more sinister force stood behind the enemy massacre— the Djinn demons drove the bloodlust and battle, on their own quest to carry darkness into the souls of mankind.

When this invading Persian army came, they seemed invincible. The Greek forces allied themselves against them, but could not restrain their masses. The Greeks were desperate for more time to plan and strategize since it was their only hope of stopping the Persian hordes.

One man, King Leonidas of Sparta, annnounced that he would provide the necessary delay; that he would lead his three hundred most elite officers to make their stand at the narrow spit of land known as the Hot Gates.

Thermopylae.

This pass, an opening wide enough to accommodate only a few men fighting side by side, would be the stage. There Leonidas and the Spartans would bottle up the Persian forces, using the Gates themselves as an advantage to limit the power of the Persians, for only a handful of soldiers could traverse the pass at one time. They would fight to the very last man in order to restrain the Persians for as long as they could—even until the very last Spartan lay dead. These three hundred would give up their lives for Sparta and Greece, for duty and loyalty, for homeland and family. And for a hero's passage to heavenly Elysium.

And so it was that for three sweltering August days this courageous, stubborn king fought alongside his crimson-cloaked warriors. There were no distinctions for Leonidas: all were soldiers, and all would drink from the cup of death as the gods decreed. Beside him, his senior captain, Ajax Petrakos, led charge after charge. Together they blocked the pass, battling with swords, shields, and, eventually, their bare hands.

The king and his captain never relented, never backed down, and on the third day, when the burning sun began to slide behind the mountains that marked the pass, only a few Spartans remained standing. It was then that the final moments came, and one by one these Spartan warriors, inseparable in life, fell together in death. With their passing the battle was lost, but their Spartan duty was fulfilled.

Captain Petrakos was the first to awake facing the River Styx, that boundary between mortal life and the mystery beyond. Next his servant Kassandros materialized beside him, linked in death as they had been in life. One by one, other Spartans appeared out of the mist:

Ajax's brothers, Kalias and Aristos, then Nikos and his fellow warrior Straton. And then, their beloved King Leonidas, battered, broken, and mutilated from battle, but standing tall among their ranks.

Beside the king another being emerged from the mist, one beyond the warriors' imaginings. Before them stood a towering golden god with a proud smile upon his face. It was none other than Ares, the lord of all Spartan soldiers, the god of war.

Ares had come to present an offer, one final choice, as the seven warriors stood at this place between life and death: They could lay down their swords and move on to Elysium and the afterlife that awaited them, or they could turn back to the world, take up their arms once more, and become immortal protectors of mankind— for eternity. They would fight every form of evil that threatened humanity; they would become battlers of demons and fighters of wars; they would serve under Ares, in the name of mankind. With this offer, these warriors could ensure safety for their families, for Sparta, and for the sons and daughters of Sparta for centuries to come. In their immortal form, each man would possess abilities akin to those of the gods. They would be stronger, and in the heat of battle would take the form of hawks, with the flight, lethality, and grace of these warrior birds. They would become dark angels, saviors of the night.

The will of warriors was in their blood and in their souls, and they knew in their hearts that it was a noble quest; but it was a noble quest for a capricious god. No matter what, they would follow King Leonidas to the ends of the earth, would follow him to Hades itself. When they looked into their leader's eyes, they knew his decision had already been made. Their king did not beseech them; the choice lay with each man alone. But these were men born and bred to fight, for the glory of war. Their duty, honor, and love for one another bound the warriors in unspoken agreement. One by one, each of the seven men drank from the River Styx, binding their immortality and their vow.

There was not time for second thoughts and no place for regrets. The seven Spartans, now the immortal protectors of all mankind, turned away from what may have been and bowed down before the voice of war.

Chapter 1

Coffee. Nectar of the gods. Or at least it should be, if Ajax had any say in the matter. Which he clearly didn't.

Strike me down for that, why don't you? he challenged with a glance at the granite sky overhead. *Come on and fight me.*

No arrows or lightning bolts scorched the sidewalk café, and slowly Jax lowered his gaze.

Too bad, he thought with a dark laugh, sipping his coffee. Quite the cure when you are nursing a pounding hangover. Sure, it was a taste that he'd acquired in modern times, this era of coffee shops and triple-mocha everything, but he didn't mind being modern on occasion. In fact, he relished it, much to his brothers' chagrin.

He'd lumbered in heavy armor, worn a cravat when fashion had required it, had even donned a kilt for about a century. So drinking a bit of women's coffee hardly qualified him as an impostor, he rationalized, and took another sip.

You have to live in the era where you find yourself. It was his number one rule, and so far it hadn't misled him on his winding passage through the corridors of time.

The King's Road bustled, shoppers from nearby Sloane Square hurrying home, with countless others making their way back toward the tube. He registered the foot traffic, the creeping chill of twilight that was so common for London in mid-April, the throngs pulsing and pushing their way past his table. And he noted every detail without once glancing up from his copy of the *Evening Standard*. No *Independent* for him. He remained a simple man to the core; it didn't matter if his well-heeled feet now walked hard pavement and not the fields of ancient Greece.

Scanning the paper's headlines, he could hardly focus. There was too much noise coming at him, an overload of sensory detail in every direction. And it wasn't the usual human clamor, like car horns or rap music. No, it was the mental din that hounded Jax year after year, century after century, growing louder every day. Lately he'd been choking on it, nearly drowning beneath the mental voices of London's entire population.

"Stop feeling sorry for yourself."

Kalias. Jax rolled his eyes as his big brother slid into the seat beside him. No invitation was ever necessary for the hulking warrior; he just took what he wanted and possessed every inch of land he walked or occupied.

"You don't know jack about what troubles me," Ajax answered coolly, his clipped British accent sounding particularly nasty. One good reason for having affected it during this recent London venture.

"I know that you've got a job to do, Brother." Kalias's own accent remained unchanged despite almost a century in the British Isles, as ancient and authentic as the Greek blood that pulsed through their veins.

"I know my place, and I do my work." Ajax gazed up at his eldest brother with a cutting glare. It was like staring into a mirror: the olive skin, the long, aquiline nose, the black hair. Except Kalias wore his own hair buzzed short, military-style, while Jax kept his long and loose, free, as he had in the olden days.

Kalias gestured toward the half-consumed cappuccino. "It's five o'clock. Surprised to see that's not Scotch you're drinking."

"I only woke an hour ago," Ajax replied, taking another lazy sip. "Even I have my standards."

His brother leaned closer. "So the only code you're

still clinging to pertains to the satisfaction of your basest desires. Very commendable, Jax."

Ajax rolled his eyes. "Oh, bloody hell. When you put it that way"—he waved to the server, a leggy Polish blonde—"who can resist?" Then, turning to the waitress, he said, "Irish coffee, darling." She smiled back eagerly and he added, "A double, and heavy on the Irish."

Kalias leaned in toward him. "You ignored our king's summoning. Twice."

Leonidas. Their once and future general. Their commander for eternity.

"The Old Man told you that?" Ajax ran a hand through his shoulder-length black hair. Silky as midnight, that was how his most recent lover had described it. They'd spent hours in that well-appointed Mayfair hotel room having sweaty, wall-bumping sex. Once done, she'd called him a god—and he'd answered by swiping a hand across her face, clearing every memory of the dark event from her mind.

He kept his gaze down, avoiding his brother's blazing, angry one. If Kalias knew that he'd taken to sleeping with mortal women in his warrior form, oh, there'd be hell to pay—and straight to Hades he'd go, no doubt about that.

And then there was the matter of Ares. Always out there, hovering on his eternal horizon like a sky full of enemy arrows.

Kalias clasped his shoulder. "So, baby brother, don't you want to know what Leonidas asks of you?"

"An assignment, no doubt."

"Not just any assignment." Kalias settled back in his chair, sipping from Jax's own glass of water without permission. "The Oracle calls you."

"Bollocks to that woman and her scheming." Ajax muttered a few choice vulgarities, thinking of the hidden prophetess and her affection for him. Too bad he liked her so damned much—and called her a friend.

He had known her, literally, for thousands of years. Back when the Spartans were originally transformed at the River Styx, the young, black-haired beauty had been assigned to the warriors as their guide. She was the Oracle of Delphi, the youngest and purest prophetess of Apollo's Oracles. Her prophecies assisted them in all their missions, but only Ajax was able to hear or see her.

"Something dire is afoot, or she wouldn't be asking for you." Kalias scrubbed a palm over his spiking hair.

"Did you tell her I'd retired from the game?"

Kalias flashed him an impatient glance. "Since you're the only one who can hear the Oracle, no, I did not tell her that you're on unofficial—and unauthorized, I might add—leave."

"Well, if I stay gone a bit longer, perhaps she'll cozy right up to you, Brother. She's quite the looker; trust me on that."

She had often determined how they drew their strength, their very life source, with her vague predictions. The supernatural law that she would be their guide in all things had never made sense, not from the beginning of their pledge more than twenty centuries ago. Still, immortal vows were lasting vows, and that had been one of Ares' rules at the outset of their agreement.

Kalias eyed him hard for a long moment, then continued in ancient Greek: "Her words maintain our warrior unity, give us needed direction. Perhaps I should mention Thermopylae ... Gettysburg ... Berlin ... Omaha Beach. Do you want me to go on?"

"Names, nothing more."

"Oh, keep telling yourself that. But we share the same memories of battles waged. Of comrades lost." Kalias sighed, his eyes filling with dark recollections. "If you won't answer our Oracle, and you refuse our king's summons, then try this on for size, little brother," he said, dropping back into English. "You do remember the name Shayanna Angel?"

"Shay," Ajax corrected hoarsely, his entire body jolting in reaction to the familiar name. Along his back, a compulsive sensation began, a ripple of power. That itchy-fingered probing of his true nature. "She goes by Shay." The burning in his shoulders spread, began to tear across his spine, threatening to burst forth from beneath his skin.

"Calm down," his brother cautioned, apparently seeing his darker temperament expose itself.

Ajax nodded, swallowing, and surreptitiously slid his palm over the center of his tailored slacks, where a swelling hard-on had quickly formed. It was impossible to think of Shay Angel and not feel that kind of achy, thick need—and he'd never met her or even glimpsed her. In fact, her name was just one out of many. But what the Oracle had said of the woman was far more than a simple name, and whenever he recalled the prophecy about what the promised human would mean to him, he couldn't help but react—physically and otherwise.

"You shouldn't talk to me about Shay out here on the street—you know better."

"I'd have figured that more than two thousand years would be plenty of time for you to master your other nature."

"Not when it comes to that little minx of a mortal." Ajax groaned, shifting in his chair.

"You have no idea who she even is." Eyebrows like winged midnight furrowed, Kalias's fury barely contained. "So I shall repeat—calm down."

Ajax blew out a breath, drew another. He crossed one expensive Italian loafer over his knee, watched a black taxi drive by. At last he observed, "You're right. This isn't about some murky future that was once foretold to me; it's about my duties."

"Well, I'm glad you concur with me, little brother." Kalias leaned back in his chair, toying with a Zippo lighter that he'd retrieved from his hip pocket.

"Why must you do that? Honestly?"

"Do what?" His brother extended the lighter questioningly, his face a mask of pure innocence.

"Not the lighter, you bastard. Why must you remind me—constantly, I might add—of our birth order?"

"Perhaps because it is my only means of containing you." Kalias's mouth turned up at the corners in a subtle grin of triumph.

"You won't *ever* contain me," Ajax shot back, staring at the darkening sky overhead. A perfect evening for flight, for soaring above the clouds, banking like the bird of prey that he was. If this conversation didn't right itself, then he would take matters into his own hands—or wings, as the case would be. He would shape-shift and leave his obnoxious and condescending eldest brother here on the street and rise to the very heavens.

"When our king requires your presence, Ajax, you comply. Immortality doesn't grant you the privilege of impudence, not with Leonidas."

"And with you?"

His brother fixed his attention on the Zippo, flicking it open and closed. "I'm not sure you ever respected me."

"Oh, please," Jax snarled. "Save the sorry guilt trips for Aristos. At least he still buys them occasionally."

Ari kept himself positioned between the two of them like the rocky pass that had once determined their battle at the Hot Gates. Their middle brother's way was always peaceful, like a trench drawn between two enemy sides.

Kalias glanced at the busy street, seeming to gather his thoughts. When he turned back to face Ajax, his expression was naked, open. "I don't understand what happened to you over these many centuries. What went wrong? You were our strongest. Our bravest. The very best of us."

Something savage broke loose inside of Ajax, the millennia peeling away as if time had never existed. He lunged forward, grabbing his brother's shirt sleeve. " 'May eternity's arms hold you,' " he pronounced coldly, repeating Ares' words from that August day so long ago. "It was a curse, not a blessing, dear brother. We're no better off than the slaves we once kept."

Kalias made a grunting sound of disapproval, but Ajax blustered on. "Haven't you ever looked at yourself in the mirror while transformed? At the blackness of your wings? At your raptor's hands, the twisting talons? We are Ares' own vile playthings, Kalias, and I am done—done dancing to his battle calls."

That was why he focused on the sex, the lusty, driven need to bed human women in his transformed body. It made him feel less dirty, less abominable. That they could worship his wings, caress his curling claws—well, it was the only redemption he knew anymore. Unless he nurtured the name of his supposed and future beloved—Shay Angel. He'd never sought her out, never tried to discern which century she might live in. That it might be this current epoch, well, it wasn't something he was ready to entertain. And yet . . .

"At Thermopylae, no one wanted to win more than you did; no man possessed a greater thirst for victory," his brother pressed. "What happened to the warrior who helped beat back four hundred thousand Persians in just three days?" Kalias shook his head. "You have the greatest calling—the most important one. You can drink yourself into oblivion, *little brother*, but your destiny won't be denied."

"It's not a destiny," Ajax answered grimly. "It was a vow."

For the first time during the conversation, Kalias beamed, his voice becoming softer. "And shall I remind you that you have always been a man of your word?"

And to that, well, there wasn't a damned thing that Ajax could possibly say in rebuttal.

"As I thought," Kalias finally murmured. "So, you will answer Leonidas's summoning. You will visit our Oracle and learn what words she has for us, the Spartan cadre."

"So why mention Shay Angel now?" Ajax persisted. "And why would the Oracle and the gods themselves have deemed her my mate? Whatever time she exists in, that's what this entire conversation is really about. We both know it."

Kalias's expression transformed, morphing into a satisfied, if not devious grin. "That much is simple. Because"—

he leaned much closer—"she's the only one who might guide you back from this eternal abyss that threatens to destroy you. If only you should finally meet her."

Jax left Kalias sitting in the sidewalk café with a quickly muttered, "I'll do it," and excused himself. Now, standing in the men's restroom, he carefully tugged his cashmere sweater over his head—the last thing he wanted was to shred one of his favorite pieces of clothing when his wings unfurled. Tying the sleeves about his waist, he hoped for the best. Traveling the heavens in his Bond Street finest wasn't his idea of great timing, but it was better just to get the visit to King Leo over and done with. *Talisao,* he thought, brushing nonexistent dirt off his hands. *Finished.*

With a final tug on the ivory sweater's sleeves—and a last check of the restroom door's lock—Jax stood back and gathered his energy. He folded his hands over his bare chest, let his eyes drift shut, and allowed the transformation to begin. Sometimes fast, sometimes a slow burn, the transition always started with a tingling sensation along his spine. Physically, it was one part pure ecstasy, another sharp pain, yet he never felt more whole than at this precise moment.

Pretty bloody ironic, he thought, as the first feather began to pierce through his warm skin. For someone who despised his calling as a warrior protector, didn't it just blast all that he loved to shape-shift so damned much?

Despite his complaining to Kalias earlier, he could hardly imagine life without his true nature. He was a hawk. A guardian. A midnight angel of sorts, charged with one thing: to watch mankind and protect it from the powers of darkness and aggression. Yeah, destiny was one son of a bitch. As if in answer, his wings began to break through, the rustling sound of feathers quietly announcing that his change was accelerating, overtaking his human body. Supernatural essence was replacing his everyday guise of mortal man.

He braced both hands against the rim of the sink. Hunching forward, he gasped and, meeting his own gaze in the mirror, watched his dark eyes turn silver. Felt the blaze between his shoulder blades intensify.

Briefly he thought of his servant and friend, River Kassandros. The two of them had been specially linked for warfare by Ares on that long-ago day. Unlike the other warriors who drank from the River Styx, Kassandros was fully submerged into the fiery waters and, transformed into a gleaming silver sword, made to serve Ajax in immortality as he had in life. Ares had proclaimed him the greatest weapon he ever created.

From the moment thousands of years past, the warrior had been called River because he was forged in the flowing waters of the Styx itself. He could shift from his human form to that of any weapon that Ajax required, and in that mode River would contain a powerful ability to kill, but if necessary, also to heal.

Ajax's right hand clenched as he recalled the feel of River in his grasp, their easy union whenever his servant was transformed into the blazing silver sword that was his preferred weapon whenever Ajax summoned him. It had been nearly a year since he'd called forth River for battle; he wondered if his powerful friend had felt useless during these months of Ajax's own rebellion. The thought brought an avalanche of guilt with it. He had abandoned and let down every one of his six fellow immortals in the past year—especially in the past few months.

With a growl, he shook off the heavy remorse. "I am Spartan," he murmured under his breath. "There is no pain. I do not succumb to human weakness."

As if in answer to the firm assertions, his wings surged forth in a powerful display, black feathers spreading wide behind him. Beyond the restroom door he could hear the clank of plates and silverware. Dozens of humans were taking their supper, having their wine. But for Jax, there was no escaping his fate: He was a winged hawk protector, duty-bound to serve mankind. To protect them above all else; to stand down the evil forces that forever whispered in the darkness. This had been his one true calling since the day he'd bound himself to Ares.

What a shame that his freedom was also his bondage: that to be truly liberated meant he was a slave for all time.

Chapter 2

She was being eaten alive, one choice bite at a time. The creatures were crowding her, crawling up her arms and legs, beneath her skirt, along her neckline. Eaten. Alive.

It was absolutely the wrong thing for Shay to focus on during the funeral, but there you had it. The rain did nothing to stop the mosquitoes' vicious advance, either. They didn't care that her mother was dead, that tears streaked her face. That life as she knew it had ended with one phone call less than seventy hours earlier. The live oaks about them seemed to bend a little lower, their Spanish moss swaying in the gusts of rainy wind. As if they were weeping along with her and her family.

She slapped at first one arm, then the other, trying to drive the insects' advance backward. No dice. Beside her, Jamie turned and gave her the evil eye, raising his eyebrows.

Yeah, well, Jamie didn't have the same body chemistry that she did. The little fuckers never bothered him or their brother Mason, who stood on her other side, oblivious to their silent interchange. He just watched the minister, his eyes glazed over with that familiar thousand-yard stare—the same one he'd brought back from Iraq four months earlier.

She couldn't think about Mason. Or Jamie. Or even her mother, whose grave yawned before her, a cavernous opening that made her skin prickle and crawl. How was it possible that they would bury Mama beneath mounds of dirt, heaping piles of it, and leave her to sleep in this dreadful place all by herself? And who the hell had ever called Bonaventure Cemetery peaceful? That was tourist talk. When it was your own mother being lowered into the dark, dank earth, there wasn't a damn peaceful thing about it.

Her skin erupted in welting bites, at least half a dozen new ones along her right thigh. As if the lecherous insects had gnawed their way through the fabric of her skirt and were mainlining from her bloodstream. As if demons had assumed the mosquitoes' minuscule forms in order to torture her. And maybe they had, she thought, with an uneasy glance about Bonaventure. Suddenly chilled, she huddled a little more closely beneath her black umbrella, watching the rain drip off the spokes with heavy droplets. Like tears, she thought, her own eyes joining in the watery swell yet again.

One call, one moment when everything had been perfectly normal, then shattered into a thousand shards of glass. She'd been practicing with her band, the Horde, when she'd happened to look down and notice that she had a voice mail on her cell. She'd ignored it as they launched into a sixth run-through of their latest song, "When Hell Strikes Twice." Three minutes later she'd set her drumsticks aside and looked down to see that she'd accumulated four more voice mails. "Better check these," she'd told the gang.

"Call me back. Right away," had been Jamie's message, his voice choked and hoarse. With shaking hands, she'd exited the warehouse already dialing the phone. Their mother was dead, he'd told her. Massive heart attack. Gone before she'd even reached the hospital.

"And so the dead meet the dead," the minister droned on. "From dust to dust . . ." She covered her left ear with her free hand, staring at the puke green Astroturf beneath her feet. She didn't want to think about the dead, or that her mother was among them now. She didn't want to think about anything, not mosquitoes or the moss-covered angel that marked their plot. That hulking statue was nothing more than some ancestor's idea of a joke, erecting a stone angel to guard the Angel family burial ground. The passage of time had even given the sculpture a tearstained cheek—or at least the appearance of one.

She slapped her own cheek, zinging one of the bloodsuckers really good. Thing was, battling mosquitoes was a heck of a lot easier than admitting her mother was gone. Or that now, at age twenty-seven, she was officially an orphan.

Bound on either side by her brothers, and staring at the open grave once again, she realized that she'd never felt so alone in all her life.

Jamie nudged her on the elbow. With a nod toward the graveside, he cued her. *Right.* This was the big moment, the one she'd been dreading all day, but who was she to deny Mama anything that she'd specifically requested? Especially here at the end.

If only she were convinced that Joanna Angel had truly *been* her birth mother, or that Daddy, buried in the plot beside Mama's open one, had been her natural father, too. The letter in her pocket put doubt to everything she'd ever known, especially when it came to family. Dirk and Joanna Angel had raised her from birth, but maybe they'd just been a pair of strangers who had taken her in twenty-seven years earlier.

The minister introduced her. "And now Joanna's daughter, Shayanna, will sing one of her mother's favorite hymns."

Shay took a few careful steps forward, her high heels stabbing into the sodden Astroturf. For a moment she almost lost her balance when her shoe staked deep into the fake grass, sinking even deeper into the damp earth below.

Jamie was at her side instantly, steadying her. "Go ahead, Sissy Cat." He nodded his approval; she gripped the umbrella and bowed her head.

With a deep breath, she began a slow, melancholy

version of "A Mighty Fortress Is Our God", a classic
Protestant hymn. Perfect for any funeral, especially
this one—no wonder her mother had earmarked it in
advance for the occasion. The first note rolled forth
from within her, but when her voice faltered slightly, she
tensed up, afraid that she'd never get through the solo.
There was no backing down; this was for Mama.

She hesitated, closing her eyes, and dove full-force
into the song. It folded its arms about her, soothing
her the way music always did. Swaying slightly, she was
aware of the hush about her, the loud pounding of rain
on the umbrella—and that every family member and
friend held their breath.

" 'And though this world, with devils filled, should
threaten to undo us,' " she sang, " 'we will not fear, for
God hath willed his truth to triumph through us. . . .' "

Her eyes fluttered open at that precise moment, and
she gasped, the song momentarily lost. On the far side
of the cemetery, a knot of demons was massing. They
were little more than a dark cloud at first, an absence of
life, a vacuum. But then their forms took shape, materializing. Threatening . . . her. No, not just her; they were
here to torment her entire family, gathered as they were
at the graveside. They might even be planning to attack
and feast upon all the mourners—right now, during
the funeral—as the ultimate desecration of her family's
name.

Or maybe they would simply do what demons often
craved most of all: sweep through the humans and cause
despair, agony, loneliness. Slip inside the weaker ones
and possess them for a few raucous hours. Shay gasped,
glancing back at the minister and her family. Everyone
stood, waiting for her to resume the song.

Panicked and empowered by her own adrenaline,
she turned to Jamie, then Mason, leading them with her
gaze toward the gathering creatures. Her brothers only
stared back at her, glancing around the cemetery, obviously seeing nothing unusual. Or demonic.

Why can't you see them? she wanted to scream, aware

that she was supposed to be singing the hymn. Jamie nodded again, urging her onward. The questioning expression on his face asked one thing: *Can you do this, Sis?*

She'd be damned if a nasty group of demons forced her to forfeit what her mother had requested. *Sing, girl, sing,* she coached herself. *Ignore them; fight them. Fight for your mama's memory, and for all that the Angel family has lost to demonkind throughout the years.*

Swallowing, choking back the fear that gripped her very soul, she glanced among the gathered mourners. They averted their eyes, obviously embarrassed that she was tanking in her funeral song. That only made her angry; of all times for the demons to come circling around her family. Did they not possess even the basest kind of manners? She looked back at the small horde, and the largest of them lifted a bony, accusing finger. Even across the distance that separated them, she heard the creature rasp, "You're next."

Like hell I am, pal, she thought, glaring back in silent aggression.

Her fury filled her, empowering her with fighting strength; she could battle the dark entities just by singing her hymn. That was the power of God's holy praise, the power to slay the blackest and evilest of creatures. Feeling a rush of spiritual strength, she launched into the rest of the refrain. She kept her gaze riveted on the demons in accusation—in the pure challenge of a demon huntress. Her singing voice would be a bony finger pointed back at them in an accusation of her own.

" 'We will not fear, for God hath willed his truth to triumph through us.' " The words blazed forth from inside of her, growing louder. " 'The Prince of Darkness grim, we tremble not for him,' " she trumpeted. At that precise moment, the ugliest of the gathering horde—clearly their leader—turned to glare at her. His hard, beetlelike wings began beating in fury, and he took faltering steps backward, limbs disjointed and ungainly. Insectlike. He staggered, stumbling; his power was obviously fading, at least for this moment. The hymn and its spiritual words were like a weapon in her hands. No demon could stand when a huntress sang praise to the highest God.

Smiling—a dark, knowing smile—she nearly shouted the rest of the refrain. " 'His rage we can endure, for lo, his doom is sure; one little word shall fell him.' "

As she bowed her head, she watched the demons vanish from the cemetery like black dust—and knew that her brothers, supposedly her own relatives by blood—had never seen a thing.

Ajax paced the great hall, rubbing his arms against the draft, a wind that seemed to edge in from every crevice of Leonidas's ancient castle. The damp cold of the moors beat at the structure's windowpanes, just as it had whipped against his body during the flight out here to the far reaches of Cornwall. Still, whenever the wind filled his wings, he was exhilarated. The cold hardly mattered. It penetrated his senses only later, like now, when he was earthbound once again.

Raking a hand through his long hair, he sleeked it into a ponytail. The old man was nowhere to be found, but the fire roaring in the hearth told him that his king couldn't be far away. Probably polishing up his shield or drinking blood soup—once the mainstay of their Spartan diet. Nothing ever changed for Leo; he was frozen in time, exactly the same king and leader he'd been the day they'd all died at the Hot Gates. Died and been brought back to life by Ares, that was.

From the corner of his eye the sweep of a crimson cloak appeared—then just as quickly shimmered and vanished. Jax turned to discover his king studying him from the arching stone doorway, his ancient image replaced by a much more modern one. The scarlet cloak was Leonidas's supernatural precursor; like a ghost, it was caught only in sideways glimpses. That slight shadow whenever he entered a room or even, sometimes, when they just mentioned his name. Leonidas hadn't actually worn the Spartan cloak in more than a thousand years. But it was burned into his being, was more a part of him than the burnished shields they still carried into battle or the eight-foot spears they used to destroy demonic enemies.

"My lord," Jax murmured, dropping to one knee, reverent.

Leonidas waved him to his feet, brushing past him. Dressed in a simple black tee and matching military fatigues, the warrior made a fierce impression. "And here he is," his commander announced quietly. "Precisely one month and eight days late. I hope the bender was a good one."

Oh, bloody hell. Suddenly Jax's decision to blow off the big guy's recent summonings didn't seem like such a grand idea. He didn't reply— no reasonable answer was to be had—just clamped his idiot's mouth shut and kept it that way.

Leonidas's dark eyes narrowed on him. The moments spread out between them like the beating of massive hawk wings, and neither said a word: Jax because he didn't dare to open his mouth; the king because he was measuring Ajax with silence. Why was it that, miles away in London, it was so easy to forget how incredibly intimidating Leonidas could be?

Maybe because he was also Jax's dearest friend. Maybe because he was a naturally quiet man. Maybe because—*ah, bloody hell*—sometimes Jax forgot the Spartan wasn't actually his brother by birth. Ari and Kalias had to put up with Jax's temper. But not Leonidas, who wielded more than enough power in his little finger to send Jax straight to Ares for a reckoning, if he chose to do so.

The endless silence was measured by the heavy ticking of a marine clock on the mantel. It had been a gift from Jax to Leonidas about one hundred and fifty years earlier. Simple, in a mahogany box, it had seemed a proper timepiece for their Spartan lord. Now, the rhythm of its metronome verged on near-deafening proportions. He'd stood down thousands of enemies, and the silence hadn't burrowed up under his skin, not like this.

One stolen glance at Leonidas. And damn it all, but the bastard was grinning. A sly half smile that basically said, *I have your number, you lazy fool.*

"I should've come when I was summoned. I absolutely should have done so," Jax blurted apologetically. "Forgive me, my lord." He inclined his head. "It shan't happen again."

"Oh, bugger that." The king snorted. "Of course it will. Time and time again; we both know it."

"I will endeavor to serve you more honorably in the future," Jax pressed, intentionally assuming a more formal speech pattern. Working to sound more civilized than he generally felt—or behaved.

The thing was, this wasn't groveling. It was a profound respect that grew out of one plain fact: King Leonidas could still wipe the floor with *all* their collective arses—without so much as breaking a sweat. It didn't matter that he was the eldest among their cadre of seven.

The warm smile faded on the king's lips. "I trust that the time off . . . was"—his voice grew even quieter—"shall we say, worth it."

All at once, Ajax was just out of the Agoge training school, barely more than eighteen. The man before him was leader of all the Spartan military—just as quiet and equally as awe-inspiring. No matter how far back you stood in the ranks.

Double damn, Jax cursed mentally, holding his tongue as Leonidas planted one combat-booted foot on the hearth. The Spartan stared into the roaring flames, both hands gripping the mantel. The emotions on his scarred face were difficult to read, but seemed to waver somewhere between concern and anger.

When he spoke again, however, Leonidas's words were gentle. "You've stayed gone quite a while this time, Ajax. Longer than ever before. Have you turned away from your old king?"

Jax winced as if he'd been slapped. "Never, my lord," he promised in a rush of breath. They worshiped the ruler, all of them. In some ways Ajax adored him most

of all—they'd been more than just king and elite guard
years before. Even more than dear friends; they'd been
brothers in every adoptive sense of the word. Jax had
even married one of the ruler's distant cousins, Leonidas standing beside him at the wedding.

The king lifted an eyebrow. "Never turn away? Or
never consider me an *old man*?" A smile played at the
edges of Leonidas's mouth, the scar that slashed through
his lower lip causing his face to assume an unintentional
leer. "That *is* what you call me behind my back, no?"

Busted, Ajax thought. "Term of endearment, my king."
He tried his damnedest to laugh.

"Of course." Leonidas dropped his hands away from
the mantel, and turned to face him. "And what are *you*
now? Thirty-one years past twenty-five hundred or so?"

Leonidas gestured toward one of the large leather
wing-backs positioned by the fire. Jax took the seat, muttering, "Leave it to you to keep count."

The king gave him a rugged smile, dropping heavily into the chair beside Jax's. "And you've got another
birthday next month."

Jax grinned back. "Rub it in. Rub. It. In. So long as
you remember that you'll always have four years on me,
Old Man."

"I'd offer you a glass of wine, but it's clear that you've
already had"—Leonidas leaned forward in his chair,
sniffing Jax's breath—"plenty of alcohol tonight."

"Oh, for all the gods' sakes. One Irish coffee is not
plenty of booze." Not by a long shot. "Just because you
still take your wine cut with water doesn't mean I have
to."

"It must be coming out of your pores, then." Leonidas
chuckled softly, and reached for a large bowl of wine
that rested on the table between them. "Here." He extended the ancient Spartan vessel. "Drink up. I know
you want it."

"I know you want it?" By the gods, did he really seem
that far gone?

"Thank you," he said, and accepted the bowl of wine,

tilting it upward just as he had in the old days at the common dining messes. They'd all shared wine together—wine and food on a nightly basis. Nothing had ever been done alone, which made Jax's recent isolation from their small corps all the more significant. Leonidas knew it, as well. No wonder he was extending the shared bowl.

The taste of the aged bronze against his lips peeled back the millennia, made him crave the simpler times. He tilted it farther back, nearly draining it—not even giving a damn that the wine had been blended with water. The liquid tasted like home; that one simple drink, and he was back in Greece once again. His eyes prickled, and he finished off the dregs.

"Now look into the bottom of the bowl," Leonidas said when Jax offered it back to him.

Not this. Anything but this. Blasted Leo and his *gift*.

"Not tonight, my lord." *Please.*

"Gaze into it, Ajax," he commanded, his voice thick with emotion. "Do it . . . now."

Jax winced, pressing his eyes shut. He couldn't deny a direct order from his leader, and the blessed Spartan knew it. With a quick intake of breath, and a prayer to Olympus, he opened his eyes. He stared into his lap, where the empty vessel rested, cradled against his knees.

At first nothing happened; no visions entered his mind. Then, slowly, a mighty wind began. The wind grew, building, whipping his long hair; his mouth went dry, grew rubbery, and his tongue seemed to stick to the roof of his mouth. When he tried to raise his gaze from the bowl's hollow depths, he couldn't, was frozen. And then everything grew quiet—eerily hushed and stilled.

Right before the very universe itself split open.

She stood on a hillside, the black sweep of her hair flowing in the breeze, and instinctively Ajax knew it was her: Shayanna. With a quick glance, he knew precisely where they were: overlooking his beloved Sparta. A place he'd never once returned to since his transformation, not in all these many years. He hadn't been able to; the crush of heartbreak was too intense, his longing for all that he'd lost much too painful.

He thought back to that time, to the battles he and his fellow immortals had waged in those early days just after their change at the River Styx. They'd been full of new power, surging with fighting adrenaline. Their very first battle had been against the same Djinn who'd been behind the Persian massacre. With their new immortal power, coupled with their desire for vengeance, it had been a complete rout, with hordes of demons tasting death that day.

One of those Djinn in particular took special notice of Ajax, noticing how Ajax led and inspired his fellow Spartans. Elblas—also called Sable by his demon followers—realized that although he might not be able to best Ajax in battle, he could still crush his soul. Sable knew that Ajax had left behind a mortal family, a wife and two sons, and he decided that simply killing them could never be enough vengeance—not when their love for Ajax would survive beyond their physical bodies.

Elblas arrived at a plan. A dark, sinister, punishing plan, one that could never be reversed once enacted: He would erase every memory of Ajax from his beloved family's minds and hearts. Nothing, not even a single caress or embrace, would remain in their thoughts. He would be as a stranger to them.

In his immortal form, Ajax always had a choice: He could either be seen or remain invisible to mortals. When he went to his family, he came as himself, in his familiar human form. But as he entered through the doorway of his home, his wife, Narkissa, had no idea who he was. His sons backed away from him as if he were a stranger, tucking their small bodies behind Narkissa's legs. No matter how hard he reached, no matter what he said, they didn't even know his face.

His heart broke in agony. His dearest and most cherished, his wife and sons . . . lost to him forever. With a wounded cry, he tossed back his head, and lost all control of his new immortal's body. His black wings surged forth; his hands curled into claws. They could only stare in utter horror.

They had no idea who he was, no memory of him at all, so of course his monstrous hawk-form terrified them. Ajax's last memory was of their screaming faces, uncomprehending of who he was as a man, or as the demon he had seemingly become before their eyes. Their last and only memory of him was of a monster they did not know.

No wonder he'd never been able to return to Sparta. The pain had simply been too great. But it made sense that he would dream of Shayanna here in this place he held most dear.

There she stood, looking exactly as he'd always dreamed she might: slender of build, with fair skin and vivid, light blue eyes. She was dressed in a modern style, wearing close-fitting denim pants and a clingy white T-shirt that accentuated every last curve of her muscular, compact body. He stood frozen perhaps a dozen feet away from her, praying that somehow this would be more than just a vision induced by his king. He'd waited for her so long, so damned long; she had to be more than a mirage on his homeland's hillside. Didn't she?

Yet she seemed utterly unaware of his presence, and turned to face the valley below them, shielding her eyes with her right hand. The sun was low on the horizon, causing the familiar Eurotas River and surrounding land to gleam in gorgeous hues of pink and gold. Tracking her gaze, he saw a grove of olive trees, then paved streets and new buildings. This wasn't ancient Sparta he was being shown; it was the modern world that had grown atop his former city.

"No wonder you loved it," she said without looking at him.

Me? She's talking to me? Leo had never produced a vision like this one, where the other participant spoke to him.

Her voice was husky-rich, and in reaction his body

jolted, his khaki pants suddenly way too tight to contain the pulse of desire she caused. "Shayanna?" His voice had nearly left him, and rasped over her name like sandpaper.

She laughed, tenderly, turning her gaze to him. "Geez, Jax, you know my mama was the only person who ever really called me that." Her accent was a lilting, musical one, all the consonants soft and blunted. He'd never visited the American South, but he still recognized her accent from the movies he sometimes watched on late-night television.

He felt unsure, as unsettled as he'd once been around girls as a boy. She was the one, his chosen and foretold. How could he possibly know how to speak to her without trembling inside?

But it was her familiarity with him that was so unnerving. At once he had the compulsion to rush her, to take her beneath his body right on this mountainside and drive into her. More than two thousand years he'd waited. For her. She'd been his only source of sanity throughout time, the only thing that had kept him from madness as he'd lived out his calling. The hope that he would one day find her.

Shayanna. His own angel.

"Aren't you going to say anything?" She laughed again, smoothing her windblown hair with an open palm. "Sparta is so beautiful, Jax, and I know how long you've waited to see it again."

"I've never come back," he told her suspiciously, still unable to believe she was real. She was, though, wasn't she? This was more than a vision; this was a teleportation somehow. Apparently Leonidas's gifts had been growing exponentially, a rumor that had recently been circulating among the corps.

"What are we doing here?" He took a tentative step closer, bunching his fists against his thighs. "Why now; why this place? You and me . . . how did we get here like this?"

She laughed, a soft and sensual sound that crawled

right up his spine and then shot straight to his groin. His khakis tightened even more in reaction, jutting outward with his prominent erection.

"You brought me here." She cast a shy glance toward him, those lovely blue eyes alight with mischief and ... *gods of Olympus* ... desire. She wanted him as much as he longed for her.

Swallowing hard, he cleared his throat. "I have no memory of it. Bringing you here, to my Sparta."

"That doesn't make it any less real, does it?" She smiled coquettishly. She might as well have purred and rubbed up against him for the way those words affected him.

He had to rein in his volatile, lustful reaction to seeing her for the first time. Otherwise, he was going to take her without warning. It wouldn't be gentle, either. No way in Hades could he be gentle with his Shay. *She* was what he'd waited so long for—even more than he'd waited to see his homeland again. He'd had plenty of rough, grinding sex throughout the millennia, and it hadn't meant anything—their first mating had to be slow and sensual, ravaging and tender. He wanted to caress her, to stroke the velvet satin of her human body with his lips, his tongue ... his cock. He wanted to worship the creature before him, inch by loving inch.

"I don't know how I got here, how I came to be with you," he told her honestly. "I was with my king, and then ..." And then what? He couldn't say, but she definitely wasn't like any vision he'd ever experienced at Leo's hands before. "Why are you here with me, Shay?"

She smiled, silent for a moment, and gazed back over the sprawling valley below. "It's larger than you and me, Jax. It's what we can do for all of mankind, even more, but we only do it together, as one. Without each other, we are just two parts without a whole." A shadow crossed her lovely face. "It won't be simple, Jax. There are choices we will have to make. Evil will never cease to hunt us down. . . ."

With a soft shake of her head, she smiled once more and turned to him, opening her arms wide. "I am yours,

Ajax Petrakos. You're the only man I've ever belonged to; no one else will ever know me like you do. I am totally yours, for eternity."

In half a heartbeat he had her in his arms, crushing his lips against hers. So many years, hundreds upon hundreds of them, he'd waited for this. For the taste of her lips against his, the heat of her pressed against his chest. His tongue probed her mouth, twining with hers; he cupped her from behind, drawing her flush against him. He didn't care how hard he was, or that she would know it instantly.

Wrapping her arms about him, she shocked him to the core when she mirrored his own action. Her palms slid over his ass, squeezing, kneading the firm muscles in both of her hands. All at once the burning began ... that familiar threat along his shoulder blades. He broke the kiss with a desperate gasp. *My wings! Oh, gods, oh, gods, not now.*

Not now, by all that is holy, not right now. He'd only just found her, after searching for so very long. But if the spasms along his spine were any indication, the wings were already breaking through, would shred his shirt. They were already about to unfurl, and his destined love would know exactly what sort of dreadful, terrible creature he truly was.

Not bloody now.

But he couldn't hold back his core nature, not with such severe heat coursing through his entire body. She was the flame, igniting his darker side. "Not now," he half moaned, lifting his gaze heavenward, imploring.

Brushing delicate fingertips against his lips, she stilled him instantly. "I'm right here; don't panic." But he *was* panicking, afraid that this vision-woman was going to vanish from his arms before he could truly taste her for the first time. The damned aching had begun all over his spine and shoulders, his hawk nature begging to reveal itself. Even his fingers had begun to twist into talons; his entire frame shook with need for her. He couldn't hold back anything from her—including his true form.

"Shay, my love. I have to take you. Now. I can't wait. It has to be right now, or I can't promise what I'll become."

"I know exactly what you are. I've seen the truth first-hand." She glided backward, seeming almost to float apart from him. "Now come, for me, Ajax. Come for me."

Oh, he wanted to come, all right—inside of her—but he knew that wasn't what she meant.

"What are you saying?" He rushed toward her, hands outstretched.

"Come find me ... and make me yours."

And then she floated away, dissolving into the gorgeous Spartan sunset that now blinded his eyes.

I will find you, he vowed mentally, staring at the empty hillside. *I will make you truly mine.*

Chapter 3

Shay glanced around the high-ceilinged parlor of her mother's home. Slowly she backed her way toward the kitchen, hoping to avoid the crush of fellow mourners who had packed their receiving room from fin to gill.

The three-story plantation house had been in their family since before the Union forces had seized Fort Pulaski from the Confederates. Right now it was jammed full of their friends, cousins, second cousins, and every other imaginable combination of relative, friend, and neighbor. It was as if the whole group had crawled out of Savannah's social woodwork and descended upon Shay and her brothers like a swarm of palmetto bugs.

This had been Mama's intention all along, Shay thought wryly, watching the tuxedo-clad waiters move gracefully through the crowd, offering flutes of champagne off of engraved silver trays. Yep, her mother had planned this entire wake, right down to the live band in the foyer and the caviar-covered oysters being served all around. The arrangement was so freaky-thorough, it almost seemed as though her mother had anticipated her untimely death. Pretty weird, considering she'd dropped dead without any warning. Then again, maybe not so weird for a family like theirs. Especially when you took into account all the varied and bizarre talents they possessed.

Her mother had first mentioned the funeral a few

weeks ago. "But we aren't Irish, Mama," Shay had complained as they'd sat down to Sunday brunch. "You're talking about a wake."

"Our people always turn the whole affair into a tragedy," Mama told them. "And my life has never been tragic. Neither is going on to meet our Lord and savior." Despite their Greek ancestry, her mother was a proper Presbyterian, and always spoke like one.

Jamie glanced up from his Sunday paper. "Damn, and here I was looking forward to chanting and flinging myself onto your closed casket."

"Shut up." Shay scowled at Jamie. "You are so rude sometimes."

He got a hopeful gleam in his green eyes. "Can I wear a toga? That's close enough to Greek, right?"

"That's the Romans, darling." Their mother smiled at him with all the patience she'd grant the idiot offspring of a Saint Bernard.

"Hardly high society," Mason added from the far end of the table, the first time he'd spoken since they'd gathered to eat. He kept his nose behind the local section of the *Savannah Morning News*.

Her mother smiled with such joy, she might as well have been planning her wedding. "There won't be togas. But there *will* be mimosas." Then she'd deposited a heaping plate of homemade biscuits on the table, along with gravy, cheese-grits casserole, scrambled jalapeño eggs (secret family recipe), and a slab of ham.

Closing her eyes against the memory, those distant aromas swirling about her like ghosts, Shay tried to imagine Sundays without her mother. Suddenly it felt as if the kitchen walls were closing in on her, as if the laughter and happy chatter were wrapping about her torso, squeezing the breath out of her.

I have to get out of here. Right now.

The second-story veranda finally offered a little space. The only door that opened onto it led off the family study, and the lights weren't even on inside that room. Shay closed the door quietly behind her, the early-evening sound of cicadas and crickets rushing toward her like a Doppler effect. Creeping along the semi-rotten floorboards, and casting one backward glance to ensure that she truly was alone, Shay collapsed against the railing.

The earlier downpour had cleared, replaced by sticky humidity that instantly plastered Shay's maroon-colored dress against her thighs. She'd come within an inch of wearing her favorite black miniskirt, but at the last minute had bowed to her mother's wishes that they not wear black. Apparently the urge to rebel against your parents continued even when they were in their graves. But then, she already knew that; she'd been bucking against her father's iron hand of authority ever since his death ten years earlier.

With another secretive glance, she made sure she hadn't been followed, and reached into the pocket of her dress. She retrieved a well-worn letter, one that she'd read hundreds of times during the past four months—and probably nearly as many times in the past few days. It was crinkled and creased, weathered by the sheer fact that Shay had handled the thing so many times.

With a deliberate gesture she unfolded it, wiping a rivulet of sweat away from the corner of her eye before she began to read by the fading dusk light.

As if that would make the letter's contents any less shocking. Any less—potentially—true.

"Whatcha got there, Sissy Cat?" Jamie's voice jolted her, literally causing her to yelp out loud.

Shay crumpled the paper against her chest, hiding it protectively. "Why on earth do you always skulk around? You want to give me a heart attack, *too*? Huh?"

"I was just coming to check on you. Mrs. Erickson is starting to tango. Had to get out while I still could."

"It's been six years since she tried to kiss you at that New Year's thing."

"Speaking of which, has she started playing for the other team?" He gestured toward the letter. "Is that some missive from the old gal that you're hiding away?"

"Sicko."

"Oh, I get it . . . it's from a guy."

"It's none of your business, that's what it is."

"Let's have it." Jamie made a dive for the letter, but she was too fast, and darted a few feet down the veranda. But her big brother had the persistence of a warrior—hell, he *was* a warrior—and before she could cram the crumpled paper into her pocket, he had it clutched within his hand.

"Dang it, James Dixon, give that back!" She hopped on her booted feet, trying to reach where he held the paper over his head. Unfortunately, he had a good nine inches on her.

Keeping the letter well out of her reach, he began reading aloud. " 'Have you ever asked yourself why they won't let you go into the family business?' " He paused, glancing curiously at her, then continued: " 'You are not your parents' daughter. Twenty-seven years ago I gave you up for adoption. That's why they are denying you the Angel family birthright—your right as a huntress. It's because you do not have their calling.' "

Jamie's hand dropped heavily to his side, the letter still in his grasp.

"I want that back." She made a move toward him, and he extended the letter, his face unreadable. She could only wonder what pain and hurt he must see reflected in her own eyes right now.

He wandered to the railing, staring out at the yard, past the trees to the river. As children they'd marked this land in every possible way, making it their own. From fishing off the dock, to kayaking on the river, to running through the groves of live oak trees—this land bound them together. But were they bound by blood? The idea that they might not be brought tears to Shay's eyes all over again. Jamie knew it, too, the minute she started to cry.

He opened his arms to her. "You don't believe that bullshit, do you? Come on; you know better than that."

Although he was trying to act lighthearted as he drew her close in a warm embrace, the intense look in his eyes said very much otherwise. Jamie had an easygoing and sometimes feckless nature that made everyone fall in love with him, but that free-spiritedness was a useful mask.

She sighed, ducking out from underneath his arm's heavy weight. "I don't know what to think," she said. "Except I need you to tell me ... as head of our family and leader of the hunters ... what that letter might mean."

"Damn it, Shay, you know exactly why you can't fight, and it's got nothing to do with that letter."

"This city is crawling with demons." She gestured at the landscape around them in frustration. "Despite all your protections, even this property gets its own fair share." He started to argue, but she poked him in the chest. "Don't deny it. I know that demons have come very close to the house. So give me one really good reason why you won't let me engage with you and Mason. With Evan and Robbie, and the rest of your little demon-hunting gang."

He lifted an eyebrow. "Little? Did you just call my team little? 'Cause I sure hope you wouldn't insult my work that way."

"You have a calling, Jamie, but so do I." She placed her right palm over her heart and searched his face intently. "And now, with Mama gone, and Daddy long gone, it's time you let me get down to what God intended me to do."

"The gift is always passed from male to male in our family. You know that."

"Now you're sounding just like Mama, with her millions of reasons why I couldn't join in the battles with you. And know what? I want in on the family business."

"You *are* involved in the family biz, Sis. You're the first one to handle the foot traffic at the downtown location.

That's right in the thick of it all, *downtown*, where most of the action happens."

"Oh, puh-lease! I want more than reassuring superstitious weirdos that they're safe at night. Little ol' women who wouldn't know a real demon if it bit 'em on the ass." She couldn't keep the exasperation out of her voice. "I want to be a fighter, just like y'all."

He shook his head, glancing down at the letter still clutched within her hands. "If you believe that letter, then you're not even called to hunt demons—that is, *if* a woman in our bloodline could ever fight them."

"Oh, shove that sexist bullshit up some other sister's ass. I don't know what to think about the letter, but I want in on your fight. Period. And it's time."

"Again, *Shayanna*, I will tell you what you've always known: The gift is passed from father to son within our family, generation after generation."

"Then tell me why I see them all the time?" She kept her voice soft, but the words themselves were simmering with power.

"Them?" He was visibly startled, taking a quick step toward her.

"Them." She nodded her head. "Our enemies."

For the past hundred years or more, the Angel family had been quirky guardians over the city of Savannah, always under the radar. Their shop in the heart of the historic district sold herbs, Christian relics, holy water, and other supernatural protections, but was nothing more than a cover for their family's much more powerful "enterprise" that never involved the trading of money. They refused payment, and always had, for the spiritual cleansings they performed about the dark city of their birth and its surrounding areas.

"Tell me what you mean about seeing them," Jamie persisted, his voice oddly chilly. "When? Where? I need details."

Shay leaned against the veranda post, too worn out from the funeral and the emotions of the past few days for this conversation. But it was time— high time—that she confessed everything to her big brother, the leader of their familial demon-hunting team.

"Today. At the funeral while I was singing." She cut a cautious glance at him. "I tried to get you to see them, too, but you didn't."

"Was that what tripped you up in the middle of the hymn?" He waved her off. "There weren't any demons there. I'd have seen 'em. So would Mason."

Her brothers always had been so sure of themselves when it came to their abilities as hunters. She couldn't help but feel just a little bit triumphant. "They were there," she said, "and you didn't see them. Maybe you couldn't see."

Jamie's expression grew tight, a flash of anger appearing in his eyes. "That's a pretty big leap there, Shay, especially since I've never known you to see demons at all."

She stared out at the yard, at the river ebbing slowly past their land. "It started two years ago, on my twenty-fifth birthday." She grew quiet, the night's events growing clear in her mind. "Remember we had that party at Kevin Barry's, sang Irish songs till way past midnight?"

He nodded, looking vaguely guilty. Of course he remembered; he'd gotten lucky that night with that pretty Irish lassie who worked the bar. His words that night, not hers.

"As I was climbing into the cab, I turned to wave back at you, and I saw it. This ... this *thing*, a monster with twelve taloned hands and brittle, scaled wings on its back. It appeared behind you like it was going to follow you into the pub. I couldn't scream, couldn't move, but I wanted to warn you so badly. Several more appeared beside it—one was even bigger, another one much smaller, but they all had the leathery wings. And then, they seemed to ... to ... I don't know, confer? They sort of bent their heads together, and with a last look at the door closing behind you, they moved down River Street."

He scowled. "Shit. That sounds like Astikas and his pals."

"Who?"

He shook his head firmly. "Doesn't matter, because you're not getting involved in all this."

"That wasn't the only time before today. It's happened at the shop, at the mall—in fact, Jamie, it happens all the time. All. The. Time. I see demons everywhere I go, and it's starting to . . .to . . ." *I can't say it; I can't. But, oh, God, how I need to tell him. He's gotta know.*

He clasped her shoulder, bending down so that he was right at eye level with her. "Starting to what?"

She shivered, pressing her eyes shut against the vision of the creatures who had almost followed Jamie into the bar that night. "I'm afraid you're going to die, Jamie. I keep picturing what they want to do to you. It's like maybe they're making me see it or something. Maybe that's why they came to the cemetery today, too . . . as a threat."

"Nothing's going to happen to me," he told her fiercely, thrusting his chest out as if in defiance of the demons who craved his blood.

"You have to train me. We can't afford to lose the knowledge if something happens to you—and besides, you may need my protection."

He said nothing to that, just asked softly, "Why didn't you tell me?"

"I knew what you'd say. What Mason, Mama, all of you would, so I kept my mouth shut."

The truth was—and she wasn't about to tell Jamie—she'd been training on her own. Reading their sacred books, the ones they stored down in the special section of the wine cellar, using the bottles as a front against anyone who might come calling, demon or otherwise. Something about the aging vintage and the bottles themselves created a barrier that the demons couldn't sense. She'd never understood why exactly, but it was all part of her strange family's demon lore.

"No way will I let you fight, and I'm not going to argue about it anymore."

"I tried to talk to Mama," she admitted softly. "About

four months ago it really stepped up . . . and I got scared, so I told her."

Jamie's eyebrows shot up toward his hairline. "What did she say?" he asked in an odd tone that she'd never precisely heard from him before. As if he were shielding himself against her—when they'd always been totally open with each other.

"She shut me down completely. Then the letter showed up shortly after that."

"You know you can't be adopted. There's no way. I remember when Mama was pregnant with you."

"Maybe somebody wanted to stop me from entering the family business, huh? Maybe it's a sign that you should *let* me get involved?"

He stared at the darkening side yard, contemplative for several long moments. "Let me think about it. Talk to the rest of the team."

"You really do remember Mom being pregnant with me? You were six years old; maybe you forgot. Maybe you just thought you remembered."

"I remember the day they brought you home from the hospital."

"But not Mama actually being pregnant?"

He remained silent.

"Yeah, what I thought. And you know what else? There aren't any pictures of her pregnant with me either. So I'm thinking there's a good possibility that the woman we buried today wasn't my natural mother."

"Then why would you see demons?"

"Good question —especially since I'm a woman. Again, that's leading me to think that I'm not your real sister."

"You're my sister no matter who your parents are."

With a strengthening breath, she laid her theory on him, the one she hadn't been able to shake all these past months. "Maybe I'm some demon huntress's daughter. Maybe my gift is handed down through the female line—and maybe I'm awakening."

The door behind them creaked, opening, and Mason poked his dark head outside. "What are y'all doing out here?" He glanced between them. "Family meeting or something? You could've told me."

"Nothing, Mace," Jamie said, putting his back to Shay. "What's up?"

"Caterer needs to talk to you about the payment. They're waiting on you downstairs."

Jamie excused himself, following Mason inside, and Shay practically collapsed against the veranda rail. As she did so, she grew faint, unsteady, and felt suddenly light-headed. She gripped the wooden porch rail, trying to steady herself, but sensations rolled over in her unexpected waves—as if someone were touching her, stroking her seductively. For the briefest moment her lips even burned, as if that someone were kissing her. Tensing, she tried to beat back her physical reaction to the unseen stroking. No such luck. Her entire body reacted, her eyes drifted shut and she lost herself in the sensation—the feeling that an invisible being was kissing her. Yet, strangely, nothing about the touch was threatening. It was gentle, yet strong—seductive. She swayed beneath the whispered touch, barely willing to question it.

Then her rational mind took over, forcing her back to reality. *It's a demon's kiss,* logic volunteered, but she beat that fear back. No, it was too gentle, too filled with goodness.

Forcing her eyes open, she gave her whole body a shake; she'd been through too much in the past few days. That had to be the reason why she felt some imaginary lover kissing her as if their very lives depended upon it. *This is a demon's tactic, plain and simple,* she thought, forcing herself to concentrate on the moment, on reality itself.

With a glance about the porch and the ground down below, she searched for intruders. The long-legged kind, the wolfish sort, the leathery-winged variety—in fact, all the different breeds she'd been pretending not to see. Had been willing out of existence for two solid years.

Despite the edgy, light-headed feeling, she saw nothing—nothing but the slow-flowing river in the distance and the mournful live oaks all around.

Why, then, did she feel raw power, dangerous electricity, held just barely at bay?

Chapter 4

"It was violent this time," he heard a man whisper, the voice filled with dark concern.

"That's because your gift is expanding, my dear Leo," a softer, feminine voice answered. "As we've known for months now."

Jax groaned against a hard surface, his bones feeling brittle and aged. His entire body ached, and for some unknown reason he couldn't open his eyes. Whoever the bloody fools were, the ones talking over his prone form, they were being too damned loud.

"Quiet," he managed to moan. Only it came out more guttural than intelligible.

A pair of small hands, firm ones, stroked the hair away from his brow. "There we go; you're coming around." The voice was feminine, solid and sure. Familiar somehow, he just couldn't place why.

"Fuck ... off," he growled, his head exploding like a grenade.

"Now we know you're truly all right," the deep familiar voice countered. "Wake up, Spartan. We need to talk."

Leonidas.

Jax rolled onto his side, grunting loudly, and had to squint against the glare of bright lights. Blinking, he realized he wasn't in the king's castle anymore. This place was more of a low-roofed English cottage, and he recognized it. But from where?

A pair of piercing blue eyes peered down into his, framed within an elfin female face. The vision quest was suddenly making much more sense.

"Oracle," he greeted, struggling to sit up. He'd been laid out on her hardwood floor, sprawled as if he'd just spent ten days on a bender. He ought to know; he'd gotten pissed often enough recently.

"Here, let me help you up." The king, squatting beside Jax, extended a hand. Jax took it and managed to sit straight up, although the room was spinning like a whirlwind.

"Are you responsible for this?" he asked his commander with another groan. "Did you drug me with that bowl of wine?"

The Oracle laughed faintly. "I'm afraid it's merely"— she hesitated, casting an oddly tender look at the king— "Leo's gift. He's growing much more powerful lately."

"You give me too much credit, Oracle," Leonidas replied, avoiding her eyes.

Wait—since when had their king been able to hear or see their Oracle?

Jax jabbed a finger in the Oracle's direction. "Hey, now. I thought I'm the only one among our corps who can see you. So what's up with Leonidas? Since when has he been in on your act?"

When neither of them answered his question, he glanced back and forth between them.

"Oh, I get it," Jax said finally. "The whole 'you're the only one who can hear her' thing has been a ruse all along. But to what purpose? I'm hardly indispensable, especially if you can hear and see her yourself, my king."

Leonidas's gaze flickered slightly, and he glanced away. "Not a ruse at all. It's just . . . well, Jax, what you've been hearing about my gifts increasing, the murmurings among the cadre. It's all true, but I don't have much control. You saw what just happened when I tried to offer you a vision. And now look at you, half-sick, shaking all over, transported to the Oracle's home. Not much control at all. Clearly." His king bowed his head, looking apologetic.

Jax was still more than slightly confused. "But *what* does this have to do with *her*?" Ajax gestured rudely toward the prophetess, who scrunched up her rhinestone-pierced nose at him like any little sister might do. He was amazed she didn't stick her tongue out at him.

"About a month ago I saw her for the first time," his king began, rubbing a hand across his curling beard. "After all these years she appeared on the cliffs beside my castle. It was morning, and suddenly I glimpsed a woman."

"Me." The prophetess flashed an impish grin and made the rock 'n' roll symbol with both hands. "Freaking A!"

Leonidas stared at her for a full five seconds—as if she were the strange twist of nature that Jax had long known her to be. Twisted *and* sexy—if you were into prophetess types, that was—and to Jax, she was more supernatural sister than sex siren. Leonidas, on the other hand, didn't have so many centuries of familiarity with their muse. Her leather miniskirt and Gothic makeup and hair were probably revving his kingly engine right up.

"I can't hear her prophesy." Leo's words were plain as he glanced across the room. Forced himself to look away was more like it, Jax figured.

"When I try to give him the words," she explained, "I disappear. Well, at least to him. So it's still all on you, Ajax. Sorry." She gave a little shrug that said she really wasn't sorry at all. "Cup of tea?" She bounced to her feet brightly, her leather getup crackling like fallen leaves.

She crossed the room to a sideboard, where a steaming pot waited, and he realized for the first time that there were vivid blue streaks in her black hair.

"New look for you, Goth Girl?"

She beamed, pouring tea for all three of them. "I'm in Delphi, England," she explained, her accent taking on a decidedly British clip. "Thought I'd do my best to fit in."

"Darling, you never blend in anywhere you go." Ajax

laughed, watching her. "And there's no such place as Delphi, England, anyway."

"There is when I'm involved. And for what it's worth, Leo was behind the teleportation, not me."

Leo? Well, aren't the two of them getting awfully chummy.

"Thank you, sir." Jax gave a mock bow in his king's direction. "Good job, I suppose. At least I'm only lightly scrambled."

"Sorry, old friend. It wasn't my intention." Leonidas inclined his head respectfully. "As I said, I don't have the proper control over my abilities these days."

"Curious. Your powers are increasing for no particular reason?" Jax addressed the question to his king, but his gaze was squared on the Oracle. Something about the whole situation was just . . . off.

Neither of them answered. Yes, curious indeed. He glanced at Leonidas.

"Warfare conditions have been changing very rapidly." The king pierced him with a hard gaze. "The time for rebellion is over, dear Ajax. The time to fight is *now*."

The Oracle had transported Leonidas back to his castle, leaving Ajax alone with her for the prophesying, which always veered into the personal and intimate realm. *Thank the gods for our king's gentler and more sensitive side,* he thought, grateful for the leader's willing absence as the Oracle placed warm stones on Jax's open palms. The two of them sat facing each other in front of her fire, knee-to-knee in cross-legged style. With a quick waving of her hands, her outfit had been transformed to something much more casual. Now she wore a Sex Pistols T-shirt and ripped-up blue jeans—still with the blue hair and black lipstick, though.

She hadn't yet begun, and spoke softly to him as she laid the healing stones upon his palms and wrists. "Tell me what your king said while you were alone." Her voice was soft and commanding, hypnotic—even her speech patterns became ancient as she spoke to him in Greek.

She placed her palms atop his open ones, squeezing the stones between their hands, creating a shared mystic connection.

His eyes drifted shut. "That he's found three dead hawks on his property in the past month," Jax murmured. "The last one right on his doorstep. He believes it a sign that darkness is coming to the hawk protectors . . . to our corps."

"He is correct. You should trust him more."

"I trust him with my very soul. I followed him into this abyss of an immortal life."

She made a chiding sound. "Your king loves you most of all—more than the others who walk with him and serve him."

"I know." Jax kept his eyes closed, nodding.

"He worries for your soul of late."

"I . . . I don't want that." Guilt put a stranglehold on him. "I've only been . . ." *Begging to be set free from my duties. Aching to die and pass to the next realm. Exhausted from battle.*

"You've been wandering for far, far too long. And your king has gazed into the coming darkness. This is why he fears for your soul."

Jax shivered at her words as she continued in a trance-like voice. "It is an honor that the gods chose you as my receiver. It may be a burden, but they have blessed you. The Highest God, the one true, He honors you. These are His words, not mine. I do not listen to angels, to the winds . . . I listen for holy words, and so far you are the only one among the Spartans who has been deemed worthy to hear them. You are their guide, even more than I."

For a brief moment, his concentration wavered. *Did she just say "Highest God"? She couldn't possibly mean Ares, so who—*

His thoughts were interrupted as the Oracle continued in a firm tone, "Ajax Petrakos, a dire fate approaches . . . a dire . . . fate." Abruptly she stopped, releasing a high keening sound. Jax's eyes flew open, and she jerked backward, jackknifing against the floor. Her entire body became racked with terrible paroxysms.

"Oracle! What's wrong?" He lunged for her, the warm stones flying across the floor. He shook her shoulders, but she kept on shuddering, shaking. Her blue eyes rolled straight back in her head.

This was totally unlike the woman, and damn it, he was scared. "Please," he begged, pinning her against the floor with both hands in an effort to stop her convulsions. "Stop this! I'm right here ... tell me how I can help you!" He would have used her name if he knew it, but he'd never been given that privilege. None of them had. "Please, I want to help you. Just tell me how."

She finally stilled, lying on the floor, gasping for breath. Reaching for him, she bunched handfuls of his sweater within her hands, pulling him closer. This woman had always been strangely like a sister to him, and he felt her current pain like a spear through his gut.

"Listen carefully, Jax. The swirling darkness surrounds your warrior band. A trial comes ... couched in fire. There is a crown of death about your head. The Highest God calls upon you to fight the ancient evil, the demonic force that stormed the Hot Gates. Your old nemesis stands ready, but you will go alone. You will fight upon the Savannah plain. The warrant comes, a death notice has been given, and when you begin your venture there, the answers will come at last. Oglethorpe upon the square, a circle of light, angels all around you."

And then, just as quickly, she snapped right back to her usual self. She sat up, rubbing her eyes, working to put her spiky hair back in place. "Wow! That was a big one, wasn't it?" She laughed, becoming totally modern, and they might as well have been discussing the latest episode of *Dr. Who*.

He gave her shoulder a shake. "Woman, you scared the piss out of me."

"With what I said?"

"With the way you acted. You've never done that before."

She gave him a weak smile, but it didn't reach her eyes. "Heavy times ahead, dear soldier. But you are strong enough to face them down."

"Did you just tell me there's a death warrant on our heads? From the Djinn demons?"

She shrugged, rising to her feet. "I only speak the words I'm given."

He rose with her. "Well, you aren't right. We can't ever be killed—remember?" He gave her a playful rap on the side of the head. "We're immortals? Hullo? No killing in immortality."

Although he argued the point, deep down he knew he wasn't being entirely truthful. An endless life didn't precisely translate to being unable to die. There were certain prescriptions, methods the demons knew how to use. *I could finally be free. Finally pass into Elysium and see my sons.* He wrestled the thought aside, seduced despite himself into the idea of meeting the Persian Djinn in battle once again.

The Oracle moved toward the sideboard, where the tea sat steaming, and he followed her, refusing to back down despite her abrupt change in mood. "You mentioned the savanna plain," he said. "I *hate* working in Africa . . . last time I was there, I came upon a particularly nasty variety of demon, the Bori. Nasty. Nas-tee, I'm telling you."

She began pouring herself another cup of tea and glanced sideways at him. "You silly Spartan, I'm not talking about Africa—which is quite lovely, by the way. Savannah, Georgia. That's where you're going. Ready to travel?"

"What in Zeus's name is in Georgia, of all places?"

She smiled at him, that mysterious little grin that he'd come to know meant she was sitting on something big. But then the grin slipped, and her lips turned down slightly, almost as if she'd just remembered some intense worry.

Ajax clasped her arm. "Oracle, there's something else.

You said something about a Highest God. What did you mean? You've never said anything like that before."

A flicker of worry passed across her eyes and she shook her head. "The rules for our interaction remain in place. No explanations or speculations on my part. You *know* those rules, Ajax."

"The rules remain in place, which is why you *need* to discuss this with me!" he insisted, in a soft but forceful tone. "I know you weren't referring to Ares when you said that, which I would say is breaking a pretty significant rule. As your receiver, I need to know where these prophecies are coming from. You owe that to me."

She dropped her gaze to the floor for a long moment, and at first he wondered if she would respond at all. Then, in a subdued tone, she began. "I work against Ares when I can because I no longer trust him . . . or his interests regarding you Spartans, who are so dear to my heart."

Ajax couldn't help but laugh. "And you've only figured out his fickle nature in recent times? Dearest Oracle, Ares only follows his own changing desires, nothing more."

The Oracle sighed and continued. "You know yourself, Ajax, that as times passes—thousands upon *thousands* of years of time—we find that certain truths begin to crumble, and some assumptions reveal themselves to be just that . . . assumptions."

Ajax knitted his brow in confusion, but nodded for her to continue. Her voice grew much lower. "There is a Higher God, a Nameless One, who stands above every god at Olympus. I can't tell you how I know this. But if He identified Himself in some way through my prophecy to you, then I suppose He wants to make Himself known, make His power known," she said quietly. "That is why, when He chooses to speak through me, I give you His words, no one else's."

Ajax stared silently at the Oracle, perplexed, but he could not shake the feeling that some part of him had already known what she just told him. He opened his mouth to respond, but the Oracle waved him off.

"Enough of this," she said brightly. "I won't say a word more. Are you ready for me to send you to Savannah?"

That he didn't possess the power to teleport on his own had always been terribly annoying, now more than ever, when his cohorts seemed hell-bent on poofing him to and fro. It would take half an hour if he winged it, but it was more than doable.

She reached for his hands, ready to send him across the world, but he thrust his chest out in defiance. "I've got it covered, thanks."

He started to disrobe in preparation for flight, but she waved him off. "Bah. No time for all that. I'm just going to send you." She raised her arms in a shooing motion, her voice like tinkling wind chimes. "So sorry. Too bad. The need is now. I will do my best to make sure Leonidas understands the stakes . . . so long as I don't disappear while telling him."

He grabbed one of her thin, pale arms. "Wait! I want to ask you about Shayanna Angel," he blurted. "I had a vision of her. . . . Leonidas gave it to me back at his castle."

She only smiled, already fading from his vision. "No time at all—you must go."

"First tell me about Shay! I need to—"

He never got to finish. All at once he was hurtling through a massive tunnel of wind. Time and space met as one, transporting him from England, across the Atlantic, right to his new battleground: Savannah, Georgia, USA.

After Jax vanished, the Oracle sank into the love seat, all energy gone. The prophesying had taken more than the usual toll on her. His questions afterward had been even more draining; their interactions always wore her out. She should be able to warn them all, in easy words, plain ones. That she wasn't allowed to do so seemed entirely unfair.

For a brief moment she thought of Leo, of his beautiful, quiet strength. Without meaning to, she placed a palm over her chest. *Oh, please, gods, protect the king from this coming darkness.* She cared dearly for Jax as well, but now that Leonidas could finally see her, after aeons of her wishing and hoping that he would ... she simply couldn't lose him. Not before they'd even been given a chance to be together.

That was, if he even felt something for her. He'd only just met her, whereas she had watched him, loved him, wanted him for more than a thousand years.

She didn't know which god had finally granted her freedom from that hellish prison, the stony place where she had been forever doomed to love the king from a distance, but she would take what fate offered.

A knock on her front door startled her. It wasn't exactly as if she received visitors here in her strange home in North Hampshire. An ancient writ declared that this small hamlet had once been called Delphi. That was good enough for her in terms of a British residence.

She cracked open the door cautiously, peering out, and a seven-foot-tall golden god draped himself against the doorjamb. This was the very last thing she needed.

"You going to let me in? Or is he still here, your lover man?"

"I don't know what you're talking about, but you may come in, yes." She opened the door and Ares breezed past her, golden hair flowing down his back. *Cocky, arrogant god,* she thought with a scowl.

Their relationship had deteriorated centuries ago; if he hadn't originally included her in his arrangement with the Spartans, she was fairly sure he would have removed her from their lives long before now. As it was, unless he wanted to violate the terms of his own agreement, the god was stuck with her—as she was with him.

"Oh, how very quaint," he said, noticing the cups of tea. "You've been entertaining." He sniffed of the air about them. "And Spartans, how glorious. I can only surmise that this would be the two warriors who are capable of seeing you—Ajax and Leonidas."

She folded her arms across her chest and said only, "What do you want, Ares?"

He tossed back his head in laughter, the draped cloak that covered his near-nakedness falling open to reveal his fantastically muscled chest. "Ah, so I struck a chord. You are mooning, as ever, after good King Leonidas."

"Jealousy does not become you, my lord."

He grabbed her by the hair, taking her roughly into his arms. Pressing his mouth against her ear, he murmured, "You warned them, didn't you? Don't tell me that you didn't."

"I speak the words the gods give me. It's the least I can do."

"I am a god." His tone boiled with fury, and he snapped her head against his chest. "I am *their* god, their master—not you."

"I know what you have planned."

"You've no idea," he snarled.

"Your boredom promises to bring great pain to many. So I listened to the other gods, my lord, and allowed them to speak through me. The Highest God of all."

"Oh, *him*," he growled in distaste.

"He can command you in a breath, so I'd be careful, Ares."

"I'm not bored," he drawled. "There just isn't enough war anymore—not the sort of epic spiritual battles, fire raining down from heaven, that sort of thing. There's been a stalemate between the Djinn and the Spartans for too long."

"So you're forcing your hand, bringing the conflict to a crisis?"

He slid his cape about her shoulders, covering them as one. "Like you said, prophetess . . . it's the least I could do."

Chapter 5

"I could have come here on my own, you know!" Jax shook his fist at the sky as soon as he was plunked down on the street in Savannah. Glancing around, he found a sign that read, THUNDERBOLT, GEORGIA. "Ah, bloody hell, woman!" he shouted to the Oracle, even though she was thousands of miles away. "You couldn't even use your *own* damned thunderbolt properly. I'm in the wrong place."

It was about midnight, he noted with a glance at his watch. The cutting-edge timepiece adjusted to local time via GPS no matter where he traveled—a helpful tool for an immortal protector who was forever flying the heavens or being teleported by his comrades, often against his will.

Up ahead he saw a small gas station with a sign that read, BOILED PEANUTS SOLD HERE and then scrawled below that, *Pork Butt for Sale.*

Pork butt? He shivered at the thought. Lately he'd taken to filet mignon, but already this was clearly promising not to be a tenderloin mission.

Unless Shay Angel awaits me here, he thought, his pulse skittering unexpectedly. Where had that thought come from? His vision of her had been in Greece, not Savannah. Clearly all the teleporting had jumbled his emotions.

"My flat had better still be in perfect condition when I return to London," he grumbled quietly. "And my Mer-

cedes Gullwing. And my clothes. Definitely my clothes."
Especially considering that the Oracle had seen fit to
give him a soldier's version of *What Not to Wear*, dressing him in the sort of practical outfit he'd avoided lately:
khaki cargo pants and a plain black T-shirt. Not exactly
Mayfair's finest, but it would suit for the mission's duration. By his calculations, the "mission" had to be a small-
time one; otherwise the whole crew would have been
deployed to this Southern city. Not just him. Definitely
small-time, nothing else it could be.

Except . . . what about the Oracle's words? She'd said
a death warrant was on all their heads. Or had she? She'd
hypnotized him so completely, there was no telling what
she'd really meant. As always, however, he knew that
her prophecy would begin to piece together as the assignment continued; eventually it would all make sense,
just not right away.

*So if I'm in bloody Thunderbolt, Georgia, how near
am I to Savannah?* He checked his wristwatch GPS, and
was relieved to discover he was only four miles away
from Savannah's downtown sector.

He set out walking; a large, hulking guy like himself
didn't ever worry about getting jumped, even when he
was new in town. Or maybe it was just the confidence
that came not only from being a Spartan, but also from
knowing he could kick any mortal attacker's ass. Being
immortal didn't hurt either. He kept to the roadside, his
gaze sweeping the perimeter, determined to find any
clue to the prophetess's words.

" 'Fight upon the Savannah plain,' " he muttered under his breath, sidestepping a broken beer bottle that
littered the pavement. " 'When you begin your venture
there . . .' " This was some venture, all right. "Thanks a
lot, woman."

He knew he should have a better attitude, but after
so many years in the line of duty, he was worn out. Was
it true that he could be killed? Perhaps he should welcome the threat and step into the golden fields of the
afterlife.

But then a road sign just up ahead stopped him in his tracks: BONAVENTURE ROAD.

Bona*venture*.

It couldn't be an accident that he'd been set down right here, so close to the sign. This was where it would all begin, he realized, feeling that first jolt of adrenaline hit his system. And then another. And another.

Until the first flush of his transformation had begun.

Shay had driven loops around Savannah, winding her way through the many one-way streets, the squares and cobblestones that comprised her city. Earlier in the evening she'd hit Spanky's for a while, hoping that a beer or two might settle her down. But the regular crowd had been too loud for her melancholy mood, so she'd started driving again. Aimlessly, as if the drone of her tires on the road and the progression of songs on the radio could soothe her tangled emotions.

Until at last she'd made the turns that would take her to her mother. She had to go to Bonaventure, had to protect her mother's memory—maybe even her body—against those voracious demons she'd seen near her grave earlier in the day. Sure, her warfare hymn had sent them scurrying, but that had been hours ago, and the idea of her mother alone in the cemetery—the thought of the demons gathering around her grave for some vile purpose—was a haunting image that Shay just couldn't shake. It wasn't exactly as though the Angel family were beloved by the powers of night, and it was obviously up to Shay to safeguard her mother's grave site.

Here it was close to midnight, and she stood staring up at the locked gates of Bonaventure Cemetery. They kept tight security around the place because the hoodoo and voodoo had escalated during the past few years—so much, in fact, that they'd had to cancel the candlelight tours that used to be a regular occurrence in the old graveyard. She gave the wrought-iron gates a tug, rattling the loose padlock and chain that fastened them shut.

With a glance upward, she figured the gates were only about seven feet high at most, surprisingly unimposing.

I guess the folks who run this cemetery know they can't keep the ghosts and witch doctors out, not even with gates as high as a mountain, she thought. Then she shivered at the image of her mother spending nights in the cold, hard ground alone with practitioners of the dark arts.

She's not here; she's gone, she tried to tell herself. *She is not inside this place.*

At least, if all that she and her churchgoing family believed was true. Ironic, but Shay's faith in God and angels had truly awakened only the moment she'd glimpsed her first demon. It was like a math theorem: If totally, horribly, evilly bad exists, then something perfect has to exist to balance it all out.

She'd been praying to see an angel ever since. Just one winged, magnificent creature, a being who watched over her, protected her from evil—and who might drag her family out of this harrowing profession of theirs. Hopefully before she lost Jamie and Mason in the same way that she'd lost her dad. At the memory of her father's murder, Shay winced, glancing back at the hard iron gates barring her from her mother's grave.

Oh, angels, are you here? she half prayed. *Can't I see just one of you before I attempt this moronic idea?*

Like some sort of homing instinct, she couldn't seem to stop herself from putting her booted foot on the metal gate. As she started over, she saw nothing. Just midnight and drooping Spanish moss as mosquitoes practically crawled right up her ass.

"Figures," she whispered aloud. "In the words of George Bailey, you're about the sort of angels I would get. Only mine are nonexistent."

Nope. She never got angels ... just demons. Hordes upon hordes of the nasty guys. And they *were* males, never females, something she hadn't quite puzzled her way through yet. Jamie said Mason had some supersecret theory as to why that was, something he'd figured out in Iraq, but in the four months since his tour ended, he hadn't given up the goods about all that. At least, not to her.

Mounting the top of the gate, she cut her knee on a jutting spike, ripping her jeans straight through to her flesh. With a cry she catapulted on over, hitting the ground hard. She crouched there, regaining her equilibrium, and gave her injured leg the once-over. Damn it, these were her Lucky jeans, too. Only they hadn't turned out to be so lucky after all.

Flipping open her cell phone, she used it as a flashlight and, sticking to the gravel road, headed toward her family's plot. She knew the way from all the years she'd spent sketching in the cemetery, not to mention the Sunday afternoons when her mama had dragged them out to visit "the family." In the South, visiting the peeps extended far into the afterlife. If her mother could have gotten away with it, she'd have left regular helpings of biscuits and fried chicken at the cemetery.

The eerie arc of light from her phone illuminated only a few feet ahead at a time, so Shay made her way carefully. One step, another; the trek was slow going without more light, and the overhead oaks obscured the nearly full moon. But then a flash of brightness straight ahead made Shay blink, then squint. At first it vanished, but then reappeared larger, a luminous orb right in the middle of the unpaved road.

Shay's heart began to slam hard, her throat tightening. *Get the hell out of here, girl. No telling what kind of witch doctors might be around this late at night!*

Her feet froze, and no matter how hard she tried to back away, it was as if something magnetic kept her glued to the ground.

"Hellfire," she mumbled beneath her breath—right as she heard the first of the whispering.

"Soooo pretty," one hollowed-out voice sang, its shrill voice off-key.

"Lovely, lovely!" a more masculine one cheered.

"Ours!" Several clanging tones sounded, the noise

seeming to come from overhead, from out of the darkness. From everywhere and absolutely nowhere, all at once.

Shay's scalp tightened, her hair standing on end. A flush swept down her arms, followed by an ice-cold sensation. Her hands grew numb, and the cell phone slipped from her grasp, clattering onto the road. The aroma of early spring flowers was instantly replaced by that of sulfur, an acrid smell, as if human skin were burning. As if her own skin were burning.

"Holy Mother!" she cried, but the words were caught in her throat. Caught just as tightly as she was, in some sort of supernatural trap.

The harsh cries of unknown animals circled about her, like something right out of the *Blair Witch* movies—only this was real, and it was happening to her. All these months she'd dodged the demons, stayed below their radar, and now she'd apparently walked right into their nest.

"Delicious . . ."

"Wholesome . . ."

And then, with the most glee of all, the cavernous voices cried in unison, *"Hunting!"*

She began to hyperventilate, struggling to move her feet, but she felt tight hands clasp her calves, even though she couldn't see anything. Not in the dark, but it was also far more than that: Whatever held her was invisible even to her hunter's eyes.

"Let me go!" She searched the blackness, reaching inside herself for anything to battle the onslaught. She dug deep, trying to find some latent talent that she'd never been trained to use. But fate greeted her with only empty hands.

The sounds grew closer, the circling of the demons like a stranglehold on her body and mind. At last she stood fully frozen, barely able to breathe, much less move her hands or blink her eyes.

Help! she prayed, eyes fixed on the sky above. *God, help me! Angels, I need you!*

Even her heart within her chest began to thud slower; her entire body was freezing, molecule by molecule.

"You'll make a pretty, pretty statue," a voice cawed from the trees above. "Pretty here in our home."

"We devour her!"

"We rape her!"

An argument broke out, wild demonic voices whipping across the inky blackness.

And all the while Shay's heart grew thicker, beating heavier and slower. And even slower still, like the fading drumbeat of a low, sad funeral march.

Something brushed along her arm, scratching. All at once her right calf erupted in sharp pain, the metallic smell of blood battling against the dreadful odor of sulfur that wrapped about her like a cocoon.

She would die soon. *God, let them make me a statue; just don't let them tear me apart alive!* she cried within her spirit. After all, at least Jamie might be able to free her from a paralysis spell. She'd been reading something about that very thing just the other day. What had it been? She tried to recall, panicking.

"A thousand years, unmoving," a new voice said, male and deep against her ear. "Now that, lovely huntress, that I would like to see."

Holy Father, they can hear me. I'm powerless if they can even hear my prayers.

"Not all of us," her captor purred, his breath warm against her cheek. "Only I am that powerful."

"Who . . . are . . . you?" she barely managed to rasp, her mouth thick, as if she'd been given Novocain. "Name?"

He laughed, a tinkling, light sound that mocked the utter blackness that his presence cast between them. "Little huntress, think me such a fool?" A warm hand pawed at her nape, lifting her hair, then let it fall to her shoulders again, but not before the scrape of sharpness bit into her skin. Long nails or claws, it had to be.

The entity was solid, formed of flesh, not like the others, who were little more than dim echoes calling from the depths of hell.

She tried to argue, but her mouth had frozen solid, cast harshly midcry. With more force and will than she even realized she still possessed, she managed to cut her eyes toward the demon. But he had vanished, and there was only the unexpected clomping of horse's hooves, the sound of trotting on gravel as the creature rounded behind her. Cloven hooves, maybe? She'd seen a few demons like that while driving down Harris Street last month. Their puckish feet had been at odds with the black leather they wore and the chains they dragged behind them along the sidewalk.

"The statue plan was clever! Thank you, brethren," Hoof Demon announced from behind her in a strong, eerily human voice. A voice dripping with horrible sensuality and cunning. He was definitely the ringleader here, and smarter than all the others—perhaps smarter than any demon she'd ever seen before. How else would he have managed to freeze her as he was doing—and so quickly?

"Oh, I'm smart indeed." Clawed fingers stroked her arm. "Smart enough to know that hard marble will never do your beauty justice. No, taking you myself is appealing. It's been far too long since I've lain with a woman. Although"—he began to laugh, that deep, husky sound again—"I doubt you'd know what to do with a *sword* quite like mine."

Sword? Surely he didn't mean . . .

She shuddered beneath her skin, every part of her reacting in revulsion—every part, that was, except her frozen marble exterior.

"Oh, indeed, you should glimpse my shaft at full mast. The length of a bronze spear, I guarantee that."

Get out of my head, you bastard freak!

An explosion of leaves and branches overhead set the demon moving away from her. The heavy sound of his clomping hooves echoed off the road; he circled beside her, staring overhead while dropping into a half-crouching posture.

At that precise moment, the branches above parted

enough that the bright moon arced down on her captor, and she would have screamed if she could have. His face was mottled and disfigured, with horns curling inward against his scalp—and, God help her, his body was half horse and half . . . demon. Or half human? She couldn't say, but *monstrous* didn't begin to describe the terrifying nature of the demon beside her.

"Elblas, stand down," a deep, commanding voice called from above, the trees rustling and swaying. "Leave the human be. She has no part in this battle." Instantly she felt safer, even though she had no rational reason for doing so.

The demon hissed, his lips curling back viciously. "Mine! Spartan, this one is claimed already!"

"Mortals are off-limits, Elblas. Leave her now or I will cast you into the depths forever this time!"

Then, with a snarl, the one called Elblas swooped back toward her, baring a gleaming set of sharp teeth. "Before he comes, I'll have you. Because he wants you, I'll consume you," the monster hissed, lowering his head to her breasts. "I sense his desperate hunger. But he'll not have you, my choice little pearl, because what Ajax craves . . . *Sable* takes."

Ajax dance-stepped out the length of the tree branch. Not that he needed a promontory in order to observe the demons hording below. He'd seen and sensed plenty already. Discovering Sable, of all creatures—after more than two thousand years—had thrown him completely off guard. He'd been ready to dispatch the gathered band of demons, right until he'd spotted Sable, looking exactly as he had the last time they'd battled it out— perhaps even more hideous,

After Ajax's devastating reunion with his wife and sons, the rage within him had been immense. Ares, always the lover of bloodlust, had told Ajax the identity of the demon who had gotten to his family—and granted Ajax free rein to seek vengeance as he saw fit.

In a godlike fury, Ajax met Elblas in battle, and al-

most immediately bested the demon's attack. To punish
Sable, Ajax took away that which was most precious to
the demon, just as Sable had done to him. However, the
only love in Sable's base existence was for his wings—
their beauty and the freedom of flight they provided. So,
when Ajax had finished with him, those once glittering
wings were gone forever.

Ares himself was disappointed by the battle, specifically by Sable's poor showing. So as his own form of
punishment, he banished Sable to an indefinite desert
exile, and cursed him with the form of a hideous centaur,
eradicating any trace of the beauty of which he had once
boasted.

At the sight of his old enemy, instincts raged within
Ajax, their voices as primal as the guardian's blood
pumping through his body. To protect the mortal would
always be his first priority, but Elblas Djiannas? In
the Americas? And set free from his eternal prison?
The danger that Elblas—or Sable, as he liked to call
himself—posed to all of mankind complicated things.
And Ajax hated complications with a fiery, determined
passion, especially if it meant he couldn't save one of his
charges. Again his gaze went to the human below, his
heart thudding loudly in his chest as he deliberated a
course of action.

He could practically hear Leonidas's charge in his ears:
*Take out the demon; then get the mortal to safe ground.
But protecting the human is your top priority.*

But something about the human made him hesi-
tate. That rounded shape of her lips, the cry frozen
there, unsettled him. Made the odds seem even more
treacherous.

Narrowing his eyes, feeling their silvered power flow
into the rest of his body, he saw the landscape below for
what it truly was: littered with demons and dark spir-
its, and even a few lost ghosts. He also confirmed the
identity of the centaur below, that he was indeed Jax's
greatest enemy.

Sable cast him a quick glance, then bared his fangs

and moved in for the kill. Jax knew exactly what the demon would do next: He would drain the woman of her life force, suck her spirit right into his own, and leave her as little more than dried leaves spread beneath his feet.

Unless Jax got his Spartan arse in gear—and lightning-fast.

Chapter 6

Jax balanced on the large tree branch and unfurled his wings, tearing through leaves and Spanish moss. Sable and his pack of Djinn demons were already well acquainted with his power, but he was outmatched—and a human life hung in the balance. Intimidation was the order of the day.

A demonic cry sounded from the distant reaches of the cemetery, momentarily distracting Sable and buying Jax extra time. The demon lifted his head from the human's breast, and then trotted a few feet away. *Thank God.* Jax exhaled, and watched to be sure none of the other demons closed in about her. They probably didn't dare, not with a demon of Sable's stature in the barnyard, so to speak.

Jax could see little of the female below except her pale arms, which extended upward toward the moon in a pleading gesture. Her face was lifted toward the sky, too, as if she'd been praying before the demons had paralyzed her.

Lovely lass, are you still praying? Do you see me here, come to watch over you?

And what a lovely lass she truly was, he thought, allowing himself a stolen moment of appreciation. Lush, dark hair fell down her back, a lock of it concealing her cheek. His hands tensed with the sudden desire to stroke that silken hair beneath his fingertips. To press his face against it and inhale her sweet mortal scent. Her pale-

skinned neck lay exposed, vulnerable, and Jax ached to
know what she would taste like, feel like within his arms.
Gods, he wanted to caress her, just like the moonlight
spilling down from above caressed her. He even ached
to swoop upon her and make her his very own, to make
her his Leda, with him as mighty Zeus.

A flood of emotion filled his heart, tightening his
chest . . . and tightening his body. He could smell the
sweetness of her skin, the very sweetness Sable sought
to rob from her—her mortality. Brevity, that brief sun-
burst of human life . . . well, the horde would stay drunk
off that for days should they win tonight. No wonder
the demons lusted so for a taste of her. Even Jax found
her scent of mortality more alluring than any he'd ever
known. If he tasted of her, surely he would be drunk for
days, as well. But at least she would still be alive. . . .

His wings began to strike at the air in near-frantic reaction, as if urging him onward in the insane plan. Silver
filled his eyes, coloring the landscape and even the air all
around him. Pure, unadulterated silver. He blinked, trying to rein in his reaction to the little mortal, but the silver
swam all through his body. With a quick downward glance
he saw it was even pulsing through the veins of his hands.
She had intoxicated him. *She* had incited this overwhelming dose of his own flowing source, the raw *lifefulness* that
Ares had served him on that long-ago day.

Together, he and his Spartan brothers had sipped from
the fire drawn right from the River Styx, and its effect
on each warrior had been unique; for Jax, the fire had
turned silver once inside his body. That, and it had en-
larged and strengthened every portion of his anatomy,
as first liquid gold shot through his veins, then a brilliant
bronze—and finally supernatural silver. Jax had studied the pulsing liquid in marvelous horror, watching it
snake through his arms and chest, feeling it scorch him
from the inside out.

"What is this? What is happening to me?" he'd wondered aloud, flexing first one bulky forearm, then the
other. The rushing silver soared through his veins, and

Jax felt intoxicated and horrified, watching his body transform into something almost . . . unrecognizable in its magnitude.

Ares had just laughed, tossing his head back for a long moment before continuing. "My splendid Spartan, that's simply the raging fire of Styx joined together with your mortal flesh."

"Inside my . . . body?" Jax had barely gasped, feeling the tightening of muscle and bone in his chest and shoulders.

Ares had planted a long, lean arm across his shoulder, drawing him near like a comrade. "I've forged you in the rivers of eternity, young one. You are my own creation. Perhaps my very best. Of that, we shall see."

Jax's heart had thudded in panic, but he refused to let it show.

"And I, for one, will admit that I rather like the look of my creation." Ares had then raked his gaze down the length of Jax's transforming body, his eyes gleaming wickedly in appreciation. Especially when the flowing liquid infused Jax's groin and powerful upper thighs—bringing with it supernatural strengthening and enlargement.

"Of course," the god cautioned, "some have gone insane after drinking from this very river. Styx has a way of . . . well, I'll just say defying control. Like you, young Ajax. Just like you."

That was how it had been ever since, with Ajax teetering precariously on the edge, with the fire always coursing, threatening to erupt like hot lava from Vesuvius. Oh, control of the source had not come easily for him, and he'd worked hard to master the mystery inside his own body. But he had done it. Eventually.

Until now, that was; until she, the waif of a mortal below him, had drawn out his silver, just by . . .

Oh, gods, she'd aroused the hell out of him.

But there was a battle raging, he thought, shaking off the tidal wave of sensations racking his body. He would take the extra dose of power and use it. Perhaps Ares had allowed it on purpose.

Master it, you bastard, he told himself. *Her life is at stake. There is time to consider her effect on you later—if you fight well and fast. Shake off the past!*

Get hold of yourself, you fool. She's one of your own, in the palm of your own hand. That was the vow they'd reaffirmed to Ares every August for more than two thousand years, ever since the day of their initial transformation.

Trusted to us, in the palm of our hands. Mortalkind, our children—demonkind, their devourers . . .

The words droned in Jax's head, both in ancient Greek and in English. Hell, for kicks Ares had made them pledge in dozens of languages over the years, and Ajax could still recite them all. As he did so now, his mind and spirit settled; all at once he was a warrior again, not confused by ancient sensations and churning powers.

"She is mine, in the palm of my hand," Jax warned in a chilling voice. "Watch yourself, demons. You have no right to touch so much as a single hair on this one's head."

"Touch!" The horde cackled in unison, laughing as if he'd just told the most uproarious joke. "Stroke the lovely, lovely."

"Ah, bollocks." Jax shook his head; why were most demons always so inane? The least they could do was grow a decent sense of humor or manufacture some cleverness. "Stop watching *Lord of the Rings,* why don't you?"

"We serve only one master!" a somewhat deeper voice howled. "Elblas!"

"Too bad you've no better taste in masters," he muttered under his breath, but then a few wolfish demons trotted closer to the human. They snarled and circled, baring long fangs. And still she stood, unmoving, but he hoped quite alive.

I have to distract them, lead them away from her, and before time runs out. Already her skin was losing all of its color; her whole being was literally draining of any sort of pigment or softness. Even her denim jeans were fading to a chalky marble color. Of course the spell was binding her rapidly—Sable possessed that degree of power. But Jax was here to stop him; this time the demon lord would not win the battle for a human soul.

Jax launched into a long, graceful dive, rushing to the mortal woman. He spread his wings wide and screeched into the night. It was the war cry of the immortals and had long ago replaced their Spartan battle hymns. Again he screamed, releasing his piercing hawk's warning, and sent the minor demons below scattering, trailed by nothing but their own gasps and titters of embarrassment.

Sable spotted him right as he reached the female. The demon cut sideways and thundered back across the cemetery, riding wild. He stormed forward like a knight on horseback ready to joust with Jax, and then veered at the last moment, heading right toward the human. Jax blocked him, putting his own body between her and the demon. He fanned his wings tall and wide, shielding her behind him.

"Don't even think about harming her, you hybrid bastard!"

Sable sped faster, nearly to the mortal. How dare that impudent little punk of a Djinn toy with her, tickling his own fancy by capturing her like a butterfly in his wicked net?

Well, Jax would show his enemy a thing or two about what his *own* wings could do. He spread them wider, to their very fullest extension, screeching into the night. A few more demons scattered into the darkness, cackling and whispering Sable's pure demon name—"Elblas! Elblas!"—in some sort of perverse worship chant. So the bastard had a following. Jax had the very power of the *gods* flowing through his own veins—and it was time to unleash that fury on his enemy.

Shay's mind screamed, but her mouth was unmoving, her body deathly cold—and it seemed that even the demon couldn't hear her anymore. Several times that strange hunter—surely he was a hunter? one of her brothers' crew?—had moved past where she stood.

But all she'd seen was a flash of weaponry, a mammoth, hulking shape; then the hoofed demon had moved past her vision. The one that the hunter called Elblas. Or Sable. Which one? The fighter had used both. And even though she tried to tell herself that the hunter was part of her brothers' fighting unit, she could feel that he was something much stronger. More supernatural and also threatening . . . yet light in intention, not murderous and dark.

She worked at her mouth, but it was totally pointless. *I might as well have been buried alive.* Her body had been converted to a prison, to a strait-jacket.

Help me! Someone! God . . . angels!

Maybe that monumental fighter *was* an angel! Why hadn't that hit her before? *Uh, probably because my thoughts are being frozen solid, too.* Then she'd better make her very last thought, the one before this horrible transformation became complete, a strong one.

That demon heard me earlier, she remembered, aware of a massive shape just in front of her, the soft breeze of some sort of movement. It was almost as if someone were slowly fanning her—or maybe she was hallucinating. Still, she was pretty sure that whatever that dark form was, it was her angel man.

If Elblas could hear me, maybe this other creature can.

Help me! she screamed as loud as she could within her mind. *You! In front of me! Set me free!*

Only silence answered; in fact, she realized that she no longer heard any sound at all.

Their spell was nearly complete.

Jax swooped at Sable, talons bared, wanting to lead the battle away from the woman. In reaction the Djinn reared up, brandishing a pair of glinting swords that he'd produced from the cosmos. A high-level summoner, Sable had once been adept at conjuring the most lethal of weapons and apparently still was. Rubies glowed along the hilt of the sword in his right hand; emeralds shone

from that in his left. For a shield Sable used his front
legs, kicking at the air between them so violently that
Jax had to retreat a few steps.

Sable laughed, lunging toward him, both swords slicing viciously through the air, but Jax was able to feint
and rolled out of the way, absorbing his wings in a fluid
movement. Sable bounded at him, slashing with both
swords, the emerald one driving hard into the ground—
barely missing Jax's shoulder.

Jax raised his own shield, averting the heavy blow
of the demon's second sword. He kept the defense in
place, buttressing it with his supernatural energy until it
gleamed silver with his immortal life force. None of the
demons would be able to penetrate the small fortress
for a full minute; after that, he would need a new plan.
Something to get him out of this defensive position and
into an offensive one.

Closing his eyes, he gazed inward, focusing on the
weapons he would choose. He laid hold of his eight-foot
spear, made sure his armor was fully in place, from his
greaves to his breastplate. *River.* He released the name
inside the swirling silver of his soul, watched it with his
sight as the single word slipped into the flowing stream,
transported by the thread that connected him with the
warrior who had once been his servant in the mortal
realm—and who now remained so throughout eternity.

River could pick off the rest of the pack one by one,
allowing Jax to face off with Sable, who, he hated to admit, had seemingly grown far more powerful during his
exile. Or maybe he'd recently been granted new power,
just as he'd obviously been given a reprieve from his desert imprisonment, if nothing else. His hideous centaur
curse remained intact; his features were even ghastlier
than they were at their last meeting twenty-five hundred
years ago. It definitely didn't pay to wind up on Ares'
bad side, not like this Djinn had done. Not that he'd win
even an ounce of Jax's sympathy, not with all that he'd
stolen from Jax.

With a prayer, Jax surged to his feet, wings open and

hostile, and came out thrashing. Clearly Sable hadn't expected such a bold move. When Jax slammed him with his left wing, the demon was driven backward, stumbling awkwardly.

"You know what birds of prey do with horses, don't you, Sable?" Jax taunted, raising his eight-footer. It wasn't just any spear, either—it carried fire drawn right out of the River Styx.

"You're actually proud to be a *vulture*?" The centaur found his footing again and hammered at Jax's raised shield. "Oh, foul lover of carrion! Beat your wings and thump your breast with that pride! Because only the vultures will want what will remain of you . . . once I'm finished."

Jax ignored the taunts, lunging with his spear, fire hurtling across the distance that separated him from the centaur. Fiery, scalding liquid splashed along Sable's rump, and he jolted, bucking in wounded agitation.

"Greetings from the River Styx, old friend. You know that you can never kill me, Elblas. Remember how that plan turned out last time? I seem to recall you lost something of value." Jax lifted into the air with a burst of energy and held himself suspended above Sable, lightly beating his wings to drive his point home. "And as for the vultures, you should want their wings. You call me that because you know you'll never soar the heavens again!"

Sable's ruined face twisted into a cruel mask of despair and hatred, his horns uncurling, then lengthening by at least a foot, his narrow eyes turning beady red. A red haze swirled about his entire body like an otherworldly dust cloud, covering him from large horsey rump to scarred chest.

The red haze was his demon's fury. His hatred. His rage. Sable had never been able to contain his manifestations when provoked—ultimately it was what had proven to be his downfall so many years before.

Jax flew a circle overhead, his entire body bulking from the power rush that he'd invited moments earlier when he'd gazed inward. Control over their supernatural abilities had come hard for the Spartans at first—hardest of all for Jax, who, like Sable, had a raging temper. Just one more reason why the two had always despised each other so much. It was like looking into a mirror that showed you the very worst of yourself, the part that you tried to deny even existed.

The muscles of his shoulders bunched and tightened, his naturally massive thighs thickened, and, as he soared over Sable's head once again, he called out, "Yes, I seem to remember that you looked a great deal different last time. But who needs wings . . . ?"

Sable reared high, lifting one sword in a full extension of his right arm and pointing it at Jax. "And who needs a *wife*?" he thundered back.

For half a wingbeat, Jax faltered, making an awkward semidrive for the Djinn who had robbed him of all that had ever truly mattered. Sable knew he'd wounded Jax, too, and in the only way that really counted between immortal enemies—by piercing the heart.

Enraged, Jax launched into a low dive, landing awkwardly on Sable's long back. "I'll fucking take your head for that." He used his wings for balance as Sable attempted to shake him off. "I'll have your life. . . ."

"And I'll mend right away. You could never take my wings now, you idiot Greek."

Sable reared and flipped backward, taking Jax with him, and in a heartbeat Jax had been pinned beneath the crushing weight of a one-thousand-pound centaur.

He cried out, his right leg and wing brutally bound beneath the heavy horse body. Sable rolled a bit, pinioning Jax even more solidly. Sable swiveled his torso, trying to get a good look at the damage he'd done, and when he did, his vicious face spread into a triumphant sneer. Jax bit back a cry of pain as the weight crushed into his thigh and wing. The wing would be fine. They were always regenerating, and unassailable because they hadn't been formed from mortal flesh. His body, however, was vulnerable to a certain extent, although no one and nothing had ever managed to kill one of their immortal band. However, that didn't mean they couldn't be hurt, and badly.

"Get up, centaur," he said, struggling to keep his breathing even. Sable just laughed, reaching for his ruby sword where it lay on the ground. Each of them struggled and stretched, straining to capture the weapon, but ultimately it remained outside both their grasps.

Jax shoved his shoulder into Sable's large side, pushing against it as he might a massive boulder. Sable didn't budge and seemed wholly undaunted. He just stretched out his forelegs, adjusting them comfortably. "I am in no particular hurry," he said. "In fact, I can sit here for quite a few hours, crushing you slowly, and all the while your little mortal"—Sable's lips twisted over the word as if it were a rotten olive—"will have turned completely to stone by the time I decide to rouse myself."

Sable began picking out bits of dirt and rocks from first one hoof, then another. "I wonder what happens to a dead Spartan immortal? 'Dead immortal'—I rather like the ring of that, don't you? I mean, it's quite the paradox." The demon took a just-dislodged rock and hurled it at Jax's breastplate, and it ricocheted off with a loud clank. "Perhaps I'll gather my horde and we'll slowly stone you to death; what say you to that?"

All the while, his centaur's weight proved more and more crushing, but all Jax could think about was the mortal whose life was draining with each passing moment. He must help her now, but he was running out of time.

River, he thought, *come to me. I need you . . . she needs you.*

Chapter 7

The early-morning sun had just begun cresting over the moors, turning the thick mist that blanketed the rolling hills into a golden shroud. The hulking figures of Spartan warriors in combat drills slowly emerged from the darkness, their armor and swords gleaming. It was always a majestic sight, River thought as he bent low, ready to wrestle Aristos once again.

Get my arse thrashed, more like it, he thought, watching the daring, aggressive gleam that filled Ari's eyes as they faced off. Ari was their very best wrestler, and it wasn't unusual for him to handpick River as his opponent for these matches. For one simple reason—River was second-best, and had been sparring with the grinning Spartan since they were boys together.

They circled each other, eyes filled with menace and boldness, sweat coating their naked bodies. River moved in fast, more eager than usual to win the match today. Ari, however, anticipated the maneuver and flipped River right onto his back, knocking the wind from his lungs as he pinned him.

"Sissy-ass!" Ari grinned as River struggled. "Throw some more of that weak shit, River, man! This marks one."

River managed to roll sideways, but Ari captured him in a stranglehold that was tighter than usual, and lights danced before River's eyes. Except . . . it wasn't just lights; it was silver—a haze of it filling his eyes, coloring the landscape all around them.

River, he heard, loud and distinct. *River, come to me.*

It was his master, and by the sound of his voice, Jax was already in trouble. "And it only took five hours this time," he croaked aloud, prying Ari's arm from about his neck.

"Forfeit?" The big Spartan's face fell, as if they were still boys and River had just stolen his favorite *ephebike* ball.

"It's Jax . . . some sort of trouble. He's summoned me." The silver swam brighter, filling his mind, churning into a whirlpool that blanked out everything else.

"What's happened to my brother?" River heard Ari ask, noting the concern in his voice. "Is he all right?"

"Summoned," River repeated in a daze, then watched as the silver formed itself into a whirling portal. None of the others could even see it, because this was the special tie that bound him to Jax. He rose to his feet, following a glowing thread that tugged him toward the supernatural doorway.

"But is he all right?" Ari persisted, trotting beside him. Aristos was extremely protective of his brothers—well, of all their Spartan corps.

"I'll find out." River focused on the spiral before him, knew that the teleportation would require every ounce of his concentration.

With a whisper to Jax of "I am yours," he tumbled headfirst into the humming cauldron that had opened, waiting only for him.

Jax had fallen into a sort of wrestling maneuver with Sable, twisting his free arm and leg into a pretzel with Sable's forelegs. The centaur grunted a bit, striking out with one hard hoof, but otherwise Jax's efforts were wasted—and served only to weaken him even more.

River, you bastard, where are you? If you're snooz-ing through this one, I'll have your head. By his calcu-lations, the cadre should already be up and training, which meant that River would have received his urgent request by now.

Sable stroked one long horn in contemplation. "We've got a bit of time, so let me pose a question: Why are you here, in Savannah, of all places?"

Jax looked past him, watching the woman who had become almost colorless in the past few minutes. "I could ask the same. Last I heard, you were humping it like a camel through the desert. Although"—Jax laughed acidly—"I don't suppose you've been getting much *humping* accomplished, not in this current form of yours. Unless you wanted to take a lovely mare, but probably even she would shriek and squeal in terror."

"I am not a horse." Sable swatted Jax sharply across the eyes with his mangy tail, snorting loudly.

"You certainly have the very wide ass of one." Jax knew enough about Sable's vanity—how much his once-legendary beauty had meant to him—to know that the insult would enrage him. "I don't suppose many queens and princes are swooning over you these days, huh? No more falling at your feet? Whoops, did I say feet? I meant to say hooves."

Sable's eyes glowed an even brighter hue of red. Jax was about to pepper the fool with more equine insults when the humming began. It started low, more like a vibration in the air than an actual noise, from about ten cemetery plots away down the main drive. Jax grinned as the noise gained momentum, became an ear-piercing tone, almost as if some god had a massive wineglass and was running his epic finger across its rim.

Demons throughout the cemetery barked like besieged dogs, reacting to the high-decibel sound.

"Stop that!" A few of them cawed.

"Madness," a low, rolling voice called from the trees.

Then a collective screech of horror: "Light!"

"What is that?" Sable demanded, raising his human torso tall so he could see better. "What are you doing, Ajax? What plan is this?"

"You've been in the desert a long time, Sable, ol' boy." Jax slapped him hard on the withers, almost playfully. "You've forgotten how many tricks we Spartans have in our arsenal. Tricky and clever, that's your opposing team."

Jax smiled, watching the silver specter step through the humming portal. The apparition began materializing, assuming the familiar form of River Kassandros. He was already sprinting before he'd even fully set foot on the road.

Sable made a snorting sound of agitation, surging upward and trotting to head him off. "I'll deal with this one," Sable called out to his minions.

Jax laughed, thinking that the demon had no idea exactly what they had in store for him. He rolled onto his side, rubbing his body to get the blood moving again. There was no time to tend to his thigh or wing; the chase was really on now.

When River spotted Sable, his green eyes widened in shock. Yes, their old nemesis was back, Jax confirmed with a nod when River glanced in his direction, eyebrows raised in question. As their gazes locked, they communicated silently, in the way they always did.

Yes, warrior, now. Go, go, go! he urged, even though River couldn't hear his thoughts. At least, not literally—and yet, as he often did, the servant knew his master's mind.

All at once River began his transition while midrun, never even breaking stride. His human features, the light brown flowing hair, and the long, agile limbs rolled together, rearranged and re-formed. And all the while, River kept hurtling toward the trotting demon. Kept flying at him until at last he had manifested his full power, had chosen the particular form that this battle required. End over end, River sliced through the air, making a whistling sound as he arced toward Sable. Sable gasped in horror as he watched River—now transformed into a gleaming silver sword—pierce deep into his demon's chest.

Thank Ares for River's special talents, Ajax thought, watching Sable collapse downward. Forelegs first, then the rest of him dropped like a leaden weight, sending pebbles spewing. River's aim had been spot-on; with his momentum and sharpness, the sword had buried deep. Sable cried out, grasping with his claws at the broad and intricate hilt. Shaped into the form of hawk wings, it still vibrated from the intensity of River's thrust.

"Oh, River, my friend," Jax said, "yours is a unique gift indeed."

"Damn you, Spartans." Sable collapsed, black-red blood oozing from the gaping wound. "I'll still heal, you know."

"But you won't heal fast. That sword was forged in the River Styx."

Jax strolled to Sable's side, and, reaching for the weapon's protruding hilt, he withdrew it with a quiet, "Thank you, my friend."

A loud screeching sound filled the trees overhead, as if all the demons had gathered at once to observe Sable's fall. "Looks like your pals are enjoying this little moment of ours," Jax told the fallen centaur, who stared up at him with crimson hatred.

Jax strode past him and took the silver sword to the mortal woman who stood frozen in sculpture form. His chest clenched as he got his first close look at her, or the best he could in the pitch blackness of the cemetery— and considering that she was no longer human in appearance. If he didn't know better, he'd have taken her for any other statue in the graveyard. Thank the gods that River had made it; hopefully he wasn't too late.

"River, another job for you. This one needs your life touch."

First he wiped the blade clean of Sable's worthless blood. Then he closed his eyes, pressed his lips to the sword's pommel with a prayer, and thrust the blade right through to the woman's stone heart.

"Work your cure, River, my friend," he whispered, slowly withdrawing the blade once again. It was dripping in melted, flowing silver.

If for warfare, a poison draft—but if for healing, the elixir of life. That was what Ares had proclaimed when he'd forged River within flowing Styx itself. Of course, that simple pronouncement hadn't touched on the specific issues of *control* that would plague River for the rest of his immortal days, but control wasn't a problem at the moment. Not until River returned to human form, and by then he'd be back with Leonidas and the others who could handle him as a berserker.

Jax watched the frozen woman, hoping for a transformation, but none came. Only the area that he'd riven with the blade regained color; the rest of her was deathly white, still stone. He pressed his fingertips against her cold lips, wishing that his own life force could revive her.

That was when he heard it: The slightest whisper trickled through his mind.

Can you hear me?

The angelic entity jolted backward from Shay, something vivid gleaming in his hand. It had to be whatever he'd used to revive her. But man, oh, man, the pain in her chest felt like a whole troop of demons had been moshing on it.

Can you hear me at all? she tried again, shouting the question within her mind as loudly as she could. If that ugly demon had been able to intercept her prayers, maybe the angel could do the same.

"Yes, mortal, I can hear you." His voice was rich and deep, accented and a little husky. Instantly she felt safer.

With all the mental focus she could summon, she telegraphed, *There is a way you can free me.*

"I'm working on that now," he answered softly. Not defensively or even reassuringly; more like he felt really . . . sad.

Oh, shit, she thought, *that can't be a good sign.* Then, to him, she said, *It's not working, is it? Your plan?*

"Not as fast as I had hoped."

Summer heat brushed against her lips again; the angel's fingers stroked her, and she could feel his touch deep inside herself. It was as if it echoed from the cold outer prison of her body, then deep down into her soul.

You'll have to leave me here ... if the demons come back again.

"No," he said, and she felt that same fiery caress down her arms, "I shan't be doing that. You are a mortal, one of my protected. I am here to guard and free you."

Then listen to me ... about my idea. It could work.

"Tell me." That same fiery heat of his ran the length of her arms, and she knew he was caressing her, waking her bit by bit. It just wasn't working fast enough, not if the demons were still out there.

My brothers hunt demons, she confessed in a mental rush. *There are books, old lore.... I came across something like a paralysis spell a month ago. About how to counteract one. I can tell you the words to the reversal spell.*

"Humans don't have such knowledge." He actually sounded affronted.

Look, dude. I don't care about your ego right now—try it. These are the words....

Oh, man, she couldn't quite remember. It was a great plan right up to the memorization part. Mentally, she flashed on a statue of Saint Sebastian that she'd studied in college. She envisioned the crown that had been carved in detail upon the figure's head.

That's it! Death crown ... something about a death crown. Wait, I remember—"When there is a death crown upon your head, your heart and soul unmoving deep within, speak this forth and death's hold will free thee...."

The powerful words spilled forth within her spirit in ancient Greek. The angel whispered back at her in ancient Greek, too, his voice wondrous. If only she really spoke the language.

I don't understand.

"I don't either," he replied, then spun from her and uttered the freeing pronouncement. All at once her body ... awoke. There was no other way to put it. She felt herself thawing from the inside out, sensed life once again coursing through every cell of her body.

"How did you know the words of the Oracle's prophecy?" he demanded as she first blinked her eyes.

"The Oracle?" she repeated numbly, taking a small step forward.

"Yes, you just quoted her with that reversal spell about the death's crown."

Dizzy, she began to crumple toward the ground, but the angel—and oh, my God, he really was one, complete with massive, feathered black wings that gleamed in the moonlight—the angel swept her up into his heavy, muscular arms and launched heavenward.

Chapter 8

Jamie stared into the darkness surrounding the house. Shay should have been home by now. She was known to party hard sometimes, or even to crash at Sophie's or Angela's instead of going home to her own place. But not on a night like this one, when the darkness that they lived with daily seemed to be even closer than usual. She always came back to the family home when the warfare got heavy and thick, when the great wall of spiritual dimensions felt like it could crumble at any moment.

Jamie checked his BlackBerry for what felt like the fifty millionth time, but the only new message was a text from one of their historic-district clients. Mrs. von Mannstein kept getting freaked by the ghost in her attic: a ghost that, by all their calculations, didn't even exist. But she was a charming, hip old lady, and her only real problem was that she watched too much SciFi Channel.

After staring at his empty mailbox one last time, he tossed the handheld onto the side table and reached for their police scanner. He propped it on his lap and adjusted the volume. *Usual shit,* he thought in disgust. Some stupid tourist had gotten blasted and gone walking in the wrong part of town. Now he'd been mugged and was mad and scared. The familiar voices of their friends down at the station cut back and forth, the dispatcher telling them to shut up, bad jokes all the way around.

With a frustrated sigh, he propped his loafers on the

porch railing. *Think of it as poker night,* he told himself. *Buckle in for the long haul, keep a straight face.*

Tipping the wicker chair back, he balanced it. His physical posture was casual—but his eyes never stopped searching the perimeter of their family land. From the edge of the river to the length of their dock, then with a sideways look down their dirt drive, he was on guard. One thing was sure—the demons would love to come calling tonight. They'd cackle and taunt, try to siphon off some of his grief for a quick high.

Cigar smoke wafted from the far end of the veranda, and although Mason kept his usual silence, Jamie knew his gaze roved the darkness, too. That was just like him; his younger brother was also waiting for interlopers, hoping for their sister's return. Yes, she should have been back long before now.

Floorboards creaked, smoke grew closer, and Mason began another turn down the long length of the second-floor porch. "Where the hell is she?" he asked.

Jamie dropped the chair back to four legs and sat up straight. "I'd like to say she's just out partying," he admitted, "but this shit's crawling all over my skin."

The end of Mason's cigar glowed red, and he puffed a moment. "Mine, too," he said, blowing out a spiral of smoke. Then he took another long drag off the cigar, propping himself against the railing in front of Jamie. "I say we go looking."

Jamie shook his head. "You know that will only bug the crap outta her if everything's all right."

"Too fucking bad." Mason folded arms across his chest, cigar between stubby fingers. "I ain't gonna lose anyone else, not now."

"Mace, we got nothing." Jamie leaned forward in his chair, staring up at his brother in the half darkness. "She went downtown for a drink. She's stayed out way later than this plenty of times."

"Not on a night like this one." Mason's features were obscured by the shadows, but Jamie knew he was scowling.

"Yeah," Jamie said, thinking of his earlier conversation with Shay. "Agreed."

Despite all their efforts otherwise, she'd awakened; the letter had only stoked that flame.

Mason stood, poised to roll. "So we go."

Jamie shook his head. "Call the station. See if there's anything the scanner's not picking up. Maybe Bubba will do a drive-by of her usual spots."

"She's grieving, Jamie. In pain." Mason's voice grew sharp. "You know what that means—even if *she* doesn't know what she is, sooner or later *they're* gonna figure it out." Mason walked toward the table and stubbed his cigar out in the ashtray. "We can't leave her vulnerable."

Jamie closed his eyes, shivering. He had to tell Mason. It was going to mess with his head in a serious way—and his mind had already gone to shit ever since Iraq. But the truth had to be put out there.

"She already knows," he admitted softly.

"What?" Mason spun to face him. "Since when? Why didn't you tell me?"

"Calm down. I don't mean she knows about the Eye. I just mean she's aware that she has a gift."

"How the hell—"

Jamie cut him off. " 'Cause she's seeing them, all right? She's open, and there's not a damn thing any of us can do about it."

"She told you that?"

"Yeah, tonight during the wake." Jamie rose to his feet and walked toward the railing.

"But not anything about the Eye?"

Jamie shook his head, planting both hands on the railing. He stared down the long driveway that led to the road, wishing he'd see the flash of her Jeep's headlights. With a sigh, he stared out at their family's long-held property. It was marked by their blood, their callings. It was protected in every way possible. No demons should be able to tread here . . . yet, just as Shay said, sometimes they did.

"What about the Eye, James?" Mason repeated, voice tighter.

"She doesn't know shit about that."

"Good. And you're not going to tell her."

And you're not going to tell me what to do. He bit the words back. As the eldest and the leader of the hunters, he gave the orders; at just ten months younger, Mason sometimes got ahead of himself.

"We'll have to see how this all plays out," Jamie said. "I don't want her unequipped."

Mason joined him at the railing. "We promised Mama that we'd keep her out of all this."

"Mama didn't tell us that she'd started seeing demons." Jamie leveled Mason with a significant look. "Apparently Shay told her that a few months ago." Jamie held his brother's gaze for several long seconds.

After a long moment, Mason looked away. "Did she mention the letter?"

"Of course she did." Jamie snorted. "She's keeping it in her back pocket everywhere she goes."

Mason cursed low under his breath. "Damn and double damn."

"Go call the station." Jamie thought about their sister, weighed her need for independence with her current vulnerability. "If they don't find her and she doesn't get back in thirty, we head out."

Why would any angel's wings be so black? Wouldn't they be white or even golden, made of heavenly fleece? Not menacing and darkly violent, like the ones her savior bore upon his back. It was a random thought, probably stupid, but as she clung to the guy, launching upward with him like some NASA experiment, it was about the only thing Shay could focus on.

With a desperate stolen glance over her shoulder, she gasped as the dark ground below them grew farther and farther away. It was like that horrible recurring dream of hers, the one where the Ferris wheel dislodged, taking her dangerously high. Only this was no dream—or if it was, she sure as heck hadn't been able to wake up from it yet.

Snap out of it! Wake up! *Slap, slap, Shay.*

The ground just spiraled farther below, the heavy wind whipping her hair across her eyes and chilling her face and neck.

Nope, not a dream, she thought, feeling every nerve ending, every muscle in her body scream its wakeful state right back at her. The illumination of Savannah spread beneath her dangling feet like Christmas lights. It would have been beautiful if she weren't scared out of her mind, practically clawing at the angel's neck in a frantic bid to hang on to him tighter.

"Oh, my God. Oh, my God! Am I dead? Is this how you take me to heaven?"

"You're very much alive, little mortal." As if dismissing her intense fear and confusion, he adjusted her easily within his arms, scooping her against his heavily muscled chest. He was bare skinned except for a kind of . . . well, leather loincloth that covered his lower body. And all that bare skin, tight across rock-hard muscle, felt fantastically warm—especially since the night air was only growing colder the higher he flew.

He held a sword in his free hand, and for a moment he adjusted it, propping it against her side. Then he lifted it upward in a sort of charging gesture. "River Kassandros, well-done!" he cheered; then—it was the most bizarre thing—he hurled the sword into the air as though he never planned to use it again. He just discarded it like so much deadweight, or a heavy, useless stone.

Shay followed the weapon's crashing descent, amazed that he'd let something so detailed and intricate go—but watching was a first-class mistake. She got instant vertigo. That, and witnessed about the umpteenth weird thing of the day: The wings along the sword's pommel lifted right off of it, growing into black, feathered ones just like her angel's. The wings' size increased and thickened until they flew right into the wind—into the wind without any living form attached to them whatsoever.

A roll of nausea had her instantly burying her face against the angel's bulky shoulder. "Oh, my God, God, God," she murmured, refusing to look again.

"I'd stop using His name like that," he said matter-of-factly. "Because my general impression is that He's not so fond of it. That is, if you mean the God Without a Name."

"Shouldn't you know who God is?" she screeched in alarm, half climbing the creature's body as he soared suddenly much higher.

"It all depends on which one you mean. The Highest God? I assume He's the one you're invoking. Then again, perhaps Apollo is more your style, or Zeus." He chuckled strangely to himself, then added, "Although I'd leave Zeus out of it." His voice grew gravelly, richer, darker. "You know how *that* went for Leda."

"Leda and the Swan" had been one of the first poems she'd memorized in AP English, years ago in high school. Yeats, wasn't it? Then all the paintings and sculptures she'd studied while at art school. Dozens of versions of the very same myth, but always with Zeus taking the form of a swan, and . . .

Shay stiffened, lifting her head to stare the angel in the eyes. What kind of angel used sexual innuendo, especially while rescuing his protected?

"You've got to set me down or I'm gonna fall right out of your arms and totally die." She tried to sound brave, but the truth was, she was shaking so hard, it made speech nearly impossible.

He stared into her eyes, soared for a moment without beating those epic wings, and a slow and wicked smile spread across his full lips. "Did I frighten you, mortal?"

"You kidnapped me back there. You've literally swept me up on some sort of journey with you—which I'm gonna assume isn't to take me to heaven, since you nixed that one."

That lovely wicked smile grew wider, revealing the

flash of white teeth and a slight dimple in one cheek. "Oh, perhaps I could show you heaven, lass, but it won't be the spiritual kind." He laughed, a low and erotic sound. "I don't see how you have much choice at the moment either," he continued, once again beginning a slow and steady rhythm with his wings. With every motion of the sleek black appendages, his thick chest filled out slightly, pushing into her, making her increasingly aware of his supernatural heat.

His skin was smooth, hairless—at least across his pectorals—but lower on his body she felt the light tickling of feathers. It seemed that near his abdomen, what would have been a trail of wiry hair leading southward was, in fact, a dusting of down.

And why did that thought make her entire body tense and ache with lust for this . . . creature? He wasn't a man, and, as angels went, he wasn't even totally good.

You are so twisted, she told herself—right before she remembered that he'd been able to hear some of her projected thoughts earlier. She pulled back, studying his face to see if he had any inkling of what his extremely male and chiseled body was doing to her.

He smiled that crooked, half-cocked grin, the same one he'd used before, looking smug and satisfied with himself. The jerk knew exactly how hot he was; heck, he probably posed for beefcake pictures somewhere on the Net.

"Set. Me. Down," she repeated. *Firm and authoritative. That's what this situation is going to take.* "Now!"

"Back in Bonaventure?"

"No . . . somewhere safe."

"The only safe place for you, little lass, is right here in my arms. At least for the time being. Those demons will want to taste your mortal blood for a while yet."

She shivered again, thinking that it was so her luck to have such limited choices.

"Besides," he whispered huskily in her ear, "I can recite a little poetry while we travel."

"Screw that! Where are we going? I mean it, pal. You tell me where we're headed."

He laughed, nuzzling her cheek. "In circles at the moment—at least until I get you to settle down."

"That's what you call this? Settling me down?"

"I had some other ideas about how to accomplish that—relaxation techniques, let's call them—but you didn't seem to like the idea of playing Leda with me."

"You're supposed to be my protector. I'm gonna seriously complain to someone when this is all over, because, well, you really have a bad attitude. You know, one of those eight-hundred numbers for truck drivers, but with you it's 'how's my flying?' Surely it's against some rule *somewhere* for you to come on to me while hying me away from a killer demon horde."

"Lucky you, but I answer to no man . . . well, save one, and he's not present at the moment."

"How totally reassuring."

"Besides, wee nymph, look at the sky about you, at the land below . . . feel the power of the air beneath my wings . . . feel it in your own body. Experience every one of my movements within your own limbs." He pressed his lips against her cheek, murmuring, "Fly with me; don't fight."

He paused, running a warm, stroking palm along her back. But his heat only made her shiver even more, made her tremble against his bare chest. Where he held her cradled beneath the knees, he began rubbing the back of her right calf, and her whole leg erupted in needy fire. "Feel our bodies, as one, here in the heavens. Why should you want to be anywhere else but in my arms, safe beneath my wings? Yes, I protect you. But, as it happens, I also want to awaken you."

"I don't think I'm dreaming," she stammered, feeling the light brush of his beard growth against her own smooth cheek. "I-I figured that out."

"I'm not talking about sleep, my Leda. Although what I'm thinking of might be best accomplished in a nice bed." He laughed wickedly, causing her face and neck to burn. Then he became suddenly tender once again. He adjusted her in his arms, pulling her a heartbeat closer, adding, "But the open air works just as well for holding you captive. Besides, besting Sable's ass has left me, it seems, a tad . . . randy."

Her heart might as well have stopped. And that was before he drew his warm mouth against her ear and began quoting Yeats. He murmured the words slowly, as if he were savoring them, offering each one of them as a delicacy, a specific seduction. Slowly he recited "Leda and the Swan." Giving emphasis to the stanzas describing the bird's wings and webbed feet, the ones that told how he used his transformed body to press her thighs apart . . . and how he overcame the innocent girl.

He stroked her hair, caught about her face from the harsh forces of wind and nature. Warm fingertips grazed her cheekbone; he nuzzled her. No sound filled her ear for long moments except for the whistling of the air all about them—that and his accelerated breathing. And all the while, his chest expanded and filled with every single wingbeat.

His warm breath filled her ear once again—right when she almost figured he wouldn't continue. "Shall I catch you in my talons, mortal?" he hissed, his voice suddenly harsh, aggressive. Urgent. "Show you my full hawk form and ravage you with my beak? I could chase you, if you'd like, pursue you. Think what that would feel like . . . all this power that you've got about you right now, caressing you, stealing you."

She closed her eyes, losing herself in his alien heat, feeling dampness form between her thighs—the total answer to his erotic questions. *Oh, yes, yes.* She wanted him to ravage her, and not in human form. She wanted wings and submission, exactly as he threatened. Promised. Offered.

"What . . ." *What are you saying to me, black angel? That you really plan to rape me? Seduce me?* Those were the words that burned on her tongue, but she didn't have the nerve to ask them.

"What . . . is your . . . name?" she just barely managed, as he swept downward in a breath-stealing dive. She cried out, burying her face against his bulky shoulder, and he laughed.

"You didn't like that?"

"I'm going to be sick."

"From me? Am I so revolting to your mortal senses? My needs that perverse?"

"You're in some sort of . . ." She shrieked as his momentum carried them upward once again. "You bastard—you did that on purpose."

"I'm memorizing your reactions. Gauging what excites you," he said, brushing his lips against her forehead. "It seems that only my highest intensity opens you up."

"Tell me one thing—you're not an angel at all, are you?"

"If you want me to be . . . I'll play that game."

She was shaking: her hands about his neck and shoulders, her thighs caught within the cradle of his thick arms. Even her torso did a sort of vibration against the man's massive body. *Man.* Because she couldn't think of him as an angel, not anymore.

"Please," she whispered at last, pulling back slightly so she could stare into his hooded black eyes. "Just tell me who you are. What you are. I . . . I'm lost right now. And so afraid."

He reared back, his wings pushing forward about them both as he halted midflight. Staring at her, he flashed that wicked grin again, this time spreading wider than ever before. "Well, sweet darling," he replied, his voice almost a hawk's cry, not nearly human. "I'm the raptor who saved your mortal soul this night."

And then his smile faded and he faced forward, eyes fixed on the landscape far below them as he began to fly once again—as if he'd never wooed or attempted to seduce her at all. As if he'd merely been teasing all along, as if he thought she might forget the way his poetry had pierced her, body and soul.

"I'll set down over there. We'll find someplace to hide for the night." His rich voice had become . . . remote, helpful. The insane thing was that Shay hated that change—it was as though he'd suddenly abandoned her. She clung harder to him in reaction, wrapping both arms like a vise about his neck.

"Don't fear," he promised, that primal hawk's cry even harsher this time. "I'll protect you."

She shivered against him, suddenly more afraid than she'd been in the cemetery, more terrified than she'd ever been in her entire life. More than when her father had been murdered by a demon pack. More shaken than she'd been while turned to stone earlier. No, the simple promise that this black angel would protect her caused her very soul to quake. Because the real question wasn't how he'd save her, but something much more threatening.

What would this . . . thing, man, whatever he was, do once they landed? With all the promises he'd just whispered in her ear and suggested, what might he do if given a night alone with her?

And even worse—what might she do in return?

Jamie's sixth sense suddenly went on full alert. Mason hadn't returned from calling Bubba down at the station, but it had been only a few minutes. It wasn't really that; more just a deep knowing. Shay was in danger. A quiet voice whispered it in his mind, and all at once the hair on his nape prickled and the top of his head went numb.

At almost that precise moment, the door to the veranda opened with a crash. Without even waiting for Mason to give him an update, Jamie said, "What's happened to her?"

Mason grabbed the hood of Jamie's sweatshirt, yanking him out of the chair. "We have to get downtown. They just found her Jeep down at Bonaventure," he said. "Abandoned. She's nowhere in sight."

Jamie was on his feet and moving before Mason was even finished. "We'll take my truck," he said. "Search all her usual spots. Maybe one of her friends met her there."

"I'm calling Sophie now, to see if she's with her."

Jamie shook his head. "I already did that. None of her friends have heard from her all night. They've been texting her, too. Checking up on her, but no reply."

Mason halted by the door, fixing him with a worried stare. "This ain't like her, James. You know it, and I know it, too."

Jamie nodded. "That's why we're going after her," he said, sprinting inside the house. "Before it's too late."

Chapter 9

"This might be a bit rough. I'm not used to landing with a mortal in my arms." He leaned forward, watching the land below approach faster than he would have liked. He worked his wings in the wind, molding it to his needs, slowing their descent.

"Define *rough*. How rough, exactly?" the mortal asked, trembling within his arms.

As rough as you'll take it, sweet one, he thought, but bit back the words. "Just hold tight to my shoulders and I'll do the rest."

The woman leaned into him, the fullness of her breasts grazing his bare chest. He would have groaned at the temptation, but their imminent landing was a very useful distraction. If he didn't plot their trajectory with precise accuracy, her extra weight could unbalance them. No, this wasn't the time for more flirtation or seduction. Just putting them down on both feet was going to require every ounce of his physical agility and concentration. Any miscalculation and they might bounce off the hard ground like a pair of copper pennies across an open pond. Only it would be their flesh tearing with every bounce, and although he would recover almost instantly, her frail human body might be flayed to pieces.

He swooped into the tree-lined park that he'd chosen upon descent, thankful that although the mortal world was perfectly visible to the two of them, not one human soul would detect their arrival. His wings cut through the top of twin live oaks, sending sleeping birds screeching, and with an awkward running tumble they skidded onto an open patch of grass.

With a grunt and a heavy topple, he kept her in his arms, but the sheer force of their arrival had him sprawling atop her much smaller body. It took a few seconds for each to catch their breath, and he was just about to roll off of her when she looked right up at him, locking gazes. As if she were truly seeing him for the first time, her pale eyes went wide.

"Oh, my God, your wings. You really have wings. Big, huge black"—she lifted both hands in a waving motion—"wings!"

He levered himself upward onto one elbow, savoring the feel of her warm, curving body beneath his much heavier one. "I thought we'd already established that fact, love. Seeing as how I carried you here with them." He kept his voice lazy, liking the idea of turning this mortal on. If she was a wing girl, then so be it. He'd bedded his share of those. He just wished that it weren't so dark, that he'd been given one truly good look at her since capturing her from the cemetery. He ached for more than mere half-shadowed glimpses in the night.

"But I couldn't tell how big they were. They're so .. massive." She made no effort to move from beneath him, just kept staring wide-eyed at him. "And I thought angel wings would be white." She sounded puzzled.

Angel? She'd said that earlier, but he'd assumed she was joking. It had been at least a few hundred years since anyone had mistaken his black form for that. Fair enough: If it worked for the moment, so be it.

With a cautious movement she reached past his shoulder, as if she planned to touch one of his feathered appendages. Ajax swatted her away; he had to act quickly, before she made a solid connection with his altered physical form. Unlike his recent lovers in London, he needed *this* one to remember so he could find out how she tied into the prophecy. His flesh body was one thing, but she couldn't touch the part of him that was purely immortal—and that would be his wings. The one completely god-endowed portion of his altered anatomy. They were the most sensitive part of his body, and if this woman touched him there, he might lose his senses entirely. And he needed his wits right now to find out how and why she'd quoted the Oracle's own words.

"I just want to see what they're made of," she told him, leaning back into the grass. He had the strange thought that they were youthful lovers, about to tup right in that park.

"Hawk's wings. Basically." Keep it simple, to the point. The less this little mortal knew the better.

Truth was, he *had* stolen her from the demons, acting as her protector, so no wonder she'd mistaken him for an angel. But now, back on terra firma, he needed to learn about her connection to the Oracle. Why was it that she'd known about the "death's crown" referred to in the prophecy?

She had practically quoted the words—well, more precisely, one of her family's books had. And in ancient Greek, no less. So no matter how badly his randy cock wanted to find out what she felt like inside, no matter how much he longed to take his wings and rake them over her naked body, he had a duty to fulfill. The fragile little mortal clearly held the key to his Savannah mission, so it was imperative that he keep her memories intact, and that meant no true touching of his one purely immortal feature—the wings. Bedding her he could do, but not transformed like this.

Besides, if she stroked so much as a single feather, traced her fingertip along just one barb or rachis across his back, he'd be given no recourse at all. The pleasure of it, the sheer arousal of her touch—her mortal caresses against his hawk's body—would be too much to resist. His Spartan discipline, corrupted lately, could withstand only so much temptation.

She lifted both hands again, the expression in her eyes a mix of amazement and hunger, but he caught her by both wrists. "Don't." He swallowed hard. "Not a good idea."

Unfortunately, she was a stubborn little thing and ignored him completely. Two fingertips nearly made contact with the feathers of his right wing, causing a jolt of wild pleasure to spear through his whole body.

I could take her—not here, but somewhere safe. Let us roll together, wing and flesh. His body tensed; his fingers spread into talons once again. With a choked cry of frustration, he raked them into the earth, tearing at the grass.

"I told you not to touch me there," he growled, his body flexing violently atop hers.

"I didn't." She hesitated, withdrawing her hands, and all he could do was stare like a dumb fool into what he could see of those breathtaking eyes. It didn't matter that they were darkened by the shadows of night and the trees overhead; he didn't need details to know just how perfectly she'd been formed.

He was beyond control, and far too willing to let her cross his boundaries. Turning his gaze toward the moon, he absorbed the wings instantly, becoming fully human in appearance once again. All that separated them was his leather loin covering; otherwise he lay naked atop her.

Unable to deny how he craved the human beneath him, he bent low and covered her mouth with his own. In an instant they were already one, her body molding together with his, their tongues twining in a maddening dance for dominance. Damn, it was too easy savoring this one . . . such a sweet taste, too, like something pure that he'd always craved. Waited for.

He thrust his hand through her long hair, brushing it beneath his fingertips, amazed that it was like pure, curling silk. Warm hands slid down his back, stroked his spine—that seam where his wings began—as if she were searching out his darker, truer nature. As if it weren't enough for him to be in human form. Damn it, but he longed to be winged again, to roll with her and wrap her in his feathered, transformed embrace.

I could take you high up in the heavens, join our bodies as one upon the winds. He had to swallow the words, they burned so hot upon his tongue. *Let me show you the wildest part of this hawk-man.*

As if she'd heard his silent words, she ran warm fingertips along his spine once again, stroking, teasing his true nature to the fore. The burn of his change began, nearly overtaking him, but he beat back the urge by thrusting his tongue deeper within her mouth. By rolling with her—not once, but twice, until he lay atop her all over again, until they clung to each other, breathless and hot. Their bodies were dampened by the dew of the grass, yet they pressed together like wildfire. Ajax felt—was sure—that if he didn't halt their kissing embrace soon, then surely they would combust into something dangerous, become dark and winged together. It seemed possible that the small mortal who lay beneath his pulsing body might even sprout wings herself.

"Help me," he murmured, finally breaking the kiss. "Gods of Olympus, you are unlike any woman I've ever touched."

"You . . . are gorgeous," she whispered in turn, and wrapped both arms about his neck, drawing his head down atop her breast. He could hear her thudding heart, its beat so desperate that it literally ricocheted into his own body.

He had to keep her memories untainted—if they made love, he could never learn how this lovely, sensual human played into his mission in Savannah. Drawing upon every bit of his Spartan discipline, he raised onto both elbows, tamping down his sexual craving.

"We can't do this," he told her resolutely, wiping the back of his right hand across his swollen mouth. "This can't happen, not here and not now."

She blinked up at him. "Then when?" So innocent and genuine—so unhindered by the darkness that ruled his world.

"I don't know," he told her honestly. "Much as I ache for you . . . for this . . . I don't know."

But I need you, crave you . . . later. Later I'll take you, sweetest mortal.

She raked a hand across her brow. "Like I said earlier: You're about the sort of angel I'd get." The woman collapsed backward, arms falling at her sides as she struggled to breathe beneath the weight of his body. "I prayed for you," she said quietly. "I asked to see you. To have you reveal yourself to me. I just never thought you'd kiss like ... man, like *that*."

The angel stared down into her eyes, seeming vaguely annoyed—no, not annoyed—confused. "Forget the kiss," he told her gruffly. "It never should have happened." Yet he didn't move from his prone position atop her, and who was she to shove him aside?

"No kidding," she agreed, shivering as she stared into his otherworldly, silver-filled eyes.

His expression grew stern. "How could you possibly have prayed to see someone you have no knowledge of?"

"Maybe I'd never seen one of your kind before now, but I've always believed. And now I know. Even if you are some weird seducing type, you're *still* an angel," she whispered prayerfully, rising up on her elbows. "And you came and helped me fight. You saved me, just like I prayed for you to."

He lifted into a push-up, staring into her eyes. His beautiful smile transformed, becoming harsh and sinister. "Well, lovely, I'd say you saved your own arse in that particular battle." He rolled away from her in the grass. "Although you weren't much good beyond the incantation."

He stood, his gaze outlining her body from head to ... well, his stare pretty much stopped and pulled a bull's-eye on her boobs. "I don't suppose you're good for much else." The boobs or the incantation? She wasn't sure, and he let his meaning dangle as a double entendre, finally lifting an eyebrow in challenge.

He sounded awfully snitty for a heavenly being. Standing in that shaft of moonlight that shot through the trees overhead, he looked far too sinful to be any angel that she'd ever heard about. Again he let his piercing silver gaze—and she was sure of it now; his eyes truly were silver, not just illuminated by the full moon above—rest on her chest. His lashes dropped to half-mast, his full lips parted.

"Come on," he said, extending his hand. "We need to get someplace safer."

And the silver eyes changed hues, turning to pure, threatening black. At that same moment the clouds overhead parted briefly, casting him in magnificent, terrifying profile. Suddenly she understood. She never saw angels, no matter how hard she prayed, but there was another kind of being that surrounded her every day in outrageous abundance.

She collapsed backward in the grass and, feeling stupidly giddy, began to laugh. Of course, nothing was funny about how much danger she'd just realized she was in, but that was what made it so darkly amusing.

She'd finally figured out the identity of her bad Spider-Man. And now that she had, it just seemed like such a *her* thing to do . . . to inadvertently attract the most dangerous being she possibly could.

The moonlight grew brighter, the creature seemed to loom even taller, and as she gazed up into his shifting eyes she became convinced of one plain fact.

This savior of hers, this winged devil, was no angel. He was pure demon. And she wanted him like she'd never wanted any man before in her life.

All of that came clear in the space of a heartbeat as clouds traced along the night sky. In the next heartbeat the demon's eyes widened, becoming like full silver moons themselves. And, staring at her, he gasped the one word she never could have guessed that he'd say.

"Shayanna?"

Somehow the baffling, sensual entity knew her name. And, man, oh, man, given his love-poem knowledge, and that angel's body, he'd undoubtedly figure out how to add it to his daunting arsenal.

"Shayanna Angel," he murmured, eyes wildly searching her face. "It's *you*. My Shay. It was so dark, so sudden. But now I recognize you."

My Shay. He'd called her *his*. "How do you know who I am?"

He shook his head. "Doesn't matter. But that *is* your name." He presented it as ironclad fact, and she didn't see where denying it would get her.

"Sure enough, but folks all call me Shay. Only my mama ever really called me Shayanna."

"Yes, of course. Shay," he repeated, as if he were rolling her name about in his mouth, tasting it. "I've been saying it wrong all this time." He kept repeating her name, accenting it slightly differently with each usage.

All this time? What, was he some kind of demon stalker? Maybe he even had a copy of *Catcher in the Rye* tucked away inside that leather loin-skirt of his.

For a long moment he said nothing, just stood studying her breathlessly. His bare chest gleamed in the moonlight; his exposed titan's thighs were solid as a pair of tree trunks. Now that he'd ditched the wings, he was basically naked except for his privates, which he kept contained in that leather wrap of sorts. Talk about the ultimate tool belt   especially if that leather cup was any size gauge in terms of what it concealed.

As if he'd read her thoughts—or noticed how hard she was staring—he parted his legs a little wider. From her view below, she could tell that the cup was even larger than she'd initially guessed, created somehow—by God, aliens, angels, Frederick's, who knew?—to accommodate his mythic form.

For the briefest moment she pictured herself kneeling before him, her hands working at that leather binding, freeing him.

"Oh, my God," she blurted, flushing wildly. *I did not just imagine slowly unwrapping him, did I?*

"I'm sorry; I've been rude," he said softly.

She rubbed a hand across her brow, sexually frustrated and a little bit frightened. "With what?"

"My lack of appropriate"—he smiled significantly, let-

ting her know that he'd noticed her visual appreciation—
"attire." In a flash of light he transformed and was wearing
a black T-shirt and black cargo pants. "This should be
more familiar to you."

Damn, she'd never said she *minded* the leather. Anyway, the black ninja look was supposed to be better how,
exactly?

She sat up on the grass—too fast, apparently; all at
once the world went Tilt-A-Whirl on her. Her heart
slammed even harder in her chest, and the dampness in
her panties grew softer, thicker.

"Shay, are you all right?" He squatted beside her.

"I just . . ." The earth spun a little wilder. "Oh, I think
it's from the flying. I'm feeling funky. Way too funky."

"Stay still a moment," he cautioned. One massive hand
reached out, brushing a loose lock of hair back from her
eyes. Unbelievable, but she'd have sworn that his hand
was trembling a little. Not as though he were cold or
afraid; as if he felt too much not to quiver. It was such
a vulnerable detail, such a human one, it made it hard
to picture him as some leather-winged raptor from hell.
Besides, he'd saved her from all the other playground
bullies tonight, so he couldn't be absolutely evil, right?
He'd been gentle with her, too.

The spinning stopped, and she stole a glance at him.
A slow, cautious smile spread across his face, the single
dimple appearing. "Better?"

She nodded and quickly looked away; she was afraid
to stare at him another moment. As if she might fall into
him somehow, get lost forever just by gazing into his
eyes.

He allowed the rough pad of his thumb to graze her
cheekbone. "You're sure you're all right, Shay?"

She laughed, pulling out of his grasp. "Dude. You really dig my name, don't you?" *If I keep things light and
casual, I won't react so much . . . won't feel so much.*

Unfortunately, the warrior hadn't gotten the light-and-
casual memo, because he sighed, a great, melancholy

sound that snapped her gaze right back to his face. He'd
sounded so lost. So alone. In that one weary exhalation.

He opened his mouth, shut it. Opened it again, hesitated. Finally he whispered, "Your name. Shay, yes, your
name is beautiful to me. I've lived . . ." He stopped, looking past her shoulder for a moment, then continued in a
much rougher voice. "There was a time when the sound
of it made no sense to me. It was too foreign. Then it
became like a rare jewel . . . so it's amusing to find that I
wasn't even pronouncing it properly."

"So how've you been saying it, then?"

"Too quickly. Like it's a short little thing, but you draw
it out. Put more syllables in the pronunciation."

"I'm nothing if not a Southern gal."

"I like your way. It's much more beautiful." He stared
down at her, lips half parted, hair wildly windblown,
black cargo pants massively tenting. Reflexively, Shay
scooted back a few inches on the grass, trying to put a
little distance between the giant and herself. He shadowed her movement, stepping forward—and looking
for all the world as though he planned to jump her in
five seconds flat.

"Look . . . how did you know my name? *Why* would
you have known it for a long time?"

As if suddenly remembering himself, he glanced about
the park. "We're not safe here. I have to get you off the
pack's radar."

"Are you part of their horde? Or I guess you used to
be, but then you and that Sable dude had a big falling-
out. That's it, right?"

He frowned in apparent surprise, pulling her to her
feet. "When did I get downgraded from angel status?"

"When you told me you weren't one," she cried, her
voice growing louder. "Duh. I know, crazy character
fault, but I tend to believe people."

"Oh, love, that's a bad one." He shook his head. "We'll
have to work on that habit if you're going to make it in
the demon-hunting game."

"You're a demon who somehow called my name from nothing."

"Underground," he said laconically. "Best protection from their kind."

"Their kind?" she asked. "*Their* kind? What makes them so different from you?"

"Trust me, love. I'm no demon."

He scooped one hand under her elbow and began walking briskly, his long, powerful legs absolutely eating up the ground. In order to keep up, she was forced into a cartoonlike scramble, her much smaller legs bicycling at the ground while he dragged her along beside him. They passed a large, gurgling fountain, and with a sideways glance Shay spotted the old fort that placed them in Forsyth Park. He avoided the main walkways, dragging her through the shadowed, darker portions of the park, toward the street.

"My brothers have got to be wondering where I am," she said, searching the darkness for demons. She didn't see a single one. Which meant that this creature who was yanking her toward God-only-knew-where was her current threat. "They're probably on your butt already."

"Shay, I'm not a threat to you. I promise."

"You're not an angel and you're not a threat—but you are a demon," she said, and when he yanked her by the elbow again, she cried, "Ow! That hurts, pal. Let me go and let's just make a run for wherever you're taking me."

He stopped in his tracks, lowering his head so he could look her in the eyes. "If I release you, you will run, Shay. I'm not an unwise man. Your fleeing, however, *would* be most unwise. Sable and his underlings are following you—they've targeted you now, and they're not going to relent."

The words formed like lead inside her stomach. He was right; whatever the man might be, he had saved her before. She had no choice but to remain under his protection.

"I won't run," she told him earnestly. "I'm not an unwise woman, either."

"Of course not. You wouldn't be." He smiled that sideways, half-cocked grin that had aroused her earlier. It did its work all over again. But the freaky thing was the way he said the words, the meaning that seemed to be behind them—as if he'd known her for a very, very long time.

"How do you know that, though?" She gazed up into his eyes, so dark in the shadows, and they began to glow an electric, otherworldly shade of silver.

His smile vanished. "There will be time later for you to know everything." He took hold of her hand and began to jog toward Drayton Street. "Now we run."

Jamie gunned his Chevy down East Park, paused at Drayton, and was thankful that the difficult four-way was almost empty at this hour. He made a sharp left, his tires screeching as he accelerated onto Drayton. Then, just ahead in the arc of his lights, he saw Shay.

Mason did, too. "There she is!" His brother slapped the dashboard. "Right up there, Jamie! Pull over!"

But who the hell was that man standing with her? He had a grip on her hand and was jerking her out toward the street. Jamie pushed the pedal to the metal, laying hard on the horn. Shay glanced up and stared at his truck, eyes wide—with relief? Shock? There wasn't time to decide.

He swerved up to a stop beside the pair and thrust the truck into gear; Mason was already in the street, running toward Shay. "Who the fuck are you?" his brother shouted, lunging for the extremely tall and bulky man who had a hold on her.

Jamie was only one step behind. "Shay, what the hell are you doing? It's almost two a.m.! And who is this . . . ?"

The dark man glanced between them, releasing Shay. Taking two steps back, he held both hands up. "She's safe," the guy said, and not as though he were defending himself. "But you need to get her out of here."

Shay ran to Jamie as if she were seeking shelter from

the worst kind of attacker. He put himself between her and the big man. "Go get in the car, Shay," he said, keeping his voice level. "We'll deal with this."

"He's okay, Jamie," she said softly, moving toward his truck. "He's not the problem."

The man lowered his hands, stepping back toward the two of them. "Like I said," he told them in an eerily quiet voice, "she's all right. But if you two are what she claims, you get her to a protected zone. For now, she's safe. Let's keep it that way."

"Safe from who?" Mason launched himself at the stranger, shoving him in the chest. "If you hurt my little sister, I'm gonna cut off your balls and shove 'em down your throat!"

Jamie stepped forward, grabbing Mason by the back of his jeans jacket. "Hold up!" he told his brother. "Step off, now. Let's hear what he's got to say." Mason growled as Jamie shoved him, sending him sprawling against the truck. Jamie turned back to the man. "Who are you? What happened to her?"

The man stepped much closer, lowering his shoulders slightly to eyeball Jamie. "You hunt demons. That's what she says. Well, I have a wake-up call for you two: She sees them, and tonight a rabid band of ancient Djinn went after her blood. So you stop the bullshit and start truly protecting her—and training her—now."

Jamie's jaw dropped. Behind him Mason shouted, "What the . . . ?"

The man gave them both a hard look, turned toward the park, and, in an intense blasting silver light, vanished completely.

"Holy Mother of God," Jamie muttered. "What in Jesus' name was . . . that?"

Jax held to the spiritual shadows; even with seers he could obscure his form. To Shay and her brothers he'd vanished like a mist, but the truth was that he'd moved into the realm of immortals to watch Shay leave. His heart was like a Gatling gun, firing off rapid, staccato beats. The work he had ahead of him—in solving the prophecy and defeating Sable—was immense. Yet watching his mortal love leave was far more difficult than any challenge that lay ahead. He would have given his wings to know for sure that he'd soon have her in his arms again. That he'd finally be able to bind himself to her, their souls joined and inseparable.

And, sweet gods of Olympus, that body of hers! It had been like cradling Aphrodite herself in his arms as they'd flown. Only more tempting, more arousing... more real than any fantasy he'd ever entertained about what the name Shayanna Angel could mean. And now that he knew exactly who she was, all his emotional and physical reactions while he was with her came into relief, made perfect sense. She was his foretold, and he'd finally held her and kissed her—and had been so ready to take her as his own, even before he'd realized who she truly was. His Shay.

He watched the truck make a sharp turn on the park's far side, now only the taillights visible, and his heart reached for her. "Ah, love, be safe tonight. Stay safe until I come to you again," he murmured as the truck vanished from sight.

He didn't have time to moon over the gorgeous human, not if they were to have a future. Every ounce of his warrior's focus had to be trained on protecting Shay, and that meant finding out what Sable's true interest in her was—especially since Jax had a sick feeling inside that the sole reason his enemy had targeted her was his own damned doing.

Somehow, some way, the bloody Djinn had learned of Jax's thousand-year prophecy—that a mortal named Shayanna Angel would be his one true love. That she would lock souls with Jax, completing his heart, finalizing his soul. That, and according to the prophecy, so much more.

"I will protect you," Jax pledged in Greek. "And nothing will stop us from being together. Just as was foretold, sweet one, we will join our souls and become one."

Chapter 10

River materialized on the crest of the hill overlooking their king's castle. With a bloodthirsty cry he collapsed to his knees, clawing the ground in agonized lust. The silvery haze in his berserker's eyes made clear vision all but impossible. Sexual heat coursed through his body—bloodlust, too, the wicked combination heightened more than usual this time because of the particularly long portal jump. He'd already been screaming in need before he'd fully returned to human form.

It was always this way, this perverse reaction. The urge for release was inescapable; if he assumed weapon form, coming back to himself was always a bitch. And sometimes the drive was worse than others, depending on how long he stayed transformed, how far away he had to jump. But one variable of his transformation never changed: Without sexual release of some kind, then his brutal, violent streak would become maddening. Could even literally lead to insanity—he knew that much from experience. *One* experience. And he'd never repeat that mistake again.

He collapsed on the ground, naked, slick with sweat, and shaking uncontrollably. Gods, he needed a woman, needed some way to slake the frantic desire that had turned his cock hard as stone. Of course, he'd never once dared to bed a female in this state, not as violent as he always became upon returning via the portal. Still, that ache, that craving to feel a woman's touch, to have her wrap her arms about his body and stroke him into oblivion ... that need alone was enough to make him insane. Even if he weren't there already.

With one sliding palm he clasped his shaft, squeezing his eyes shut against the rage that pumped through his body and soul. Doubling over, he pressed his face against the dew-dampened earth, hips lifted so he could stroke himself. Blind with silver haze, hips jerking furiously, he worked his hand back and forth over his cock.

Release came almost instantly, his hips dropping low— and just as quickly he stiffened again.

The shaking took hold of him harder, reached down to his bones as he tried to glance about the landscape. The warriors were nearby: He sensed them and knew that they would still be in the midst of their morning training regimen.

Gods of Olympus, don't let them see me like this, he half prayed. *Not again, not this time.* The shame of his state swamped him; with his palm he began stroking and teasing himself toward release once again. *Maybe only three times this journey,* he told himself, working his loins against the ground, his hand, anything to come down from the frenzy.

Again his warm seed shot into his palm and coated his fingers. For a long moment he lay still, panting against the wet grass, and he counted off the moments, wondering if by some miracle it would be only twice this time. His hopes were short-lived as a cinching sensation wrapped about his hips and loins, driving into his manhood like a sledgehammer.

Enraged, he roared onto his knees, transforming his arms into glinting-sharp methods of violence. The sex wasn't calming him this time; he needed destruction, needed to take life, search out demons and slay them. An ax as his left hand, a broadsword as his right, he stalked naked down the moor, stepping through the mist like a harbinger of death—not caring at all if the brotherhood saw him fully berserk.

"Whoa, there, friend." Ari. Off to his right, approaching him cautiously. "You going Lizzie Borden on me?"

River snarled at the man who was more than best friend, truly a brother. "Away!"

Without warning Ari was right in his path, fully outfitted in his Spartan uniform and with shield extended. "Not going anywhere. Not until you come back down to earth."

The shield went up; his Spartan comrade was in full defensive posture. The thought seemed odd, until River realized he'd raised the ax and was rushing Ari. As if from a distance, the clank of bronze against bronze filled his ears.

Help me, gods! But he couldn't stop himself, not with the way he tasted blood, hungered for it.

Ari met every single lunge and thrust that River made, hardly breaking stride. "There ya go, big guy. Get it out. Get. It. Out."

"Damn . . . you . . . Aristos!" River went wild, a naked blast of fury and flashing weaponry as he attacked Ari over and over. The big warrior dropped low, his familiar black eyes filled with a very *unfamiliar* nervousness.

"I . . . make . . . you . . . afraid!" River shouted the words, drunk off the reaction he was evoking in his lifelong friend.

"Never!" Ari laughed in his face, his ballsy warrior's bravado only enraging River again. "I've kicked your ass since we were kids. We've danced this dance too many times before."

Too many times? Suddenly River stilled, weapons held aloft in both hands. "Before?" he asked in a hoarse voice. "We've done this before?" The thought seemed right, yet he couldn't think, couldn't remember.

Slowly he lowered his weapons, his head erupting in a blazing headache.

From behind, broad arms clasped him, wrestling him backward. "Here we go," one of the warriors said, sounding much more annoyed than Ari did.

River whipped his head sideways and saw that it was Nikos. "You," he barely rasped from between parched lips. "Fucking perfect." The one Spartan who couldn't stand his ass had just seen him in the worst of his berserker nature.

Nikos's lips curled backward in a sneer. "You jump my brother, I'm gonna jump you."

"He's not your brother," River spat.

"He's my fellow Spartan, and in that, he will always be my brother." *And you will not.* The unspoken words echoed across the rocky, wind-whipped moors.

River stilled slightly, breath heaving as Nikos kept him pinioned in his grasp. Ari walked toward him, shield lowered, staring down into River's face.

"You back, friend?"

River relaxed at last, blowing out a sigh, but Nikos didn't release him yet. "I'm all right," he assured them both, glancing over his shoulder and into Nikos's eyes. "You can let me go."

Ari spoke up. "It's all right now. He's calm now."

Nikos didn't look convinced of that fact, and it took Ari's nodding his reassurance a few times for Nikos to finally release him.

River doubled over, trying to find his breath. The silver faded from his vision, and he could see that the morning mist still hovered across the landscape, the sun only slightly higher on the horizon than it had been when he'd received Ajax's call.

"Ari, what time is it?" River gasped, sucking in air with desperate gulps.

"You left thirteen minutes ago." Ari slid a hand onto his shoulder. "You sure you're all right?"

River nodded, straightening. With a slight nod to Nikos, he murmured his gratitude. Nikos's expression didn't change, but he gave River a slight slap on the shoulder. It was more camaraderie than he usually got from the brutal warrior, who disliked him for reasons River had never fully understood.

"I need to speak to Leonidas," River said, beginning to trot down the hill toward the castle. Ari and Nikos took off with him, and they crossed the distance easily.

Reviewing his portal jump, the transformation, and its price, River found it hard to believe that only thirteen minutes had passed. Still, it had been just long enough for him to perform a standard in-and-out maneuver for his master. Although this one had turned out to be anything but standard.

A thought hit him headfirst, almost threatening to reawaken his berserker: What if Leonidas and the others didn't believe his report about Sable? Stupid, he knew, because apart from Nikos, the cadre always displayed unshakable faith in him—faith that River knew he'd earned. But that outsider feeling still had a way of blindsiding him when he least expected it.

If he were one of the Spartans, he never would have worried. Not that the corps thought of him as a servant or ever treated him as anything less than a fellow warrior. Except Nikos, and River had some theories about why the brutal warrior despised him so much. Leonidas had once murmured something to River privately, indicating that there had been bad blood between River's own helot father and Nikos's Spartan one. When River had begged his king to elaborate, the quiet commander had clapped his mouth shut. No matter how many times River had tried to gently approach the topic again over the years, there'd been no cracking the fortress of silence that was their king.

Like his father, River was a servant, a helot, yet the corps treated him with equality and respect. Still, River felt his role like heavy armor, always weighing on him, never allowing him to be quite sure of his true position with the corps. And it wasn't like Jax still wanted him as his servant—he'd asked Ares to dissolve their unequal relationship that day when they made their vow by the banks of Styx, but the god had refused point-blank. Still, River loved Ajax and served him with reverence. Even in mortal life his Spartan master had been good, fair, always giving extra food and wine during festivals, abundant wood in the winter. It was no wonder that in this afterlife of sorts, Ajax had never wanted to keep River as his helot servant.

"Let me release you," Jax had begged him thousands of years ago. "Please, friend. You are my equal, my brother, my comrade in every way."

River had refused, adamant. Their relationship had been set in silver, bronze, gold—every form imaginable, in fact—when Ares had first placed River, in weapon form, in his master's grasp. River had been gleaming and hot, drawn right out of Styx, when Jax took him in his hands for the first time.

"You will wield him," Ares had promised his Spartan master, placing River's sword form in Jax's hands. "Your servant, so faithful in mortal life, will be the most powerful weapon you ever take in your hands."

River had lived for little else since that day, no matter how barbarically reckless and stubborn his master could sometimes be. In fact, he took pride in watching over the wild man's ass. Which made him think of what he'd discovered in Savannah, and so he sprinted the rest of the distance down the hill. Jax was going to need him on this mission—probably more so than any other in his immortal life.

"Tell me my brother's all right," Ari said as they approached the training ground.

"He's safe. And he didn't even instigate the trouble this time." River skidded to a stop and bent double for a moment, catching his breath. He was more winded than he'd realized. Not from the transformation or even its brutal aftermath—the deep weariness was from the spiritual warfare he'd performed back in Savannah, the shape-shifting, too, but most of all the portal jumping. That was what Ari always jokingly called him, Portal Jumper, or PJ when they were really hanging close.

The immortals formed a circle about him—Ari and Nikos closing in behind him, the others in full battle gear. Leonidas approached slowly and the circle parted; he wore his helmet, the red brush waving slightly with each of his steps. No cloak, though. Even after so many years, the absence of the flowing crimson garment stabbed River in the heart. The fabric should be billowing in the wind, inviting their enemies into battle.

But it was gone, as lost to them as their mortal lives.

Maybe that fact pierced him hardest because he'd once secretly prayed for the day when he, too, would bear the Spartan crimson.

Years ago—hundreds? A thousand? River couldn't even say how long it had been, but sometime after Thermopylae the cadre had made a choice: They'd abandoned their scarlet cloaks out of respect for the dead. It had been the ultimate tribute to fallen brothers and friends, to lost families and children.

River would never forget the image of King Leonidas in the firelight, each of the immortals gathered in a circle, their faces dancing with the golden red flame. It was the same color as Hades, River had thought as he sat along the circle's far edge. One by one, Leonidas had received a folded, frayed Spartan cloak from each of his men—then, one after another, he'd placed each treasured garment on the funeral pyre.

River was certain that he'd heard several stifled sobs from around that bonfire, in spite of the stoic demeanors each presented. Ari had played a mournful accompaniment on the flute, tears gleaming in his eyes the entire time. At the very last, Leonidas himself stepped forward, unpinned his own cloak, and with a quiet prayer folded it—slowly, end over end, as if he were going to shelve it for just a while. As though it were an honored battle flag that needed protection from the elements. Then, with only a moment's hesitation, he'd tossed it onto the flames as if it were nothing more than a kindling stick.

"Guess we won't be getting so lucky with the ladies anymore, will we?" he called out with a hearty laugh. "And as for quick bedding when we do the deed . . ." He waved at the burning bonfire, stacked high with their scorching cloaks. "Perhaps a bed of flowers for you poetic types."

"That would be Ajax!" Ari snorted and glanced around for the others to join in. "I hear he's all about the sweet talk."

"Talks them to death, more like," Kalias groused.

Just like that, Leonidas had turned the mood. The honor had been given—to the past and to what had once been. "The future," Leonidas said, "is what we are about now, men. Pass the bowl of wine!"

It should have eased the eternal pain. Maybe it had for the other warriors . . .

But River knew things about his master that the others didn't—including Ajax's own brothers. Fighting hand in hand as the two of them did . . . well, there weren't many barriers when it came to thoughts or fears. Those walls dissolved while in battle, the two of them melding into one complete warrior. And what River got firsthand at those times wasn't pretty.

For all his master's recklessness and bluster and swaggering pride, the truth was that he'd never recovered from what Sable had done to his family. No amount of pageantry or sex or booze could fill up that hole, either. There'd been only one thing over the endless lonely years, ever, that had eased Jax's pain—the hope of Shayanna Angel.

Oh, his poor bastard of a friend and master. How had Sable found out about Shay? River had realized who she was the moment his sword form had run her through the chest, had sensed her mind and thoughts. *Oh, Ajax, Ajax,* he thought. *This is gonna be one hell of a fight.*

"I don't want to talk about it." Shay stared out Jamie's truck window at the familiar downtown sights as they sped quickly past them. Savannah, a city that barely slept, was almost shut down this late at night.

"We have to know what went down," Jamie said. "It's clear that you're in a lot of danger, so you need to talk."

"Not now." She rubbed her tired eyes, feeling tears threaten.

"I know it's tough," Jamie pressed. "We get that, but

tell us who that guy was. He vanished right before our eyes. Vanished. Did he hurt you in some way? He didn't look like any demon I've ever seen, but—"

Shay didn't let him finish. "He's not. A demon. I don't think."

"Then what happened?" Jamie persisted, glancing back and forth between the road and her gaze in his rearview mirror. "Who attacked you?"

"I can't talk now." She barely got the words out, because her throat tightened up on her.

Mama, why aren't you still here? I need you to hold me and tell me everything's gonna be all right.

"Give her a few minutes," Mason told Jamie in a low voice that he didn't intend for her to hear.

"I'm not deaf and I am still here. So don't act like I'm not."

Mason turned to look at her. "I'm telling him to ease off. You take your time, sweet pea."

Sweet pea. Mason had nicknamed her that the year he'd gone off to the Citadel. She'd been a freshman in high school, and in those days she'd been closer to Mason than to anyone else in the family. When he'd come home on occasional weekend leaves, she'd practically hurled herself at him in excitement. He'd always indulged her whenever she'd rubbed her hand back and forth across his nearly shaved head, and let her tease him mercilessly for how short it was.

She'd lived for those brief visits with Mason. Being the last of the Angel kids still at home had been lonely, and even though Daddy was still alive then, he'd been gone more and more frequently with the family gig. Her mama had stayed preoccupied a lot in those days, worried about the increasing danger her father was in. Mason had been her only lifeline.

But he'd changed in the past two years. The last stint with his marine battalion in Iraq had left him with an honorable discharge that he didn't discuss. And not just that: He'd returned uncharacteristically withdrawn and moody, a darkly changed man who was inaccessible to her right when she needed him the most. So now all of a sudden he was pulling "sweet pea" on her? The term of endearment only made her mad.

She'd never felt more alone than she did right now, with her big brothers right there in the front seat. Until a few years ago they'd been the definition of safety and protection in her mind. That had been before she'd started seeing demons—and before they'd locked her out of the family calling. And what she'd experienced tonight? The attack, and then the strange erotic attraction—and connection—to that winged warrior? They would never understand. At the very best they'd go researching, try to explain his existence away—but deep in her heart, she knew they'd never even come close to the truth.

"I just want to go home," she said dully. "And, Jamie, can you turn up the heat? It's cold."

Jamie sped up. "No way in hell are you going back to your apartment tonight."

"No, I mean I want to go *home*. I want to sleep in my old room tonight." Her apartment was only a few blocks from Forsyth Park, and didn't have the long-standing protections that their family land did. Even she knew that. "Just take me home," she repeated, tears welling in her eyes.

In the passenger seat, she could hear Mason tapping away on his BlackBerry. "Okay," he said. "The team is on their way over there now to check your apartment."

"Good work," Jamie told him; then, glancing at Shay in the rearview, he assumed a reassuring tone. "Sweetie, the Shades know exactly what to do in situations like this. They're gonna look after you, make sure you stay safe."

"The Shades," she repeated, and rolled her teary eyes. "What a stupid-ass name."

Jamie kept his silence, looking back at the road. But in the mirror she could still see the seriousness in his eyes. A few generations ago the Angel family hunters had named their elite circle the Deadly Nightshades. Over the years the name had been shorthanded to just the

Shades. Shay had a life filled with memories of hushed mentions of the elite fighting squad, midnight phone calls to her father, all veiled in mystery. Her mama had done the best she could to shelter her as a child, to keep the dark fears their family's activities—and secret band—invoked. In adulthood Shay had come to associate the name with being left out, with being overprotected. She despised the term now.

"The Shades," she repeated disdainfully. "How lame. Sounds like a wannabe college secret society or something. And you know what?" She leaned forward, gripping the back of Jamie's seat. "You care more about your stupid *team* than you do about me."

"Pamela Shayanna, that's not fair," Mason piped in.

She slapped the back of his seat. "Wow, he speaks! Four months of silence since you came home, and now you're talking to me? Big freaking deal." She glared at Mason, who looked at her in surprise.

She continued, "Yeah, you know what, Mace? Maybe I would like to know all the big supersecrets that you picked up over in Iraq! Maybe I'd like to know why you're in so much pain all the time that you won't even talk to me, your own damned sister."

She sank back in the seat, folding both arms over her chest. "You two want me to talk? You want to know what happened tonight? Guess what . . . you two talk first. You can start by telling me what and who I really am."

"Do you mean the letter?" Jamie eyed her in the mirror again.

She threw both hands in the air. "I don't even care about that stupid letter. Or what my supposed birth mother said."

Mason cast a glance at Jamie, but said nothing.

"Yeah, it's clear that both of you know all about it. But, see, I really don't care about the letter at all. What I want right now is to get on home, go down into the cellar, and do a buttload of research. I have to get some answers about what I saw tonight."

Jamie shook his head emphatically. "No way. You don't know anything about what's in the lore."

Shay leaned forward again, gripping Jamie's right shoulder. "Look, one thing that guy said was right: I know a whole lot more than you think I do. And one of the things that I know right now is that whoever I am—whatever I am—it's time for me to fight."

Leonidas felt a strange sensation crawl over his spirit as he waited for River to catch his breath. The young servant had been struggling for a full minute, unusually weakened by whatever he'd just encountered on his portal jump to Savannah.

"Get him a cup of water," Leo commanded Nikos, who was standing at his right. The wrestler trotted away, returning with an overflowing wooden bowl. Leonidas believed that in training they should stay true to the old ways, right down to the food and drink.

River guzzled the liquid. "That was a hell of a battle, sir," he finally sputtered, water and spittle flying from his mouth. "It drained me."

Then he stood upright again, and relayed the details of what he'd seen, his words tumbling forth clipped and fast. When he reached the part where he lanced the demon while in his sword form, Leonidas's eyes widened.

"Through the heart I took him, and down he went." River made a stabbing gesture at his chest, his eyes bugging out. He had always been the dramatic sort. "But we all know he won't stay down for long."

Leonidas hesitated, thinking about the grave implications. "You're certain it was Elblas?" he asked at last.

"I'm telling the *truth*, my lord," River said in a louder voice.

Leonidas silenced him with a patient smile. Of all the men in the corps, truth was most important to River—enough so that he'd get worked up about it sometimes, especially if he feared they wouldn't believe his word. As if any of them ever had any reason to doubt.

"Go on," Leonidas encouraged.

The servant bowed his head. "I know what I saw and what I heard. Even if I'd not taken the demon for Elblas, Jax himself kept calling him by name. I returned to camp because he sent me, but if he summons me to Savannah again, my lord, I request permission to remain with him in the fight."

Ajax's older brother Aristos stepped closer, his well-oiled body gleaming. "Not just River, Commander, but we all need to go, and now," he said, his tone unusually serious. "He can't take on Elblas by himself. All of us know the history there, how deep it goes."

From the outset, Leonidas had wondered about sending Jax alone to America. The Oracle had tried her best to explain the prophecy to him after the fact, and although much of it was vague, on one point she had been absolutely clear—that the mission was to be conducted without support from the other Spartans.

"The prophecy required him to venture alone." Leonidas knew his men wouldn't like his verdict, but destiny had already been determined. If time had taught him anything, it was that he and his immortal fighters were kindling in the hands of almighty fate.

Ari's thick black eyebrows cranked downward; his usually jovial expression darkened. "With all due respect, my king . . . the two nearly destroyed each other the first time they squared off. Sable got turned into a centaur because of my brother. You don't think that Sable's nursing some serious payback in his nasty little Djinn heart? We should fight as a unit on this one. Again"—the hulking soldier inclined his head—"with all my respect, sir."

"We stand by the Oracle," Leonidas reminded him in a quiet voice. Even the long-ago battle at Thermopylae had been guided by her prophecies. "And the word was that Jax travels alone to Savannah."

"Jax summoned River, and he was part of the fight," Kalias argued, stepping near. The tallest of their gathered group, the soldier made Leonidas look up into his eyes. "He's already violated the terms our Oracle outlined by pulling River into the fight."

Kalias had a good point. Besides, it was highly unusual for Ajax's big brother to argue a counterposition to that of his king, so Leonidas gave the request some additional thought.

"The binding tie between River and Jax is unique," Leonidas explained after a moment's consideration. "They were specifically joined by Ares when we made our vow. So Jax fighting with River in his *grasp* isn't the same as Jax fighting with a fellow Spartan."

River glanced up at him, deep emotion glinting in his green eyes. "I was another warrior joining the fray," he said in a thick voice. "Surely you can send the cadre. He's in grave danger."

Leonidas planted a hand on River's shoulder, choosing his words carefully. "Young River," he said softly, meeting his gaze, "when Jax draws upon you in battle, he calls upon a part of himself. Not another warrior, but his own right hand."

Again, the odd look in River's eyes as he responded. "Then let me go back. I can shadow him, be closer in case he gets in trouble with the horde."

River blinked, and Leonidas finally identified what he saw in his eyes—fear for his master. River, who had been the very first of them to agree to Ares' proposal, the one who would bluster into any situation without fear or a second thought, was frightened by what he'd seen in Savannah. Not a good omen.

River pressed on, his green eyes locking on Leonidas. "If I am part of Ajax, then I should be allowed to serve him on this mission."

Leonidas considered that angle, but if they were found even slightly in defiance of the Oracle's prophecy, Ares would be furious. They weren't allowed to play semantics with their instructions.

He pinched the bridge of his nose, mentally searching for any loophole. "I'm not entirely comfortable with that, River," he finally admitted. "Supporting him one time and in the heat of conflict was one thing. The toll it takes on you is magnified by such a long portal jump, and it's too much to risk again so quickly. It's too dangerous for you, and therefore for us."

River stepped close, looking up into his eyes. "You need to know something else. About the stakes and how seriously Jax will take them. It's more than the vendetta between Jax and Elblas."

Leonidas nodded him on. River sucked in a breath, then released a long, agitated explanation that Leonidas had a hard time following in its entirety. About the woman Jax had saved, how she'd been a statue before River had revived her.

"He saved the mortal by using me, my lord. He ran her through with my blade."

A bit odd, but not entirely unheard of. There were many ways that River could be turned into a healing instrument, but actually using him in sword form was one of the rarer usages.

"The thing is"—River stood taller, sweeping the circle with his gaze—"Jax took her with him . . . after saving her. I don't think it was just for safety. I think there was something else he was after."

"Oh, my gods, was he thinking with his big sword?" Kalias snorted. "Are you joking, man?"

River shook his head, emphatic. "I think she had special knowledge. He recited something in ancient Greek that broke her out of the chant, something she seemed to have given him, but I couldn't make the words out because of my changed form. And that's not all." River paused, swiveling his gaze only on Leonidas. "Let's just say this: That was no mortal . . . that was his soul mate. I knew it the moment my blade touched her form." River grinned, stepping even closer. "For better or worse, my lord, our boy has found Shayanna Angel. She was the one Elblas turned into a statue. She was the one I pierced with my blade. Ajax has found his great love. But so has Elblas, it seems . . . and before Jax himself could."

*   *   *

Shay stumbled up the stairs toward her room, Jamie and Mason right behind her. They'd let things go during the drive, but she could sense a big-brother gang-up was brewing. She reached the landing and made the left turn by the polished wooden banister that led down a long hall to her room.

"Not so fast, Sissy Cat," Jamie called after her. She stopped, didn't turn. Waited in silence. He took hold of her elbow, gently turning her to face the two of them. Jamie's green eyes locked with hers; Mason stood a bit to the side.

"I told you," she said, "I'm not ready to talk about it. And, as it turns out, I'm also too tired to head to the cellar. But in the morning I'm starting my research."

"You'll have to get past me first," Jamie cautioned.

"Fine. Watch me." She glanced at Mason. "Are you going to barricade me out, too?"

Mason dropped his gaze and held silent. She wasn't sure how to read him, but that was hardly new these days.

Jamie reached out and brushed a long lock of her hair out of her eyes. "I'll help you, Shay, if you'd just tell me something about what went on."

"I want to sleep." Her limbs felt heavy; her eyes burned. "We can have this out in the morning."

"I'm going to pour you a vodka," Mason volunteered, moving toward the study.

"That's *your* drink," she called after him. "I hate vodka."

He turned back and with surprising warmth gave her a very comforting smile. "But you don't hate sleep, and you need it after tonight. You go on to your room; I'll bring it to you."

She shuffled down the polished-wood hallway, thinking that her entire body was being pulled down by gravity. And then the oddest thought hit her—that the heavy, weak sensation was the very opposite of how she'd felt soaring the heavens with her demon-angel just hours before.

All at once she missed that man, the sensual, unholy

creature, as if she'd known him her whole life—for many lifetimes, in fact. The thought of being in his arms was the one comfort she'd been aching for during the entire drive back—and even now, in her childhood home.

After such a brief time with the man, she yearned for him with her very soul.

She stepped into her former bedroom, still decorated as it had been when she'd moved out on her own five years earlier. The framed drawings she'd done in high school, the antique canopy bed, the signed movie poster of *Midnight in the Garden of Good and Evil*. All of it so familiar, yet it glared back at her as if it belonged to someone else.

All she wanted to see right then was her winged savior. With a panicked gasp, she collapsed on her bed and buried her head in both hands.

What if she never found him again?

A compulsion hit her—one that she'd known for the past few months. She reached beneath her bed and found her sketch pad, her coal drawing pencils. She flipped through the book, seeking an empty page, images of demons and otherworldly creatures flashing past. She'd been drawing visions—she didn't know what else to call them—more and more frequently recently. She just didn't know where the urge or even the desire to do so had come from. One day she'd been playing around with a sketch idea and suddenly a dark vision had begun to fly forth from her fingers.

As she flipped through a few more pages, her gaze landed on something startling, a sketch she had completely forgotten. It was of an angel, massive wings practically exploding forth on his back. The way she'd drawn them, with the heavy emphasis on shadow, the wings were undeniably . . . black.

Black angel wings, and although the being's face was obscured, his body looked shockingly familiar. For a long moment she stared in disbelief; then, driven by the same compulsion she'd been experiencing lately, she flipped to a clean page.

In a frenzy she began sketching; her pencil moved back and forth across the page, whiplashing almost, and as she sketched something new emerged, something other than what she'd seen and experienced tonight.

An image of her flying the heavens with her protector, smiling broadly and holding him by just one hand. She was free. They were free together, but it was a memory of something that hadn't happened yet.

Chapter 11

The human's scent trail veered all over town, marking the brick sidewalks and squares, the shops and courtyards, and it had made tracking her after the cemetery a challenge. Until this afternoon. Sable trotted back and forth down the one particular street where Shayanna's sweet mortal aroma intensified.

"Little vixen," he cursed under his breath. "Slut of a huntress . . ." His insults grew more and more profane as he searched the street, sniffing for her.

Above him, Krathsadon and Mirapish flew, their wing-beats clipping quickly, marking pace with his earthbound, plodding steps. He despised his minions for the very fact that they—unlike him—could fly. Not on beautiful wings as he'd once done, but still, they possessed that freedom.

You can walk through walls, scale mountainsides, bound across half-mile rivers, he reminded himself. *You possess at least some of your former strength and independence.*

His own dark soul whispered back at him, *A shadow of what you once were, glorious one.*

A bitter sneer formed on his lips, forcing them over his sharp teeth. Shayanna was his chance for redemption; if he kept to the prearranged plan, then he might have a chance at being freed from his cursed centaur form. The work-beast form had grown almost impossible to endure, the heaviness of it, so awkward and ungainly. The fucking stink of the manure—the inconvenience of having his minions brush his coat every day. And, gods damn it all, not being able to clean his own private parts.

All at once his heart began beating furiously. For the pure pleasure of it he summoned a sword and lanced it upward, pricking Mirapish through his right wing. The smaller demon warbled in the air, and Sable laughed raucously.

"Stay on guard, little one," he cautioned his follower, who yelped and, with an offended look, finally began flying correctly again. With a threatening glare, Sable extended his sword toward the underling's twin, who gave an obsequious smile.

In their demonic hierarchy, the less powerful Djinn had no choice but to serve Sable; he'd acquired them fair and square in a desert battle, and now he owned them. He could torture them all he pleased, and when he got annoyed or bitter or frustrated, that was exactly what he chose to do.

"Shayanna has spent time near here," Sable declared, ushering the twins to the street. They landed with a buzzing of wings and a graceless thud.

Sable continued, "She probably lives here, right in this area."

Mirapish's red eyes narrowed to pinpoints. "How do you know, my lord?"

Sable sighed. *The little moron.* "Surely even you can smell that annoying stink of her? The perfume of her"— he spat the last word—"*goodness.*"

Krathsadon's mouth opened, fangs lengthening. "Pretty, pretty huntress." It was about all the idiot could say about Shay, but then again, Sable had bought him from a sex-lord demon, so he'd been raised on a steady diet of lust.

"Huntress, whatever," Sable hissed back. "Not that it matters. The bitch only knows the basics."

Not totally true, he had to remind himself as he turned and paced the street again. She'd freed herself from his paralyzing spell the other night, and such counterwarfare had been the stuff of bigger guns. Undoubtedly she'd been taught a few useful tricks. In the huntress-and-hunter game, it all came down to words. Sure, knives and switchblades, throwing stars and swords, all those things were useful to their kind in battle. But in the end it all came down to words—living words of power.

"What shall we do, my lord?" Mirapish asked, his twin bobbing his head in unison.

Sable shook his head. "I'm going to find her dwelling. It's here, right here close by; I scent it. Just follow me."

Shay sat behind the long wooden counter of their downtown shop, surfing the Net, which, so far in the past few days, had been her only recourse for information. The morning after the insanity at Bonaventure she'd awoken late, only to find that her brothers had pad-locked the cellar. Plenty of hollering and arguing had ensued, but they'd proved an implacable force.

She'd even thought about getting her best friend, Angela, queen of all things technical and mechanical, to pick the lock. But her brothers never left the house at the same time, so that plan had been a bust. Besides, Angela hadn't stopped bugging her about why breaking into the cellar had suddenly become so urgent. No way was Shay ready to tell her the truth, either.

To say that she was seething, hopping mad would have been the understatement of the century. So they'd arrived at a stalemate—she wouldn't tell them what happened; they wouldn't let her into the family archives. She figured that eventually she was the one who would win, given that she held the primary information.

Still, she wasn't about to take the chance that the de-mons would come back for her, so although she'd in-sisted on returning to work today, she was still staying out at the house. Her apartment was a one-bedroom over a carriage house, and she'd asked her landlady to look after her cat, Sunshine. Lydia had assumed a sym-pathetic voice on the phone, telling her they were all so sorry to hear of her mama's passing. Shay had been more than happy to let her think that she'd been staying with her brothers because of their recent loss.

In the past two days she'd looked at every painting of angels, demons, and winged men that Google would spit out at her. She'd read about spiritual beings she'd never even heard of, some mythical and others supposedly real, but nothing she'd found came close to the entity that had taken her in his arms and flown her through the night sky.

In a pathetic attempt to re-create the emotions he'd stirred inside of her, she'd also saved dozens of pictures of Leda and the Swan paintings and sculptures—in fact, one in particular was now displayed on her screen. It was erotic, more so than any of the other artistic representations she'd unearthed. Leda lay on her back, legs spread wide, while Zeus, the mighty warrior come to Earth, draped his wings atop her belly, his bill nuzzling beneath her bare breasts. Shay stared at the painting again and began to laugh. The pair's satisfaction was so obvious, Leda might as well have held the proverbial postcoital cigarette in her relaxed hand.

But more than any other image, she was drawn to the sketch she'd made the other night, after arriving at home. The drawing had seemed to spill forth out of her, almost like automatic writing, except it was a picture, an image of something that hadn't happened. At least, not yet.

With an upward glance to be sure she was still alone, she opened the drawer underneath the counter and retrieved her sketch pad. There the two of them were, flying together, she holding his right hand, her feet floating behind. Beneath them the marshes and river flowed, and the landscape seemed lit by golden late-day light. Lifting a careful fingertip, she reached to touch one of his wings.

Suddenly her fallen angel's voice filled her mind, recalling the stirring poetry whispered in her ear. That voice. It had been as rich as Belgian chocolate, soothing and arousing at the exact same time. She sighed, and for one long moment she let her eyes drift shut and actually heard the sound of his beating wings, *felt* his supernaturally warm chest against her own, imagined herself on her back as his mighty winged body pushed between her bare legs.

Get a grip, girl, she cautioned herself, and slid the sketch pad back into its hidden spot within the drawer. The bell over the door to the shop chimed, and she jolted, reaching for her laptop. Her Google searches were ten deep, and she was about to tile them shut when she saw that it was Jamie sauntering toward her. *Not here, not now, James.*

"You're supposed to be closed," he told her. He was dressed for going out on the town; it was Friday night, so he had on a button-down Polo shirt and khakis. For Jamie, that *was* dressing up.

"I've got band practice at seven. Figured I'd hang out here and see if any Friday-night stragglers came strolling in. Tourists, hippies . . . demons. You know, regular foot traffic."

"Is that supposed to be funny?"

"Aren't you supposed to be out combating the forces of evil?"

He draped himself on the other side of her counter in a forced casual posture—as if she didn't know exactly why he'd suddenly deigned to show up at the shop. "I have a date."

"Well, that really is battling evil, if it's that chick from Thunderbolt you've been seeing lately." Jamie's taste in women ran notoriously toward the booby, blond, and not so bright.

"You know why I'm here." He tipped his head downward and hit her with a kick-ass stare. "I'm done messing around about this. You were attacked the other night. I want to know who that man was who did it."

"He didn't attack me!" she blurted in an outrage, and leaped to her feet. "He's the one who protected—" Shay snapped her mouth shut and slowly sank back onto her stool across from him.

Jamie's eyes widened slightly, and he smiled in triumph. "I see," he told her in an annoyingly patient voice. "Now we're getting somewhere."

"No," she told him, closing her laptop protectively. It wouldn't do to have him snooping in her cached files. "We're not. Not until you give me access to the lore. It's tit for tat, dude."

He tapped his fingers on the counter and glanced at his watch. "I'm meeting Candy in ten minutes, so I gotta jet. But this thing between us? This standoff? It's ending tonight. You're going to tell us exactly what you saw, experienced, whatever."

"So you're willing to unlock the cellar?"

"Not until I know what we're dealing with." His BlackBerry rang, the theme to *The Good, the Bad, and the Ugly* cutting them off loudly.

He put his back to her, talking in low tones, and it was clear that it wasn't Candy calling on the phone. He glanced at his watch impatiently and murmured something about canceling his plans. When he finished, he pocketed his phone again and turned to her.

"Candy's going to be so bummed," she offered brightly. "And pretty soon she'll get tired of dating a warrior."

"Shay, I just want to help you." He reached for one of the satchels of sage and rosemary they sold as spiritual protection and sniffed it, holding it close to his nose. The packets were stacked high in a basket on the counter, and he dropped it back in, pawing around the other neatly tied bags. "I'm really worried about you," he said, "whether you believe that or not. What can I do to make all this better?"

"Pretty simple there, James. One, you can tell me what you know about that letter." She raised two fingers. "Two, you can tell me why I seem to have a unique calling, and three"— she held up a third finger —"you can give me some information."

"What kind of information?" Of course, he'd ignored points one and two, but she was just desperate enough— just obsessed enough with her winged hottie—that she was willing to give a little ground. She placed her hands flat on the counter, sucked in a deep breath, and went for it.

"Have you ever heard of good demons?" she asked, sounding as nonchalant as possible. "You know, the kind that actually protect humans for some bizarre reason?"

He shook his head. "No such thing. It's not in the lore . . . just not possible."

She shook her head, too. "Maybe there's more information than what we have in the family archives; ever think of that?"

He reached for another packet of herbs, sniffing those, too. His fidgeting was his poker tell, even though none of them had ever cared to point that out to him. Either he was hiding something or he was just plain nervous. "Yes, of course," he said after a moment, "but all the demonic varieties have been thoroughly documented over the years, and I've never come across anything like that."

She'd known he would say that, but she'd been chasing a thought over the past few days and figured she might as well hit him with it. "What if there's something like a good demon in the Bible? Would you believe it then?"

"When it comes to spiritual warfare, I've studied the scriptures intensively. There *are* no good demons," he said in an emphatic voice. "They are the fallen angels from heaven, period."

"Explain the Nephilim then." She leaned back in her chair. "The Old Testament mentions them several times . . . maybe they were good demons. It's possible."

"Nobody knows what the Nephilim were. But it doesn't matter, because they don't exist anymore—at least, not according to the texts. They were destroyed by God."

"The Bible doesn't actually say they were destroyed," she argued. "You're leaping to conclusions."

He snorted. "So, what are you, a Bible scholar now?"

"I went to Sunday school, same as you," she told him in annoyance. "And *unlike* you, I actually listened."

"I conduct spiritual warfare based on the holy texts. Don't give me shit."

"And you bind demons with that mouth?" She gave him her best incredulous look. "God must be ashamed of you for talking like you do."

He scowled and answered defensively, "Been working on that."

"I'll ask again," she said as calmly as she could. "Is there any precedent whatsoever for a good demon?"

Jamie gave his head a slow, emphatic shake. "Shay, there are angels and there are demons, and as far as I know— with my limited, apparently *disdained* knowledge— there ain't nothing in between."

"Uh-huh." She forced her expression into a neutral one.

You didn't fly the heavens with a winged demon who was, no pun intended, hell-bent on protecting you.

The door chimed, interrupting them, and Shay looked up to discover a middle-aged man with a panicky expression on his jowly face. She moved around the counter and met him halfway toward the door. Hers was a profession of calming the worried and fretful.

"I'm sorry to bother you," he began, eyes searching the shop nervously. His right eye betrayed a tic. "But I've been hearing these noises in my house late at night...."

The man proceeded to chatter anxiously about the paranormal activity at his home. As he launched into his tale, Jamie made a motion that said, *Don't bring me into this,* and pointed at his watch. She put her back to him and spent the next five minutes reassuring the man and teaching him some sacred prayers. When his wife entered the shop, she chastised him for being superstitious and he left, thanking Shay profusely.

Finally she had them out the door and turned the latch, flipping the sign to CLOSED.

And found Jamie hunched over her laptop, snooping.

"Hey, don't look at my stuff!" she said, storming toward him. She grabbed hold of her laptop and snapped it shut. "That's rude to read someone else's private things."

He glanced up at her slowly, smiling. "You think he was an angel, don't you?" Excitement twinkled in his green eyes. "That's what the guy was, some kind of protective spirit with wings? You actually saw wings?"

You don't know the half of it.

"Trust me," she said, unplugging her laptop and powering it down, "he was too twisted to be any kind of angel. That's why my money is on good demon."

"Twisted . . . how, exactly?"

"He tried to seduce me." She dared a peek at Jamie, whose eyes narrowed furiously. "I mean, not really, but he was just very . . . persuasive."

Jamie leaped off the stool and began pacing. "That fucking bastard. What did he try on you?"

"He saved my life, all right? He's not your problem," she argued, wanting to defend her strange protector. "Really, Jamie, I wouldn't be here now if he hadn't shown up. So he's not my problem either. . . ."

"I'm not following. You just said—"

"What he told you about the ancient demons?" she said, talking over him. "They surrounded me at Bonaventure that night. I was a goner, and by all rights I shouldn't even be here right now. But then out of nowhere that guy showed up and battled them off. Then"—she took a deep breath, because she knew the next revelation was really going to freak Jamie out—"he flew me to safety and put me down in Forsyth Park."

Very quietly, Jamie repeated, "He flew you to safety. Flew. You."

"In his arms," she added in a whisper.

Jamie dropped his own voice just as low. "In the sky?"

"I don't know . . . it felt like Neverland—okay? I could see the earth below, the lights of the city, but we also seemed to be moving through some spiritual dimension or something. Very surreal."

Jamie began pacing all over the place, practically

jumping with excitement. "You encountered a new type of entity, Shay. That's what you're telling me. Something that's never been documented by anyone in our family or even mentioned at all in any of our texts or scriptures."

She shrugged, thinking how irrelevant that fact was to her. "I guess." She sighed softly. "He was amazing, the most beautiful creature I've ever seen. And he made me feel . . . safe. So totally safe."

Jamie halted in his tracks. "You sound like you've got a crush on this thing."

She tilted her head sideways, scowling. "He's not a thing; he's a man. Or a creature or . . . hell, Jamie, I don't know what he is. But he's not part of the pack that attacked me, and he did save my life."

"Demons don't save lives, so you can rule that guess out."

"Maybe it's like you said—he's a new breed or something."

Jamie slapped a hand on the counter. "Wait until I tell Mace. This defies everything we've ever been taught. This is a sea change for the Shades. It's huge."

She shook her head, taking a step backward. "Don't tell Mason."

"Why not?"

She pressed her eyes shut. "Because he's already so distant from me as it is, ever since he got out of the marines and came home from Iraq. He tells you everything and tells me nothing, and it's not like I don't want to hear about it. I know it was traumatic, but that's not a good enough reason for him to be so shut down to me."

"Shay, look, it's not . . ." Jamie began, but then he dropped his gaze and said nothing more.

"It's not me?" she prompted, anger rising inside "Apparently it's entirely me, since he can talk to you. I can't risk his pulling away any further."

"Shay, what Mace is going through has nothing to do with you."

It was bad enough that Mason had shut her out lately

after coming home from Iraq. The marines had diagnosed him, citing an acute case of post-traumatic stress disorder as the reason for his honorable discharge. Still, Shay couldn't shake the hunch that something more had happened to her big brother overseas. Something that was so spiritually dark that he refused to talk about it. Or, at least, not to her, and her only hope was that eventually Mason would start to open up about the experience.

So what would happen if he suspected they weren't even blood related? If he figured out that she was different from the other members of the Angel family? That she saw things they didn't, sketched entities when they didn't? No, Mason could never know about everything happening to her right now.

"Jamie, I know that I'm special. I mean, not like I'm so wonderfully amazing, not that." She paused, trying to gather her fast-moving thoughts. "But I think there's something different about me . . . that I'm not like you and Mason. Those demons I saw at the funeral . . . the sketches. I'm a *woman*—in this family—seeing demons? I'm not like y'all."

He said nothing, just glanced away—it was another poker tell at a time when she was trying to read him more deeply.

"I'm right, aren't I? I have some kind of unusual calling?" she persisted. "Because I'm adopted?"

Reaching into the pocket of her jeans, she retrieved the well-worn letter that she'd been carrying for the past few months and slapped it onto the counter. "Who was this thing from? Huh?" She smoothed out the creases in the paper, flattening the now-familiar epistle. "You tell me who sent this to me."

Jamie stared down at the paper and seemed ready to answer, reading the handwritten words once again without speaking. Studying it, he opened his mouth, and Shay steeled herself, knowing that whatever he said next would surely change her life. But all at once his damned BlackBerry rang again, and he whipped it to his ear, letting the letter flutter out of his hand.

She stood waiting, expectant and painfully curious, but when he hung up he was already jogging toward the door.

"I've got to roll," he called over his shoulder. "The team needs me. But we'll talk all about this tonight."

"The ol' 'team' excuse again, huh?" She busied herself with gathering her papers. "Same revolving door of testosterone recruits these days, or have you actually gotten a few women involved?"

He leveled her with a stare. "Don't give me shit, okay? The lineup hasn't changed in the past couple of months. You saw everyone at St. Pat's while we were patrolling downtown. You took care of Evan that afternoon, remember?"

"No, I helped nurse Evan back to consciousness after three Asian demons had just about soul-sucked him dry. You were lucky you didn't lose him that day, poor guy. And what would Emma have done?" Their second cousin Emma was best friends with Evan, and had absolutely no idea that he was a member of Jamie's team. "I wouldn't have wanted to look her in the eye and tell her why Evan died."

"You sound resentful, Sis." Jamie studied her hard. "You always do when it comes to our family enterprise. St. Pat's is critical; you know that."

The demons loved St. Patrick's Day in Savannah; it was almost as much of a field day for them as Mardi Gras in New Orleans. And every year—at least, according to Jamie and his Shades—the demons visited for the holiday in ever-expanding numbers, gallivanting wildly among the human masses. It had become a regular Disneyland for demons. They raped, body-jumped, soul sucked . . . generally had their way with the human fools who'd become too inebriated and lost control of their senses.

"I know that someone had to protect the civilians. I just wish I'd been one of those somebodies."

"Shay, even if it weren't about your seeing demons or not—"

"Which I do—"

"You're my only sister, and I have to protect you. I have to do that; don't you get it? What if something happened to you on my watch? I would never get over that. The level of fighting that's involved . . . it's hard on us, and we're men."

She popped a hand to her head as if just remembering. "That's right . . . still 'men only.' I forgot."

"It's dangerous, Shay."

"You're sexist, Jamie."

Jamie shook his head vehemently. "I have Charlotte; she works calls, dispatches, all that stuff. She's been in demon fights a few times."

"Great. One woman." Shay twirled a finger in the air. "You're a regular Rainbow Coalition in the demon world."

Jamie opened his mouth to say more, but then his phone rang once again. He cut her a glare and, with a muttered, "Later," was out the door and answering his fighters.

The Shades always needed her brothers; meanwhile, she needed someone else—something else—and, closing the door after her brother, she wondered if that *someone* hid in the shadows of the encroaching night.

Jax kept to the spiritual shadows across from Shay's shop, watching her through the glass windows as she closed up. For two days he had tailed her, never releasing her from his protective guard, always keeping to the dim places that her seer eyes couldn't penetrate. And for two days he'd waited for Sable to strike again. So far there had been no sign of the Djinn or his minions.

Jax wasn't fooled, however. No way in Hades would his ancient enemy give up so easily, especially not after being soundly trounced in their last confrontation. The centaur would be out for blood now—both Shay's and Jax's. It was only a matter of time until he struck again.

Shay opened the door, stepped out onto the sidewalk, and, casting nervous glances in every direction, quickly locked the shop and began walking briskly down the street. Jax shoved off the wall and followed her on the opposite sidewalk. What he wanted was to go to her, to slip a protective arm about her shoulder and escort her openly wherever it was she was heading. But there were many reasons why such boldness wasn't going to cut it, not the least of which was that she undoubtedly viewed him as a threat.

Or maybe not, he thought, his heart giving a hopeful leap. *Perhaps, if you're lucky, she views you as her savior. Perhaps she craves you as strongly as you do her.*

She had seemed awfully aroused by his wings—and his almost-bare body. He'd been with enough women in his endless lifetime to know when one was attracted to him. Oh, yes, he knew he had her in *that* category, but it didn't mean she wasn't terrified of him as well.

Even in mortal form he made human men glance away nervously: his strapping height, his broad chest, his menacing face. In full warrior glory? Wings pounding at the air, body half-naked? He moved from threatening to absolutely petrifying, and so far that was about all of him that Shay had seen. She didn't know about his gentler qualities, and after all, he did possess at least a few.

She held a pair of drumsticks in her hands and tapped them together nervously as she moved down Bull Street, shoulders hunched forward as if she faced a hurricane wind. With quick glances all about her, she never stopped studying her environment while she walked. She arrived at the corner of what Jax now knew was Liberty and Bull, shivered a bit—there was a chill coming off the river tonight—and turned left.

Jax was only a few paces behind, but when he crossed the street, following in her footsteps, what he saw chilled his blood.

A black curtain formed about her, from the front and behind, blocking her from Ajax's sight. A temporary circling, one that couldn't hold fast around any human, especially not one with Shay's calling, not for an extended length of time. Yet Sable had still managed to barricade Shay from Jax's protective watch.

* * *

"Shayanna Angel. You didn't think I'd forgotten you, I hope?"

The centaur blocked her path on the narrow sidewalk; he'd waited until the foot traffic thinned, obviously. He'd caught her alone, unprotected—except for her stupid drumsticks, a new Vic Firth pair. Great for drumming, lousy for beating back ancient demons. She waved them in his face, pretending they were a pair of matching swords—and trying to tell herself that they would serve as true weapons.

"You back off, Sable!" Her mind whirled like a tornado, rushing for any weapon that would truly work on the demon. Nothing came to mind except the paralyzing fears of what this band might do to her in retaliation for the other night in the cemetery. In reprisal for all that her family full of demon hunters had wrought on demonkind over the years.

Sable's scarred mouth twisted into a bitter smile. Under the streetlights she could see more details than she had in Bonaventure. The demon's human portion looked as if he were a severe burn victim, his skin mottled and puckered all over his face, neck, and chest. "Please, Shayanna, call me Elblas. No need for informality among enemies."

He trotted closer, a smug, hateful expression on his face, yet somehow she had the impression that he might have been attractive at one time. Or at the very least, that he could have been. And as horses went, he was big as a Clydesdale, but with the grace of a powerful stallion, a terrible combination. It also put his human torso far, far above her middling height.

"I mean it, demon." She extended both drumsticks like rapiers, wishing to God that she'd brought some weapons. "You know what I am, right?"

Months ago she'd secretly "borrowed" a pair of Jamie's daggers and even a throwing star of Mason's— some absurdly ninja-esque piece out of his armory. But they were at her apartment, where she'd been practicing and teaching herself by watching mail-order paramilitary DVDs. None of those items were in her current possession. Why hadn't she armed herself better today?

"I *said*," she repeated when they circled closer, "you do know exactly what I am, *right*?"

"Huntress," Sable snarled, drawing the word out distastefully over teeth that seemed to lengthen. Behind him she heard the echoing cackles of other, as yet unseen demons. The horns atop the centaur's head suddenly uncoiled in reaction, then lengthened into a pair of razor-sharp protrusions. Shay shuddered at the thought of being gored to death if he decided to head-butt her.

"Huntress pretty," a smaller demon snickered.

"Our pretty one. Lovely, lovely."

She'd heard the same from them the other night, in the cemetery, and their taunts chilled her blood just as cold now. Maybe even more so, because she knew what they were truly capable of doing to her. They might freeze her again, turn her into a cold-blooded statue, and this time she might become their prisoner for eternity.

"Huntress," Sable repeated with another sneer, his lips curling back to reveal long, knifelike teeth. Her gaze was drawn to those razors, and they elongated dramatically as she stared. So did the curling horns atop his head, unfurling from their tight position into sharpened pommels standing high and gleaming. He could skewer her with either one, could stake her straight through the heart.

Maybe she should launch into a praise hymn, use the holy words as a battle sword—but she couldn't find her voice. A vise coiled about her throat, preventing her from song.

She only barely managed to rasp out a counterthreat. "That's right," she hissed back, vocal cords already raw. "I destroy your kind. While you may have caught me off guard the other night, I'm ready for you now."

Sable trotted right up to her, his thick human chest just above her head. "I take exception to your threat, little *huntress*."

Once again the unseen forces behind him laughed uproariously, a dry, cackling sound that made her hair stand on end. "Huntress, huntress," they chanted gleefully. "Ours to take. Ours to lose."

Nearly paralyzed with fear, she reminded herself of her spiritual power, kept telling herself that they were liars by nature, not capable of an honest word.

"Liars," she spat over her tight throat, clutching at her neck in an effort to dislodge the unseen hands that were strangling her and trying to keep her huntress's words from spilling forth. Her words were her greatest weapon—spiritual words, hymns, incantations. That was what she kept reminding herself of as the tight hold of Satan himself cinched her throat harder.

In a ridiculous gesture of mock strength, she kept the drumsticks extended, praying that Sable and his minions would buy into her masquerade, the idea that she had enough power to kick his ass with nothing but a pair of wooden sticks.

Damn it, Jamie, you should have trained me! If he had, she would have more fighting power and strength now. As it was, she had only the knowledge she'd gleaned from their family lore over the past months. That and her calling as a huntress, which did give her a certain amount of natural strength as she stared up into the centaur-demon's face.

He inclined his head with mock politeness. "Let me rephrase my answer," he said, his twisted mouth curling into a cruel smile. "*Untrained* huntress. You have the sight, but not the power." Sable sidestepped slightly, revealing his motley horde right behind him. "You must be stopped before you gain more knowledge."

"You are wrong!" She jabbed at the air between them with the sticks, straining her vocal cords just to shout back a challenge. Her heart was in her throat, too, adding to the tight sensation, making her nearly breathless. "You have no idea of all that I've learned, Sable," she taunted baldly.

Sable reared up, rising to a spectacular height, and

struck the air between them with his hooves. The sheer force of the motion sent her sprawling against the brick wall beside them. As he lunged earthward again, he seized her drumsticks, breaking them into papery wooden shards.

Sable chortled at her attempt to seem ballsy. "Your neck, little human, is next." With one muscular arm he scooped her into his grasp, hauling her right onto his back.

With a grunt she struggled, kicking at his horse's side with first one foot, then the other, and Sable jolted in jittery reaction.

"Stop her squirming!" the centaur commanded, and a flying demon landed atop Sable's hindquarters. The smallish creature reminded her of one of the flying monkeys in *The Wizard of Oz*, with its cackling screeches and the way it hopped along Sable's back, pinioning her there.

"I have her, Elblas," the thing squawked, and Sable began to trot forward, Shay dangling awkwardly across his back. The trot gained speed, became a rolling canter, and no matter how Shay struggled to dismount, the monkey-demon managed to hold her firmly against the center of Sable's back.

Shay watched the blurring street, struggling for breath, her eyes fixed on Sable's fast-moving hooves. He was gaining speed, the night becoming nothing but a shadow of blackness—not from the lack of daylight, but from the draining absence of goodness that had somehow encircled her. It was like an evil halo all about their moving band, and it held Shay captive within its boundaries.

She gave another kick at Sable's ribs, and another, digging her nails into his flesh until he reared up in a furious display. *Ha, not a smart move,* she thought as she rolled off his back and landed on the pavement. She'd grown up riding horses with her cousins, and the emergency dismount came easy for her.

At once she took off sprinting, never looking back. The sound of hellfire itself chasing on her heels definitely gave her extra speed. Her carriage apartment was only two blocks away, if she could just make it there.

A clawlike hand ripped into her back, snagging her by the shirt and lifting her into the air midrun. She cried out, wrestling in Sable's grasp, kicking and flailing in an attempt to make him drop her.

Bending his mouth close to her neck—hot, smoky breath wafting across her face—he panted for a moment. She could practically taste his hunger for her.

"Huntress," he murmured, "not quite so fast."

They'd taken her right to her apartment. The early Friday-night traffic on the sidewalks had been brisk, but as they were demons, they were completely unseen. And as she was in their clutches, that meant none of her neighbors whom they passed could see her either. As they entered the courtyard that led to her carriage apartment, they walked right past Lydia, who sat by the fountain, Shay's own cat, Sunshine, in her lap.

Sunshine hissed, hair on end, the moment the demons neared her.

"Little bitch of a creature," Sable cursed, and Shay—strapped across his back with snakelike cordons—dug her fingertips into his withers. After all, you didn't let a demon insult your very own kitty without a fight.

Sable lunged up the steps, taking them several at a time, and as they reached her apartment door Shay wondered if they'd make her unlock it. Like hell she would.

But like all the other shocking moments of the past days, the door apparently meant nothing, and Sable passed right through it, bringing Shay with him. She blinked at the familiar sight of her kitchen and breakfast nook, and when Sable's demon servants began unstrapping her, she had to bite back an absurd urge to laugh.

All these months she'd been wanting in the game, to really fight the demons that caused murder and pain and mayhem in her home city. She'd gotten her wish, all right—she'd just never imagined they'd be standing in her kitchen beside the cans of cat food, the molding bread, and her stack of bills. The real world colliding with the surreal world, right where she'd made scrambled eggs only three days before.

She slid to the floor as the last of her restraints came loose. Sable planted a hoof atop her belly, not leaning any weight on her, but the threat came through loud and clear.

"Now you talk, Shayanna." He bent his torso low, meeting her in the eye. "You talk—then you die."

She blinked up at him, confused. "Talk about *what*?" she snapped.

Sable began stroking each of his horns, and applied just a hint of weight to that hoof on her belly, enough that she had to yelp in slight pain. "Think, Shayanna. What would I want to know about?"

She leaned back against the floor, trying to find her breath or even to get her racing heart to settle down. It wasn't hard to figure out what the demon wanted— information about her angelic protector. As if she had any!

"I don't know anything about him," she announced flatly.

Sable lifted his threatening hoof and circled her slightly. "Ah, but you know and understand where my interest lies, don't you?"

She rolled onto her side, sitting up. "I just told you, pal: I don't know anything about him other than what happened the other night."

"Yet he saved you, how convenient." Sable reached a clawed hand to her face, and although she jerked sideways, he still managed to tangle his hand through her hair, giving it a painful jerk.

She managed to pull her hair free. "I thought . . . I don't know . . . that he was an angel." Drawing on a hidden source of bravado, Shay bolted to her feet. "Coffee, guys? What sorts of beverages do demons favor?" She moved toward the fridge, falsely peppy and bright. "I have wine, milk past the expiration date, vitamin water. Whatever you want."

Sable eyed her as if she were insane.

She sidestepped a millimeter at a time, edging her way toward *the spot*.

"What about your friends? They want something?" she offered, sliding a finger into the edge of the drawer in front of her.

"They don't warrant it." Sable watched her suspiciously, his red eyes narrowing. "What are you up to, Shayanna?"

She held up both hands. "Nothing, look. I'm just my mama's daughter, and no matter who comes into our home, we offer 'em something to drink. Well, and to eat, but my pantry's bare."

Sable leaned his elbows onto her bar. "I already know what I plan to devour, thank you."

She shivered, lifting her right knee and using it to wedge the drawer all the way open. From where Sable stood across the counter, he couldn't see what she was doing. Slowly lowering her hands, Shay reached for a sponge that sat on the counter and began wiping the surface. "Wow, lots of crumbs. How rude of me," she singsonged, working the sponge with her right hand as she eased her left hand into the drawer and made contact with one of Mason's throwing stars.

Bingo.

Just as the DVD had taught her, she tossed the star from her left hand into her right, and before Sable knew what was coming she hurled it across the bar, right at the center of his forehead. He screamed in pain, and she launched herself past the stunned demons and toward the door to her porch. Fumbling with the lock, she managed to fling the door open right as the centaur closed in on her.

On the balcony she turned with her back to the railing and extended the dagger that she'd also grabbed from the drawer. Sable closed in on her, the throwing star jutting out of his forehead like some kind of sharp handle.

"I'm going to punish you for that act of rebellion," he thundered.

"Not if I punish you first, you bastard." She leaned against the railing, striking at the air between them with her dagger in threat.

"I'm going to take that dagger from your hand and gut you like a pig. I'll hear you squeal and screech like one, too, before I'm done ... or maybe that's screech like a dying hawk, perhaps? Either way, I'm taking your blood tonight."

"No, Elblas, you are wrong about that one," a deep, wonderfully familiar voice said. Shay let out a tight breath as her hawk protector swooped onto the porch and inserted himself between her and the centaur. "I'm not letting you touch Shay, not ever again."

The protector-demon spoke to her over his shoulder. "You stay right behind me, Shayanna." Briefly he extended his right hand behind his back in a reassuring gesture, easing her away from the railing and against the brick wall of the carriage house. Holding her in his protection, her protector reassured her. "I've got this one."

She gave him room to fight, planting her back against the brick wall so that no other demons could take her from the rear. Studying the courtyard below and the street beyond it, she watched for demonic reinforcements—and marveled that none of the normal humans driving along could see a thing about what was really going on. One man walking by glanced up at her curiously, probably since she was backed up against the wall, hands splayed beside her, looking as though some nightmarish beast were about to eat her alive. Which was exactly what was going down—the man just couldn't see the rest of the picture. Finally he looked away, shaking his head in confusion.

The demon taunted her protector, and at one point she thought he said something like, "I followed her here to punish *you*."

She wondered what that meant, but didn't have time to analyze it as the two beings launched themselves at each other.

Beneath the courtyard lights—and not in statue form

this time—she was able to really watch her protector fight. She was amazed at the pure grace he displayed as he battled. He moved with the lightness of a dancer, yet assaulted with those same feet as if he held a black belt in karate. Sable actually retreated a few steps along the porch under the sheer force of the attack.

Yet the most amazing thing about her guardian's fighting skills was that he never used a sword, didn't summon his wings; the entire assault was carried out using only his hands and feet. Oh, and his head—he butted Sable hard in the chest, driving him backward again. The other demons began to make their move then, no longer holding back in deference to their master.

That was when Jax took hold of her in a fast-forward silver motion. One moment he was wearing black combat boots and fatigues, reaching for her elbow—the next his wings were erupting from behind his back as he swept her into his arms with a running leap off the balcony's railing.

Just like that she was lifting heavenward in his grasp all over again. And just like that, she flung her arms about his neck and clutched him closer, tears of gratitude filling her eyes.

"You came back," she murmured, pressing her face against his shoulders.

"I never left, sweet one," he replied, shushing her.

The wind tunneled about them, whipping her hair against her cheek. No wonder he had his own long hair drawn into a ponytail. Maybe she should start planning ahead, she thought with a ridiculous, girlish giggle. You just never knew when a winged demon-angel was going to kidnap you from downtown.

Although he hadn't soared very high—barely above the rooftops—his wings were pounding at the air much harder than before. She looked up into his face and saw a thin sheen of sweat on his forehead, and she wondered if flight was much harder on him, carrying her like this.

"There," he said, swooping downward, "there's our

spot. Hold tight to me, Shay; I don't want to hurt you when we land. I'm aiming for both feet this time."

She burrowed against his chest, shutting her eyes. "Thank you."

When he hit pavement he absorbed the impact by running, just like an airplane touching down and then braking hard. He finally came to a resting stop and searched the surroundings. "This is farther down Bay Street," she observed.

"Right where I intended," he told her in a serious tone. He took hold of her elbow. "Come on! We have to move fast; they're not far behind us."

Shay held her ground, unmoving. As relieved as she was by his protection—and at his having found her again—her emotions were in turmoil. She couldn't be sure whether she should truly trust him, much as she already wanted to—or fear for her very life.

"I need to know who you are," she insisted, "what you are, before I go with you."

He gave her a disbelieving look. "No time right now," he finally said, tugging on her arm again. "I'll explain when we get underground, where you'll be safe from them."

His ebony wings gleamed beneath the streetlight, and for the first time she could truly see how fierce his face was, beautiful and horrifying all at the same time, with its sharp planes, the long nose. "I don't know if I can trust you," she admitted softly. "I keep thinking that I can, but I can't figure out what sort of demon would protect me."

"The kind who doesn't care if you like *this*." With a cry in an unknown language, he transformed into a new set of street clothes, wings gone. Then he literally picked her up by the waist, held her aloft, and sprinted down the sidewalk. Like a dancer he sidestepped as he ran, dodging tourists and pedestrians, who, she was beginning to figure out, had no idea the two of them currently moved in their midst.

"Why can't these people see me?" she cried as Jax nearly tripped on a baby stroller, but managed to swerve past at the last minute.

"You're under my protection, so you're not visible to the mortal world at the moment."

She squirmed in his grasp. "Put me down," she argued. "I'm not a flipping sack of potatoes!"

"No," he said, barely winded as he ran. "What you are is noncompliant, quite a dangerous problem at the moment. So I'm taking control."

For some reason she thought of Linda Hamilton's character in *Terminator 2*, the way she'd skidded and clawed to get away from Arnie—until the moment she realized he only appeared to be the bad machine. He was still a machine, and he looked like a Terminator, but he had a different mission. He was there to save them all. Maybe her fallen angel was the same sort of thing; maybe he truly was what she'd been thinking ever since their first meeting, what he'd said from the very beginning: her protector. He had saved her not once but twice now, after all.

Resolved, she shouted, "I'll go with you. Just put me down!"

He stopped abruptly, depositing her on both feet. "Come on." He grunted, giving her arm a firm yank. "We've been exposed too long already." He moved purposefully, his gaze sweeping the landscape, his footsteps slowing sometimes, speeding at others. But he never let her away from his side, clasping her arm or her elbow with the death grip of the Terminator himself.

He watched the ground, studied the sky, sniffed at the air. Then he did the darnedest thing—beelined right into the middle of Bay Street, ignoring the oncoming traffic.

"Watch out!" she yelled as a car missed them by a hairline fracture's width. The car didn't swerve, and she remembered that, of course, they were invisible to the passing drivers. It was just that seeing him wander right into danger like that had really scared her. And what would have happened if he had been hit? She hated how much the thought unsettled her.

"First, they *didn't* hit me. Second, as I said, you're under my protection right now, so they don't even know we're here," he told her dismissively, and dropped to his knees. "Only someone with your special sight would be able to see us here right now."

"So you've got like, what? A supernatural umbrella around me? Or, like, a bubble-type deal?"

"That's one way of putting it."

With a bizarre conjuring of burning fire, he created a pothole in the street. He tested it by sliding into it. Then, climbing back out, he widened it a bit more and tested it again. Seemingly satisfied, he hoisted himself back out of the hole, and just narrowly missed being plowed down by a Range Rover in the process.

"Now we can go in together," he explained, crouching beside her. With a pat of his shoulders, he said, "Climb onto my back."

She gave her head a little shake. "You ... go ... first. Yeah, you go."

He stared at her incredulously, then jerked her out of a dusty Volvo's path, up against his side. "I understand that I'm confusing you with all this."

" 'All this' isn't confusing me. You're confusing me. *You.*" She waved her hand up and down his shirtfront in explanation. "Now a black T-shirt; before a breastplate; before that, bare skin and wings," she singsonged, aware that she sounded a little hysterical. "Yeah, sorry, dude, but whatever you are is confusing the *hell* out of me. Whoops, bad choice of words."

"I saved you before. Ergo you can obviously trust me. So let me give you a status check. As I see it right now"—he paused, sniffing the air—"and smell it, for that matter, Sable and crew will be on you in less than five. Plus, there's a hot little Benz starting down the street, moving, oh, about eighteen over the speed limit. You either bolt to the sidewalk or come with me now."

He stopped, giving her a significant look suggesting

what exactly *alone* might mean if the demons found her and she wasn't under his protection. "Or we both get rolling and you let me do my job. But I can't keep this pothole open for long, not if we don't want to cause a car accident that endangers the lives of innocent people."

"Job? Someone pays you for this?" She jabbed him in the chest with her forefinger. The muscle was so hard that she actually had to shake her hand in pain.

He sighed, glancing down the street. "I'm your guardian, Shay," he said, "like we discussed before."

She suddenly forgot their quarrel and remembered the Benz—which was closing in on them. *We're invisible, so maybe it won't hurt so much,* she rationalized mentally. *Or maybe we're* only *invisible and that Benz could crush me like a mosquito.*

"But you wouldn't want to find out for sure," he warned, knowing her thoughts without missing a beat. With another pat of his shoulder, he bent low enough that she could climb onto his back.

She didn't budge. "I don't want you getting in my head like that."

"Then perhaps you should think less loudly."

She slapped him on the arm. "Wait! That's how you knew my name. You plucked it right out of my own head the other night, just like that Sable freak knew my thoughts."

He gave her a shockingly gentle smile. "Come on, Shay," he urged. "We're almost out of time."

With a sigh of surrender she slipped both arms about his neck. "Just gotta know one thing," she said as he slid powerful forearms under her legs. "Are you a *Terminator* fan?"

"Not the third one," he said. With a catlike movement he slid down into the hole, swinging from the opening. "The others, yes. Why?"

"Tell me you're here to fight the T-1000s." She clung hard to his neck. "Just promise me that."

His answer was to drop with her like a heavy stone

into the utter blackness below—fathomless darkness. Maybe even into the depths of the underworld itself.

Jamie stood with Candy beside him. She'd clearly been confused when he'd taken off running down the street a moment earlier. She had no idea, of course, that he'd just seen his sister in the middle of a supernatural crisis, but she'd kept up behind him, sort of, high heels clacking on cement.

His emergency call from the Shades had turned out to be a false alarm—the real issue, he now knew, was his little sister. In disbelief he watched as she disappeared below Bay Street clinging to that demon—or angel—from the other night. Jamie had been too far away to glimpse much. But he'd seen enough, transfixed as he'd watched the winged creature fly earthward with Shay cradled in his arms, then land right on the sidewalk.

Jamie had been too late reaching them, however. By the time he'd caught up with them, she'd been sliding below Bay Street with that *thing*.

"Wait here," he told Candy, who, of course, hadn't witnessed any of the supernatural action. "I need to go check something out."

He started to walk into the street, but Friday night traffic was nonstop, and the light was green. *That hole could lead anywhere,* he thought. *You have to get to it before it seals.*

Tapping his foot, he kept waiting for a break in the traffic, and hit speed dial on his BlackBerry. It was time to gather the Shades in earnest now.

Chapter 12

The manhole, it turned out, was really a laundry chute right into a dark, creepy-ass tunnel. Shay screamed the whole way down, burrowing her face against the warrior's neck. It was a five-second whirling plummet that was worse than any Six Flags ride she'd ever been on.

When they landed, he absorbed the full impact with supernatural grace. He stood still for a moment, breathing heavily, then swung her off his back and onto the ground.

"You stay here and don't move—I'll be right back." As if that were going to reassure her? Hello, she wasn't five years old.

"Don't leave me down here!"

But he was already gone, blackness and heavy wing-beats letting her know that he'd transformed again and flown back up to the manhole where they'd entered. She stared upward, trying to make out what he was doing. "This better not be a trap," she called out, standing on tiptoe.

What a trap this would make, too, if he were one of the bad guys. *Oh, crap,* she thought. *Maybe this is what they've all been after this whole time? Use hottie demon boy to lure stupid human girl into hidden underground space? Check. Take said tunnel straight into hell? Check again.*

All he's done is protect you, she reminded herself. *Whatever he is, he's one of the good guys.*

Still, staring up at the tiny shaft of light that filtered

in from the opening, then glancing at the darkness all about her, she had the overwhelming sensation that she was being buried alive. Trapped in the underworld without her dark angel's protection.

"Don't leave me down here! Please!" she cried, gazing upward.

Her breathing accelerated; her pulse went crazy; all at once a full-blown panic attack hit her. Once, as a little girl, she'd followed her father into the cellar, hoping to find out what all the family secretiveness was about, and had managed to get locked in. For hours and hours she'd been enclosed alone in that dark space, no windows, no good light. It had seemed forever until Mason had heard her crying and screaming.

"Help!" she now screamed, clawing at the walls around her, unable to breathe. Hot tears burned her eyes. "Come back—*please*!"

At that precise moment even the small amount of spare light she had was extinguished as he sealed the overhead opening. She glanced first one way, then another, but it was impossible to see a thing. Panicked, she groped at the air all around her, tears burning in her eyes. All she knew was that she had to start moving, that she had to get free somehow. She stumbled into the pitch blackness, feeling as if she were going to throw up; her heart was beating that fast.

The sound of booted feet landing echoed behind her. "Shay? Where are you going?"

She moved faster, her hysteria rising. Her outstretched hands met what felt like a crumbling stone wall, and she clawed at it, crying harder.

"I have to get out of here," she shouted. "I'm trapped. You trapped me!"

Groping along the hard surface, she managed a few steps, and tamped down a rolling wave of nausea. Some dim part of her mind told her she was reacting irrationally—but the suffocating, claustrophobic feeling choked at her throat, driving away any faith she had in the threatening creature behind her.

"Just stay ... away." She sobbed, pressing her forehead against the cool stone surface. "I need out. Have to get out."

She heard his clomping footsteps behind her, coming closer every moment. "Shay, stop! I haven't scouted this area yet. Where do you think you're going?"

"As far away from you as I can!" Hyperventilating now, she struggled to pick up her pace, but it was a losing battle. The warrior was practically on her.

"You're acting crazy," he said. "You're safe down here. Safe with me."

"I'm not safe." She ran blindly into the darkness. "I have to get out!"

One large forearm came down across her chest, and she was dragged to a sudden halt. "Not a good idea." He breathed the words in her ear, pressing his face against her cheek as he'd done when they were flying that first night. But this time he sounded truly pissed, not as though he were toying with her.

"You've trapped me down here." She squirmed in his grasp, gasping for air.

"No, Shayanna." He sounded anything but patient. "I've gotten you out of our enemies' crosshairs. For the moment."

He held her from behind in a sort of wrestling maneuver, his forearm firm about her. Yet he didn't hurt her or choke even an ounce of breath from her lungs. He treated her more like a delicate butterfly that he'd pinned rock-solid against his chest. For many long moments he kept her close, just letting his own even breathing calm her, settle inside of her. Gradually the steady beating of his heart against her back slowed her own erratic heart. Breath by breath, beat by beat, he soothed her without speaking a single word.

She exhaled, feeling the panic ease. She wasn't alone, wasn't trapped. She kept repeating that to herself until her nausea and tears began to subside.

But as rational thought returned, she became increasingly aware of a new problem—the strapping creature had her in a tight, intimate hold within his arms. Thank God he was back in the T-shirt and pants, at least. Lord knew what she'd do all cozied up to his bare-chested self. Or if his wings were brushing near her once again.

"Better now?" His voice was whiskey-rich in her ear.

She bobbed her head obediently and then released a tight breath. "You're not going to hurt me?"

"Shay, I may be dangerous to you—but not the way you're obviously thinking. I'm your guardian." He sighed in apparent frustration. "I don't know how many ways to say it."

"Then *how* are you dangerous to me?" She hadn't missed that comment.

He laughed, a low, rumbling sound that vibrated through his chest and into her own body. "Because of how I want you. And when I take you, sweet Leda of mine, it won't be easy or gentle."

She trembled at the words, shaking slightly against him, and still he didn't budge.

Didn't move that arm of his or even shift so much as an inch in the way he kept hold of her. *You're making sure I won't run again,* she thought, realizing what it was he seemed to be waiting for.

"No." He ran his other hand down the length of her hair, the gentlest touch for such a giant man. "I'm making sure you feel *safe.* That you trust me."

She twisted slightly, wanting to see him, but he wouldn't allow it. Neither would Satan's black armpit, aka the tunnel where they presently stood. "I don't really have a choice, do I? It seems you're hell-bent on saving my life." She smiled, realizing that she did feel safe with this man. Safer than she had in a very long time.

"I would fly to the ends of the universe to keep you safe, sweet one."

She shivered slightly at his words, her whole body tightening with craving for him. "But," she whispered, "I don't even know anything about you ... or what you even are."

The moment seemed to suspend between them, one

endless breath, one eternal heartbeat that they shared somehow. He didn't answer at first, just kept his mouth right against her ear, breathing in and out. So warm, that breath of his. Comforting in a perverse sort of way.

"Ajax," he finally murmured in a quiet voice, stroking his fingertips across her cheek. "I'm called Ajax."

"Like the household cleaning product?" she blurted with a stupid snort of laughter.

He snorted back, but it wasn't a playful sound. "Like the great warriors of old." He tugged his arm even tighter around her. Payback, she supposed.

"Sorry, pal." She twisted in his grasp, apparently an exercise in futility when battling any guy named Ajax. "But my 'great warriors of old' knowledge isn't really that up-to-date."

Seeming truly indignant, he slid his other palm atop her hip, tugging her flush against his body. "Ajax the Great, cousin to Achilles." He burrowed his face against the top of her head. "Don't you know anything about the Greeks? The name Ajax means nothing to you?"

"I know that a *man-being* named Ajax is holding me captive right now." She pried at his hand where it rested against her hip, but he didn't budge. "And that I want him to let me go. My hip says so, too."

He moved his hand and began stroking her hair with it again. "This man who holds you, Ajax Petrakos, will never hurt you, wee lass," he promised in a quiet voice. "But neither will I release you. Not until you're convinced that I'm telling the truth."

She sighed, shaking her head—or at least the best she could, since he had her in a full nelson, or whatever this wrestling maneuver of his was. "See, that dog just ain't gonna hunt."

"What dog?" His grip on her loosened a little. "You want me to hunt food for you?"

She couldn't help it; she rolled her eyes, even though nobody but God and the angels themselves could see.

Non-Southerners. Sometimes, they just didn't speak good English.

With all the patience she could possibly summon—
and that wasn't much, given the circumstances—she explained things. "It's an expression down here in Georgia,
Ajax. So I'll put it in words you'll recognize." She made
her voice a high falsetto, as if she were a medieval prin-
cess held captive in some dark tower. "This situation absolutely will not do! You must release me posthaste!"

"This dog *will* hunt," he told her in an intense, fer-
vent voice. One that totally cracked her up, because he
just sounded so sincere. And sweet. And unintentionally
stupid. The fact that he'd botched the ridiculous saying
only made him seem even more endearing somehow.
She sighed, her whole body relaxing against his.

As she melted into him, he loosened his hold on her
slightly, shifting his forearm so that the wrestling hold
became an embrace.

"So you're Greek?" she asked softly, feeling breathless.

He replied in a flowing, elegant sentence that made
absolutely no sense to her. Too bad her family had abandoned their Greek heritage several generations earlier.
She could have used a little fallback info right now.

He murmured in her ear again, the flowing, hypnotic
words soothing her this time.

She closed her eyes, not that she had to in the consuming darkness, but she did it anyway. Focusing on the feel
of his body, the rhythm of his breathing ... the rise and
fall of his chest ... all of it felt right. Instinct told her
that she could trust this man with her very soul, even if
it literally flew in the face of rational thought.

So, here in the dark with nothing but those same instincts to guide her—and with the distractions of fear
and survival fading into the background—she knew beyond any doubt that the gorgeous creature holding her
could be trusted. No—should be trusted.

She let her head relax against his chest; he stroked
her cheek with the back of his knuckles, whispering in
Greek a bit more. The words sounded earnest, like a
pledge from the heart. The longer he held her, the more
she became aware of his solid, muscular body, of the

nuances of it. How massive it was . . . although it didn't seem as big as when he'd been flying. Could it be that as he shifted forms, his physical proportions actually altered, too?

She slid a palm onto that forearm that he held about her chest. His skin was warm, hairless, just like his chest had been. She stroked her fingertips down the length of his arm, ending at his hand, and then caressed a slow path back up again. His muscles were so heavy, the lines could literally be traced, each ridge and crest forming a mountainous landscape.

He shivered at her touch, moaning softly in his language.

"I-I don't speak Greek," she replied, dizzy from all the physical sensations he was arousing inside of her.

"You knew the incantation the other night. That was Greek. Oh, sweetness, your body is divine." His large palm moved across her abdomen.

"It's phonetic, from family stuff. Books." She gasped as his hand trailed lower. "I told you."

Brushing her long hair off her nape, he pressed his lips to the exposed skin and kissed it. "Your body?" he half groaned. "Quite obviously it's from your family."

Sadness washed over her as she thought of her mother's death—and all her fears about being adopted. "Maybe . . . maybe not," she told him quietly. "But I meant that reversal spell, those ancient Greek words. I learned them from my family."

"How did your family have a book in the old language?" he asked in surprise. "Apart from being in the demon-fighting business, why would they?"

"My great-great-grandfather changed our name from Angelopolous so we'd seem more American. It was the South, you know, and folks down here were more inclined to trust someone who sounded Anglo. Still are. Plus, Angel's just shorter."

"*Angelopolous?*" he repeated in a wondrous voice. "From the Peloponnese? I never even thought you might be Greek."

"There we go again." She laughed. "With this whole you've-known-me-forever thing."

He purred in her ear. The sound of his breathing was heavy, hot and fast, and it electrified every part of her body. She felt her nipples go taut beneath her baby-doll shirt.

"Would a good Greek girl believe in the ancient oracles?"

She stroked his arm again. "Not if a sexy and dangerous Greek boy tried to tell me anything about them."

"Ah, Shayanna Angelopolous." He kissed the top of her head. "I like the sound of *that* name best of all."

And maybe, just maybe, I like you whispering it like that.

A low thunderclap of laughter sounded in her ear, and she knew that he'd just read her thoughts —again— which suddenly didn't seem like such a bad thing.

Slowly he pivoted her within his arms until they stood face-to-face. Or face-to-chest, to be more accurate. He dwarfed her with his colossal height and size. Not that she could see well in the darkness. It was more a matter of sense—where his voice came from, the strength of his chest against her cheek.

"You feel safe now," he observed in a whisper, sliding both his large palms along her shoulders, then lower along her back. "I've made you understand."

"No, I don't understand anything at all." She laughed, leaning against him. "But I do know you've got my back in a big way."

"Just remember that. No matter what happens, remember how protected you feel right now, right here with me."

She bobbed her head, wrapping both arms about his substantial torso, and suddenly felt incredibly small by comparison. Her arms—long enough and strong enough for drumming—could barely reach about his tremendous body. It was more than just height he had on her. It was the tree-trunk chest, the wide waist that narrowed only slightly from his hips; it was just the sheer volume of the man who embraced her.

She sighed, loving the rough, woodsy smell of his body. It was a natural scent, the sort a hawk-man would have, as if he'd been touched by the early spring itself, by the wind that carried him high into the clouds. Oh, what *was* this guy who held her right now, who made her want him to the point of confusion and stupidity?

"The feel of your body . . ." She couldn't say it, couldn't put into words how luscious it felt to touch, to hold.

A rumbling laugh vibrated through his chest. "You like my wings; you like my body. It's possible that you might even like me, at least a little bit." He laughed again, a lighter and happier sound than she'd heard from him before. "I think, Shayanna, that we make a good match already."

"Already?" She clutched him tighter, despite herself.

"Yes, imagine once I've taken you beneath my body. When I've filled your ears with the beat of my wings." His husky voice dropped even lower, becoming thick and rough. "Imagine when I've glided atop you like the wild hawk I truly am, and you've given yourself over to me. Ah, sweetness," he purred, his Greek accent suddenly emerging. "You've not known the pleasures I will show you."

She opened her mouth, feeling helpless and dizzy, but all at once a flash of silver illuminated the area around them—like a lightning storm contained right in their small space. "What was that?" she asked, squinting as the light quickly dissolved.

He released her, cursing under his breath. "We need a plan . . . and some light," he mumbled, suddenly all business. "I can make a torch." She heard him take several steps away from her.

"But what was that silver flash?" She followed him in the darkness, determined to know, and felt her way by gripping the jagged stones of the wall. "I saw a flash of lightning . . . bright silver, then it vanished. Ajax? Damn it! Where did you go?"

"I'm summoning my spear to use as a torch. It carries fire from Styx itself," he called back to her.

"I'm coming with you." She followed the sound of his steps.

"Shay, stop where you are. We haven't investigated the terrain down—"

She cut him off with a loud cry when sharp pain sheared unexpectedly through her right calf. She'd rammed into some kind of metal, slicing her leg on it. She bent down, feeling the already bleeding gash.

"Shay? What happened?" The heavy sound of his booted feet moved swiftly toward her.

"I don't know. There's some kind of metal. . . . I don't know." She felt along the stones with her hands, and a long rounded and rough shape moved back and forth in her hand. With her fingertips she traced the metal conduit all the way up the wall. It was loose, and as she outlined it in the darkness a slight sound began from inside the wall. *Crap,* she thought. *That doesn't sound good.*

Making her voice sound falsely bright, she called to Ajax, "It's a pipe!" Cold, trickling water began to flow over her hands.

"Are you all right? Did you hurt yourself?" Jax's steps were nearby; he was almost to her.

But she didn't have time to answer, because all at once—from seemingly everywhere—she heard the sound of rushing water. Damn it, that pipe had been old and corroded, no telling what damage she'd just caused.

"That pipe broke loose!" A rolling tremor hurled her through the blackness and up against the wall. "It sounds like it broke off. . . . I dislodged another one, I think, I'm not sure."

The roaring sound intensified, the entire tunnel began to rumble, and stones began falling from the sides, the ceiling. Such an old and sealed-off passageway was fragile at best. She fell to her knees, covering her head as the entire place threatened to come down around them.

"I'm almost to you," Ajax called back to her. "Hold your position."

His words were cut off by an absolute deluge of water that dumped down onto her head. The force was so strong it swept her away, taking her down the tunnel along with it.

"Ajax!" she screamed, trying to keep her head above the flowing torrent. But no matter how hard she fought to grab hold of anything stable, the fast-flowing water shot her farther along, stones and debris scratching her back and her arms.

"Shay, take hold of anything you can find," he shouted, sounding much farther behind her than before.

Thank God the water at least smelled clean, she thought vaguely. River water maybe. Both hands wide, she clutched at anything she could find, imagining being shot right out into the cold of the spring river if she couldn't stop herself.

"Ajax! I can't stop this!" Panicked, and feeling her skin scrape and burn, she flailed in the rapid current. She tried calling again, but managed only to suck down a lungful of the water. She sputtered and coughed, her hands sweeping all about her, and, when she was truly becoming terrified, she made contact with another pipe. For all she was worth she gripped it as more torrents of water whipped at her body.

"Shay, I'm almost to you," he shouted above the rushing noise. "Don't let go!"

There was heavy splashing beside her, and then his now-familiar hands seized hold of her, swinging her out of the gusher—and into a cradling position within his own warm arms.

He worked his hands across her body as he sloshed back up the tunnel. "It's still dry back there; just hold on to me."

She nodded and coughed some more, swiping a wet tendril of hair out of her face. Her clothes were plastered to her, and her whole body smarted from abrasions and cuts.

He sloshed heavily through the flowing water; the current had died down now. "You're bleeding on your arms ... your back." He sniffed lightly. "And your leg smells like blood."

"I cut it pretty badly," she admitted, bending within his grasp so she could touch the gash. The ragged pipe had sliced right through her jeans. "But I'll be all right. And I'm all caught up on my tetanus shots, thank *God.*"

"Elblas will pay for this." Ajax's tone grew intense, his voice boiling with unconcealed fury. "For every scratch on your body, for every tear he causes you to shed, that demon will suffer, too."

She shivered, feeling confused. "Do you mean he made that water rush in here?" She tried to glance about them, panicking. "Is he already on us again?"

"No, but you wouldn't be down here in the first place if he hadn't attacked you earlier. You just dislodged a pipe of some kind," he explained. "River cities like this one have all sorts of channels underneath them."

"We have pirate tunnels, too. They'd use them to get their booty straight to the ships."

His rich, silken laugh rumbled in her ear. "They can't have *your* booty. I already plan to claim it as mine."

The image of being tossed across his winged back as he set sail for the heavens themselves entered her mind: a hawklike pirate, stealing her to the other side of the cosmos. Yeah, and he was a lot fiercer and darker than Johnny Depp, and way bigger than Orlando Bloom.

"Ahoy," she said, and promptly wilted against him.

Chapter 13

Jax busied himself with exploring the tunnel, using a lit spear that he'd conjured in order to illuminate the far end. "We should be safe here for now," he informed Shay. "Just for now." There was no relaxing or letting their guard down. He'd chosen the underground space—had scouted it earlier in the day after following Shay to work—knowing it could provide temporary shelter if they needed it. But it wouldn't protect them for long.

In the past moments Ajax had investigated every inch of the dank space. Although he couldn't truly relax, not until he was convinced he had her permanently out of Sable's reach, he dropped down on his haunches beside the wall. He stayed in that crouching position, ready to launch into combat at even the slightest scent of demon's sulfur. Battle-ready, he bore his breastplate and kept his shield against his left knee, his sword by the right.

"So what's with the silver?" Shay sounded exhausted. She sat propped against the wall opposite him, her head drooping.

"Silver?" He kept his tone and expression bland. The truth was, every part of his body jolted at her question, reacting violently both to the question and to her.

"Yeah, your eyes keep changing colors." She sat up straighter, leaning forward slightly. "They were silver when you saved me. Then they turned pure black, and now"—she peered up into his face—"now they're sort of both all at once. And a moment ago I saw the veins in your hands glow."

"I don't know what you mean," he lied, casting his own gaze downward. He couldn't meet her genuine, honest stare, not while racking his brain for some invented excuse to pacify her.

"Listen, I get the wings. I get the talons and the whole hawk-protector thing you've got going here, sort of. I mean, I don't understand it, but it's obvious you're one of the good guys—"

He jerked his gaze upward. "Don't count on it. At least, not in the traditional sense."

"—and I realize that even though you *aren't* going to hurt me, you're probably not an angel, not like I've been praying to see."

"You're dead right about that one."

"And you're definitely not a demon."

He remained silent.

She only got louder, crawling toward him. "But what I *don't* get, at least not so far, is why your body keeps lighting up like a Christmas tree. Not the traditional variety, by the way, but the metal-flocked kind my mama got secondhand. Tacky bright."

His jaw dropped slightly. "Are you calling me *tacky*?"

She pushed against both of his knees. "No, I'm wondering why you keep lighting up like that."

"My kind are a crafty, cunning breed, Shay. Tread carefully." He flashed a menacing gaze to really demonstrate his point—and that one look into her lovely, sleepy eyes destroyed him. Like a hawk barely clinging to a sheer cliff face, he lost his gripping hold. Went free-falling, dangerously tumbling toward the emotional rocks below.

A flare lit his beefy forearms from the inside out, illuminating his long body like lightning in a distant stormy sky.

"See!" She gestured excitedly. "It happened again. Right then, your arms." She reached for him, but he jerked backward.

Turning his profile to her, he stared down the length of the dank tunnel, anywhere but into her pale eyes. The immortal source was running dangerously hot and wild in his veins. It was too soon to explain about that to her; he didn't want to frighten her off.

He rose to his feet. "I'm going to build a fire farther down there," he said. "A small one that won't attract visitors, just to help you warm up a bit. You're shivering and soaked." He brushed past her, all business. "I'll keep it small so as not to attract demonic attention."

"But how could they even see the fire down here? I don't get it."

He turned back, smiling. "Persistent, aren't you, love?"

She shrugged. "When it comes to riddles and mysteries, yeah. Guess that comes with the family legacy. So how *would* a demon horde see your campfire from aboveground, Boy Scout?"

He tapped his nose. "Smell it. They're not human, remember. That asphalt overhead means nothing to them."

"Then don't worry about me. It's not worth the risk; I'll warm up. I'm just having a little sinking spell or something."

"A sinking ... what?" He cocked his head, curious. Long ago he'd memorized most English colloquialisms. Then again, his only ventures into America had been up north and in the Midwest.

A faint smile tugged at her mouth. "I'm tired and a little sore, that's all."

He smiled back. *Tired* sounded like *tarred* when she said it, but at least he got her meaning this time.

"I could warm you up," he offered softly, intentionally keeping his expression neutral, his body on a restraining leash of his own making. "There's a lot of heat in this body of mine." He laughed seductively, staring at her through his lowered lashes. "Plenty of heat for you, Shay."

She tensed visibly, shifting her crossed legs. "It's way too dangerous."

"Is that me or the fire?" he teased, letting his voice

fall into a low, wicked vibration. "Or perhaps you mean both."

He moved closer, dropping to his haunches. He approached her as he would a wild wolf in midwinter, aware of every muscle tensing in his body—and of every one reacting in her own. "Shayanna." He fixed her with his gaze, feeling heat rise to his face. "You are worth far more than a warming fire. If you had even an inkling of what I want to give you, show you . . ." He reached for her, but she recoiled slightly, straightening against the tunnel wall. "I'm frightening you again."

She gave her head a slight shake. "No. Not frightening me . . . not exactly."

"Then why were you suddenly afraid for me to touch you?"

She stared at the stone floor of the tunnel, avoiding his gaze. She trailed her tongue across her lips thoughtfully, and it was all he could do not to cover that mouth with his own. "You make me feel powerful . . . things." She peeked up at him, her thick black lashes shadowing her eyes. "When I'm with you, my heart goes nuts, Ajax. It's almost too intense. So, yeah, you do frighten me. It's only natural."

The words made his own heart turn over inside his chest. How he'd longed for the day when he'd lay himself bare before this woman; now the time had come. Even though he wanted to rush headlong at her, wanted to make love to her body, caress her soul, he had to remember that she'd never known about him until a few days ago.

He propped his spear against the wall, still squatting in front of her. "Before, you felt safe with me. Why are you afraid again? I would never hurt you, Shay." He made his tone as gentle as possible. "Think about it—all I've done since we met is protect you. Let yourself feel safe with me."

He reached toward her again, this time managing to capture one of her hands. "Ah, you're chilled. Your hand is so cold—give me the other." He waited until she slowly gave in. Forming a cave with his much larger hands, he enclosed hers, then lowered his mouth and blew warm air into the small opening, an old battle trick that had served the Spartans well on many a winter campaign.

Her eyes widened in surprise. "Oh, you're good, all right."

He bent his head low again, softly blowing between his palms, allowing his breath to caress her, to heat her chilled body and soothe her aches with his own primal warmth. Then, unable to help himself, he slid his tongue across her fingertips, trailed the tip of it over each of her knuckles, one at a time.

"I'm warming up, so why am I still shaking so hard?" she asked as he leaned in closer, his head nearly against her breast as he turned her hands within his grasp.

Drawing first one palm to his lips, then the other, he nibbled her flesh. A raptor's instinct, to bite and taste that way, but this level of desire—so intense, so untamable—always awakened his hawk instincts.

"You're shaking, too, Ajax."

Careful, you're losing control too fast. Calm down, you randy fool.

Briefly he glanced upward, staring into her eyes, looking for some promise of absolution or release. He flinched slightly at realizing that his vision was awash in silver.

"Your eyes," she murmured, gesturing toward his face. "They've turned again."

"It's what they always do." He clenched his teeth, leaping back to his feet. He had a duty to this woman, and what was he doing? Losing control, surging with dark power.

"But why do they turn silver?" she persisted. "What does it mean?"

"That I've lost hold of the beast." He turned from her slowly, watching the tunnel electrify with his own perverse life source.

She rose to her feet, favoring her injured leg slightly, and started walking behind him as he took off down the tunnel. "Are *you* the beast? Is that what you mean?"

"It's not meant for mortals to know these things, Shay." He rounded on her, his body ablaze with need for her. "Watch yourself."

What did she think she was going to prove, anyway? She already knew he wasn't a human, so why the big deal about what flowed inside of him?

She touched his arm again, much gentler this time. "I want to know. I won't hurt you either."

"Hurt *me*?" he thundered, the cry echoing off the walls that enclosed them. "Hurt me? Bloody hell, woman, how can you worry about me? You should feel the pressure inside this hawk's chest of mine." He thumped his breastbone hard. "If you could, you'd know you're the one in danger here, not me. I'm just trying to protect you from all that I am."

Again, the untamable power surged inside his body, spilling out through his pores, across his skin. *Damn it all to hell.* So many years of control, all smashed to nothing by the dark-haired beauty in front of him.

"Just a moment ago you were telling me how safe I am "

"And let's keep it that way," he managed through clenched teeth. Bathed in his silver light she looked like a vision or a fantasy . . . even a lost memory. "I can't lose you . . . not by my own hand, or otherwise."

Their gazes remained locked, silent words flying between them. She begged him with her eyes; he beseeched her with his own. Clenching his hands, he turned them back and forth. He wasn't surprised to see every vein pop with bright silver power. Shay had him in a physical and emotional tailspin. Like the great hawk that he was, she'd shot him right out of the sky, and he was plummeting helplessly toward her. His body no longer listened to his commands or obeyed his efforts to control it. Instead, his immortal essence seemed to be amping up, intensifying wildly—and so was his libido. As if that needed any extra fuel.

Her eyes grew wide, but she said absolutely nothing. Neither breathed or moved or blinked. Hell, not so much as a droplet of water deigned to fall from the ceiling as his human body turned into a raging furnace.

This was the cost of Ares' gifts; Jax's inability to master his own power. The benefits of his oath to the war god had been abundant: immortality, safety for Sparta and their families, survival for all of Greece. But they hadn't come without a severe price, one that had required a choking portion of Jax's Spartan discipline ever since.

Ares later told Jax that he'd overloaded him on purpose. That he'd intentionally given him a longer draw on Styx's goblet than he had the others, thereby allowing more of the source to meld with Jax's mortal flesh.

It was the only sure way I could handle someone as spirited and strong as you, Ares had explained jovially in the beginning. His god's body gleamed that day, shining bright as the Greek mountainside where they met: brilliant, luminous, juxtaposed against the clear cobalt blue sky above. Studying Ares there on the hills of Parnassus, Jax had known how small human temples really were, their constructions all chalky white, a wash beneath any god's eyes.

Ares' skin always reflected light, despite his seeming so human in many ways; he was a sun unto himself, the full moon at night. The god's body sparkled, shone like gold, wavered like sun-brushed wheat. Ares knew he was perfectly beautiful, with his long blond hair falling over his shoulders, a cascade of locks that reached his lower back; teeming muscles that formed his lean and long body. The god swam in his own beauty; it only added to his heavenly confidence.

I had to have a way to bridle you, he told Jax then, clasping his shoulder in the same familial way Jax's own brothers so often did. *Using your own power seemed as good a way as any.*

Ares had visited him often then—sometimes on Greece's hillsides, other times in her caves, depending on where Jax had hidden himself. Those had been his lost days, the insane time, as he'd later come to think of it—when he'd been maddened by that long, hard drink from Styx. Quite literally Ajax had woken with the hangover from hell.

You placed an untamable beast upon my Spartan back, Jax complained, desperate for a reprieve from the constant churning of the source in his veins. *All my years of training in the Agoge, my hard-earned discipline ... it means nothing now.*

Exactly as I wanted it, Ares agreed, tossing his long golden hair down his back. *You, a disciplined man in every way, have been saddled with uncontrollable power.*

It had served as the challenge that Ares no doubt intended, urging Ajax to gain control. The god had watched like some cosmic coach, sometimes chiding—and sometimes praising.

Now, so many years later—and after mastering his supernatural nature—Shay had unraveled all the careful control he'd managed to wield when it came to his immortal source. Just glancing at her, he felt his changed body shake with lust and longing; the swirling power was roaring in his cells, maddening him. Making him crave Shay even more.

Had Ares sent Shay into his life in an attempt to bridle him yet again? To keep him bound by the uncontrollable immortality in his male veins?

Well, he'd be damned if Ares would sacrifice Shay's mortal life with his fickle game playing. Not this time, not again.

Jax took Shay's hand and squeezed it imploringly. "I can't control it, the silver, not around you. Don't you see? My power is raging inside of me because it's you, Shay. *You*."

She cocked her head, stroking him lightly on the arm. "What is it about me that's so important?"

"I can't explain that now. I have to get away from you," he barked, leaping to his feet. Striding toward the tunnel's end, he began deep-breathing exercises. Worked to relax his forearms, his face, his neck—all of his body, one muscle fiber at a time. These were the techniques that had served him well in the past, but as his breathing came faster and harder, he realized he was powerless in Shay's presence. *She was supposed to save my soul*, he wanted to cry and actually beat at his chest in frustration. *She's meant to be my destined one. Not my undoing.*

Flexing and relaxing his hands, he willed the source flowing in his veins to calm down. No such luck for Ares' finest, he thought with a grim laugh. The dark tunnel itself began to glow like the flowing River Styx. His groin tightened; his T-shirt pulled sharply across his chest, his full body morphing and expanding.

He ripped at his T-shirt, tearing it off; with an anxious motion he pulled off his pants. The seams would have ripped to shreds right off his body otherwise. Transformation of any kind—even just to ditch the clothes—would only have accelerated his power load. But nudity didn't exactly help his current state, either.

He stood, naked and panting, his back kept to her. Helplessly he palmed his cock, aching for release of any kind . . . from the silver rushing inside his body, from his lust for the human behind him. He closed his fingers about the erection, yearning for the feel of her hand about him. After a gasping moment he dropped his hand away—and his shoulder blades began to itch and burn. There would be no stopping the wings from piercing through his skin, not now. He was completely out of control, a danger to Shay with his power surging so wildly inside his body and soul.

A prickling sensation teased across his back, feathers pierced skin, and, unable to halt the transformation, he felt his tremendous wings burst forth. It was a wild display of what he wanted, how badly he craved her.

What you should be doing, you bastard, is apologizing. Not lusting. He should be on his knees begging for her forgiveness, pledging to protect her—saying he was sorry again and again that he'd somehow gotten her into this dangerous mess.

Not that *she* realized that he was responsible for her current predicament. She believed that she'd done her own job of attracting the demons' interest just by entering the cemetery. A workable theory; unfortunately, Ajax knew better. As he'd replayed the events in his mind—the precise order of them, starting with the Oracle's words and ending with Shay herself—Ajax had become convinced of one fact.

Elblas Djiannas had come to Savannah for only one reason—no, for one person: Shayanna Angel.

It was a horrifying, gut-wrenching realization: that the Persian demon horde knew of Jax's long-ago prophecy, that she was the great love he'd been promised. Yet the coincidences were too crazy otherwise: that ancient Persian Djinn would pop up in her hometown, that Elblas himself would have attacked her so aggressively twice now. No matter which way he outlined recent events in his mind, the road map always connected his mortal enemy with his one great love.

He was more convinced than ever after the earlier fight, when Sable had taunted him about her.

Besides, even if he hadn't, Jax was smart enough to figure out the facts. Why else would Sable have gone after Shay? Especially since he'd just spent the past twenty-five hundred years languishing in a desert exile, imprisoned there because of Ajax. Ares had punished Sable because Jax had bested him so easily in battle in the hours after the Hot Gates—it was the sort of poor fighting that Ares had no patience for. And so it was Jax's fault that Elblas no longer had his wings, Jax's fault that Sable had been transformed into a centaur. Or at least that was how Sable would tell the tale. While adding, no doubt, that he'd been a graceful demon before they'd met—sensual, beautiful to behold as he'd traversed the heavens with his glittering wings.

"Ajax?" Shay began walking closer, her footsteps echoing off of the cold tunnel walls.

"Stay away!" he squawked, his voice no longer human-sounding.

"You're not gonna hurt me." She kept moving toward him, confident, and he was momentarily stunned. How could she be so sure that he wouldn't turn on her—fully raptor, fully transformed—and devour her as hungrily as the demons still wanted to do?

"I'm not safe for you right now, Shayanna." His wings sprang wider, fuller, even larger than usual. He dropped to his haunches in an effort to keep balanced, allowing the appendages to serve as a shield of protection for her. A barrier between his naked warrior's body and her own, much frailer human one.

At first he thought she was going to give up. He could have sworn retreat was imminent. But then the one thing that couldn't happen, the one thing that he'd been so careful to avoid until then, came like the gentlest whisper of wind.

A small, cautious hand reached out and touched his right wing.

"Don't do that!" he roared, the wings fanning wider and higher and bigger between them. The force of his reaction, and the motion of the wings themselves, was so strong that a wind actually kicked up between them. The flame of his spear flickered, then roared to life once more.

Shay stared in amazement, her hair tangling across her face. Once again she reached out to him, only this time she flinched as her hand made contact with the feathers. She jerked it to her mouth with a sharp cry of pain.

"You burned me. Your wing just actually burned my hand." Staring down at her palm in shock, she watched raised welts appear. Silver welts.

He stood and pivoted slowly, folding his wings down his back, a majestic, awe-inspiring motion. "I warned you not to touch them, to let this be."

"So you burned me on purpose?"

"I had to do something to make you stand back." He gazed at her with a pained expression. "I'd never hurt you on purpose ... except to keep you protected from me."

The words made perfect sense: *Stay away, stay safe. Let me guard you.* That was what he'd been saying with words, sure. But ever since they'd entered the tunnel his words, his eyes, his body—now his wings—were screaming an entirely different message. One that she found impossible to resist. With a shiver she thought of his whispered promises as he'd flown her through the heavens the other night. And now here he stood, a towering hawk of a man who filled the tunnel from top to bottom and side to side, eyes blazing silver-black, golden body bare and gleaming.

Erection thrusting toward her, nearly begging her for what he really wanted.

And, man, oh, man, she just couldn't help herself—she had to steal the smallest glance at his full, glorious body. And at the soft down of ebony feathers that dusted low across his pubic bone. For the briefest moment she even allowed her gaze to travel his hardened length; he was without a doubt the most beautiful creature she'd ever seen. She raised her eyes to meet his once again. His lips parted as he released a soft moaning sound, stepping closer to her.

She held out her hand. "All I want is one thing, hawk." She kept her gaze steady, unblinking. "Just one small thing, and then I'll leave you alone."

He swallowed, his Adam's apple bobbing visibly. "If I can, I'll grant it."

"It really is a small thing," she said, sliding her palms over both her hips. "Probably a fair trade." She allowed one of her hands to trail low across her belly, rubbing slightly.

In reaction, Jax took another step toward her. "Nothing about my body is small, as you can see." His voice was like sandpaper—no, like the sound of his talons on the stone wall—a rasp more than a whisper. "In fact, you're only making me bigger, Shayanna." He laughed in a low, threatening tone, suggestively moving his hand up and down the firm length of his shaft. "Surely you can see what you've done to me. How this body of mine swells for you." He rapped a hard fist against his chest, his wings fanning wider.

She took her time answering and let her gaze drift low again, appreciating every detail of his honed figure, studying the soft path of feathers along his muscled abdomen. "No arguments there, hawk," she said, finally meeting his sharp gaze again. "You're a *really* big boy, and I like that."

"Then tell me," he begged. "What is this one small thing you need?"

"Simple," she said, meeting his strong gaze head-on. "I want to know exactly what you are."

Chapter 14

"My brother is too much of a hothead these days to face a trial like this alone, Commander." Kalias had pulled Leonidas away from the other warriors, who were gathered around the bonfire. He'd been arguing his position for the past several minutes. "I doubt he's even trained in months."

Leonidas planted a boot on the bottom step that led to his castle, nodding thoughtfully. They'd been debating the same issues for days. Now here it was, well past midnight, and they were no closer to solving Ajax's current crisis. It had been a long time, aeons, since he'd lost a man in battle. The last time had been at the Hot Gates. This situation with Ajax put him in mind of the days leading up to that battle. The same heavy dread had settled in his belly, the same sense of disaster on the horizon. It had been more than two days since Ajax had contacted them at all—not by summoning River, not by a phone call, not even a modern text message. Very concerning, indeed.

Leonidas turned to Ajax's eldest brother. In the old days, the bonds of family were far less important than those of the Spartan brotherhood. In some ways that still held— no, *did* hold true. Yet Leonidas could only imagine what it must be like to have your true family with you in the eternal battles they waged. That bond the three Petrakos brothers shared was also a potential chink in the their armor, at least if they weren't careful.

Kalias continued, "Commander, his discipline is shot to hell. It's no secret to you that he's had a sort of . . . breakdown these past months."

Leonidas smiled. "Other men would go insane or worse from the duties we've all borne up under. Ajax's version is to toss every bit of his discipline to the four winds."

Kalias nodded. "Without it, what will happen to him as he battles the Djinn? He needs us all, my lord."

"If we go, we defy the prophecy," Leonidas reminded him again, his mind made up. "Don't forget that he does have millennia of training and discipline to fall back on, both in our former life and this one. He draws on that now in Savannah."

"Maybe this is a test of unity," Kalias suddenly volunteered, thick eyebrows shooting straight to his hairline. "That could be it! The gods want to be sure we still fight as one, so the challenge is to draw our cadre behind Ajax." The hulking warrior's voice held an edge of panic; he was reaching wildly in an effort to protect his little brother.

Leonidas slid a hand onto Kalias's shoulder. "It is a test, no doubt, Kalias. Not one I intend to fail by defying the Oracle and sending support troops."

At this his captain stepped backward, pain in his eyes. "So be it." Then his face brightened suddenly again. "If only *another* one of us could see or hear our Oracle. Could summon her. Perhaps then she would give us more information, more revelation."

Leonidas averted his eyes. So far Ajax was the only one of their corps who knew that he'd recently begun to see and hear the Oracle. "I will ask the gods before I sleep," Leo said simply, inclining his head as he made to enter the castle.

"Ask and you shall see," came the Oracle's saucy, English-accented reply. Leonidas nearly bowled right into the lovely prophetess as he bounded to the top step. She stood, hand pressed behind her against the doorknob to the castle's great wooden door, blocking his entrance.

All at once his body was flush against hers, pushing her into the door. He moved to step back, but she caught his arm, anchoring him close against her.

"I-I ... didn't ... expect ... Oracle, you are ..." He'd never had words when it came to beautiful women—or at least, beautiful women whom he secretly hoped to woo. He'd been the same speechless, stammering idiot when he'd first called on his wife, Gorgo, so many years before. "I'm surprised to find you here," he added at last.

She tilted her heart-shaped face upward, her eyes teasing. "King Leo, speechless? The man with the razor-sharp zingers for every battle occasion, without the perfect words for me?" His shyness had pleased her; he could see it gleaming in her light blue eyes.

He inclined his head, smiling faintly. "Few words as ever, I suppose." He laughed in self-deprecation. "If they'd relied on me to create the dictionary, it would have been a thin volume, indeed."

"Ah, but see!" She wagged an elegant finger at him, and he noticed that her nails were painted glittering blue. "The fewer the tools, the mightier the man who wields them must be. Clever and strong, outwitting his opponent."

Leo smiled slowly. "If you are ever in a battle of words, my lady, I would not want to be on the opposing side. You have ten sentences to every syllable of mine."

He planted a hand on the door, steadying himself—which put that hand within just a few inches of her shoulder.

"Few, but powerful—like you and your brave, bold warriors." She glanced past him, and only then did he remember that the gathered Spartans couldn't see her. He jerked a glance in their direction, and they were all looking skyward, earthward, and beyond. Collective cries of confusion filled the bonfire area in front of the castle.

"But how did he leave?"

"Where did he go?"

Slowly Leonidas turned to face her, smiling despite the gravity of the situation. "You hid me from them."

She reached for his hand. "I wanted you to myself. All to myself. Just for a moment."

Their fingers laced together, and he had the inappropriate urge to lower his mouth to hers and kiss her. Not a holy kiss or a friendly kiss, but the kind that would make her cling to him and beg for much more. For a moment he gave it serious thought, but remembered himself almost instantly; they were at war. The kiss would have to wait.

"Perhaps you *will* kiss me. One day." She smiled back at him, the tip of her pink tongue darting across her lips. "But not today."

He dared to reach a hand to her cheek, the rough calluses of his palm scraping her soft skin. "Perhaps one day, my lady, you'll grant me the honor of your name. I'm not sure I could kiss you and call you Oracle."

Her eyes sparkled mischievously. "You do realize that no one knows my true name—that is, no one with even a hint of mortal blood or essence within them. Not unless they are an Oracle."

He pressed his knuckles against her cheek, feeling its flushed warmth. "I'd like to be the first."

She drew in a sharp breath, leaning back against the door; after a moment he let his hand drop.

"If you're not here for my kisses," he said, "then I can only assume you know how desperately I need your help."

" 'Desperately need'?" she repeated seductively, gazing up into his eyes. "Oh, dear Leo, let's talk like that on a better day."

He leaned closer to her, bending his head to her ear. "You have my word." Reaching around her, he opened the large castle door. "For now, let's talk about Elblas and how Jax can possibly defeat him."

Leonidas knelt at the Oracle's feet—not that he needed to beg, but some part of his soul hoped that

showing enough deference to the gods themselves—
and to their messenger—might grant him favor. After
all, they had deemed him worthy to converse with her
lately.

*Better not wind up cursed because what I mostly want
is to hold her in my arms,* he thought darkly, but shoved
the idea aside.

He took her right hand, squeezing it in supplication.
"My lady, might the gods allow you to speak their words
to me in Ajax's stead? So that I could know whether or
not to send support to him in Savannah?"

She stared down at their joined hands, and then gently
gave his a warm squeeze in return. "I want to help you,
Leo. All of you. But we both know what the prophecy
said—that Jax must endure this trial alone."

Leonidas bowed his head. "I know. I know."

Another squeeze of her small, dainty hand, and she
added, "But in this instance, Ajax has gotten himself
into a right mess. Of course, then again, that's hardly
a big change." Her black eyebrows quirked into a concerned frown.

"I am worried," he confessed, averting his eyes. "His
brothers are worried also."

Her tone grew even more serious. "This is the test of
his life, my lord. You're right to be concerned. And we
do need more guidance," she said intensely. "Not from
the gods, but from the Highest God—the One who has
sent Jax on this mission."

Leonidas glanced up, surprised. "It wasn't Ares who
spoke to him through you? Nor Apollo or Zeus?"

Her eerily light blue eyes narrowed significantly. "The
Highest, Unnameable God. I think that maybe, just possibly, if I speak the words to you, you'll be able to hear
my prophecy this time."

She slid onto the floor beside him, and the sleek leg-
gings that she wore brushed against his bare right thigh.
He was in battle gear, which meant that while kneeling his upper legs were exposed. For a moment they
both froze, staring down at the place where their bodies

touched. They were transfixed like foes, as if each were waiting for the other to charge ahead—to move either closer or farther apart. But neither even breathed for a full moment.

Their gazes locked, and he knew that the small woman could see the heat flaring in his own eyes. How long had it been since any woman had brushed so intimately close to his war-battered body? Thousands of years—time that he'd never questioned—but the mysterious Oracle captivated his heart in ways that he'd not thought possible. His heart, in matters of romance and desire, had felt dead inside for centuries. He shifted his hips uncomfortably, not daring to glance downward lest she notice how his longing had speared straight to his groin.

He noticed the slow ticking sound of his clock on the mantel, the way it punctuated their frozen stance. *Damn it, take action,* one part of him demanded. But this was their Oracle, blast it all. One of Apollo's own. If he should kiss her, the god himself might strike them both dead. Not to mention Ares . . .

"I want you," he said, simple and direct, the only way he knew to speak of such things with any woman. "I've wanted you from the very first, when I saw you on the moors, my lady."

She dropped her head instantly, but her short hair couldn't conceal the rush of color that touched her cheeks. Her hands twisted anxiously in the hem of her T-shirt, but she said nothing.

"I've made you uncomfortable?" With his scarred right hand he cupped her chin, forcing her to glance up at him. When she met his gaze, her eyes were glimmering with raw passion, an undisguised need that he'd never seen in the eyes of *any* woman before. It was real, that look; it was honest and unconcealed. She closed her eyes slowly, knowing that he'd read her heart and mind . . . and body.

Abruptly, she scooted sideways. "Whoops." She clamped a hand over her mouth, eyes big and wide and dramatic. "Sorry, dear Leonidas. So sorry!"

He nodded, saying nothing, and she made an awkward little fanning motion, as if to overcome embarrassment. But despite all her theatrics, the daring gleam in those pale eyes of hers seemed to be saying something else entirely; as if perhaps she'd slid halfway atop his lap on purpose.

She began to inch a bit farther out of his reach, but he clamped her arm within his grasp. "Don't do that," he said firmly.

She glanced upward in surprise, almost alarmed.

"I want you close to me," he explained in a voice much gruffer than he'd ever used with her before.

She stared back at him, blinking speechlessly. "Leo, we *have* to be close for what we're going to do next...."

Gods, woman, he wanted to thunder, *let me take you here. There will be divine inspiration in the taking, for both of us.* But in his heart he knew there was no place for such passion—not now, not today, with Ajax's life at stake.

He swallowed hard, bowing his head. "Yes, Oracle." He cleared his mind completely, let the distraction of the woman before him fall away from his thoughts. There was only the moment, like every other battle in his life—just the words that he needed to hear. His thoughts stilled at last, and as if reading his mind, the Oracle gave a resolute sound of confirmation.

She lifted up onto her knees and began a little edging motion toward him, a funny duckwalk. "I'm going to kneel in front of you while I prophesy," she explained with each bit of ground she covered. "We're going to face each other."

"Is that how it's done?" He'd always imagined smoke and incense, trances and fire. And snakes, plenty of them.

She planted her hands on both his shoulders, steadying herself once they were barely an inch apart. They would have been a mirror image except that he was so much larger than she.

"It's different every time... well, sometimes. I've never spoken the words in this position before, but it's what I'm hearing I should do." She gave a little shrug. "So we kneel together."

He shifted slightly on his knees, the old war injury from Thermopylae aching the longer he held the prone position. He'd never changed out of his uniform after training earlier; it now felt awkward and heavy as he faced off with the petite woman before him. As he adjusted position, the brass of his breastplate clanked into the side table; the leather bindings creaked around his chest. The Spartans called him *old man*, a joking term of endearment. He'd been only thirty-five at the Hot Gates, and was frozen throughout eternity at that age. Still, he felt every moment of his endless and immortal years on some days.

He glanced down, tugging his breastplate into position, and when he looked back up, the Oracle had leaned forward and was gently unfastening its bindings. "Here, you should be more comfortable," she said matter-of-factly. In a flurry of dexterous movements, she had him out of the armor—and breathlessly imagining being fully undressed by those same graceful, fast fingers for a very different purpose.

She froze, one hand still against his back. Gathering a handful of his tunic, she avoided his gaze. For a glorious moment he honestly thought she would tug it over his head. He had no words; the only sound between them was that of his *very* heavy breathing. And perhaps his half-muttered prayer, his hope that he would one day take her in his arms. She shivered as if she heard his thoughts, and brushed a hand through her wildly blue-streaked hair. Then slowly—bit by bit—she released his tunic.

He racked his brain for anything—a joke, a pithy remark, the right comeback—that would break the sudden awkwardness between them. "I like the blue," he finally told her, reaching out to stroke one of the vivid locks.

Her gaze flew to his, a beaming smile forming on her face. "Really? I'd noticed that you liked this color . . .

the bowl in your kitchen, the comforter on your bed . . ."
She glanced around, gesturing at various other items
that he owned in a similar shade, and then clamped her
mouth shut once again. Blue eyes went wide; pink col-
ored her cheeks.

Leonidas fixed her with a slow, knowing smile. "The
comforter in my room? Interesting, dear Oracle, for
you've never entered my chamber. At least, not with
my permission or knowledge. Nor do I recall you in my
kitchen, for that matter." He leaned close to her, pressing his lips against her ear. "But I daresay it's the secret
visits to my bedroom that seem most dangerous and
damning of all."

"I didn't spy!"

"At night, I suppose? When I slept, you came then?"
He nuzzled her, letting his beard scrape her cheek. "Secret visits . . . oh, that is tantalizing indeed. But let us
keep those hidden times our *own* special secret. Perhaps
one day you will come again and make your presence
known to me."

"I never looked at you while you were naked; I promise." She flung both arms about his neck, half climbing
atop him as she blurted apologies. "I would never com-
promise you or violate you. I revere you too much, dear
king. I wouldn't, didn't, couldn't—"

He silenced her anxious babbling the best way a truly
quiet man could think of—he covered her mouth with
his and delivered the very best kiss in his arsenal. A kiss
worthy of an ancient Oracle, worthy of the goddesses
themselves. She twined her arms about his neck, her thin
limbs stretched long to encompass his barrel-chested
body. Her chest pushed hard into his, almost as if she'd
lost her balance in her giddiness at being kissed. He
could feel the firm warmth of her breasts, delicate like
the rest of her, but round and pert.

Her hands wound all through his hair, brushing at his
thick curls, fingertips stroking down along his beard. He
wrapped his own arms about her back, tucking her even

closer against his immense chest. It was like a bull taking a wee fairy to its breast.

With a gasp she broke the kiss, arms still tangled about his neck. "Oh, Leo!" She was radiant, pale blue eyes sparkling; he'd seen many beautiful women in his days, including his share of happy, just-kissed ones, too. But he'd never imagined—not with all the many times that he'd hoped to kiss this little Oracle—that he could make her so luminous and happy.

"The thing is, you see," she explained, tugging her Union Jack T-shirt back down about her hips, "for all those years I could see you ... when you couldn't see me. I'd get lonely sometimes when Jax wasn't around."

He couldn't believe what she was telling him. "You came to me?" he asked incredulously. "Before I first saw you out on the moors a few months ago?"

She smiled sheepishly. "I'd been trying to get your attention for a long time. A *very* long time."

He ran a fingertip down the end of her nose, securing her atop his lap with his other arm. "You have it now—but I still don't have your name."

"In Oracle land, that's third or fourth base," she said lightly. "And I'm not that fast. In fact, I should mention that I've never gone that far ... landed a homer or even gotten a base hit. I'm not that kind of girl."

"Are you saying that you've never given anyone your name?" She'd lost him with her twisting metaphors. He laughed to himself, figuring this must be how Ajax often felt after hearing her complex prophecies.

She ignored him completely and rubbed her hands together. "We must get busy now. Chop-chop. Time to work." Sliding off his lap, she held out her hands, palms flat toward him, and he mirrored the gesture, pressing their flesh together. An electric jolt blasted through him, and he found himself focusing not on her eyes, but on the full, swollen shape of her lips.

"Leo, Leo." She stared at him through lowered lashes, calling his attention back to the task. "Time and place, my lord. Time and place ..."

"...for every battle," he completed with a hearty grin—and laced his fingers together with hers. He thought she'd argue; instead she let her eyes drift shut and squeezed his hands in return.

"Now, let's see what we hear from the Highest One. I am feeling very inspired, I must say. Like I could ride on the winds. Perhaps that will help us find favor today."

Every prophecy was unique; she likened hearing the words to deciphering a puzzle, one that was different every time. Many times she got pictures, flashes of images that she had to name in quick succession, stringing them together like a pearl necklace. On other days it was literally a voice in her ear, and she had to blurt out the words as quickly as she could.

And other times, the ones she liked the least, she literally transported into a dream state, somewhere else entirely. Those always left her frightened, with the sense that she might not ever make it back from the spirit realm.

Leonidas's thick, calloused palms felt divine against her own. Even the barest touch of his skin was more than she'd hoped for in the past thousand years. The last thing she wanted was to be carried away from him, even to retrieve the words he and Ajax so desperately needed. But as fate would have it, that solid, human feeling of his hands began to dissolve, to fade away.

She closed her eyes, accepting. It was what they had in common, she and Leonidas: They would always be obedient in their divine callings—even to the death. Even if it meant an eternity of being alone.

The first thing she saw was a long, torchlit tunnel. She held her hands in front of her, but Leonidas was gone; she was feeling her way through the half-dark. It was dank and smelled like mildew. Then, at the far end, she glimpsed Jax in full warrior form, and he appeared truly terrifying. It had been hundreds of years since she'd seen him lit from the inside out by his power that way.

A mortal, smallish—but bigger than her. Something happening between them ...

She heard the name Shayanna. Yes, it was Shay. ...

They came together, kissing, all tangled in each other just as she and Leo had been moments before.

What am I to see here, Highest One? Show me, your servant, that I may help them.

A pair of ancient and delicate scrolls appeared in her hands. She knelt on the tunnel floor, ignoring Ajax and Shay—not even clearly able to see them—and unrolled one of the prophetic parchments. In long, flowing ancient Greek, the first prophecy continued the one she'd recently given Jax. It had the words she'd spoken about the death's crown, but then went past what she'd heard spoken before.

"Leave it," a voice said, and she nodded, searching the tunnel. "Over there by the wall, away from the fire, but where they will see it."

She bounded across the dark distance, afraid that the trance would end before she could complete the task. Dropping to her haunches, she positioned it against the wall in just the way she'd been instructed.

Now what?

"Take a few strands of your blue hair and wrap it about the scroll as a sign that the words are from you." As always the voice was rich and warm, full of authority and strength.

Again she nodded her willingness, and with a wince plucked a few of her brightly dyed strands, winding them about the prophecy.

She still held the other scroll in her hand and, gazing down at it, wondered what to do. The voice anticipated her question.

"That one is for the others. Take it back to Leonidas."

Anything more, Nameless One? There was almost always more, and He seemed to be making quick work of her today.

"Obedience is everything. Go now."

With a stab of shame and fear, she fell face-first. *Are*

you mad about the kiss? she blurted, unable to help herself. *I meant no disrespect, my Highest One. None whatsoever! It's just that Leonidas . . . Leo is . . . special. So special.*

She felt a rush of warmth fill her chest, such love that her eyes prickled with tears. "Little daughter, your faithful heart will be rewarded. But not without a hard test."

Oh, she prayed, pressing her eyes shut in relief. *Oh, okay. Okay. Just so you're not mad.*

Again the soothing touch of goodness filled her heart, a place that had felt empty and lonely for such a long time. Her tears began to fall in earnest now; she couldn't hold them back as the sense of clarity and warmth and perfect love rose up in her chest.

"Leonidas's kiss," He said at last, "was pure. It's what gave you the strength to make this long journey. Now go forth and take the scroll back to the warriors."

Without even a second to transition, she came sputtering out of her trance and found herself cradled within Leonidas's arms. She'd apparently collapsed against him, and he held her close, crooning an ancient melody in her ear. She flailed as she jerked out of the dream state and rolled out of his arms onto the floor. Gasping, she sprawled flat on her back, staring at his wood-beamed ceiling, at the ancient weaponry and armor that decorated his great hall.

"Are you all right?" Leonidas asked, leaning over her. His dark face, even when he was troubled as he was now, always comforted her. "You're shaking all over."

"I'm more than fine." She reached to wipe away the tears that still brimmed in her eyes. She smiled up at him and presented the rolled parchment with a flourish. "Heavenly FedEx, my king. No signature required."

Then she collapsed back against the floor, hoping she could rest there a very long time.

Chapter 15

Shay stood, waiting. Watching him expectantly. Her question should have been an easy one: What and who was he, precisely? He'd already offered enough hints. Revealing the full truth was only one more step beyond. Yet the less she understood the odds in this battle—what they really meant to her and for him, for their future, too—the better.

"It's only fair that you tell me," she offered, her voice surprisingly gentle and patient.

"If I do that ... if I confess it all ..." Ajax raised his heavy arms out to his sides, gesturing to his full warrior's body. "The demons might use that knowledge against you. Might try to get to *me* by using you. The less you know, Shay, the better."

"My brothers have tried that maneuver on me my whole life, the protection routine. My mother, too, plus my dad, when he was still alive. You've brought me into this battle, so I need answers."

"I saved you twice," he reminded her, letting his arms fall back to his sides. "I never wanted you in this fight."

"You of all people realize that ignorance has almost gotten me killed twice." She held her hands out in frustration, groaning. "If you were just gonna shelter me, then why in the world did you tell my brothers that it's time to train me?"

"So you wouldn't be unprotected," he admitted roughly.

"Because you do have a mighty calling, a role to fill as a huntress—just not in my current battle with Elblas."

"But I was already part of it somehow, wasn't I?" That thought had been nagging at her for the past minutes, a little kernel of an idea that had begun to bloom into full life the longer he refused to tell her the truth of what he was. *Who* he was.

He said nothing at all.

"Then who is Elblas to you?" she persisted. "That should be safe territory. Why does he despise you so much—and what was he talking about the other night in Bonaventure, what he said about your wife?"

He growled, baring his teeth. "I don't talk about Narkissa."

"Sable obviously does," she snapped. "At least, if she's the woman Sable was referring to."

"You want to know about my *wife*?" Ajax hurled the words at her like an accusation, glaring. "You're daring to ask about her? Oh, sweet mortal, you don't know how dangerous that ground is."

She wasn't going to let his obvious pain or his theatrics daunt her. She kept her voice low and quiet. "Narkissa? That was her name?"

He didn't answer, not the way she thought he would; his reply defied usual human speech. Almost as if in slow motion, he tossed his head back and released a piercing, shrill cry—an eerie sound that trespassed somewhere in those dark borderlands between beast and man.

Ajax pounded a fist against his breast, releasing a second agonized screech—one that was wrought with such loneliness and heartbreak, it instantly caused tears to fill Shay's eyes. She'd spent a lifetime on land surrounded by all sorts of wild creatures ... not to mention living with her two warrior brothers. But Ajax's wounded cry had to be the most tortured sound she'd ever heard—from *any* being, human or animal.

Slowly Ajax bowed his head. He stood before her, ebony wings barely visible along his back, blazing torch clasped in one hand. Dark and light, evil and goodness, all the contradictions formed the man standing before her—a living Michelangelo sculpture.

He wants you to walk away; he's trying to drive *you away.*

Shay hugged herself, struggling to chase the chill from her body. "He must've really hurt you," she said. "Elblas, I mean."

Ajax's wings beat slightly at the air, an agitated motion that she'd already realized was a nervous twitch of his. After a moment he said, "I gave as good as I got. There was retribution."

She kicked at a loose stone, wanting to seem casual. As if she could, as if anything about their interchange were mundane. "Did he go after her or something? Are you still married, Ajax?"

Blazing-bright eyes flashed upward, locking with hers. "I am bound to no one."

Her brothers always said she never knew when to let something go, and this was probably going to be one of those times when she'd kick herself for not keeping her mouth shut. "Bound to no one . . . but you *did* have a wife? Narkissa."

Before she could blink he was upon her, those wings high and threatening, his hands twisting cruelly. He grabbed her by the upper arms, sharp talons biting into her exposed flesh. With a slight shake of her shoulders, he glowered down at her. "Isn't it enough that I already lost one good woman? And my sons? Don't you see why I don't want *you* to know the truth of me?"

She winced in pain at the force of his hold, at the light scratches his talons caused on her arms, but she didn't budge or back down. She tilted her chin upward, meeting his otherworldly glare.

"The demons killed your family?" she persisted, her face flushing hot just from such proximity to his alien body. "But why was that because of you?"

His face, bathed in lightning, morphed like the rest of him. His nose lengthened, his eyes became beadier, and, although still human overall, he transformed into something fiercer than he'd been with her so far. The raptor had fully emerged.

His now deep-set eyes swirled with glowing power. "They weren't killed," he said, the words a rasping noise along his transformed vocal cords. "They were taken ... from me. Stolen ... Elblas ripped them away."

Extending his talons, he made a sweeping motion, tearing at the air between them. "Tore me out of their hearts."

"That can't be true," she said, horrified. "I don't understand."

The talons flexed against her arm, their texture ridged and rough. Jax stared down at his transformed hands, seemingly surprised to see that they shook as hard as she did. Slowly he released his hold on her, dropping his head.

"Tell me, Ajax, please," she urged, reaching out to touch one of his twisted talons. She kept her touch as gentle as possible, terrified that he might bolt away if she didn't.

He jerked at the physical contact and turned his radiant silver eyes on her. "Elblas stole their memories— every memory they had of me. After our deaths, and days of fighting, I went to them, but it was too late."

She blinked hard. "You're dead?"

He screeched at her, his vocal cords tightening as his hawk form emerged. "I told you it wasn't for mortals to know!" The wings spread high over his shoulders, bearing down on both of them, and he seized her with his talons once again.

She winced as he tightened his hold. It took every bit of her willpower, but she tried to block out the surging image of his wings and the way they seemed to beat out his painful emotions. "You can't be dead ..., you're holding me right now. You're physical and real!"

He continued, his hoarse voice an eerie monotone, eyes even beadier as he spoke. "He reached Narkissa before I could. She didn't recognize me, and when she saw me in my true form it terrified her; it terrified my sons. I was no longer her husband, and no longer their father, just a horrific demon come to instill fear in their hearts. I knew eventually I would lose them to their mortality, someday, but I never even got to say good-bye. . . ." He stared down at her with his mystical eyes; his talons still scraped her arms.

Lowering her voice, she planted both palms against his fiery chest. "How could Narkissa forget you, Ajax? *You?*"

Jax slowly released her, taking several steps back. His emotional outburst had filled his entire form with that odd, liquid power of his. Silver shimmers shone off his wings, outlining every line and detail of the feathers. They'd assumed a jeweled appearance, gleaming and glittering like icicles in sunlight.

He was exquisite.

The pulse and flow within him glowed like priceless diamonds. Or like a rare metal, only it flowed through him—visible in the veins at his neck, pulsing with every beat of his heart, and visible along his forearms, then particularly in his hands. He skimmed scalding palms over her shoulders, her arms. He simply loomed above her, towering to at least six-foot-six or -seven. Maybe even more.

"And even if she did lose her memories, how could she ever fear you? How could she help but fall in love with you all over again?" she whispered softly. She felt his heavy pain in the very center of her soul; it tore at her the way his talons could, shredding her heart into pieces.

In a single motion he covered her mouth with his, tilting her head back. He lowered her slowly in a graceful arch, sweeping her within his hold. His warm tongue thrust into her mouth, demanding all of her, letting her know that he'd never accept less than completion. Trembling at first, she barely held to him. But as he twined his tongue deeper with hers, plumbing every bit of her warmth and wetness—and as she felt brazen talons scrape between her shoulder blades, she surrendered.

She slid her hands about his neck, combing fingers through his tangled, silken hair. It was shockingly soft, and she thought again of the light down that covered his groin. Bringing her fingertips between their two bodies, she made contact with his abdomen, stroking fingertips along the ridges of those taut muscles. They were inseparably close, but she had to feel all of him; the curiosity and desire was driving her to the brink.

Wedging her hand low between their bodies, she felt the first brush of hawk's down, then traced the line all the way to his groin, where it thickened somewhat, spread wider, just as his pubic hair would have done. The feathers curled slightly beneath her fingertips, shockingly pliable, so soft—impossibly soft, just like the long black mane atop his head. For a moment she thought of how much more hawklike he'd become in the past moments—and wondered if he ever changed completely.

Those damned paintings of Leda and Zeus with his wings spreading her legs wide paraded through her mind, scalding her body, scorching her fantasies of being held in his arms.

She played her fingers through the tickling softness between his legs, her fingertips trembling at how unexpected that hawkish detail was—even though she'd already seen it with her own eyes earlier.

"You know, your body is just amazing, every bit of it so glorious, epic. You're like something out of my dreams. Or my . . ." She let the words trail away; it couldn't be true.

"I dreamed of *you*," he whispered in her ear, carefully combing his talons through her hair. "You've always been in my dreams."

She pressed her cheek against his bare chest. "I drew you the other night. After we met, but you weren't frightening in the sketch, not like it felt that first night."

"Each of us has been waiting for the other, yes?" His Greek accent had grown thicker, and she knew they were approaching something key to the very core of this warrior.

She closed her eyes, some unremembered dream tugging her below the moment's surface, almost taking hold of her. Yes, she had dreamed of this man, just as he had of her. Many times, she was sure of it. She'd just never remembered it after waking.

"I dreamed of you, too," she said, drawing in his scent. The freshest, most natural aroma bathed his body, washed over him and made her feel one with the winds, as one as he was when he flew. "I wonder why I never remembered until now?"

"It doesn't matter, now that we've found each other."

His monumental arms wrapped about her, but he kept his talons carefully away; those muscular arms felt like granite, his body a well-honed weapon. For a moment she imagined how he used that body to destroy demons and evil creatures in the night, and the thought made her shiver with lust. His power and pure strength were downright erotic, the way they made her feel intoxicatingly hot.

She pressed her mouth against his right nipple, suckling it until he moaned a rasping sound of pleasure. *Oh, yes*, she wanted to purr back at him. *I want to cause all your sexy sounds.* Licking and tasting that nipple, she used her hand to arouse him even more. She smoothed her fingers across the light feathers between his legs, stroking his stretched cock at the same time. It was her turn to moan loudly in desire and need; the way he affected her was almost too much, and she began shaking as she closed her hand about his erection, stroking it gently.

Yet her fingertips were drawn back to the curling feathers that dusted his groin; over and over again she had to caress them, was compelled to feel that part of him that was transformed.

With a growl of deep pleasure, he shifted his hips to give her better access, spreading his thighs slightly. "You love the feel of me, don't you, sweetness?"

She swallowed, not sure how to answer, driven to touch him over and over again.

"This down . . ." She swirled her fingers through it, loving the way it tickled and curled over her fingertips.

"It's like the last thing I'd imagine about you, these soft feathers here."

He flashed a gorgeous, lopsided smile at her, clearly pleased with himself. That sexy dimple popped into view, too. "Now that I know how you like them, I'll keep it in mind."

"What does that mean?"

"The down feathers are for insulation. When I'm particularly cold, my chest is sometimes covered as well."

"Oh, wow." She felt her legs start to tremble. *Don't swoon. Don't swoon.*

He bent low and nipped her ear with his teeth. "Might come in handy on those chilly nights, when your human body needs warming. The brush of my wings, the thrilling softness of my chest feathers. I can see you wrapped within me, love. Feather and mortal skin blending as one. Yes, I see it. First one of my wings between your parted legs, then the other, caressing you to the realm of pure ecstasy."

"When I touched your soft feathers, they didn't burn me. So maybe I really can touch your wings." She'd already begun reaching over his shoulder, hungry to make the intimate contact.

He captured her chin, forcing her to look up into his eyes. "The only reason my wings burned you before was because I didn't *want* you to touch me."

"Great. You *meant* to burn me. Wonderful." She jerked her head sideways, forcing him to release her, but he wouldn't have it.

With both hands he grasped her face, eyeing her hard. "I meant to keep you away," he said softly. "That was then. I don't want you to stay away, not anymore."

She shook her head, pressing her eyes shut. "It's all so absurd. None of this can be happening. Clearly I watched *Flash Gordon* and those Hawk Men too many times growing up. Someone must've gotten me stoned at the funeral the other day. That's the only possible explanation for all of this. Well, of course, it doesn't explain right now. . . ."

He jerked slightly. "Funeral?" His voice suddenly seemed very intense.

"My mama died. We buried her two days ago. At Bonaventure. That's why I was there the other night. I just had to be there, with her somehow. Well, more than that—I saw demons in the cemetery during the funeral while I was singing." Still Ajax studied her, his eyes narrowed. She frowned back. "I don't get why you . . . Why are you *looking* at me like that?"

His eyes drifted shut. "You should've told me, Shay. That you were grieving."

"Yeah, we've had so much time for chitchat. Besides, I didn't see how it was all that significant"—she slapped his chest, voice rising—"in comparison to *a demon brawl!*"

"They feed off that pain, Shay. That's what Sable and his crew are like, how depraved. They're probably still half drunk off what they siphoned from you in the cemetery. And again out on the street tonight. Or much more likely, they're rabid and hungry for more of your suffering. Right now they're already searching out another taste of you, wanting to drink you dry. A huntress in emotional pain like that, Shay? It's a feast to them. That's how they were able to overtake you at the cemetery. You're weakened and vulnerable to them because of your loss."

She blinked up at him, trying to understand. "Isn't it bad enough that I lost my mama?" she finally whimpered, feeling tears begin to streak down her face. All day she'd held it together. All the past few days, really, ever since her mama's death.

He drew her into his arms again; she could feel the thunderous beat of his heart. The warm velvet of his chest became damp from her tears. "I understand, Shayanna," he told her in a soft voice. "I do. It's how Sable attacked me . . . all those years ago. How he used my own family against me."

She let her eyes drift shut. "Because you were grieving?"

"Because losing them was the only thing I still feared

in the universe." Jax released her and, in a blink, transformed his appearance to a more appropriate one.

"I had no control yet." He paced the length of the tunnel, wingless and dressed in his standard military attire, all black. "When I realized what had happened, that someone or something had manipulated my family's minds, my grief overcame me and my true form emerged. My wings were so mammoth, alive, like they sometimes still are now. But back then they were new to me, a heavy ship on my back, mast and sail swinging wildly. I couldn't retract them or be graceful, couldn't bow them to my will. . . ." Ajax hesitated, the memories assailing him. "I can still smell the soup cooking on the fire, hear the clay pots I upturned, the crash of them on the tile floor."

He winced, afraid to continue, but somehow he needed to tell Shay all of it.

"Imagine a feral hawk or eagle, suddenly in a very small house, wings untamed and flapping," he confessed heavily. "The raucous sounds, the chaos. That feral raptor was me, with wings that gleamed like midnight and were the length of our kitchen table. Of course I was a demon to her. Narkissa—kept screaming and praying and flailing her arms. My twin sons, they were so small, so frightened. I can hear their cries as though it were hours ago, not centuries. . . ."

"When, Ajax? When did this happen?" Shay's soft question called him back to the present, to the tunnel where they stood deep below Savannah. She had no context for any of what he shared; how could he expect that she would, someone so innocent?

Yet he'd begun his tale, and she needed to know.

"I was something right out of our people's worst stories, their most sordid visions of what Hades might bring."

"I don't believe that could ever be true of you."

"Do I look like a normal man to you? The sort you might encounter out on River Street? No, sweetness, I am not any sort of man you've ever encountered, gods help you."

She backed against the wall, eyes widening. "The breast-plate," she said softly. "And your weapons, the spear . . ."

"Yes." He smiled slowly, aching to touch her. Once she knew everything, what would be left to stop him?

Shay wrapped her arms about herself, shivering; he should have felt guilty for torturing her this way. For telling her the sordid details in such a cruel manner. But if he slapped her with the truth of his monstrous nature, the burden of his duties, perhaps she could still save herself.

Shaking so hard that her voice quivered, she never even opened her eyes. "So when you died, you became an angel? Is that what happened?"

Something broke inside of him right then, something he'd not even realized he'd been holding inside for such a long, long time. His eyes burned and his throat tightened. "Shayanna." By all rights she should be fleeing him now, but there she stood, tears streaming down her lovely face. "Shay," he said hoarsely, "look at me. You are not Narkissa and you will not run; I know this, and so I'm trusting you."

She bobbed her head, tears rolling down both cheeks. "I won't turn on you, I promise."

"No . . . you won't, little mortal. I'm certain you won't." He reached a hand and stroked the tears away, loving her already. As he'd always been told he would. Adoring her for her acceptance of every feather and wing along his back, for the vow he'd made with Ares, even though she didn't know all its gruesome aspects yet. "Then I shall tell you who and what I am."

Her eyes flew open, her lips parted, and she breathed, "I need you. I need to know."

In a rushing wind of transformation his warrior's chest filled out and his wings unfurled. His gleaming shield appeared in his left hand, a blazing sword in his right.

With two backward steps from her, he urged his form to change completely, growing, bulking from head to toe. When the alteration was fully complete, he presented himself to her proudly.

He knelt before her and offered himself to her as he would his very queen. "I am Ajax Petrakos, adopted son of Ares, immortal protector of humankind. A fallen warrior reborn in the flowing fire of Styx." He paused, breathing heavily as he stared at her across the small distance that separated them. Her own eyes were wide, but not shocked, as he'd expected. "But all you have to know is one thing, Shay Angel," he said, panting.

He thrust his shield high and raised his sword toward the ceiling. "I, Ajax Petrakos, am a Spartan!"

Chapter 16

" Maybe we should search for him," Ari argued, settling on the castle's bottom step. "He's been gone a good fifteen minutes, no warning whatsoever before his departure. This isn't like the Old Man."

Kalias scrubbed a hand over his short-cropped hair. "You know how Leonidas gets. When he needs to think things over, he has a way of retreating inside himself."

"But not of vanishing well after midnight," River disagreed, chewing on his lip. "I'm with Ari. We send a search party."

Nikos gave River a vaguely petulant look. "Search *where*, genius? Wait, I know! Why don't you transform into a metal detector and go looking for the commander's shield?"

Ari shoved Nikos in the shoulder, sending him stumbling toward the dying bonfire. "What?" Nikos cried, trying to look innocent. "I'm just saying."

River turned back to the group, ignoring the guy; Nikos was always on his ass for some shit or another.

"I say we break into two groups," Ari continued, his gaze sweeping the gathered men. "Half of us take to the sky; the others walk the moors."

Straton gave a thoughtful nod. "Agreed," he said in his usual monosyllabic way of speaking. The man was truly Spartan in his laconic choices of words. "The moors."

"Not in search of me, I hope." Every head jerked toward the castle doorway, where Leonidas had suddenly emerged. With a soft movement he closed the heavy door behind him; the hinges didn't even creak at his touch.

He turned to the men gathered below him. River decided that he appeared a little flushed. And strangely excited. Actually happy. He sat up straighter on his step, aware that something extraordinary must be happening for Leonidas to appear so . . . flustered and animated.

Every pair of Spartan eyes riveted on their commander, a murmur of surprise rolling through their gathered core of six. River wondered if the others noticed how changed their king seemed, how different from the way he'd been before he'd vanished from their midst.

"I was blessed by the gods." Leonidas held out a rolled parchment. "I made contact with our Oracle—and was given this."

They erupted like a volcano, voices rising and mingling as they barraged Leo with questions; he held up a silencing hand, turning back toward the door. River got the distinct impression that Leo was conversing with someone, *hearing* someone. Their king nodded, whispered low, then turned back to face the warriors gathered on the lower steps.

"Our Oracle has given one scroll to us, the other to Ajax," he explained, meeting each of their eyes meaningfully by the firelight. "But the words all reiterate what we knew before. Ajax is to fight alone—at least for now."

Then Leonidas turned his gaze on River. "Except for you," he explained, his gaze never wavering. "River, you will await a portal, then join Ajax and Shay Angel in Savannah. If you can conjure a gateway on your own, then do so swiftly. These are the words from our divine lady."

"I've never been able to do that, my lord," River admitted, feeling the burn of the gathered men's gazes. "Not alone. The portal has to be opened by Ajax himself."

Off to his side he thought he heard Nikos laugh derisively under his breath, just loud enough that River alone could hear. River lifted his head higher. "But I'm willing to attempt it, sir."

"The Oracle thinks this situation is unique, that it might work this time. She has spoken; let us show our gratitude."

They all bowed their heads, some planting helmets over chests, others their fists. After a moment Leonidas told them, "She's gone now, our Oracle."

River studied the king closely; he seemed a little . . . disappointed by their guide's departure. Apparently her support had meant a great deal to the king, he decided, as Leonidas urged them inside and into the great room, where they would inspect the parchment.

As they filed into the castle, River last in line, Leonidas stopped him. "This battle of Ajax's . . ." He hesitated, seemed to think a long moment. "Be the strongest you've ever been. He's going to need you."

River nodded. "Thank you for letting me back him up, sir. For believing me about the seriousness of the situation."

His king smiled, squeezing his forearm. "I always trust you, River, with all our lives. You are a worthy, honorable man. And now I'm trusting you to form that portal and get to Savannah. Not to wait, but to take action now. Unless, of course, Ajax summons you first."

A tornado is coming, Shay thought vaguely. But down in this tunnel? The freight-train sound had come from nowhere, and now roared from one end of the shaft to the other. Her first thought was that it was a cosmic reaction to Ajax's cosmic-size confession.

Yet he didn't seem to expect it at all, and leaped out of his kneeling posture and right to his feet. Wind knocked her face-first against the ground, and, just like the rushing water had earlier, the tornado began rolling her down the tunnel. Blowing her like a discarded feather, tossing her like a dust mote.

Jax grabbed hold of her arm, pulling her to her feet. Shouting over the tumult, he said, "Get behind me,

Shay!" He shoved her against the wall, spreading his wings in front of her. "Whatever happens, whoever comes down in here, don't move unless I say so!"

She grasped at his back, but only came up with a handful of feathers. "Is that Elblas?"

He didn't answer, but performed an unusual folding maneuver with his wings that literally caught her between both feathery appendages. Suddenly she found her cheeks being brushed by otherworldly magic, by sheer sensation, as every prickle from every single feather elicited a cascade of raw physical reaction inside her body.

In any other situation it would have been the height of eroticism, the most awakening moment of her life: if she weren't so flipping terrified, that was.

· "Stay behind me," he hissed. "Hide within my wings. I will guard your body with my own." Then, in an unearthly voice he shouted, "River! *River!*"

What river did he even mean? She didn't have time to think about it.

She heard snarling and vicious barking sounds gaining on them. It was obvious that a band of demons was circling close. Not just that, though. Even with her eyes pressed closed she could see bright flashes all around.

"Take her with you—away from here, to safety." That was Ajax's voice, but who was he talking to? Something made her look down, a gut instinct, for lack of a better term. Beside her feet, nearly getting trampled by Jax's heavy dance steps, she saw a rolled-up parchment. It hadn't been there moments before; she would have noticed it. They both would have!

She reached for it, doing a limbo motion that kept her hidden within Jax's wings but allowed her to take hold of the scroll. It was tied neatly with what looked like blue threads.

"Jax, I found something," she shouted over the tumult.

"Later, Shay!" he screamed back, and a sudden gust knocked her back against the wall. "Tell me later. You're going with River."

River. Wait! Hadn't that been the name of the flying sword, the strange thing that had grown wings and left them—after Jax had stabbed her with it in the cemetery?

"Who's River?" She pressed her face against his wings, never wanting to leave their safety. The rabid sounds of demons on the hunt swelled higher and louder within the tunnel. "*Where's* River?" she amended quickly, leaning into Ajax for one final moment of safe harbor.

Her heart hammered a frantic rhythm. If only she could see Jax, could look into his eyes. If only this crazy whirlwind around them weren't making it impossible to do anything except hide behind her protector.

The wings parted without warning, exposing Shay to the violent, whipping torrent that had filled the tunnel. Right in front of them, she glimpsed a rolling silver opening forming, a large ball of energy and power. In front of it, a long-haired warrior stood, reaching toward her.

"River's taking you to safety," Jax shouted loudly. "He and I have formed a portal so he could get you out of here."

"Shay! Come with me!" the man called, obviously the one Jax called River. In human form now, he was of somewhat slighter build than Jax, but certainly not small, and every bit as muscular as Ajax. His blondish brown hair was shot through with shimmering silver, as electrified in appearance as Jax's wings. "*Come on!*" River insisted, reaching toward her with one strong arm.

Then, as if in slow motion, Jax moved out of the way, his wings shunting her toward River—and protecting her from the screeching, howling demons that had advanced upon them. Without a word she lifted the wrapped scroll toward River, her eyes questioning.

He pointed toward Ajax, shouting above the din, "Give it to him! To Ajax! Come now!"

Ajax shoved her by the shoulders. "I'll find you. Go, go, Shay. Now!" As her hand brushed his in the pass-off, she slid the parchment into his grasp.

"Take this!" she said without looking back. River was

already pulling her forward, the snap of demons' jaws right on her heels.

Oh, Ajax, be safe! she shouted in her mind, hoping he could hear. *Stay safe for me, my dark angel. Be safe for me, please!*

She never knew whether he heard; everything happened too fast. One moment she'd been hidden in Jax's wings, and the next River yanked her headfirst into the swirling silver gateway that waited for them. Once inside the flowing maelstorm, she tried to turn back, to make sure Jax was going to be okay. But the gateway closed before she could find him, shutting them off from each other with a terrible and final roar.

How in Hades could a centaur have squeezed his way into a subterranean tunnel? Yet there Elblas stood, snorting right in Jax's face, looking pretty fucking proud of himself. Jax puffed his chest out, drawing on the deepest parts of his immortal source; it was the only way he could battle Elblas in such a small space, and surrounded by at least ten of the lower Djinn.

Jax flexed his talons; they lengthened and filled out. He'd kept them slightly tamed while he was around Shay, but Elblas didn't deserve that kind of respect.

"So you got her to safety. Good for you." Sable's tone was jovial, perversely approving in its condescension. "Good for you, old friend. Too bad I'll chase her to the ends of the earth now that I've found her." He stamped a hoof on the hard stones and stroked one curling horn. "Now that I know what she is to you, I'll never let her go. Your little slave boy can't protect her for long."

"Fine words, considering how that slave ran you straight through the heart in our last battle."

Demons circled Ajax in wolfish form; their long jaws opened, hungry and snarling. A couple of them lunged, but Sable established his authority by calling them back. One of his dark Djinn hands extended, and the beasts bowed down by his hooves.

"There will be time for devouring later," he told them

softly, his voice that of a loving master. "There, there. Time enough for sure."

"The human is not part of our battle, Elblas," Jax cautioned, pointing a talon at his old enemy. "She's under immortal protection, so if you even think about harming her, you'll bring down the fire of Hades on your beastly head."

"Ah, look who is calling whom a *beast*." Sable clucked, his mottled face twisting into a snarling grin. "From where I'm standing, you look more animalistic than I do at the moment. Dripping with feathers, eyes beady and black. By the gods, what a hideous form Ares chose for you."

Ajax felt fury build in his chest. In reaction, his vocal cords tightened and he released his screeching hawk's warning. The shrill sound ricocheted all the way to the tunnel's end. He'd lost himself with Shay, given over control, and in the process the hawk had emerged totally. Again he tossed back his head and pierced the tunnel with his warrior's song.

"Are we meant to feel threatened?" Sable trotted a little turn in front of his gathered, seething minions. "Do not forget, Ajax Petrakos—you are outnumbered and outflanked down here in your own private little hell."

Sable returned his gaze to Ajax, clomping lightly across the stone floor. Jax had tucked the scroll safely beneath his right wing the moment Shay handed it to him. He held it close against his side, hoping it would remain hidden from the demons' eyes. It had to be the Oracle's handiwork, some new bit of guidance. The Djinn would barter one another's very souls to lay their hands on such an item—although it was unlikely that even King Leonidas would be able to read her words. And if their king couldn't, then why would the Djinn be able to? Still, that wouldn't matter to them—the scroll would be a prize, a precious jewel snatched out of the hands of their enemies who needed its contents.

At least he'd gotten Shay to safety; the horde could not step onto Leonidas's property. It was one of the laws that Ares had established upon their creation day.

"I've waited for this moment a long, long while, Spartan." Sable took slow steps toward him, folding both arms across his scarred chest.

"I have, too." Jax took a step forward, spreading his wings in a menacing gesture—which wasn't as easy as it should be, because of holding the scroll against his side. "You're the one who stole my family from me; I'm the one who deserves revenge."

"You took your vengeance long ago!" Sable reared, striking harshly with his front hooves. Jax sidestepped, barely missing a violent strike to his face. The demon continued: "You had your revenge, warrior . . . I am ruined! Look at me, Spartan, at what you made me. It was thanks to you that my own god, Ahriman, sold me into Ares' slavery. Because of *you* that Ahriman urged Ares to punish me . . . curse me for the shame you'd brought on me and the other Djinn."

Sable dropped his forelegs back down to the ground, his voice suddenly much quieter. "A winged angel transformed into a work animal? What demon would crave the form of half a beast? Your doing." Sable snorted at Jax, keeping his eyes on him for a meaningful moment. "And now it's yours to pay for."

Sable's sword smashed downward, nearly slicing Jax's arm if not for his careful feint. Furious, Jax met Sable's pounding sword thrusts with raised shield, lunging with his own sword at each opportunity. But the longer and harder he fought, the more demons joined the fight, circling him back against the wall until he was completely hemmed in. There was nowhere to go, no means for escape. But he'd known there wouldn't be from the moment he'd been left alone down here with the Djinn.

Breathing heavily, Ajax stood poised, back against the stone wall. For several moments he and Sable eyed each other, neither willing to break the staring contest.

"I have you, Spartan," Elblas taunted, his scarred lips forming a sneering smile. "None of your brothers are coming for you. This is it, the moment when I torture you as you once did me." Then, hideously, Sable laughed for a long moment. "By Ares himself, I do believe my shoulders are burning! A sign, of course, that my long-lost wings are about to be avenged."

Sable gave a light, almost joyous buck of victory, then swung to face his minions. "Take his weapons; search him completely." Then, with a searing glance up and down Jax's exposed front, he added, "And if he manages to generate more weapons, or summon that shape-shifting slave of his, strip them from him as well."

From out of the darkness, a pair of leather-winged apprentices emerged. They appeared to be identical males, demon twins; Jax held steady, shoving every memory that he possessed about the ferociousness of demonic fighting pairs far from his mind. The males stepped toward him, the chains that linked them clanking on the hard floor. One of them shoved Jax hard in the right wing. "Humph," the Djinn said, baring fangs. "Girlie wings, of course." Then he flapped his harsh, beetlelike appendages right in Jax's face.

"You're Ares' handiwork, not mine," Jax called after him. "I only claimed your wings; he's the one who made you the monster that you are."

Sable rounded on him, brandishing one of his jeweled swords. He dragged it down Jax's bare chest, slicing the skin with slow precision. A surface cut; Sable would save Jax's true punishment for later, and he would take his time about it.

"How does this sword feel against your flesh? Sharp? Cold?" Sable waited, cocked his head while studying Ajax, then continued: "Imagine, Ajax, how my wings bled for those four days. Imagine the pain of being staked through each one, pinioned to that mountainside and left for dead."

"You ripped away my family!" Ajax bellowed as the sword reached low down his abdomen and began a dangerous slide toward his pubic bone.

"You stole my beauty, my power . . . my freedom." Sable stared down at Jax's groin, shaking his head.

The blade slid, cold and solid, down the length of Ajax's cock, pricked his sac. Jax sucked in a breath. Sable kept the tip there, poised between Ajax's thighs, eyes riveted on Jax. "You left me to die, and I had to burn off my own wings, had to consume myself in demon fire lest I truly die."

Sable moved forward, blade held carefully in place. "Twin wings you took from me, and now . . . now shall I seize a pair for a pair?"

Jax's groin felt as if lava were being applied to it. Sable was releasing fire into the sword's tip, slowly scalding Jax between the thighs. "I'll burn off your male parts as you forced me to burn off my own wings."

The scorching sensation intensified. Jax feared making any motion with the rapier-sharp blade tipped against his groin. But the pain was increasing. He felt sweat erupt on his brow; at his sides the demonic twins held each of his wings and anchored him against the tunnel wall. As they manhandled him, he struggled to keep the scroll hidden beneath his feathers. He struggled even harder not to move so much as a groin muscle.

Sable watched as they pinned him firmly against the wall; then, glancing at his sword, he told them, "Until I'm finished, hold him down."

And at that precise moment, the bloodred rubies on the weapon's hilt began to glow.

Chapter 17

Shay rolled over in the large, decadently soft bed, and hoped that she could stay there forever. The pillows were so silky, the sheets and blankets plush. Yes, all she wanted was to keep her eyes closed for hours and dream. She was beyond exhausted, so weary. *Sleep, sleep,* she thought she heard a light female voice whisper in her ear. *Don't wake up, not yet.*

Good idea, she almost groaned in answer, pulling a fluffy down comforter close to her face and sliding back into the strange dream she'd been having, the one where the sensual angel was wooing her, kissing her.

She sat up in bed with a panicked jolt. "Ajax!" she screamed, as all the events of the past few days rushed back to her. He was in terrible danger from the demons!

"You're all right," that same soft, British-accented voice told her. Shay whipped her gaze in every direction. A woman sat beside her and, placing a warm hand on her chest, urged Shay to lie back down. "You still need more rest, I'd say." She had sparkling blue eyes, matched by vivid blue streaks that shot through her black hair.

"What's happening? Where am I?" Shay glanced about the room, trying to get her bearings. The windows were large casement ones, the walls weathered stone. The place looked downright medieval.

"River brought you back here, to safety," the woman told her matter-of-factly.

Shay clutched at the plump comforter within her

hands, squeezing it. "But Ajax . . . that demon Elblas . . ." She stopped. "Who are you? How do you know Ajax? And, again, where am I right now?"

Goth Girl—well, more like Goth Woman—smiled, staring out the windows. "Would you believe me if I said those are the moors of Cornwall just out there?"

"Uh, no, I would not."

"Take a peek," the other woman told her, strolling to the windows. She peered out, then, taking her shirt-sleeve, wiped it across the glass. "It's so cold out there, the panes have fogged up. It's April, but these are still the moors." She shivered in demonstration.

Shay crawled across the mattress. The casement was near the bed where she'd been sleeping, almost at the end. Kneeling there, she planted a hand on the wall—it was cold, the stones smooth beneath her hand—and gazed outside. It was daylight! No matter what the time difference from Savannah—five, six hours? It still should have been nighttime here, too.

"How long have I slept?" she asked in a panic.

"Awhile," was the woman's vague reply. "And you still need more rest."

Shay had no clue how long she'd already been sacked out, but her questions became insignificant as she stared at the landscape beyond the windowpanes. Long, rolling hills covered in large, craggy rocks and flowing grass spread as far as she could see. Nothing at all like coastal Savannah. More important, a few stories below her window a small group of men were gathered in heated discussion.

Large men . . . dark-skinned men . . . most with black hair. Impossibly large men, a few of whom were wearing breastplates and holding swords. Large, sexy men who just so happened to look a lot like Ajax. In fact, there was one with short-cropped hair who so resembled Ajax that she'd have bet her recent magic-carpet ride that they were brothers.

"Oh, I am in such mega, mega shit, aren't I?" she voiced aloud, not even expecting the universe to answer. "I don't even have my passport with me."

"You're in the safest place you could be right now, actually," the mystery woman told her. "These grounds are warded and protected against any demon entering. Leonidas saw to it himself long ago."

Shay whipped her head around. "Leonidas? As in *King* Leonidas, the famous Spartan?"

The other woman's face broke into a beaming, adoring smile. "The very one!" Then she clapped her hands together gleefully. "Shayanna, we have to talk. In fact, there's a lot we must talk about, especially before the others get here. But it's not the time for that just yet."

"Is Ajax safe? Are those guys"—she pointed out the window at the warriors gathered below—"going to help him? We just left him there, all alone and surrounded by an entire demon horde. So they'd better be hauling ass back to Georgia, like, now."

Blue Streaks sat on the edge of her bed. "You need more rest, Shay." Her voice was soothing, lulling. "Here, come lie back down a little bit." She patted the mattress, folding the blankets back. "You look *really* knackered, and this bed looks *really* cozy," she told her, eyes bright and twinkling. There was something about those clear blue eyes in particular that really just wasn't human.

For some reason all Shay's urgency began to melt away; it was as if the warmest sunshine had suddenly begun to lull her into sleep. She sighed, yawned, and crawled back under the covers.

"Are you a fairy? Is that it?" Shay asked, feeling groggy. "Like some sort of ancient Greek Spartan fairy?"

Blue Streaks kept quiet as she tucked all the edges of the blanket around Shay. After a moment she beamed at Shay. "There, all tucked in, comfy and toasty."

"What should I call you?" Shay asked, drowsiness wrapping about her like a safe cocoon.

"Blue Streaks works fine for me right now," she told her, even though Shay was sure she'd never called her that aloud. Then, smoothing out the comforter, the woman continued, "As to why you should rest . . . because a few hours ago you were yanked through a portal—one that weakens even the strongest immortal of that bunch out there—and because you withstood a demon attack. Plus it looks to me like you're covered in abrasions and scratches—I put some medicine on that one big cut, by the way. You're doing fine." Shay felt her arms and for the first time realized she'd been bandaged.

"I'm not a weakling or anything," Shay protested. "I can get up and fight, too."

Blue Streaks swatted her lightly atop the head. "Why do you think I'm trying so hard to rekindle your strength? You're going to need it, little one."

Little one. Now, that was just plenty ironic, coming from a five-foot-nothing fairy with blue hair and blue fingernails ... wearing a T-shirt that said, ANARCHY, on the front.

"Blue Streaks, are you a fairy?" Shay rolled toward her. "I'm asking again 'cause, ya know ... I've lived through the weirdest few days of my life, and nothing would surprise me anymore."

"I'm not a fairy." She clasped her hands beneath her chin, planting both elbows on the edge of the bed.

"Then what are you?"

"That answer will come in time; all of your answers will. For now, know that I'm watching over you—and that, oh, by the way ... the boys can't see me at all, except for Ajax. . . ." She dropped her gaze suddenly. "And Leonidas, too. He can see me every now and then." Then she grew emphatic again. "But right now you rest, Shay-anna Angel."

A heavy mental blanket fell across Shay's mind, dousing her thoughts so fast that her eyelids began to droop.

One last time she turned to Blue Streaks. "But Ajax," she tried to argue. "What's going to happen to him? Aren't they going to help him?"

Blue Streaks patted her arm. "*Ajax* is more than twenty-five hundred years old, Shay," she told her, eyes bright and twinkling. "He's been at this for a very long time. Let *him* worry about *you*, okay?"

*   *   *

As soon as the bloodred rubies on Sable's sword hilt had started to gleam, the atmosphere in the chamber changed. Gold light flooded from everywhere as a familiar, rich voice drawled, "Not down here, boys. Aboveground. You both know how I abhor the dark."

Ares had paraded between them and, placing his hand atop Sable's, had cautiously guided the sword toward the ground. Jax released a breath, resisting the temptation to rub his aching balls and make sure everything was still intact.

"I won't let him harm your unmentionables, Ajax." Ares shook his long hair, letting it cascade loosely across his shoulders. "But I do want something in return."

The world flashed bright, no warning at all, and Jax now found himself falling face-first onto a cobblestone street. He blinked. How long had he and Shay been underground? Morning light was filling the distant sky.

With a glance around, Jax realized that Ares had transported all of them to the riverfront. He could hear distant horns from passing ships and freighters, the clanking of bells. It was early morning now, yet he and Shay couldn't have spent more than an hour in that tunnel. In dealing with a god, progressive human time meant nothing. Ares had probably taken a nap or drunk a full bottle of wine while transporting them. By Jax's calculations, some twelve hours had just elapsed in the blink of his eyes.

Jax shivered, realizing he was naked and winged. Summoning his power, he transformed into his mortal guise, clothed once again in black fatigues and shirt. None of the humans would be able to see him or the others, but after Sable's swordplay, he wasn't about to present any obvious vulnerabilities. Rolling to his side, he leaped to his feet; Sable and crew stood a good twenty paces down the street.

In a panic he realized the scroll that he'd held so carefully beneath his wings was missing, totally gone.

He was interrupted from his searching when a heavy,

firm hand came down on his shoulder, one that held the warmth and fire of eternity.

"Looking for this?" Ares extended the scroll, but as Jax reached for it, the god lifted it overhead. "I have something for you, Elblas," he called out to Sable.

Jax lunged, but the war god had already hurled the scroll through the air like a spear. Too bad it wasn't a boomerang that would circle back around and slice Ares in the throat. He was through serving as his god's plaything. All the resentment that had been building in him for the past hundreds of years had finally reached a boiling point. This moment had been a long damned time in coming. Once, he'd considered himself Ares' adopted son—just as he'd told Shay—but that time was long past. He could no longer conjure even an ounce of respect. Besides, Ares was far more interested in toying with the Spartans than he was in making good on his threats to transform them into beasts or objects if they displeased him.

With a war cry Sable bounded forward, his hooves clomping loudly on the cobblestones. He leaped high, snatching the rolled parchment in midair. Shouting in ancient Persian, he declared himself the victor.

Jax spun to face Ares, sneering up into his golden face. On the river beside them a long barge moved by, horn blowing. Jax raised his voice to be heard above it. "Why would you? *How* could you? That was given to me by the Oracle, a relationship you established, if you recall. Now you toss her words like garbage toward that . . . thing?"

Ares said nothing. His full lips turned up at the corners, a faint, unknowable smile forming. It was often impossible to read the god's expressions, a fact that he obviously enjoyed.

Sable held the scroll overhead like a prize, preening in front of his leather-winged twins and several other demons as if he'd just been garlanded at Olympus. With a glance in Jax's direction, Sable gave an almost courtly bow, extending his hand with a dramatic flourish. "Thank you, Ajax, for this most fortunate gift."

Jax cupped a hand over his mouth, shouting as the passing barge blew a long, bellowing sound again, "You won't be able to read a word of it, you fool!"

"Don't be so sure about that," Ares said. He clasped Jax by the arm, his warm fingers a sharp contrast to the early-morning chill from the river.

"What's that supposed to mean?" Jax whipped his gaze upward, only to find that Ares' eyes had narrowed to catlike slits, nothing but the golden electricity of his god's body moving between the two of them.

Jax wasn't about to be intimidated, not after his years of servitude to this master. "Is that why he's here?" Ajax jabbed his forefinger in Sable's direction. "And what about his companions? Are they Djinn, too? I can't tell because of the"—Jax's voice rose, and so did his anger— "*stench* they're giving off."

"Careful, Ajax Petrakos. Do not forget that you're in the presence of your god."

"Then act like one!"

The cat eyes turned dark as onyx, and the reflective goldenness of Ares himself darkened, almost as if the sun had suddenly dipped behind a dark thundercloud. "Again I say, Careful, little one."

Jax clinched his hands at both sides, using every ounce of his Spartan discipline to keep from coldcocking the insufferable being.

"It was your oath many years ago," Ares said in an offhand tone, offering a shrug. "And now you burn with fury toward me about it." Another shrug, and Ares reached for his woven-gold cloak, wrapping it about his shoulder. "You've only yourself to blame for accepting the terms."

Jax got right in Ares' face, unafraid of what punishment might come. This battle of theirs had been intensifying for more than a thousand years. "I was peacefully moving near the glowing fields of Elysium when you came knocking on my departed back. What Spartan wouldn't have given his soul for his sons? His wife? For Sparta? For humanity?"

All at once, warm fingers encased Ajax's throat, bruising his windpipe. He tried to breathe but couldn't draw in even the tiniest amount of air. "Listen to me carefully, servant." Ares lifted Jax slightly off the ground until he began to see stars and images of Shay. Why had he chosen today to argue with the god? Why hadn't he considered protecting his love?

Ares continued: "At this time I have decided to even the playing field. Elblas and his companions will indeed be able to read the transcript." Ares let Jax back down to the ground, but he tightened his warm-fingered grip, squeezing. "I've decided to change the rules, and there's not a damned thing you or the other Spartans can do about it. They are my rules, you are my creation, and you will do as I command."

Jax's world began to blacken at the edges from lack of oxygen. Dimly he cast a prayer toward the Highest God. The one who could smite the powerful yet lesser god who held him captive, who was choking the life out of his body. Although Jax was currently immortal, the god who'd birthed him could strip that immortality away at a moment's notice.

"Do you understand, immortal?" Ares dug long fingers into the cordons of muscle that lined Jax's neck. Although Jax tried to answer, only a choking gurgle escaped his lips.

Ares released him without warning, shoving him away. Jax stumbled backward slightly, his boot catching on a cobblestone. Off to the side he heard the demons chortle and snicker like some foul chorus.

Ares smoothed the front of his long, glowing robe — he'd turned bright and shimmering once again—and flicked his blond hair across one shoulder. "Gentlemen, gather near—and please, do manage not to claw each other to death just yet." For a moment Jax eyed Sable suspiciously. The centaur did the same, his scarred face mildly curious, definitely distrustful.

"Boys. Please." Ares kept still as a statue, waiting.

Folding both arms over his chest, Jax moved back toward Ares; Sable trotted the small distance that separated them. The leather-winged duo stepped closer, as did several wolflike creatures that emerged from behind them.

Ares pointed at the leather twins. "Not you," he said, staring down the barrel of his forefinger. "Only these two. The leaders. The rest of you stay back."

They retreated obediently, snarling and muttering in that hollow drone that so often accompanied gathered demons. Ares watched until he was satisfied that they held an appropriate distance, then turned back to face Jax and Elblas.

Jax immediately began his argument. "From the beginning, it has been said that I alone will see the Oracle or hear her words. If you change that, then you're breaking the compact." He kept Leonidas's recent visits with her to himself. Maybe they had been Ares' doing. . . . Then again, maybe not. Perhaps the Nameless One had allowed a back door.

Ares lifted his nose with an aristocratic air. "I never said that *I* wouldn't break our arrangement." Long blond lashes lowered. "Sloppy negotiating on the part of you Spartans, especially considering that you knew you were dealing with a god."

Jax was aghast. "Wh-what? You're saying that you built in the right to break your own word?"

"You should have secured the back path that wound behind your rear flank," Ares stated simply. "Seems you keep making the same mistake—once at the Hot Gates and now again."

Jax closed his eyes. The world seemed to literally spin off-kilter as the rules of their long-standing agreement crumbled to dust in his hands. "You're not honoring your word," he whispered—a statement, not a question.

Beside him Sable's rich, melodious laugh rang out. "I'd say this is even better than slicing off your damned balls. A level playing field, lovely."

When Jax turned to the Djinn, Sable had already begun unfurling the prophetic scroll. Jax made a grab for it, but found Sable's conjured sword flashing right in his face. "Don't even think about it," the centaur drawled, those damned rubies glowing once again.

Feeling furious and more helpless than he had in hundreds of years, Jax put his back to Sable and faced Ares. "If you want an even playing field about these prophecies, then I should have our scroll as well. So give it over."

Ares stroked his tuft of blond beard to a point, looking a bit like Pan all of a sudden. "You have your matching parchment; it's already with the Spartans . . . besides, I am more than fair. I made sure that you found your Shayanna to serve as a guide."

Jax's eyes widened, fear like lead in his stomach. "She's not part of this!"

"Ah, ah," Ares clucked, wagging a corrective finger. "Don't speak when you don't know. The lovely lass is indeed crucial to this battle. You will see."

They couldn't hurt Shay; Jax wouldn't allow them to touch her or make her a part of any of this. "I won't let you," he said, knowing how ridiculous the threat seemed to all who were present.

Ares lowered his head, bringing his lips near Jax's ear. Slipping one large arm about his shoulder, the god spoke softly—but not so faintly that Sable wouldn't hear. "I have an offer for you, Ajax Petrakos. A sweet, tempting one. Shall I tell you?"

The god paused, waiting, still stooped to Jax's level— Ares was right at seven feet tall, a giant even beside Jax's colossal height. After waiting a moment, Jax gave a brisk nod of assent.

"There is an item of mine that I lost some while back A treasure that belongs on Parnassus, but somehow it's managed to go astray . . . traveled the world once and back again, touched by Marco Polo. Sought by the Knights Templar. Ultimately, a few pirates got a tad greedy a few hundred years ago, and this item—this pre cious, important item—is hidden somewhere right here in Savannah."

Suddenly the circuitous, strange mission to America made sense. It wasn't just about Sable seeking out Shay and harming her, or just the Oracle's prophecy. All of it was being guided by the master puppeteer who was now standing beside him.

"What is it, my lord?" Sable asked, placing one mottled hand atop his chest. "Whatever the item, good Ares, my servants and I shall find it."

Ares dropped his arm from Jax's shoulder, strolling toward the railing along the river. He kept his back to them both, and in a fleeting moment of kinship Sable and Jax looked to each other. Were they supposed to follow? Hold back? Sable stroked one of his horns and shrugged. Jax rolled his eyes and walked to the railing, taking a place beside Ares. "What do you want me to find? I'll get it done. Without Shay's help, no less."

Ares smiled faintly. "You love her already, don't you?"

The loud echo of hoofbeats signaled Sable's arrival at Ares' other side. "Oh, is he blabbering about his"— Sable made quotation marks in the air, scowling as he raised his voice an octave—"prophesied love?"

Jax lunged at Sable, but Ares blocked him, holding each at bay with his hands. "Restrain yourselves, boys. The time for the battle has not yet come." When they'd calmed back down, Ares lowered his hands, adjusting his cloak and composing himself before he continued: "It's the Looking Glass of Eternity."

Jax pulled a big flat zero. He'd never heard of anything like that. From Sable's silence he figured that the demon hadn't either.

"It allows the possessor to step into Elysium. One simple glance into the small mirror and one is set free from mortal life." Ares cut his eyes significantly at Ajax. "Or *immortal* life, as the case may be. Your Shay will live only her allotted years, Ajax, and you will be left here to continue eternally without her. Why give up this opportunity when you can be released from your immortal prison? She can join you on the other side once her mortal days are done."

Ajax could hardly breathe. All these years of warfare, all this time of wandering, lonely, aimless—the battles never ending. It had been hell disguised as eternal life. But with this looking glass? He could pass on; he could go and wait for Shay—perhaps even see his sons. Maybe even find his wife.

His mind churned with thoughts, questions—he almost missed Ares' next words, which were directed toward Sable.

"... will be freed from your desert exile once and for all, Elblas," the god was saying. "And not only that—if you find this object for me, you shall have your wings once more."

Jax focused his thoughts to a pinpoint. "So the key lies in the prophecies? And they're exactly the same?"

"Indeed." Ares smiled, revealing gleaming white teeth. "The search begins tomorrow morning, seven a.m. Not a minute before, since I am a god of infinite fairness"— Ares glanced pointedly at Ajax—"and will allow Ajax time to fetch his Shayanna. But only she—not any of your fellow Spartans—may assist you."

Jax stepped as close to the god as he could without touching him. "And we have your oath that you won't change the terms of this bargain? That you will honor it and not go back on your word?" He wouldn't be fooled twice.

"Of course." Ares tossed his head back, releasing a tinkling peal of laughter. "Yes, quite fun! It's a race, dear boys. And let the games begin!"

With a quick snap of the god's fingers, Jax found himself transported again. Skidding to a stop on his backside, he landed back on the training field at Cornwall, right in front of Leonidas himself.

Chapter 18

Shay woke again, but this time instead of Fairy Woman, two massive men were at her bedside. The one closest to her had spiked black hair and looked disarmingly like Ajax. "You're his brother," she mumbled groggily, blinking her eyes. "I saw you from the window . . . earlier."

The guy from the window!

All the details of her location came crashing back once again, and she launched upward in bed, instantly sorry for moving so fast. She groaned, sliding back onto the mattress. Her entire body felt like a load of bricks, too heavy to carry. She lifted a hand, gesturing, then let it fall beside her on the comforter. "You have to be . . . related."

The guy scooted his chair closer, his expression cautious but friendly. "And you are Shay Angel." He glanced at the other man who stood propped against the wall, and who looked slightly younger—and even more like Ajax. In fact, he could have been Jax's twin, with his long black hair, thick dark eyebrows, and monumental height; except his expression held an easiness that she hadn't yet seen in Jax. Then again, they'd spent their entire time together running for their lives. Or sparring. Or nearly falling into each other's arms.

She gave her head a clearing shake. "I see . . . you're both his brothers. Right?" She blinked again, her gaze flicking between them.

"It's not important who we are," the guy sitting beside

her replied, his dark eyebrows knitting together. "We have questions for you."

The standing one shoved off the wall, positioning himself right by her bedside, but not before slugging his companion in the shoulder. He extended an olive-skinned hand toward her and in a slightly accented voice said, "I'm Aristos." Then his face opened into a wide smile that revealed white, even teeth. One of those smiles that practically beamed sunlight at you. "But you can call me Ari. And yeah, I'm Ajax's brother. And this one"—he clapped the short-haired man on the shoulder—"is Kalias. You can call him Kalias." Ari laughed a moment, facial expression still sunny even though Kalias kept a straight face. "He's our big brother. Our serious, intense brother, but don't let that fool you."

Shay rubbed her eyes. "Is Jax back?" She glanced about the room, assuming that if his brothers were gathered at her side, he had to be here at the castle. The brothers coughed, looked a little awkward—and she panicked.

Jolting upward in bed once more, she ignored the answering gyrations inside her head. "He's not back? Still? We left him with that demon—"

"No, no!" Ari held up a hand. "He's fine, truly. He is well. He's returned and is meeting with our king."

"Leonidas," she said softly, chill bumps chasing down her arms. It was an eerie, unreal thought. "Is Socrates around here somewhere? What about Plato? Bet he could give us some good advice."

Ari smiled, ignoring her chatter. "Yes, there have been developments. That scroll you brought back—did you have a look at it?"

She shook her head. "Never had a chance."

"Well," Kalias jumped in, "we can't see it. We're not gifted in prophetic words. Only Ajax can actually read it—unless somehow Leonidas is able to make a bit of sense of it."

She slumped forward, pressing a hand to her temple. "Oh . . . wow." She groaned slightly. "Feeling *blech* here, sorry."

"I'm forgetting my manners," Ari blurted, and moved across the room to pour her a cup of cool water. "This will help. The portal jumps can be a real bitch, especially if you're a virgin, but you'll recover soon."

Shay couldn't help it; she blushed as she accepted the water from him. Nothing like a hunky ancient warrior playing fast and loose with the word *virgin* to make her get a little flustered. It also reminded her that Jax wanted to literally play fast and loose with her.

She sipped for a moment. "So what made you think I could read the scroll? It's a prophecy?"

"From the Oracle . . ." Ari hesitated, scratched his eyebrow. "Well, you'll get used to all of this. But the thing is, we can't see or hear her, and we thought that perhaps if you'd had a look at it, that you might be able to."

"Why?"

Ari's smile slipped a bit. "Something Jax said. About the scroll and you being able to help interpret the prophecy."

"I know demons, period. I can see 'em, maybe fight 'em, but that's it."

Ari settled a hip on the side of her bed. Reaching gently for her hand, he drew it into his own much darker one. "Shay, did Jax get a chance to mention anything to you about a prophecy he once received . . ." His voice trailed off; he drew in a breath and added in a gentle voice, ". . . about you?"

Shay thought a long moment. Everything had been happening so fast, and now, with her mind feeling muddled after the portal jump, it was hard to remember what he'd said—but she was fairly certain he'd not mentioned anything like that. Except in the beginning, he'd known who she was, recognized her name. He'd been waiting for her.

Her heart turned over in her chest. "He's been waiting for me?" Tears instantly stung her eyes. "He knew my name. Was it because the Oracle told him about me?"

The brothers exchanged a glance, and she noticed it. "Look, I should know."

Kalias held his brother's gaze, shaking his head as he

said, "And Ajax should be the one to tell you. About the Oracle and . . . the rest."

The rest. Those words were always heavy-duty, either meaning that a big threat was coming or that someone had died or, in her particular family's case, that some butt-ugly demon thugs had harmed someone she cared about.

"I hate those two words—'the rest.' They never amount to anything good. And just so you know, I'm fixing to hurl here if you don't give me at least some little bit of good news."

Ari squeezed her hand. "The rest, in this case, Shay, is all good. It's not a bad thing. But it's Jax's story to tell, about what the Oracle once prophesied concerning you."

Oracle. When Shay thought of *oracle* only one other word popped into her mind: *Delphi.*

"Which oracle?" She kept the question simple; better that than reveal herself to Jax's brothers as a total blathering idiot.

Kalias smiled faintly, taking her emptied cup from her hand. In a smooth move he rose and refilled her pitcher, answering, "The Oracle at Delphi. *The* Oracle."

"Okay, okay, okay." She guzzled the water this time, closing her eyes. "So not only did you strapping dudes make a deal for immortality—the Delphic Oracle got swept into it, too? Or wait . . . was she always immortal? I don't get it. I always thought there were a bunch of oracles at Delphi and that they were human."

She heard twin sighs and finally opened her eyes again. They began to explain in the kind of cross talk that only close siblings ever shared. "She was Apollo's favorite," Kalias explained.

"That's all we know," Ari continued. "We're not sure why she lives forever, like we do."

Kalias talked over him: "But she's our guide in all things. That was part of Ares' arrangement—which you already seem—"

"To know about," Ari finished.

"You two are making my head spin even worse than it already was. Okay, got it. She's your guide in all things. Check. But you can't see or hear her—except Jax. Check."

They stared at her a long moment, serious as they studied her, then in a shared voice agreed, "Check."

"Don't you two go trying to muscle in on my girl." The rich, deep voice was achingly familiar. Shay's heart went triple time as she dared to glance and confirm that Ajax was standing right in the doorway. There he stood, smiling at her in an almost shy way. It was the first time she'd seen him in good, clear light, and he was a sight to behold. His long, lean body filled the doorframe—from his broad shoulders and long hair all the way down to his jeans-clad legs. He was so muscular that the jeans clung to his thighs, hinting at the massive definition and sinew hiding beneath denim.

Their gazes were riveted on each other, and she knew her smile had to be as dopey as she felt inside; his was as beautiful as he *looked* on the outside.

"Just taking care of your girl, little brother," Ari announced jovially, and strode across the room. Slapping Jax on the shoulder, he said, "She's all yours. Feeling much more chipper now that you're here, quite obviously."

Kalias didn't move, even when Ajax began slowly walking across the room. Ari whistled. "Kali, come on, man. Leave the lovebirds."

Kalias rose from his seat, faced Ajax, and did the most surprising thing—he opened his arms wide and pulled him into a hard, solid embrace. "You had us worried, Brother. I am glad you are all right."

Jax folded his arms around Kalias. She had a good line on his face, and his expression was surprising. His eyes widened at first, his mouth opened, and then he bent his head against his brother's shoulder, relaxing. They stood like that for several long seconds, then released, stepping away from each other.

"It was touch and go for a bit," Ajax told them, then

smiled and glanced at Shay. "But it turned out damned well in the end."

"The end," Kalias repeated with a nod.

"It will be over soon," Ajax pledged. "I'm going to see to it. I'll have Elblas's horse's ass back in the desert and a bow tied to that mangy tail of his before I let him hurt Shay." He shook his head. "I'll die before that demon or his horde touches her—or any of my Spartan brothers."

Ari walked back from the doorway, sliding a hand onto Ajax's shoulder. They locked gazes. "Just be careful, Brother. If anything happened to you . . ."

"Nothing will happen to me," Jax insisted, waving them out the door. "I want a few minutes with my Shay-anna. Go!"

Shay tried to drive the brothers' fear from her mind, but their concern had been palpable. Undeniable. They knew far more than she did, and they clearly thought Ajax was in a great deal of danger.

He ambled toward her bed, sort of picking his way across the room; all the while he kept his hawklike gaze locked with hers. A sexy, seductive smile played at his lips. Yet he took his time about crossing the distance that separated them.

"You're teasing me," she said, surprised by how rough her voice sounded. Between her legs dampness pooled. Just a moment with the man and she was already wet for him. How could any one guy hold so much power and control over her body? Her soul?

"Correction," he said laconically. "I'm appreciating you. First time I've seen you in good light."

She averted her gaze, staring into her lap. With a tug of the comforter she brought it close about her breasts. She wore only the T-shirt she'd had on the night before. It was grimy, probably smelly, too. That and her underwear were all she had on.

"Hope it's not the big disappointment of your life." She forced a laugh, not looking at him. "You know, finally getting that good look at me. I sorta felt that way about my Jeep. Bought it one night after work, and bam, the next morning I realized it had some serious scratches. Wow, *that* really sucked."

"You're babbling."

"I'm a babbler."

"Look at me, Shay." He'd arrived at her bedside. Still, she just couldn't meet his gaze; it was too intense for daylight. Too overwhelming for being half-clothed. A long, rough fingertip slid beneath her chin, forcing her to look upward. "You are exquisite," he pronounced. "The loveliest woman I've ever beheld . . . and I have lived many, many days, as you well know."

"Now I know you're lying." She laughed, meeting his eyes. "You, on the other hand, really are the sexiest, most gorgeous man I've ever seen in my life. But, see, I've lived twenty-seven years and you've lived twenty-five hundred, so who's more reliable?"

"Twenty-five hundred and nineteen."

"What?" She scrunched up her nose.

"That's how old I am. I was thirty-one when we made our deal with Ares." He settled his hip on the side of her bed, planting one hand along the ornate wooden headboard so that he was in her personal space.

"I wonder how my mama would've felt about my dating an older man." She practically gasped the words as he gripped the headboard with his right hand, framing her between his arms.

He bent closer; she could feel the warmth of his breath. "Shay, love, this isn't dating. No, it will never be dating for us. That's too simple, too casual." Their gazes locked; she noticed the beard stubble along his jaw and chin, black as the hair atop his head. Black as his wings. "This, sweet one," he said, lowering his mouth toward hers, "is *claiming*."

Chapter 19

"Claim away," Shay told him, staring up through lush, lowered lashes that were the color of black velvet. "I like the sound of that. Much better than dating, which—historically for me, at least—has tended to suck."

She frowned at some memory, and he wanted to wipe that look from her face. Hear about every competitor for her love that he'd ever had, but not now.

"Hmm, fools, every one of them," he murmured, letting his lips brush against hers teasingly. "Besides, sucking *can* be good, depending on the body part involved." He drew her lower lip between his teeth and suckled it, illustrating his point. "Although I'd be hard-pressed to find any body part of yours that I *don't* adore."

Perfect. The woman was absolutely perfect, idealized beauty in every way. The ancient philosophers would have held a symposium just to describe her many facets. He let his hand drift across her right breast, caressing it gently within his grasp.

She arched upward in pleasure, her hips lifting against his torso, and he felt a surge of unstoppable desire. He needed Shay Angel like he'd never needed any woman before in his life, but that was hardly a surprise. It was what he'd counted off the centuries praying for, waiting for: this very moment, humbled and helpless at her slightest touch. Bending lower, he kissed her again, deeper this time, with his mouth wide and opened to hers.

Their kiss in the tunnel had been aggressive, desperate, and those same raw emotions came crashing back on him in the space of a heartbeat. He felt the silver in his veins thrum wildly as it sent a power surge straight to his loins. But unlike in the tunnel, he didn't fear her seeing his life source, or his eyes changing colors, or even his wings bursting forth uncontrollably.

None of that mattered any longer. Although she didn't yet know all his terrible, eternal secrets, she *had* seen what he was and had not run. He had to believe she wouldn't turn on him as Narkissa had, had to hope that he could love her enough to keep any possible fear at bay.

No, the only thing that mattered was that they were finally alone in each other's arms, safe in Leonidas's castle. They could roll together until the sun rose, and he'd still have time to prepare for the Savannah battle that awaited him tomorrow. For now, there was only the scent of his greatest love, the silky-hot feel of her body beneath his palms, his lips.

Gripping the headboard with his left hand, he cupped her cheek with the other and ran his tongue across her lips. She tasted like nectarines, sweet and natural. She opened her mouth eagerly, matching the driving hunger he felt inside as she lifted toward him. With a gentle moan she slid her arms across his shoulders to the nape of his neck, the fingers of one hand twining through his hair. Her other hand kneaded the muscles of his upper back, urging him closer. Her unvoiced words of pleasure trailed through his mind like a meteor shower across the midnight sky. There were no barriers; she was totally open to him, even, it seemed, murmuring to him within her mind.

Closer, he heard, the word practically a caress across his soul. *Come closer . . . come inside me.*

Yeah, sweetness, I plan on it, he thought, knowing she couldn't read his own thoughts. At least, not yet. There was no anticipating how intimate their bond would become as their bodies and souls joined. And he was through waiting to find out; one thousand years of aching for this mortal were finally over. *Now* was the time to take her; *now* was the moment for the claiming he'd just promised.

"Shayanna," he purred in her ear, brushing a tangle of long hair away from her cheek. A rush of the old language passed his lips, and she lifted upward, capturing his mouth greedily yet again. Their kiss grew hotter, with hands twisting about each other, fingers memorizing the feel of skin and curves. Her rough tongue thrust deep into his mouth, seeking more of him, and he met her urgent, deeper kiss. A battle began between them as tongue snaked against tongue.

Power swamped his body like a lightning strike from Hades itself. He saw silver, even with his eyes closed, felt his body tighten like a fist. *No predicting this one,* he thought, feeling suddenly vulnerable—and as though he could leap out of his skin just from the sheer magnitude of his rushing power. His cock ached, hard and thick inside his pants, and he wondered how fast he could get inside of her.

Slow, you randy fool. Make this special . . . you have time

Opening his eyes, he kept kissing her, but stole a glance at her face. Her black hair appeared to be silver gossamer; her beautiful peaches-and-cream skin glittered magically. His vision had gone wild, and he knew his eyes had probably already begun to change hue.

"I-I should warn you," he admitted roughly, breaking their kiss with a gasp. "All that . . . you saw in me before . . . I won't be able to stop it. Not when we make love . . ." He shook his head, trying to calm his pounding heart, but it was a useless endeavor. "Definitely won't be able to control myself, what I am . . . not when I'm with you."

He stared into her eyes for a beat, waiting for her to recoil or become afraid.

She didn't say one word, but what she *did* do made him want to fall at her feet in pure worship. She looked up at him and smiled. *Smiled.* The most open, glowing look he'd ever seen on any woman's face in his life. The smile seemed to have been beamed from Mount Parnassos itself; it was that pure, that adoring. So accepting.

"You love me," he whispered wondrously. It wasn't even a question; he was that certain of her feelings for him, knew them down deep in his very soul. He gazed at her, his heart gyrating insanely, the rhythm as strong as his wings when he climbed on the wind. "You already love me."

She dropped her gaze shyly, and he noticed that her cheeks were suddenly light pink. Pink touched with glowing otherworldly power. "You're a cocky thang, aren't you, Petrakos?" she whispered.

Thang. Oh, that sleepy Southern accent only stoked his reaction even more. He felt the immortal source rush white-hot inside his body; he began trembling in response, and dropped his hands from the headboard so she wouldn't see the tremors that were racking his body. They weren't even naked yet, and he already felt control slipping from his grasp.

She slid both palms down his forearms, the satin skin of her hands electrifying every inch of him that she caressed. "Of course," she said, closing her eyes pleasurably, "you have very good reason to be cocky. So I'll give you a pass."

"Wait until you see exactly how cocky I can be," he promised huskily, sliding one large palm beneath her hips. "When I have you naked and panting beneath me." He squeezed her bottom, stroking it languidly with his thumb. "When I have you crying out my name, begging for more of this warrior's touch. Ah, lass, what will you do with me then?"

"I'll tell you to fuck me like mad," she blurted, pale eyes wide and filled with hungry need.

"Neh, parakalo," he murmured, slipping into Greek all of a sudden; after all, it was his true voice of passion. *"Yes, please,* but be merciful, sweetness." He bent his mouth to her ear. *"Neh,* and be kind. Know that you have me free-falling here."

"But you're not scared." She slid her hand about his nape, rubbing the thick bands of muscle there. He was wound tight, but the feeling of those fingers working at his tension ... well, he practically melted beneath her human touch. So long—so long he'd waited.

"Not scared, no. I'm *starving* for you," he admitted hoarsely. "But even this Spartan has his limits, you know."

She leaned back into the fluffy pillow and reached a hand to his cheek. For several long seconds she brushed her fingers against his beard growth, back and forth with her fingertips, studying his face as if seeing him for the very first time. "What about when I ask you to become a hawk for me? What will you do then?" She dared a look at him, the flushed color in her cheeks growing deeper. "Still cocky then? Or just more out of control?"

He couldn't believe the tempting, coy tone in her voice. But she'd hit the mark she was going after, straight on like a bull's-eye.

"My little minx. You can beg me for anything, and you'll have it."

Still sitting on the edge of her bed, he turned back the sheet that covered her body and bent lower over her. Ready to kiss, to claim, to take. With a possessive growl he sank his fingers into her hair, twining it within his grasp as he thrust his tongue into her mouth. *Mine, all mine.*

As he settled his chest atop hers, she shoved at his shoulder with a little cry. And for a moment, despite all her promises, despite how safe he felt—he panicked. Fear came crashing over him, and he jolted upright, staring down at her. He half expected to see anxiety in her eyes or some kind of regret. But no. She simply sat up, facing him for a second, then extended one finger as if she were holding a physical place for herself right between them.

"Hold up," she said. "Just one teensy-tiny sec, big boy." She smiled again, perfect sunlight, and his thundering heart stilled a little. Keeping her gaze locked with his, she took the hem of her baby-doll shirt and tugged it right over her head. With that flash of fabric she suddenly sat before him wearing only a white cotton bra and underwear. "This should make things a little easier for you." She tilted her chin upward, looking proud of herself.

But, beautiful as her face was, it didn't have his attention at the moment. His gaze was riveted lower, right on that chest of hers. He was fairly sure he had to be gaping like an adolescent boy. It was like a first glimpse of what a woman should be—could be—the perfect roundness of her breasts, the way the nipples jutted with arousal, protruding through the fabric of her bra like small pearls.

She snorted with laughter. "You've got the mind of a poet, and there's not one word you can say about *these*?" She grasped both breasts within her own palms, bouncing them in invitation. "Yee-haw, baby, they're ready to play ball. You bring that bat on over."

He returned her joyous smile, then did just as she had, yanking his black T-shirt off. He hurled it over his shoulder, still staring at her with the hunger of a predator, with the urgent beat of the raptor crying out inside his chest. Along his shoulders the burning itch of his wings began, a tingling that ran from the base of his neck to the very tip of his spine.

"I can't promise . . . I can't . . ." He couldn't say it—shook his head and tried again, but came up empty-handed.

She tilted her head sideways, a slight furrow forming between her black eyebrows. "Promise what, Jax?" She seemed exposed all of a sudden, sitting before him half-naked, clearly wondering what in Hades' name he was trying to say.

"I don't expect forever, if that's what you mean," she said, hurt evident in her voice.

"I do," he promised fervently, grabbing her hands. "Oh, gods of Olympus, I only meant that I can't promise I won't transform while in your arms, that I won't be far fiercer than anything you've seen me become yet."

"Oh." She sighed in obvious relief, and he hated that he'd made her suffer for even a second. Her eyes brightened all over again. "Oh, I see. The wings and the—"

"Talons," he finished, "the full-on change . . . or more so—I don't even know what you'll bring out in me." His hands ached, the bones in his fingers tight, as they always got right before his talons emerged.

She sat up taller in bed and opened her arms to him. "I already told you I'd beg for that. For all of you. So get on over here."

For a moment he just looked at her, some ridiculous part of his mind telling him that she wasn't real. That she was a mist or a vision sent by the Oracle again. But that unreal thought served to do only one thing: propel him into action.

All at once they rushed each other, as if after waiting so long, they finally had permission. It wasn't even rolling into each other's arms; it was more like they literally charged at each other, a tangle of limbs and movement. The sheet went flying—blankets did, too—and they went tumbling together, first Jax on top, then Shay, then back in the other direction, and they laughed like fiends the entire time.

Finally they rolled to a stop, Shay sprawled atop him. Her small body was lean and curving. She felt so light, pressing against him, and as he wrapped his massive arms about her back he held to her as if life itself depended upon it.

Don't ever leave me . . . I'm begging you.

A flash of memory assailed him; that look on Narkissa's face when she'd seen him fully transformed. The horror at what he'd become. Those dark eyes that had loved him for so long had grown wide and terrified. He'd reached for her, thick wings dragging across the tile floor of their home. She'd screeched louder than he ever had while in hawk form. She'd screamed and stumbled backward, falling onto the floor.

Get away from me, monster! she'd cried, scooting frantically away from him.

It's me. Ajax, he'd tried, extending both hands in supplication. But his wings had always had a life of their own, one that matched his inner tempo, and they'd begun to flap in a horrific, possessed display. He reached for her again, but she'd rolled out of his grasp, fleeing toward their sons. His ungainly appendages had upturned pots, shattered flower vases—had destroyed everything in his path as he'd tried to follow his family out of their home.

By the time he reached the door to the courtyard they were already gone; and he hadn't bothered following. He'd already seen that horrified, primal fear in all their eyes and knew that they were lost to him.

He tightened his hold on Shay, pressing his eyes shut against the unwelcome, heartbreaking memories. "Sweetness . . . mine. Tell me you are mine."

All the urgency between them suddenly stilled, grew hushed like the quiet earth after a new snowfall. Very gently she cupped his face, forcing him to look up into her eyes. Their gazes locked, everything so silent, so electric. In those blue eyes he saw reassurance . . . true acceptance. She nodded slowly, just holding his face tilted toward hers.

"I won't leave you, Ajax," she said, and bent to kiss his forehead. She kept those full lips pressed to his temple and repeated the promise. "I won't run . . . not from you. Not ever. I *am* yours."

His groin grew thick and tight in response to her vow, the blue jeans barely able to contain their true secret: his cock pushing hard against the abrasive fabric, nudging her thigh. Her legs were bare—she was clad only in a modest pair of cotton panties—no lace, no frills. As if she weren't used to being a temptation. Well, he'd change that, he thought, sliding fingertips along the panties' elastic edge. With a deft maneuver he rolled them down, tugged them lower. She finished the job, kicking them off, and he eased her onto her side. He needed to reach her, touch her freely.

Shay wanted out of her bra, too, and, sitting up slightly

in bed, she reached behind her and in a breath was completely naked. "Lose the pants, Ajax," she ordered, gesturing down at him. "Now."

She liked the feeling of commanding him—maybe because she was pretty sure nobody else ever got away with pushing him around.

"Yes, sir," he said with a smirk, and was out of the pants and grabbing for her before she could think of a snappy comeback.

She watched in amazement as his normally inky black irises swirled suddenly, then altered to brilliant silver. By the light from the windows, eyes that had seemed so threatening that first night now looked more beautiful than anything she'd ever glimpsed in her life.

"Just so we're clear"—she slid her palm along his hip—"I think your silver eyes are gorgeous." She scooted closer until they lay facing each other, skin to skin. "And that your wings are the most erotic thing in the world."

He nuzzled her, sliding fingertips between her thighs, stroking her in just that spot, the one that made her grow even wetter. With a moan she cried out, "All of you. I want all of you."

He pulled back, staring into her eyes, his face flushed with arousal, his eyes brilliant-bright with desire. "You promised you'd beg," he told her, his voice deeper than usual.

She met the sliding touch of his fingers. "I am begging!"

First one finger, then another penetrated her, riding up deep inside. "Love, by the time I'm done with you, you'll have learned what begging truly means."

"Like this?" she teased, and without warning took hold of his erect length. It felt heavy between her fingertips, a warm, hard weight. Slowly she stroked his tip, tracing her fingertips about the pulsing vein that ran the length of him. With a groan of pleasure he released her and rolled onto his back, opening his legs wide.

Talk about a guy who knew how to ask for what he wanted, she thought, and rolled right along with him without releasing him from her grasp. Pulling up onto her knees, she used her other hand to cup his sac. If he'd been in pleasure land before that moment ... well, his piercing cry of longing had to mean he was now in totally uncharted territory.

Jax kept his eyes pressed closed, swimming in the sensations Shay was evoking. Too many interchangeable women he'd lain with over the years, too many heartless, mindless joinings had been his habit. And not one of them he could remember had ever been concerned with pleasuring him. It had always been about his wings, the eroticism of what he was ... and yet here he lay, thighs wide-open, and this angel of his seemed to want only one thing: to take him past the brink of any pleasure he'd known in his endless life.

Those soft fingers closed about his tip, released, worked a friction back and forth. And meanwhile her other hand squeezed and rolled him, tantalized. ...

"Oh, Shayanna!" he shouted when she trailed fingertips low behind him, touching that forbidden spot that was so erogenous that even the thought of her stroking it had had him releasing a little seed within her hand.

"And who," she murmured, pressing her mouth to his right nipple, "is begging whom?" She didn't even wait for his grunting answer, but took the hot tip of her tongue and swirled it around his nipple, suckling, nibbling. He wound his hands through her hair; it had fallen across his shoulder, tickling his bare skin. Loose and wild, it was like this moment, like their freedom with each other.

Flat on his back wasn't typical for him—not in bed, not anywhere. Yet she made him feel safe and worshiped. Utterly adored. Wrapping his arms about her, he pulled her close and wished for words to make her know what she was doing to his body.

There were none. All he had to offer was his touch ... his heart.

Along his backbone a tingling sensation shot through his bone and muscle. Burning fire rolled like lava across his shoulder blades. Any second now, any moment, he would be too far gone to halt his transformation.

And it would hurt like a bitch if it happened while he was flat on his back.

"Shay." He gasped, moving to roll her off of him, but she didn't realize how urgent things had suddenly become. She resisted playfully, sliding her mouth back down to his chest, working even lower with that tongue of hers.

White-hot, burning waves reached a fever pitch, centered through his middle back and shoulders ... then swirling low, almost to his buttocks. *I'm changing,* he realized, unable to stop, needing to get off his back if the wings weren't going to be smashed beneath their combined weight.

Panicked, he cried, "Shay, please—"

She glanced up, surprised, and with a near-violent motion he flung her onto her back. Lunging upward onto his knees, he was only a moment ahead of the wings that surged from inside of him with a primal force.

Their weight was so sudden, so overtaking that he lost his balance and toppled forward, bracing both hands on the pillow beneath her head. They kept spreading wider, fuller; he could feel feathers tease at the bare skin of his upper thighs, along his buttocks.

Beneath him, Shay stared in wide-eyed shock ... her mouth forming a silent O of ... what? Wonder? Revulsion?

No, she wants you, he reminded himself. *She's not running. She promised.*

But the old emotions were so suffocating, too real. As he panted down into her face, braced just above her, their gazes locked. Wordless, each stared into the other's eyes, the only sound the faint rustling of feather against feather.

Shaking hard, she slipped her arms about his neck, drawing him nearer—and with first one hand, then the other, did what he craved most of all: She raked her fingers all along his wings, feeling back and forth as she'd done with his beard earlier.

The only difference was the one thing she didn't

know ... that his wings were the most erogenous part of his body. Tossing his head back, he let loose with a hawk's cry, and his full nature overcame the rest of him in the space of a moment.

Talons replaced hands; wiry pubic hair gave way to feathery softness; his face ached as bones realigned into hawkish ones.

Gulping, he tried to find his human voice, but his vocal cords had seized up on him; the only sound he produced was another harsh bird's cry. Beneath him, he felt certain Shay would begin to scream.

He waited, knowing it would come soon, her terror. Panting down into her face, he watched like the raptor he was, ready to gauge the slightest movement.

But she did the damnedest thing: She opened her mouth and mimicked his cry, or the best she could with her human vocal cords. Leaning back into the pillow, she extended her hands with a twinkling look of mischief in her eyes, and reached to touch his wings again. He braced for the sensation, pressing his eyes shut, but her caress never came. His eyes flew open, his gaze riveted on her in expectation.

Her arms were held, suspended in their reach. "I don't want to hurt you," she told him softly.

He shook his head. "Hawk wings are strong as steel."

"Of course they are." She smiled. "Sensitive?" She lifted a shaking hand past his forearm, stretching to make contact.

"Erogenous," he breathed against her ear, right as her fingertips grazed the first feather of many along his wing. She trembled in his grasp, stroking the full length of that portion of wingspan, feeling the prickling resistance, thrilling at the touch.

In her ear he released a shattering groan of desire. "Ah," he moaned, burying his face against her shoulder.

"Here." She gasped, trying to get her hands around him. "Open them up. I need more."

Her simple request caused him to release a shattering cry of desire, his whole body quaking. Overhead, to their sides, even around her, his wings spread—probably at least six feet of glorious, gleaming power and beauty. When they were fully extended he lay atop her, carefully poised like a beautiful mythological creature, the full range of his ancient power coiled tight before her.

"Please, Shay," he begged, closing his eyes. "I'm ready."

With both hands she reached upward, caressing, stroking, feeling the long length of each wing. Beneath her hands his appendages trembled, beat the air, reacted, but she wouldn't pull away. She explored every feathered inch of what he offered, and the longer she appreciated him, the more he stilled. She recalled a horse she used to ride as a girl, Pegasus, who had been jittery and untamed. Yet when she'd brush his side, the silvery beast would always grow still, as her hawk did at the moment.

"You like this, don't you?" she asked with a sigh of pure delight. He nodded, saying nothing, but she saw him swallow hard. To see how he'd react, she withdrew her hands, and his eyes immediately snapped open, silvered with desperate desire that he made no effort to mask from her.

"More," he growled, then, pressing his eyes shut, added, "Please." The man's wings weren't just erogenous—they were, in some way, the absolute seat of his sexuality. She knew it in that moment. With one final caress she found the location along his back where bird's wing met man's flesh. It was like a long, thick seam, the place where the dark and the light of what Jax was joined.

Like they were about to join.

She trailed her fingertips down that erogenous zone, stroking it just as she would that thick cock of his. He practically squirmed atop her in obvious pleasure, shivering and groaning as she reached his tailbone and the feathers stopped.

Their gazes locked right then, a sort of battle moment between their naked bodies. In a clawing movement Jax had her rolling onto her belly. The feel of his talons was harsh—yet deeply erotic somehow. She was pretty sure he'd lost his ability with speech, since he said nothing apart from the occasional warlike cries she'd heard from him in the tunnel. Even then he'd still been able to speak, even though his voice had been ragged and changed. Now he spoke with only the touch of his hawk's body, urging her up onto her knees.

If she'd wanted him on his back, it would have been impossible because of the wings—she'd gathered that much from the way he'd practically tossed her off of him as his transformation began. No, it was pretty obvious how he wanted to take her—how he planned to accomplish it; from behind, with her spread beneath him. She leaned forward, her hands splayed against the mattress, her back arched, giving him eager access. He wrapped one forearm about her belly and balanced with his other hand, the talons digging into the mattress. He was trying to control himself, to hold back a little.

"Don't try to control it," she said, moaning as she felt his hips push up against hers, then the first penetration of him right inside her. She felt his tip slide in, gliding with her wetness, but then suddenly he was much bigger, impossibly big as he filled her fully. Clutching at the mattress beneath them, she gasped, her eyes watering. She felt her body stretch to accommodate him, and for a brief moment there was a sharp flash of pain.

Then just fullness, deep oneness. That forearm tightened about her ribs, pinning her against his body. He was so careful with his talons, too, keeping them away from her skin—yet managing to cradle her against his massive body with utter possession. Gentleness and harshness, the two twined together in the man, each facet inseparable from the other. Light and dark, roughness and tenderness.

Breathing heavily in her ear, he withdrew slightly, and it left her aching for him already. She lifted her buttocks, showing him what she wanted—more of him, deeper, harder. He answered by thrusting inside of her again, sheathing himself with an eerie hawk's cry, low against her ear.

"You're . . . amazing." She panted, and, carefully moving her right hand so she kept herself balanced against the mattress, she managed to cover his raptor's talons. She felt that altered hand curl beneath hers, heard him hiss sharply.

"You . . . touch . . . me," he rasped against her ear, warm breath fanning her cheek—yet she shivered in reaction.

"Your body is amazing," she said, not really sure what he'd meant.

"You . . . touch . . ." He moved the talons beneath her fingertips, illustrating, then with a helpless moan finished, "what no . . . one would."

Then those hawk's claws bunched beneath her fingertips, and she heard a ripping sound; he'd sheared the sheets with the razor-sharp appendages. Out of the need to stay controlled? To show how dangerous he really was?

"I'm not afraid of you," she said, as over and over he levered his hips behind her, beginning a driving, hungry rhythm. Whereas he'd been careful until now, she sensed him letting loose completely.

She let her eyes drift shut and focused on the feel of his heavy body, half draped across hers: the speeding rhythm he was establishing, the way his groin began to slap against her buttocks, the sweet sound of it. Bending lower down onto the mattress, she let him ride her; turning her head slightly, she rested her cheek against the cool sheet. The position gave him even deeper access, and as he plunged far into her, she felt slick pleasure. It was as if he wanted to erode the separation between them.

She worked her hips, lifting toward him, and this produced a rumbling groan of absolute pleasure. He took hold of her hip, the rough talons scraping against her flesh, and sped his rhythm wildly. She met every thrust and pull with her own body, working the friction he was creating. His thrusting intensified. Became more focused, deliberate. Then hard and consuming.

The wings ... the wings were a critical part of it all, she thought as if through a haze. She could hear them, the way they moved the air about their joined bodies; it was as if the wings were beating out his pleasure with every motion.

As they pressed onward, their words giving way to cries and muffled groans and stabbing sounds of wonder, something shifted—something substantial between them that Shay didn't understand and didn't bother to question. His wings suddenly stilled, wrapping about her arms, securing her hard against his chest. She ached to touch them, but it was all she could do to keep her balance, both hands planted on the mattress beneath them.

She lost herself, muffled in the feathers and his hard, large body.

This had to be more than simple lovemaking. He was *owning* her somehow. Taking something—at last—that had always belonged to him anyway.

"Shh," he whispered hoarsely. "Don't question! Give it...."

At that exact moment her whole body quaked, tightened about him, taking her to the purest release she'd ever known in any man's arms. Over and over she rode the tidal waves that he'd released. Throwing her head back, she moaned uncontrollably, tears of release filling her eyes.

As she reached the final wave's crest, he wrapped a forearm about her waist, gripping her against him. With a helpless cry, more of a raptor's song than shout, he shot into her; it was different than with any human man she'd ever had sex with. Whatever Ajax truly was, his seed was as lava-hot as the rest of his transformed body. For a moment they still rocked as one, hips pressed to hips. Then together they panted, slowing the motion as his cock relaxed inside of her. He slipped slightly, but she adjusted her hips, not wanting that separation. Even now, with both of them totally spent, she wanted to feel him there, inside her opening.

"Sweetness," he murmured, the word tight and abrasive as it passed his vocal cords. He pressed his forehead against the center of her shoulders and used his wings to wrap about her. To caress her with a cautious, loving motion. His chest and skin were slick with sweat, and she was just as damp along her back where he half rested. Stroking her hair, he whispered in a more normal voice, "You gave it, Shay. Thank you. You gave it." He seemed struck by wonder at whatever this *giving* he was referring to meant.

"Gave what?" she managed between heavy inhalations of breath. There was silence for a moment, and she had the sense that he was wrestling something intense inside himself. "Your heart," he said at last. "You gave it to me completely."

"Yes." She sighed, beaming as she leaned into him. "You have all of me now."

"Thank you. I treasure it. I treasure *you*." He pressed his lips against her nape. "I love you."

Chapter 20

"What time is it?" Shay propped her chin on her steepled hands. She was lying on her belly, hip to hip against Ajax, who, like her, was sprawled facedown. He had his left wing spread across her back, keeping her tucked underneath it in a sweetly protective gesture. Propped on his elbows, he'd hardly glanced away from her in the past twenty minutes, ever since they'd collapsed as one, completed in each other's arms.

That look in his now-black eyes just about unraveled her. There was a shyness there, a bold vulnerability that she'd never seen in any other man's glance—especially after making love with *her*. Her boyfriends had tended to be of one variety: the leap-up-and-dress-*really*-fast type, the sort who would tousle her hair afterward, treating her like some hapless tomboy with their friendly pecks on her cheek. None of that sad parade had ever really *gotten* her—not even Bobby, the guy she'd spent the past several years involved with. They'd finally clanged that relationship's death knell six months earlier, admitting to themselves and each other that they were a terrible match.

Bobby had been an art school poser, all intellect and not very heavy on emotionality. All four years she'd dated him, she'd been groping to be something she wasn't—the girl he'd made it clear he *wanted* her to be.

Not so with Ajax. He already understood her ... he got everything about what drove her passions, what made her live. And now, unlike her postcoital times with Bobby, Jax's entire posture was that of a protector. It was as if he'd just returned from the hardest kind of war and was hell-bent on keeping her totally safe, utterly satisfied. He was a man, and she realized that every one of her lovers until this exact moment had been only boys. Those guys hadn't known what it meant to really love a woman . . . to love *her*.

Still, the real world was a problem at the moment, intruding upon their little Eden.

"Ajax?" She nudged his calf with her toes. "Did you hear me? What time is it?"

"Time doesn't matter right now." He smiled, a slow, beautiful grin that revealed that single dimple of his. The one that made her half-crazy with lust every time she saw it. The man was . . . beyond beautiful. That word was weak, didn't even begin to describe how truly gorgeous Ajax was.

"Well," she disagreed, sliding her toes along his leg, "some of us are just plain ol' mortals. So I really do need to know what time it is."

He reached toward the table on his side of the bed. His hands were human again; in fact, all of him had shifted back to human form except the wings. She had a gut feeling he'd kept those around just for her benefit. Glancing at the clock, then looking toward the window, he made a low sound of dismay.

"What?" she asked, leaning up on both elbows in slight alarm.

"It's just later than I'd hoped. Noon Saturday back in Savannah . . ." His voice trailed off, his black eyebrows knitting together.

"Oh, my God." She scooted out from beneath his wing, and he rolled away from her, instantly absorbing both wings into his body. "My brothers must be freaking out. What happened to Friday night? We were only in that tunnel a little while—"

"Ares monkeyed with time on my end," he explained, leaping from the bed and searching for his clothes. He found the T-shirt first and shrugged into it as he moved about the room. "I lost twelve hours. And from what I gather, you had to sleep off that portal jump in a pretty serious way. You slept almost the entire time I was gone."

She sat up in bed, her thoughts racing. Mason and Jamie had to be going nuts right about now, calling in the National Guard—or their demon-hunting version of it. "I have to call my brothers," she told him, searching the room for any kind of phone.

Ajax picked up his pants and tossed her a BlackBerry. She caught it in midair and stared at it in disbelief, then burst into laughter. "Oh, puh-lease. You do not use a BlackBerry."

He raised an eyebrow, stepping into his pants.

"Isn't that a little . . . I dunno, *pedestrian* for you? Not exactly traditional Spartan fighting gear."

"We avail ourselves of all possible technology—why shouldn't we? Spartans always use good tactics, no matter what century we inhabit." He fastened his pants, then sat down on the edge of the bed. "It's a U.K. phone, so you'll need to put in country code first."

She gave him a blank look. Like she was supposed to know what her own country code was? The farthest she'd ever been from home—under her own steam, not stepping through a mystery portal—was her senior-year trip to Nassau in college.

Jax took hold of the phone, his fingers moving quickly across the keypad. "There." He put the BlackBerry back in her hand. "You can call the U.S. now, no worrying about the country code."

She stared down at his background image, which was priceless—a picture of Optimus Prime from *Transformers.* She began dialing the phone, but suddenly he took it out of her hand. "Your brothers can wait, actually," he said. "I think you need debriefing before you check in."

She shook her head. "By now they're afraid I'm dead."

"Text them," he said, and she took hold of the BlackBerry again.

With all the brevity she could muster, she tapped out a note to Jamie. *In England, totally safe. More to come. Love, Shay (aka Sissy Cat, just so you know it really is me!)*

Oh, Jamie and Mason would wind up framing that one and using it for target practice, at least once she got home.

"Okay, so talk," she said, turning to face Ajax. He patted the spot beside him on the bed, and it hit her for the first time that she was totally naked. Completely bare in front of Jax, and yet she felt perfectly comfortable. Safe.

She crawled beside him and mimicked his posture, leaning against the headboard. Jax slipped one heavy arm about her shoulders, tucking her close against his side. He smiled sheepishly. "I wasn't ready to share you just yet."

Her heart gave a full turn within her chest. Could this huge man be any sweeter when he chose to be? She didn't think so.

She settled against him, figuring that by now Jamie knew she was all right, so she might as well enjoy this peaceful moment. Lord knew when the two of them would have another, she thought, a wave of sadness crashing over her.

She glanced about the room and noted that, oddly enough, it was awfully plush to belong to a Spartan warrior. Maybe that was because Leonidas was a king, she decided. "This place is pretty nice for a Spartan bedroom," she remarked. "I would've figured there'd be wood beams for a mattress or something."

He chuckled to himself over that one, then said simply, "It's a *guest* room."

"Great, so you really do sleep on beds of nails or some such crap?"

"We've made our allowances over time," he told her, and wrapped one of her loose curls about his fingers.

He drew the lock to his nose and gave it a sniff. "Smells like roses," he said offhandedly, then let the lock fall free again. "Many things have changed over time. We've been in and out of the British Isles for the past couple of centuries. We did some serious time in Scotland." He smiled, a distant expression coming into his eyes. "I liked it there. It was a bit like Greece, oddly enough—a rocky land peopled with fierce warriors."

Shay stroked the length of Ajax's side, lingering on his hip. It felt large and solid, filling her whole palm. "Ya know, I've got a weird question for you."

"Fire away." He kissed the top of her head. "I'm an open book to you now."

"All right. I always thought people were smaller a long time ago. You know, George Washington was really five feet tall."

"Actually, as I recall, he was quite large for his time."

She wondered if he came by that knowledge firsthand or from books. "Okay, whatever, but you always hear that people have gotten bigger over time. *Taller.*"

Jax smiled down at her, stroking her cheek. "Your point, sweetness?"

"You are so flipping big, Ajax. Humongous." She shoved at his chest to demonstrate, and he didn't even flinch. But he did look pretty darn proud of himself. "How big are you, anyway?"

"Depends." He gave her a slow, sinful smile. "Are you talking about my height or my other . . . special endowments?"

She slid her palm across his very solid chest, lingering over every plane of hard muscle. Then, with a wicked snort of laughter, she pressed that same palm up underneath his buttocks and gave him a little squeeze. "You are such a bad boy."

"And I just got bigger, by the way." He nodded toward his groin, which, sure enough, had tented in a big way. "The ass hold was a good trick," he told her huskily.

"Ass hold? Is that like *asshole*?" She laughed, leaning back into the crook of his arm. "Or more of a wrestling maneuver?"

"No ass holding when Spartans wrestle."

"I've heard lots and lots of rumors about you Greek

boys." *Rumors about taking male lovers,* she wanted to add, but didn't dare.

He gave his chest a proud thud. "Only the good claims are true."

For a moment she actually felt insecure, wondering if he *had* taken male lovers somewhere in his distant—or not so distant—past. After all, he was an ancient Greek man. She cringed internally, because that thought fed images of other lovers—female, too—and an ugly shot of jealousy slammed her out of nowhere.

"How would you define good rumors, exactly?" she pressed, trying her best to whisk away all the mental images of her Ajax in bed with other women. Other *people.*

He stared down into her eyes, instantly noticing the change in her mood. "Shay . . . what's going on with you?"

"I bet you've had tons of lovers over all these years; that's all I'm saying. Lots of women . . . and were there men, too?"

"My sweet little babbler," he said. "Your jealous streak turns me on."

"You've lived a long time." She could hardly keep the pain out of her voice, and he instantly changed his attitude.

He gave her a sympathetic smile, bent down to kiss her, then rolled onto his side. He drew her up against him, fitting them together face-to-face, tight as puzzle pieces.

"Look, I'm going to tell you a story. First, easy answer—when I was mortal, I was a little taller than most of the Spartans. I was five-foot-seven."

She stared back at him, eyes wide. "Okay, you are seriously joking. You? Barely taller than I am now?"

"Leonidas was only five-foot-five. People *were* smaller back then. We still towered over our enemies; you can be sure of that."

"I have to tell you . . . that just shatters all my fantasies. I'm picturing the Spartans—the scary, badass Spartans everyone lived in fear of—running around on hillsides like a bunch of olive-skinned leprechauns."

He scowled at her, looking truly insulted. "I'm a foot taller now, so why does it even matter? Does it make our deeds any less heroic? Our history any less stunning?"

"Of course not." She swatted him playfully on the chest. "Seriously, though? You're six-foot-seven? For real?"

"In the heat of my change, yes. In my guise of mortal man, I waver between six-foot-four and six-foot-five. Depends on the day, how rested I am. A variety of factors."

She rolled onto her back, giggling as she mimicked him, " 'In my guise of mortal man.' You sound like a walking poetry anthology. Of course, don't color me surprised about *that* one."

"I've been quoted in a few. Anthologies, I mean."

"You're so full of it."

"I'm telling the truth." He stared into her eyes, not blinking. "Who do you think actually wrote that 'Leda and the Swan' poem, anyway?"

She had nothing to say. Was he bullshitting her? Revealing some great literary secret that would tie English professors all around the world into knots?

But then he burst out laughing. "You are so sweetly guileless, love. I am joking now."

"What about my other question? About the lovers?"

He sighed, a deeply melancholy sound. "Too many, I'm afraid—all of the female variety." Watching her, he continued slowly: "I'm not proud of my past, Shay, but I've been wandering lost as Odysseus these past many hundreds of years. I'd given up ever finding you."

"You really were waiting for *me*?"

"The Oracle promised you to me a long time ago."

She sat up beside him, pulling the sheet up over her bare body. "What was it about me? Why was I such a big thing to you?"

He wouldn't look at her, just rubbed his large fingers back and forth along the edge of the sheet for a full minute. She knew to give him room on this one, too. In the short time she'd spent with Ari and Kalias, she'd gathered that Jax's prophecy concerning her was a very important thing—not just to Jax, but period.

"I was told you would answer the endless questions in my soul," he told her softly. "That you would be my greatest love. That every bit of this eternal prison would be worth having endured ... once I found you. Once we joined our souls as one."

Shay shivered at the last sentence. "As one ..."

"It's not a small thing, sweetness. It's far more than being lovers or soul mates. It means that Olympus itself—the Highest God above that place, even—decreed that we had a destiny. A destiny of oneness."

She felt tears sting her eyes and bobbed her head like a compliant child. Her mind was flooded with thoughts and questions, but she was certain they'd all sound inane to this man—this incredible warrior—who had battled time for so long. And had done so all alone, emotionally at least.

"You waited for me," she whispered, clarity hitting her. "You could have taken another wife. Wives ..."

"No. I could not. Not after the taste our Oracle gave me of you." He cast her a cautious glance, then took a deep breath and continued: "You see, it wasn't just the words. That would have been too ... vague. I was made to feel, to truly experience ... all that I just knew in your arms."

"Oh ... wow." She couldn't begin to imagine what it would have been like to wait one thousand years for what he'd just given her. "I'm so sorry." The tears in her eyes began to fall freely. It almost seemed too cruel, what he'd been made to hold on to, this totally ephemeral hope that somehow, some century, he'd eventually find her. "That's not fair."

"Not fair?" he cried, sitting up tall beside her. "You kept me alive. The promise of you. Without that ... There are many types of hell for an immortal like me, Shay. Trust me, I could have found my way into any number of them. Could have been made a demon, could have died an eternal death." His words came out in a rush, but rather than soothing her, they just made her cry harder.

Finally she sat hunched beside him, staring into her lap. She wiped her eyes and gave him the only thing she could, the only real exchange for the faithfulness he'd given her all these years. She told him the truth.

"I love you," she said simply. "Maybe somehow, just like you've loved me ... maybe somehow I always have."

Chapter 21

Jamie bent over yet another bound volume, searching for any clue as to what sort of entity had kidnapped Shay. Had not only kidnapped her, but had taken her to England, for crying out loud—even though her passport was still sitting untouched in their family safe. When he got his hands on her, he was gonna throttle her. Issue full payback for that asinine, annoying, and thoroughly unhelpful text message she'd sent. What he'd written back had been a shorthand of expletives, punctuated by the demand that she phone him. Then, when no call had come, he'd punched in the mysterious U.K. number.

Of course, no answer. And of course there was no record of the number, not in any database he could access.

Jamie sighed, rubbing a palm over the top of his head. All their efforts to protect Shay over the past few years had yielded just one result: disaster. Now she was separated from their power base, vulnerable—and worst of all? She had no idea who she actually was. Ignorance, far from being bliss, had reached out and bitten all of them on the collective ass.

What made the current situation most infuriating was that he'd never wanted to withhold the truth from her. He'd always believed they should tell her about the Eye. In fact, he'd been the one member of their family who'd argued—aggressively—that they should share with Shay every detail about her true identity. To hell with familial consequences and the broken vows it would have meant.

He made a mental note always to trust his instincts from now on, no matter how frightening the potential consequences might seem. It was one of his best strengths as a hunter, so why hadn't he listened to his inner compass when it came to Shay?

Because you wanted to spare her the calling. You wanted to give her a better life, a freer one.

Good intentions—fuck 'em, he thought, flipping another page in the book of lore. The ancient writings and drawings were useless to him, nothing but a blur. There was only one image in his mind's eye at the moment, and that was Shay in the arms of that winged creature, dropping down inside the very earth itself. He could only pray that the looping mental film clip wouldn't haunt him for the rest of his days as the last time that he ever saw his sister alive.

The truth was, he felt powerless, and it wasn't something that ever sat well with him. Since watching her vanish through that hole in the middle of Bay Street, he'd employed every one of his hunter's weapons, availed himself of every strategy in his arsenal. He'd started by doing what he knew best, what had worked in the midst of so many other supernatural battles: He'd brought his team together, uniting their unique and special gifts as they conducted a full-on search.

By midnight they'd wasted five hours and had absolutely nothing to show for their efforts. But why had he even bothered bringing the Shades into this crisis? They were demon hunters, after all, and Jamie was becoming more and more convinced that the creature who'd captured Shay was something totally unique, not demon, not angel, but walking a dangerous in-between place, a forbidden zone within the spiritual realm.

Shay had mentioned the Nephilim from the Old Testament, and so he'd chased that lead exhaustively. He'd pulled out various translations of the Bible—had even made a stab at the original Hebrew text. But that had been fruitless, because he wasn't as proficient with the ancient language as he needed to be. It had been a weak spot of his back in theology school. After that, he and Mason had pored over the Apocrypha, and especially focused on "The Book of Giants," part of the Dead Sea Scrolls that detailed the Nephilim. All of their efforts had been a wash.

"Check this out," Mason called over to him. His brother was crouched beside one of the tall wooden bookshelves that lined this hidden cellar room. The antique cases sagged against the brick walls, almost as if it were their job to keep the place standing.

Mason's back was propped against one of the most heavily weighted bookcases, its shelves drooping beneath the thick volumes it held. Mace squatted there, encircled by at least a dozen stacks of books, and Jamie suddenly pictured his melancholy brother as an island. Mason was the solitary center point, the books his isolating sea.

He hated the sadness that his brother carried around like an anchor. Mason had revealed only a few scant details about Iraq, but it had been enough; Jamie had a pretty good idea of why his brother stayed locked inside himself these days.

And Shay . . . Jamie knew just how close she and Mason were, and how much it had hurt when their brother had begun shutting her out. At least, that was how Shay no doubt saw it, but the truth was more complex. He and Mace had seen things over the years, dark, horrific things that they never wanted her to know about. They had pledged to protect her innocence, and an oath was an oath.

Of course, now that she'd *opened*—now that her gift had come crashing down on her—there wasn't a damned thing they could do to protect her anymore. In fact, Jamie thought with a heavy pang of guilt, whatever she'd gotten involved with was probably their fault. If they'd equipped her, then she would have known how to fight—and she certainly wouldn't have trusted the winged being who had her in his clutches right now.

"Shay was convinced he was good," Jamie observed aloud, annoyed that Mason had gotten lost in the book again.

His brother slowly lifted his gaze, his thumb holding his place in the text. "What made her think that?"

"She said he saved her life. That he protected her from an attacking demon horde."

Mason glanced at the page as if he were lured back to it against his will. "Doesn't sound like the act of a hostile demon," he said absently.

Jamie slammed his own book shut. "Would you set that fucking book down and talk to me?"

Shaking his head as though awakening from a dream—an expression he had assumed too many times over the past few months, Jamie thought—Mason let the leather volume slip closed. "Sorry," he said in a haunted voice. "This is some spooky shit, man." Slowly he rose to his feet and walked toward Jamie, holding the book in front of him. "And the weirdest thing is that I've never seen this book before in my life.

That *was* weird, considering how many years the two of them had spent reading the family lore.

Jamie flipped the book sideways so he could read the spine. The title was in Greek.

" '*The Final Crossing*,' " he translated aloud. Not that Mason needed the help; he'd learned ancient Greek on their father's knee. Jamie hadn't been so adept at languages; it had taken years of formal schooling to fill those gaps in his education.

Even now, as he flipped to the page Mason had marked, the translation came to him too slowly. With a burst of angry frustration he said, "Just tell me what it says. Okay?"

Mason slid into the vacant chair beside Jamie and quietly retrieved the book. He cleared his throat and began to make the translation.

" 'But of winged beings, I was shown and told of four types, three that hold significance for this present discussion.' " Mason paused and turned toward Jamie. "The writer—no name given—claims to have gotten all this by divine guidance. He's prophesying here. Or so he says."

Jamie felt a rush of adrenaline pumping into his system. Whatever Mason quoted next was going to be crucial information. He felt it, knew it by his innate instincts. "Go on." He nodded eagerly.

Mason squinted as he read, lifting the book closer to his eyes. Even though it was midday, the only light in the musty room came from an old-fashioned library lamp over in the far corner of the room. It sat askew atop a weathered wooden filing cabinet that housed all their father's research and notes. The drawers contained the sum of his life's work as a demon hunter.

" 'We know of angels and we know of demons, and the holy texts tell of the Nephilim.' " Mason hesitated, meeting Jamie's eyes significantly. " 'Although no living man, no woman, no child, has ever seen one of the fallen ones who were once called Nephilim. It is thought these giants perished with the Great Flood, or perhaps, some speculate, they created a kingdom of their own here in mighty Greece.' "

"What does that mean?" Jamie scratched his head in exasperation. On normal days he was more than content to spend hours thumbing through their family archives chasing down arcane knowledge. But this was no ordinary day, and with Shay's life on the line he was out of patience.

"The scriptures indicate that the Nephilim were children of fallen angels and mortal man." Mace continued to stare at the open volume, his eyes scanning the pages.

"And that's what this protector of Shay's is?" Jamie sighed in frustration. "That's what you're saying?"

"Hang on." Mason ran his fingertip along the page, searching for some bit of text. "The important part is . . . here." He continued reading much more quickly. " 'The fourth winged creature, the one shrouded in mystery, has no given name. These are the mighty warriors, the ones who were born beside the great River Styx. If any vow is taken upon that river's shadowy banks, the vow will stand forever. Seven warriors of unknown caste pledged such a vow there—a vow that placed dread wings upon their backs.' "

Slowly Mason closed the book and slid it toward Jamie. "That's all it says about the topic."

"You're saying you don't think Shay's entity is one of the Nephilim, after all?"

"How did he strike you ... when we met him the other night?" Mason leaned back in his chair, folding both hands beneath his chin in a thoughtful posture. "The way he addressed us ... his authority? Seemed like a military guy to me. He had the *bearing* of a warrior, like the book says."

"You're basing that impression on what, precisely?" Jamie shook his head. "A ten-second exchange where he tried to tell us how to take care of our own damned sister?"

"Just saying my money would be on military background, that's all." Mason shrugged, thoughtful. "Not just that ... I've seen things in the past few years that I'd have sworn couldn't exist. Daddy gained all kinds of knowledge as a hunter—new information. Who says that we can't?"

Jamie drummed his fingers on the book, recalling his first instinct about the winged man when Shay had described him last night: that the being was a new revelation; something never before cataloged by the Nightshades. Until now.

"Shay was convinced that the winged entity was her protector in some way," he said, repeating his earlier thought. "That he was good."

Mason leaned back in his chair. "Here's a radical thought: Maybe she's right."

"Your book tells us nothing of real value, just raises more questions," Jamie argued. "We have nothing to go on beyond what Shay told me."

Mason smiled. "Yeah, well, here's radical thought

number two: Maybe, after all the mistakes we've made, we should start listening to Shay for a change."

River descended the upper stairs of Leonidas's castle and rolled his eyes when he heard laughter coming from the main guest room. They'd spent days worried about his master's ass, and now the man had holed himself up to *get* some ass? Loud sex. Bumpity-bump sex that the whole bleeding house couldn't possibly tune out. They had work to do, strategies to enact—each of them did. Work that didn't happen to include sheathing the broadsword, either.

Besides, it wasn't exactly like he'd been getting any himself lately. Not like *certain* warriors, who managed to dip the quill in every inkpot they could locate. His body still thrummed with sexual need from his portal jump only hours earlier; the last thing he needed was to overhear the act itself.

He growled, feeling a painful amount of sexual frustration as he jogged down the steps two at a time. So the bastard had found Shay; good for him. But the least he could've done was talk strategy before bedding the beautiful human.

He grumbled some more, made for the main door that led outside, and then stopped in his tracks. The loneliness and heartbreak Ajax had experienced all these years had been immense. River knew that acutely, understood it more than any of the others in the cadre. So why was he begrudging Jax this moment, this long-awaited happiness?

You're jealous, you idiot. You're fucking jealous because you have no one of your own. Because your only release, time after time, is to spill your own damned seed into your own hand.

"Get over yourself," he mumbled aloud, and left the castle.

Outside, the late-afternoon sun sat low on the horizon. After being inside the gloomy castle for so long, River had to squint against the sharp brightness as he searched the training ground. Leonidas had gotten his debriefing, then cautioned River to take some cooling-down time in isolation; his king knew all too well how volatile River could be at times. Sometimes it took days for his blood to run normally in his veins, for the berserker inside of him to go fully dormant.

River felt mostly stabilized, and too much planning was required for him to hide out any longer, so he was ready to join the ranks. But a quick glance about the training area and it was clear that none of the warriors were around. So he trotted down the hill toward their weight-training complex, a modern building that Leonidas had made them construct by hand—much to the lads' complaints. As he got closer, River spotted Leonidas and the other warriors. They were outside the exercise facility, gathered on a long stone patio, spread out among the tables and chairs. On sunny days they often took mess right there. Today it appeared that Leonidas had converted it into a temporary command center.

The king bent over the long stone table, brow furrowed as he studied the prophecy. The parchment was unrolled, Kalias holding down the top edge with his hand. River strode toward the gathered Spartans, thankful that it looked like Leonidas was able to literally *see* the prophecy—he'd wondered how that would shake out. Sure, Ajax could certainly read the prophecy aloud to each of them, but River for one thought there was security in having more than just one of their corps who could accomplish the job. A little built-in redundancy was never a bad idea.

As River joined the gathered men, he caught a bit of their conversation. They were deliberating about the meaning of a key phrase in the document, something about "Oglethorpe on the square." Everyone seemed genuinely puzzled about it.

River stepped into the circle, taking a place beside Ari, who smiled at him. "James Edward Oglethorpe founded the colony of Georgia," River volunteered. Except for

Ajax, the full crew was present, and they all looked at him.

He should've kept his trap shut, he decided, given the way they were all staring at him. "I mean, I'm sure you already know that about Oglethorpe." River had always admired Oglethorpe's efforts to create a colony for a ragtag, forgotten group—people not unlike him and his fellow helots.

Nikos shot him a snide look. "We did just spend the past two hours inside the castle researching, *Cassandra*."

Nikos loved feminizing River's surname—in fact, the bullying warrior loved taking jabs at him any way he could think of.

River took an angry step toward his foe, the unstable heat in his blood boiling forth once again, but Ari caught his elbow, holding him subtly back. River swallowed hard, took a deep breath, and willed his darker nature to settle down. After an edgy moment he relaxed, and Ari released him.

Nikos ignored the movement and continued a little less sharply: "We've chased every possible lead on this thing." His eyes narrowed on River. The message was clear: *I've got this one covered and you're not invited onto my team.*

Leo's private study had long ago been transformed into a techno-junkie's paradise, and it was Nikos himself who kept them wired for the future. Which pretty much sucked a big one, since River's favorite pastime was research. He could happily Google and Wiki and chase crazy leads through cyberspace all day long and never get bored. But Nikos generally ran those operations, so if River wanted in on the research team, he usually had to cross Nikos's drawbridge. It got old always having to be the one to make nice, especially on days like this one, when his reactions were so volatile.

Leonidas gestured toward a map of the city. "Oglethorpe Square is right downtown. This should be the starting place for Ajax and Shay tomorrow morning. Then this bit"—Leonidas leaned over the prophecy and read—"has us speculating. 'Where the bird flies east and west, held in balance by a young girl's hand, eternity stands to balance, too, held affixed upon the square.' "

"So that's why you think it's Oglethorpe Square?" River asked.

Leonidas nodded. "It's mentioned earlier in the prophecy."

The cadre had already done their research, and River figured it would take Shay herself—and some fancy footwork on all their parts in Savannah—to solve the prophecy anyway. Besides, he had pressing business of his own with Leonidas, so he decided to hold his tongue.

They went back to combing over the prophecy, with several of the warriors deliberating over the part about the bird flying east and west. Ari maintained that it was a trick phrase, because none of them could fly in both directions at the same time.

The discussion went on for some time, and River listened and speculated in silence—and waited to have just one moment alone with his king. He prayed for the ideal moment when he would somehow manage to get Leonidas to hear his plan. It was a radical strategy, what he wanted to propose, but despite his earlier moment of irritation with Ajax, he loved his master. And more than any of the other Spartans, River had a dark, dire feeling about what the outcome of all this might be.

Every time River tried to picture the face-off, instead of the usual silver portal he visualized a black hole. Empty, gaping space . . . a dark maw that wanted to suck all of them down into its destroying power.

River fought the dark, foreboding sense that instantly shadowed his spirit as Leonidas broke from the group. River scrambled to catch up with the large man's strides. "My king," he began, "may I have a moment, sir?"

"What troubles you, young River?"

River stopped for a moment, surprised that his mood had been so transparent to his king. "How did you . . . ?"

Leonidas chuckled. "It's a commander's job to be

aware of the thoughts and moods of his men," he said. "You've not been yourself since this entire Savannah venture began." He stopped and looked River in the eye, his gaze as always a mixture of sternness and warmth. "Since you returned from fighting Elblas."

River said nothing. Slowly they began walking again, Leonidas guiding them back toward the training ground. How could River explain to his king the power of the bad premonitions that he kept getting about his master?

"Ajax is in jeopardy right now, my lord," River began, the words pouring forth as if liberated from deep inside his heart. "I believe that facing Elblas again is the battle of his life. Jax's mind isn't clear because of Shay ... too many factors are colliding." He slapped his palms together in demonstration. "But it's Ajax himself who has the most at stake, who has the cruelest history with Sable. He wants to protect Shay from Sable ... at all costs."

River thought of the feral look he'd seen in his master's eyes back in the tunnel. He'd been half-crazed with his need to protect Shay from the ancient Djinn. "I am very uncomfortable with the way this is proceeding, sir," River said simply. "I just had to say it."

Leonidas rubbed a hand thoughtfully across his curling beard. "But you have a strategy in mind?"

"It's radical." River held his breath, keeping his posture rigid, as if bracing for a slap to the face. Leonidas slid an arm about his shoulder, and slowly River released that tightly contained breath.

"I like radical." Leonidas gave him a slow, conspiratorial smile. "Let me hear it."

The plan *was* radical—and it was dangerous—but River couldn't shake the feeling that it was the only way to keep Ajax safe ... and truly defeat Elblas at long last.

"I need to tell you something else." Ajax glanced at Shay, anxiety obvious in his eyes. That expression on his face—a face that she'd already come to associate with protection, worship, safety—caused her belly to tighten nervously, because the apprehension there could spell only one thing: incredible pain. It was like a bad omen written right into the onyx depths of his gaze.

It was more than his eyes, more than the guardedly nervous expression she saw there. It was his tone of voice. She'd heard that same tone enough times in her life to recognize it. Her own family had talked to her that same way plenty of times—and almost always on painful occasions, awful and scary ones.

Danger dead ahead. That was the warning flag that Ajax had just tossed right in her face with his carefully chosen words and edgy tone.

"Oh-kay." She braced herself physically for whatever he would reveal next, her entire body tensing against his. Suddenly she wished she weren't naked anymore, that she weren't that vulnerable. "Bring it on. Whatever *it* is."

"Don't look at me that way, sweetness." His voice managed to sound even more heavily burdened, sadder, as he tucked the sheet up over her exposed chest. That he was physically covering her proved what she already knew—that he wanted to protect her from the inevitable, from whatever the dreadful thing was that he would tell her in the next moment.

"Just do it already." She clutched the sheet beneath her chin, shivering.

He rolled to face her and bent close, kissing first her nose, then the edge of her lips. "It's not completely bad news, I promise. Ultimately good news ... or at least, I hope you'll feel that way."

She wrapped both arms about his neck, tugging him closer, flush against her body. Whatever he was going to reveal, it couldn't be that bad, not if he was lying here, kissing her so calmly. "I like good news." She tried to sound cheery, but totally missed the mark. "Well, so long as it's not actually *bad* news pretending to be good."

"A bit more complicated than that, I'm afraid."

She gave a nod for him to continue, practically begging for the truth. "Just go on."

He curled his forearm over her side, nuzzling her closer against him. "There's a trick to this immortality game, you know," he finally began. "I've waited so long for you, searched forever for you. Year after year, it just seemed endless." He paused, tentatively looking into her eyes.

"And now you have me." She gave him a bright smile, terrified of where the conversation was heading.

He smiled back at her, a genuinely radiant and happy look that gave her a momentary surge of hope. Maybe he wasn't about to tell her something awful after all. Maybe Earth really wasn't going to spin off its axis and land on the other side of the galaxy.

"You *have* me, Ajax," she repeated, holding him a little bit tighter in her arms.

"Oh, and finding you is such perfection, I don't want to lose you. Not ever again." He stroked her hair, fingertips brushing her cheek. The rough pads were scratchy against her skin, but she loved the pure maleness of him. "Shayanna, I can't lose you. Do you understand what I'm saying? I will not go through the waiting and longing and searching. Never again."

His hold on her had become like a death grip, until his fingers practically dug into her naked flesh. She could feel how his hands trembled, how desperate his grasp on her had become.

"I don't . . ." She was confused. What was he afraid of? Why was he shaking so hard? Especially if he was declaring his love for her and his intention to always keep her in his life. His fear was at odds with everything he was telling her, except . . .

I can't lose you . . . .I can't lose you. Lose you. His words began droning in her head until they crystallized, hypnotic and chilling. That was when it hit her, the terrible truth he was dancing around.

Down deep into the marrow of her bones, a chill hit her hard. She began to shake all over, and as she closed her eyes a sharp rivet of pain stabbed her like a blow to the chest. Because she knew. Knew what had this ancient warrior holding her as if she were his only lifeline, trembling uncontrollably as he clung to her.

"I do not ever want to lose you again, love." He buried his face against her shoulder, the swath of her black hair obscuring his eyes. Yet she heard tears in his thick voice.

"You don't want to lose me," she repeated, tears filling her own eyes.

"Never, by the gods. I can't."

"But I'm not gonna live forever. Not like you." It had been staring her straight in the eyes from the moment she'd first met him; she just hadn't wanted to look deeply enough.

Jax shifted on the bed, rolling onto his back. "I always believed, all those waiting years, that it wouldn't matter to me," he said, staring at the ceiling. She had the sense that he didn't want her to see the powerful sadness in his eyes, but it was too late for that. She'd already glimpsed—and heard—more than enough. "That although you'd be mortal, I would accept that limitation on our love ... that I would take whatever years with you the Highest chose to give me. That I'd accept the pure gift of you ... no matter how brief our time together might be."

She was going to wither and grow old in his immortal arms; her face would assume lines and furrows and then eventually sag, while his remained eternally the same. Her body would toughen like leather, betraying them both. It wasn't a proposition she could accept, not for either of them.

"I don't want that," she admitted in a hoarse voice. "I want to be with you ... always."

He rolled back toward her, his own face set in harsh, grim planes. Those lines aged him, and for a brief moment she imagined him weathered by the years. She wanted to grow old with him—or not—but either way, she wanted them on the same time progression. Anything else would only be cruel.

"Yes, sweetness, that's what I want, too. And there is

a way—there is only one way, in fact—for us to walk eternity together."

"Tell me what it is. I'll do it, anything. Anything you ask, Ajax, and I swear I'll agree," she blurted, words rushing forth. "If we can just be together." She squeezed his upper arm, trying to give it a little shake of determination, but, of course, he didn't budge.

It was a crazy, irrational statement—that she'd do anything and everything he might ask of her. They'd only just met, and her pledge should have been a ludicrous one ... and yet she felt a sense of total completion with him. She'd dreamed of him before—she knew it now—perhaps more times than she even knew for certain; she'd sketched him, too. In her heart and soul, the literal number of days or hours they'd already spent together meant nothing, not with the way she already loved him. The only thing that did matter was that somehow, supernaturally, the two of them had already walked eternity together.

He stared at her, and that look in his eyes' black depths—oh, God, it tore at her heart. It was pure grief that she saw there, harsh pain. He wanted to protect her against the heartache that he himself already felt. She could see it in his eyes.

"Shay—"

"Don't try to spare me this!" She shoved him hard in the chest. "You tell me what I've gotta do," she ground out, already battling time itself just to stay with him.

"We have to follow this latest prophecy, the one given us by the Oracle herself."

This big *Romeo and Juliet* buildup was about the prophecy? That didn't seem right. "That scroll from the tunnel?" she asked in confusion.

"It will guide me—guide *us*—to find a priceless object that the gods demand."

That sounded easy enough. Sure, big-ass treasure hunt, just her sort of thing. "I'm in."

She raised her fist in a *take-one-for-the-team*-style gesture, but deep inside she already knew the truth. This object was only going to spell some horrible form of doom. You didn't grow up on a solid diet of Hollywood sci-fi and adventure movies without being able to recognize the tragic hero's journey when it knocked you upside the head.

"So why are we rolling around in bed? We've got a treasure to find," she stated, throwing the covers off her body in a frantic move to get ready. She found her shirt hanging from the back of the doorknob, still damp and hopelessly dirty. "Ugh, my shirt is a no-go."

"I've got clean clothes for you."

"Really? How'd you pull that one off?" She marched about the room, searching for those supposedly clean clothes, pacing first one way, then another. She felt trapped, crazed, and suddenly she just couldn't stay still for another moment. If she could only keep moving, then maybe he wouldn't tell her just how bad things really looked for them.

"I need to find something to wear," she continued, looking under the bed for one of her errant shoes.

He caught her by the crook of her arm. "Shay, please stop babbling . . . and moving around this room like a frantic hummingbird. Please just come and sit down beside me on the bed so I can explain."

She pulled out of his grasp and kept searching for the other shoe. "Nope. We just keep going and stay happy-happy, and then it won't be real."

"What won't?"

"Whatever it is that you haven't told me yet," she said, shaking out her shirt. It was beyond repair, ripped in the back from when she'd taken her wild water ride down the tunnel. She held it up toward the light, frowning.

All at once Jax let loose with a loud, angry burst of ancient Greek. She slowly lowered the shirt, staring at him.

He volleyed another round of less angry—but more emotional—words in his native tongue.

"In English?" she half whispered, dropping her shirt to the floor. She walked, barefoot and naked, to settle beside him on the bed.

"I wanted you to hear me." His voice was desperate, aching. He sat there beside her, his chest heaving as if he couldn't even find his breath.

She lifted a hand to his face, stroking his light beard. "I'm scared, okay? I know it's bad. That whatever it is . . ." She shook her head. *No more running. No more allowing others to protect you.* She met his gaze resolutely. "Tell me."

"It's a mirror." Jax took her hand in his much bigger one. He squeezed their palms together, staring at the way they joined. "It's called the Looking Glass of Eternity. And if I can find it—if I can discover its hidden location in Savannah before Sable does—I'll be set free from my immortal prison."

This wasn't the terrible news she'd anticipated; it was a miracle. He could become mortal again, just like her. There would be no inconsistency between their two worlds, and they would age in the same progression.

"Really? Oh, my God, Ajax!" She flung both arms about his neck, burying her face in the tangle of his long hair. "That's amazing, incredible. Yes, I'll help you find it . . . of course I will." She held him even tighter, releasing a little squeal of excitement.

But he didn't shout along with her—didn't even try to kiss her or wrap those big arms about her equally tightly. Slowly she disengaged and stared up into his eyes. "You *are* saying that if we find this mirror that you'll be set free. Right?"

His black eyes drifted shut. "I am."

"But obviously not like I'm hoping."

He remained silent.

"So you're not saying that we get to live together, in the here and now, and grow old together like any other normal, *mortal* couple would do?"

"I leave you here, sweetness," he said in an emotion-filled voice. "It's the only way."

She had to swallow several times before she could speak. As she studied their clasped hands, her vision grew blurry. She blinked, swallowed again. "You'll have to die. That's what you're telling me," she whispered. "That you'll find this mirror and ... and what? Step into the afterlife and leave me here on my own, without you?"

"When your days are done, you will join me. The separation is only for this life, Shay. But then we'll be together for all time."

"And you'll be set free; I get that. Very big thing." She sniffed as heavy, rolling tears streaked down her face. "After all the years you've had to fight as a warrior, the endless time of loneliness ... I can't be selfish. I know." The tears fell harder, and she made a disgusting sniveling sound.

Jax laughed gently and reached to the side table, where he found a tissue. "Here, love. Here." He wiped her nose, then pressed his forehead against hers. It was as if he wanted to absorb all her sadness.

"I have to let you die." She sobbed.

"I pass to the afterlife, that's all." His voice grew choked, and he held her for several long moments before continuing. "I go and wait for your mortal days to end. This way we are together forever."

She bobbed her head in agreement even though her heart was breaking into bitter pieces. "And together eternally, not just for a brief period here on Earth, me getting old and haggard, you staying like you are now, so beautiful and virile."

"I go and wait for you, sweetness," he repeated softly, stroking her hair. "It's only for a brief time."

Compared with the sands upon sands of eternity that had already passed for him, yes, it would be brief. But she would be alone—potentially for the next fifty, sixty, or even seventy years. It was too much for even Ajax to ask of her.

"I can't help you with this." She shook her head violently. "You're asking me to help you die. I won't. I can't do that. It's too much."

"You're wrong, Shayanna. I'm not asking you to help me die." He seized her by both shoulders, forcing her to look him in the eyes. "I'm asking you to set me *free*. I can't stay here, can't live here for eternity . . . and only have you for just this little while. I, of all people, know how brief mortal life truly is. You'll join me again on the other side. Trust me . . . help me find the mirror. Help set me free . . . help *us* be together. For all time."

"And what happens to me? I spend all those years alone? Wandering and waiting? I won't do it. You take me with you. When this mirror frees you, I go, too."

He bowed his head, shaking it. "No. You live here—without me—for only a short time. There's a world still waiting for you here. Maybe you will have children. Maybe you will love again—several times." Then he jerked his gaze to hers. "But they won't be me. You won't be lonely in this life, but it's me you will cross over and join when your life is done."

Burying her face in both hands, she sobbed. "It's too much. You're asking too much."

He drew her into his arms, held her close against his warm chest. She thought of his endless wait for her, a thousand years. Couldn't she wait just another sixty or seventy?

"I'm asking you to believe in us," he whispered against her ear. "To believe in me."

You're asking me to help you break my heart, she wanted to cry. But in that same heart, she knew that he never would have asked for this, not if there were another way. And she knew that he asked only because he loved her. That realization left her with only one option. Because she did love him, there had never been any real choice, not from the first moment they'd met.

"I'll do it," she promised at last.

Chapter 22

Leonidas sank heavily onto the edge of his bed. Over the past few days he'd spent the bulk of his time guiding the warriors, strategizing. It always drained his solitary nature to go so long without a quiet moment alone with his own thoughts.

His heart beat heavily in his chest. What River had asked of him had been radical indeed, and although he'd consented, his approval now weighed on him like a bad omen.

The young warrior planned to shape-shift into weapon form before Ajax created the portal that would transport them back to Savannah. And, not only that, but he intended to *remain* in that altered state for the mission's entire duration. They had no precedent for what such a long-term transformation might do to River's immortal body. Or how it would impact his return, that feral berserker nature that literally served as River's double-edged sword. So long transformed and the young warrior might return to human form insane, fully berserk, without a hope of regaining his rational mind.

There was even the possibility that he'd never be able to revert to his human body again; that he'd be cast forever as a silver knife or dagger . . . whatever clandestine form he chose to assume for the journey.

But Leonidas had given his okay, because the gravity of the mission demanded it. With a sigh he rose to his feet. Perhaps a warm shower would calm him, he thought. Many things had changed over the eternal years—one of them being that the Spartans did allow themselves minor measures of comfort, like long, soaking showers or satisfying meals. Still, he knew that none of their recently acquired pleasures would satisfy his current restlessness. No, there was only one person who could work a spell over him right now, and she was quite literally nowhere to be seen.

Stripping out of his shirt, he wished his lovely Oracle carried a cell phone. If she did, he would make an exception and use his own that generally sat untouched on his nightstand. More than that, he wished that she lived in the realm that he walked on a daily basis. As otherworldly as his own plane was, the Oracle tripped her way along on another one entirely. He smiled, thinking of the joyous bounce she almost always had in her step, the way she made that constant heaviness on his shoulders a bit lighter.

It wasn't that he yearned to take her out dancing or to a pub, or any of those predictable courting sorts of things. All he really wanted was to curl beside the fire with her in his arms and make love to her. To stroke her crazy blue streaks and kiss them; to entwine his heavy body all about her petite one.

He laughed to himself chidingly. *I need a shower, all right, but not a warm one.*

Walking toward his bath, he caught a glimpse of his bare chest in the mirror and winced at the image that met him. There were more scars on his body than he could count, the worst of which was a brutal band that encircled the top of his right arm. Of all the Spartan immortals, his body had been most abused at his death—and after. He'd been put on display as a war trophy, carried and tossed among the Persian throng. Or so he'd been told. His essence had already been deep into its journey toward Elysium before all of that happened. Thank the gods he hadn't truly lived it.

As for the thick scar about his arm, it was a memento of the blow that had ended his life. A gleaming Persian sword had sliced the thing right off. The arm had been restored, of course, like the rest of him, at the moment when Ares had dipped him into the River Styx. But the pain and the evidence of his mistreatment would linger throughout eternity.

He continued staring at his reflection, at the ribbed and puckered war wounds that he carried with him like threadbare baggage. The other Spartans had been luckier, their wounds healing neatly at their moment of immortal transformation. Not so for him. This battered form was the best he'd ever get.

Normally he didn't mind the facts about his appearance. Maybe it was the edgy expectation he felt about the Savannah mission that had him so unsettled. Maybe, if he dared to admit his deepest fear, he worried that the Oracle would never find him physically appealing: not like this, stripped of his armor, out of his linen shirt.

"You're much too old to be thinking about all of this," he told his reflection, laughing faintly to himself.

"Old, shmold, I'm so tired of hearing that talk from you."

He jolted physically, actually lifting onto his tiptoes as the Oracle appeared just beside him in the mirror's reflection. Spinning to face her, he immediately remembered his half-naked state and folded both arms protectively across his chest.

"You said . . . you came to my chambers sometimes, but . . ." He let the words dangle, not even sure how to finish.

She beamed up at him, slipping both hands onto his forearms, rubbing his sore muscles. "I also said I never peeked."

He lowered his eyes. "Fortunately enough."

Gently she pried at his arms, trying to get him to relax his physical stance. "So this is my big chance," she announced brightly, even as he resisted her efforts.

He gulped despite himself. "Big chance for what exactly?"

She slapped him on the chest. "Let those mighty arms drop, Spartan."

He smiled slowly, still gazing into those pale, mysterious eyes. "I won't."

He shivered; it was so unlike his Spartan nature to react to any change of temperature. But the chill of his room made a sharp contrast to the heat of her hands—hands that seemed absolutely determined to slide across his chest in a truly wanton manner. They wrestled together for a full minute, a playful battle of push and pull, a forbidden dance between the king and his Oracle.

Until she changed her tack. Quite suddenly she stopped her tussling, wide-eyed. Staring at his disfigured upper arm, she reached out and touched his thick scar.

He jerked away from her. "Don't do that," he snapped in shock.

But she made such a soft, soothing sound as she reached toward him again—and her fingers felt so tender as they came into contact with that always-heated mark—that he fell right under her spell. Somehow it no longer mattered if she saw the vicious scars that covered his body.

"My dear, beautiful king," she murmured, fingers still massaging his worst mark. "Why did they treat you so cruelly? This body of yours was worth more than any human treasure. Much beyond its weight in gold. Oh, my sweet, brave Leo . . ."

The words seemed to catch in her throat. She bowed her head for a moment, coughing slightly. When she did meet his gaze again, her eyes—those normally joy-filled, *playful* eyes—were brimming with tears on his behalf. He reached for her, unable to tolerate that kind of pain in her sweet gaze.

"Don't, please," she murmured, the tears falling freely down her cheeks.

By the gods, he'd not wanted her to know his private pain. Then again, what had he expected? She was his Oracle, after all—of course she'd experienced all his memories when she'd touched his scar. With her higher vision she'd known every moment of his torture, how viciously the Persians had treated him. The triumphant way they'd paraded his dead body among their thronging masses, passing it from shoulder to shoulder in jeering victory.

"If you cry, my lady, I just might cry, too." He cupped her chin, forcing her to look at him.

She forced a halfhearted smile. Then all at once it grew much brighter and genuine. "Kiss me," she commanded.

"Is that why you came here, to my bedchamber? Because of what you wanted me to do to you, wanted me to touch you?" His heart thundered like a pack of wild horses as he thought about how close his bed was to them. How easy it would be to take her, finally, to strip her clothes off and slide inside of her. "You came for me to bed you," he whispered hotly, one hand already moving toward his belt.

"Alas, no." She gave a graceful little bow and his hand froze. "I'm here on official business, but you can't blame me for trying to steal a kiss . . . or, or . . . whatever I can."

She wasn't even finished talking before he'd covered her mouth with his, wrapping her fast against his bare chest. In an awkward walking tangle, he moved them toward the bed, neither of them breaking the kiss. They hit the mattress like a body slam, collapsing backward in each other's arms. As they bounced from the fall, she bit his lower lip upon impact, and he wanted to laugh when the tangy taste of blood filled his mouth.

She gasped in horror, sitting right up on the bed. "I am so sorry," she told him earnestly.

He leaned on one elbow, watching her, heat absolutely boiling in his blood. "For what?"

"I bit you. Okay, that's beyond awful. I bit—*bit*—the great King Leonidas." She shook her head and bounded to her feet, blurting, "Gotta go, gotta go."

"Oracle!" He reached for her, laughing. "I don't mind that you bite!"

She buried her face behind her hands, clearly so mortified that nothing he said would rescue the situation. "I came to say that Shay should remember these words," she rushed, never dropping her hands. "Shay should remember to 'tell thee fair.' It's in the scroll, but remind her of those words in particular. If I'd told her, I would have been trespassing too much on the compact with Ares. So I'm telling you, Leonidas. *You.* Be sure to remind her, please."

She peeked out at him from behind fanned fingers, face bright red. "I wasn't supposed to come," she added, "so it's not just the biting. I must go before ... *he* finds out."

And she did, just as swiftly as she'd arrived. Only, with her absence, a hollow sensation filled Leonidas's chest. He sank back down against the mattress, imagining that the Oracle was still there with him, that she was kissing his scars, caressing his ruined body. Then, with a flick of his tongue, he tasted the metallic bite of his own blood one more time.

"No way, Kassandros. No bloody way I'm letting you do it," Jax said.

"Leonidas has already given his approval," River replied sharply. "You plan to defy the Old Man?" River stared at him, clearly aghast. But Jax wasn't about to allow his friend and servant to risk what he'd just suggested.

"We have no precedent for this." He clasped River by both shoulders, staring hard into his familiar eyes. "We don't know what might happen to you, and I won't risk your life. Not for mine, not like this. And I won't risk your sanity either."

River wriggled free, pacing first one direction, then another in front of the fireplace, his extreme anxiety more than obvious. A blaze roared in the stone hearth; so many times Leonidas's great room had meant safety and protection. But tonight Jax wondered if it would be the last time he ever warmed himself by the hearth.

If he found the Looking Glass of Eternity, Jax would step into the afterlife. He would finally be at peace as he waited for Shay, as he counted off the days until he could be with her for all time. But if he failed in his mission, the result was almost unthinkable: Sable would be freed from his desert exile permanently, and no doubt his first order of business would be finding a way—some way that none of them had yet imagined—to end Jax's life for good. When an immortal died at a demon's hand, it was an extinguishing, not simply a passing to Elysium. The immortal's soul existed no more.

If Sable defeated him that way, snuffed out his life force, then undoubtedly the Djinn's next move would be to strike Shay down out of pure, evil spite. Suddenly the words from the Oracle's prophecy rang in Jax's ears, and seemed to refer not only to Jax himself, but now to Shay, too. The words buzzed in his head like flies on a slain warrior.

There is a crown of death about your head. The Highest God calls upon you to fight the ancient evil, the force who stormed the Hot Gates.

"... it's a risk to her, as well," River was saying. "Don't forget Shay's place in all this."

"A risk, you say? As if I've given no thought to my Shayanna?" Jax seethed, circling the younger servant, who didn't so much as flinch. "Watch yourself, Kassandros. And know this: When it comes to Shay's safety and welfare, I refuse to *risk* breaking the very rules that Ares himself established for this engagement. The potential consequences for defying them are too dire to even contemplate."

With an intentionally nasty glance, Ajax dismissed his servant with a sniff. "I've made my decision and it stands," he said.

He knew River's buttons and could play them like a melody when he had to. The chief hot spot for the younger man was his uneasiness about their eternal relationship as master and servant. Not that Jax liked doing it one bit, but talking down to his warrior friend would serve his purpose for the moment.

He tried to ignore the blatant hurt that flashed in River's eyes—and the way the man dropped his head, wordless, staying still as a statue. Great, now one of the last memories River would ever have of him was this sharp display of his bastardly streak.

Jax marched to the far side of the room. Shay sat in one of the large leather chairs in front of the fire, and he felt her gaze on him as he moved. It was as though his wings had been clipped, as if some spiritual collar had been put around his neck. No matter what direction his mind went, the end result was the same: They were trapped.

Jax pretended to study Leo's library of leather-bound books, thumbing through them, but his senses were on full alert. Behind him he was aware of Shay's curiosity and unvoiced questions. For the first time in his warrior's life it wasn't enough to be decisive, brutal, fierce, brave. The importance of all his fighting attributes shrank in the face of what he needed most right now: He had to be wise. Shay's life and the lives of all he cared about depended on it. When all was done, he just hoped his choices would be the right ones.

"Too bad we can't get the Oracle to come back and translate her own prophecy," Ari boomed as he entered the great room, tossing his field jacket across the back of the sofa.

Jax kept his nose in a book. "If it were that easy, big brother, we'd have solved all our problems aeons ago."

"Nobody's seen her then, I take it?" Ari asked.

Why did his elder brother have to look so damned jovial right now? "Obviously not," Jax nearly snarled back.

"Temper, temper, *Jax-ass*." Ari laughed, warming his hands by the fire.

Shay burst out laughing at the insult, and Ajax wanted to kiss Ari for his reliable comic skill. It always had been the Spartan way: pithy humor when things were bleakest.

His heart clenched. He would miss his brothers—not

just his natural ones, but his Spartan ones—when he passed into eternity. It was the main reason he hadn't told them the rest of Ares' promised reward for finding the looking glass. All of his brothers would open Hades itself in an effort to hold him here on Earth. He blinked quickly, wrestling aside the unwelcome regrets.

Ari shoved his chest out and did a little pass-by of the room. Kalias always called that strut Ari's "turkey jaunt," and Jax smiled wistfully as he watched it—perhaps for the last time.

With a grand, sweeping gesture, Ari addressed all of them. "Yeah, so if you see any pixies running around here with blue streaks in their hair—"

"I did," Shay volunteered, raising her hand. "Earlier, when I woke up that first time. This fairy woman came and bandaged me up."

"I thought Ajax did that," River said, scratching his jaw perplexedly.

Ari chuckled, raising an eyebrow dramatically. "Huh, and I figured on Kalias for such . . . ahem, careful tending."

"Nobody sees the Oracle but me," Ajax stated as he replaced the book and moved back toward where the others were gathered by the fire. "And sometimes Leonidas. That's it."

Ari began to laugh. "Somebody's getting replaced," he sang in a gloating tone. "And looks like the list is growing longer every day."

Jax whipped around and glared at his brother. "Why would a mortal be able to see our Oracle?"

"Beats me." Ari shrugged. "Maybe she's bored by your sorry ass. There's a guess."

Shay sat up tall in her chair. For the first time since Jax had been acting sour and temperamental, she matched his tone. "I *saw* her. I'm not an idiot—oh, and thank you very much, but I already have two grown men back in Georgia who have a corner on the market of treating me like I'm fragile and stupid. Don't join their ranks, Jax."

Ari tossed his head back and let loose a belly laugh.

"No wonder the gods prepared this one for you, Brother. Sweet."

Jax scowled at his brother. "Outmatched and outclassed. A paradise for a fool like me." Then he glanced at Shay with a sheepish smile. "I get moody sometimes. Should have warned you about that."

She smiled back and reached for him. He settled on the edge of her chair and began stroking her hair. Together they stared into the fire, quiet while Ari and River sparred verbally about an upcoming soccer match.

Tugging on his arm, she pulled him closer, and he bent low. "Why did I see her, though? If only you and Leonidas are supposed to . . ."

He sighed. Just one more unsolved riddle among all the many others. "I really don't know. But maybe we'll find the answer to that in Savannah as well."

She gave a nod, but he could see even more confusion in her pale blue eyes. He would make sure of one thing, he vowed, and that was to heal the sadness and pain inside of her before he passed into eternity. Somehow he'd find a way to ease all the hurt he was causing her.

"When do we leave?" she asked.

Jax gave a nod in River's direction. "We're waiting until nightfall. Makes forming the portal a little easier—why, we've never known. But our recovery time should be much shorter if we wait to leave then."

An hour. They had one last hour when he could sit with Shay like this. Just be in her presence. He'd take every second the gods granted.

Chapter 23

River sat on the stone hearth and watched Shay, maintaining a cautious distance even though Jax had left the room for a moment. Mortals made him uneasy, especially ones of the female variety. He'd spent so long apart from her kind, he wasn't sure he'd even know what to say should she address him directly. But that sadness in her eyes haunted him, made him want to think of something witty to chase her visible pain away.

She and Ajax had been laughing earlier when he'd passed their room, and although he'd briefly resented that fact, they were supposed to be happy now that they were finally together. Damn it, it was their right after such a long path in finding each other. Yet neither of them had *looked* very happy since they'd emerged from that bedroom. He could only guess at what she might be feeling right now, how she feared losing Jax, worried for his safety in the upcoming battle.

He suddenly felt like an intruder, as though he had no right to speculate about her personal pain, and so he made a great show of retying his bootlaces. Hell, of doing anything to avoid her vulnerable, mortal gaze. If only he could come up with anything worthwhile to say, but he was as tongue-tied as he always was while in the presence of a mortal woman—and a beautiful one, at that.

When his laces were triple knotted he sat up straight, and it was Shay who finally broke their awkward silence. "You're River." She leaned back in her chair, studying him openly. "You're the one who helped save me in the cemetery and then again in the tunnel."

"Oh, yeah." He met her gaze boldly. "Sorry I didn't introduce myself properly." He extended a hand, and she leaned forward in her chair to take it. Her grip was firm and light, her hand shockingly soft. She had sat in silence during his discussion with Jax.

"I'm Shay Angel. But you obviously know that already. Thank you for what you did." She smiled at him, such a lovely, open expression. "I owe you big-time."

Gods of Olympus. As he released her grasp, he wished he could morph into an arrow and shoot right out of the room, because she'd instantly made him blush.

"My duty." He gave a curt, dismissive nod and rose to his feet, breezing right past her.

"You look after Jax. I heard you earlier." She rose and followed after him. "Thank you for taking care of him like you do. If only he'd agreed with you, huh?"

River halted. He stood frozen, then slowly pivoted to face her.

"You heard my plan?" Although he hadn't wanted to admit it, he'd felt wounded by how brusquely Ajax had dismissed his strategy—one that Leonidas had already endorsed. Especially because in his mind it had been a damn good plan.

Her eyes brightened. "I think it's brilliant."

He blushed even more and, staring at his feet, despised himself for the weakness. What kind of warrior reddened when a lady deigned to speak to him? Only a servant would react so awkwardly. Just more proof that in his heart, no matter how his circumstances changed, he would always be just that. And that, no matter how violent his transformation might make him—how it made him crave and lust for a woman like Shay—he'd never find fulfillment, not even for that blackest part of his soul.

Shay's eyes narrowed on him. "I mean it, River. Your strategy is pure genius. It manages to circumvent both Ares' rules *and* the prophecy."

River couldn't help himself; his heart quickened with the possibility that she might help him convince Jax to go along with the idea. But his hope crashed earthward the moment he remembered how particularly nasty his master had just been about the whole affair.

He shook his head resolutely. "Ajax won't go for it. I can already promise you that." He shrugged like none of it mattered. "He made that much perfectly clear earlier. You heard him yourself."

She peered up into his face. "What if I helped?"

"Helped how?"

A conspiratorial gleam brightened her eyes even further. "You could ride in my hip pocket. I mean, that was your plan, as I understood. That you'd transform into your weapon form *before* the portal opened, and you'd go in Jax's possession so that you'd be there with him, ready for his fight with Sable. That he'd take you pre-transformed . . . that was it, right?"

He smiled despite himself. "You pick up on things fast. I like that in a fighter."

"Trust me—I've had a lot of curveballs thrown my way over the years. Jax is just the latest in a series of them. Well, more of a line drive, you could say."

"Are you talking cricket?" River didn't fully understand her metaphors, but it sounded like the English game to him.

She giggled, brushing a lock of hair out of her eyes. "I'm saying this: that you transform soon—now—whenever, and that I stick you in my pants, or maybe my bra—"

She stopped, interrupted no doubt by the choking gasp he'd just emitted, then continued. "Just basic transport method . . . pants, bra, whatever works best for hiding you."

River tried to talk, but only a rasping sound came forth as he rubbed his burning face. "Very few . . . ladies have offered me that sort of access . . . to their undergarments"—he coughed, clearing his throat—"in the past . . . ever."

"Okay, so we go with the hip-pocket plan. It's agreed."

She bobbed her head, eyes locked with his until slowly he began to nod along in agreement.

"He'd never forgive us," River warned, thinking of the possible repercussions he'd encounter because of deceiving Ajax. "There could be serious consequences for me as well," he added heavily. "And for you. Like I said, forgiveness might be slow coming on this one."

"A calculated risk." She matched his serious tone. "But if we succeed, we just might save his stubborn soul."

"We might indeed." River glanced about the great room; all the other warriors were in Leonidas's study. It was the perfect moment.

Shay extended her hand again, this time offering the iron grip of a fellow warrior. "So we agree, then? We do it?"

"Yes, my lady." River swallowed hard, battling the edges of fear that threatened to smother him if he didn't act now. Yes, there were many potential consequences— some even far more serious than Jax's anger. But his inner voice was practically screaming that this was important, that all their lives depended on it. Consequences be damned.

Gathering his internal energy, River dropped to his knees. The power rush always sent him sprawling at the beginning. Shay knelt beside him, placing a warm hand on his shoulder. "Are you okay?"

He couldn't even answer at first. His physical reaction to the impending transformation was just too intense. Glittering silver washed across his vision, morphing everything around him to the same otherworldly hue, and he turned back to Shay one last time.

"A dagger," he rasped. "I'll assume the form of a dagger. Elegant . . . a lady's weapon, but with a grip made for a warrior."

She smiled, eyes narrowing, catlike, and she squeezed his shoulder supportively. "A perfect form of protection," she agreed. "I will protect you, too, River . . . while you're in my care, I promise."

I know, my lady. I'm certain you are worthy of my master's love.

He didn't have a chance to utter the words. His flowing source, the silver itself, exploded through his entire body, but not before she pressed a brief, chaste kiss to his forehead.

"Thank you," she said. "I'll owe you my life for saving *his*."

Jax glanced at his watch. It was past eight p.m. here in the U.K., which meant it was just after three p.m. in Savannah. He and Shay needed to get a move on. Their first order of business, she'd told him, was to visit a museum on Oglethorpe Square. She believed it would hold the first clue toward solving the prophecy.

To mark their departure, the full cadre had gathered in the great room, circling Jax and Shay—all except for River, that was—and Jax wondered if his friend was still angry because of how roughly Jax had treated him earlier.

Leonidas stepped forward, placing both hands heavily on Jax's shoulders. "You fight well, Spartan. Remember who you are, the many battles you've waged and won. You will defeat this foe as well."

"Yes, Commander." Jax bowed his head, tightening his hold on Shay's hand. She stood just beside him, waiting calmly for the portal that would transport them back to her home city.

But Leo wasn't finished; he moved down their line of two, stopping in front of Shay. She lifted her head, surprised as he addressed her. "You, our Shayanna, are a warrior now as well. Fight hard, be strong for this Spartan who stands beside you. I . . . All of us . . . are depending upon you."

Jax felt Shay's hand tremble in his grasp; she bowed her head as he'd done, murmuring, "Yes, sir."

The edges of Jax's lips curved upward into an inadvertent smile. What must it be like for Shay at this moment, being charged for warfare by one of the greatest warriors and kings in history?

"The portal?" Leonidas directed. "Are you ready?"

Jax searched the gathered warriors once more, hoping to see River, but he searched in vain. After a moment's hesitation, he answered, "Yes, my king. We are ready."

Shielding Shay close against his chest, he heard a humming sound fill the room, an almost high-pitched wailing sound that he'd long ago learned to associate with a portal's appearance. Clutching Shay even closer, he welcomed the change in atmosphere, and offered a quick prayer that this journey would save all their souls.

Jax couldn't believe it. Shay held a gleaming silver dagger in the palm of her hand, wings engraved from the hilt right down to the tip of the weapon's blade.

They'd been walking down the busy Savannah street toward their first stop, a museum house that overlooked Oglethorpe Square. Together they'd been hurrying so fast that he'd nearly tripped several times, his boots catching on the uneven bricks that formed the sidewalk. She moved much more gracefully, although, of course, she'd had a lifetime to grow accustomed to her city's eccentricities. Now she'd stopped him in his tracks with a mild, "Hold up. I need to give you something."

"What the hell is that?" Jax demanded

She shifted her grip on the dagger, trying to put it into his hand. "Just take it, okay?"

"No. Not until you answer me." He jabbed a finger at the weapon, not wanting to believe the evidence before his eyes. "I shall repeat: What in bloody hell is that?"

"*Who* do you think it is?" She made her eyes wide and big. "If I were you, I'd be a bit more polite to him right now. He worships the ground you walk on."

Ajax sighed, shook his head, and decided that going the wrathful route would accomplish precisely nothing. Taking the dagger from her, he sheathed it against his hip, where he'd already stored a much simpler blade. "You went behind my back and conspired against me. Both of you."

She pointed a finger at him accusingly. "We simply forced you to obey your king."

"My decision—not yours." He could hardly contain his fury at their betrayal. "And certainly not River's," he spat.

"Excuse me. Are you saying that I have no say in this fight? That River doesn't have any vote? Think again, Petrakos." She tilted her chin upward, met his gaze head-on, then shocked the hell out of him with her next gesture. She shot him a bird, waving her curved fingers right in front of his face.

He lifted an eyebrow. "Not very ladylike." Truth was, her ballsy side turned him flat on.

"The flying salute seems perfect for you, hawk," she snapped.

Cupping her face, he bent down and planted a fiery, wet kiss on her lips. He didn't care if they were standing on a public sidewalk or in a bedroom; he wanted this woman every moment he was with her. Besides, he was at least cloaked by his immortal's protection, so at the moment there wasn't anyone who could see them together—kissing or otherwise. Unless a band of demons suddenly appeared, that was.

The thought sobered him, and even with the temptation of her tongue halfway down his throat, and those greedy little hands of hers winding up underneath his T-shirt, he forced himself to break the kiss.

"Although I'd far prefer to kiss you blind right here and now, we'd better get this mission over with." He nodded toward the Telfair Museum, their current destination that awaited just a block down the road.

They'd arrived on Savannah soil only fifteen minutes ago, but Shay had already offered incisive thoughts about the prophecy. She was convinced that the Oracle's emphasis of the one prophetic line, "Tell thee fair, doubting Thomas . . . ," was a reference to the Telfair Museum's Owens-Thomas House. Especially since, as she'd pointed out, it sat right on Oglethorpe Square.

Even though Telfair was not pronounced in the way that the Oracle had spoken—"tell the fair"—but rather Tell-*far*, such were the vagaries when it came to their lady's pronouncements. Therefore Ajax agreed with Shay's instinct that the Oracle had been referring to the Telfair Museum.

They hurried down the sidewalk, nearing the carriage house entrance. "You'd better hope they don't have metal detectors at the entrance. Otherwise they're gonna go wild with the way you're packing."

He sniffed. "I'm not the one who smuggled River Kassandros along for the ride."

She skipped several steps ahead of him on the sidewalk. "You know," she called over her shoulder, "I bet he's ready to stab you through the heart, the way you keep talking."

He caught up with her and spun her to face him. She needed to hear what he was about to say, not dismiss it as just more of their flirty banter. "I love River," he told her intensely, hoping that perhaps his loyal servant could hear him as well. He wanted both of them to know the real reason behind his previous hesitation—that it wasn't him treating River like a second-class warrior or dismissing his strategies.

"But the thought of River staying in his weapon form for so long—across a portal jump, no less—makes me very nervous. He's never attempted such a lengthy transformation before, and we don't know how it will affect him. That's why I tried to keep him out of this fight."

Jax patted his side belt, letting his palm come in physical contact with the hilt of River's dagger. He knew from experience that sometimes River only sensed impressions as they fought together—felt the emotions present more than understood the actual words being used. He hoped that the touch of his hand against the silvered blade would transmit his true feelings.

"It's not just my concern for River's safety I'm worried about," he explained. "Ares made it clear that only *you* could be part of solving the prophecy. Trust me—you don't want to see an ancient Greek god angered." Ajax shivered just thinking about the proposition. "What if Ares punished you somehow for my own indiscretion?"

The anger in her eyes melted away, replaced by such a tender, sweet look that he had to kiss her one more time. Less restrained, he pulled her flush against him, arching her slightly backward. They kissed like a pair of lovers in the midst of great turmoil, hungry and needing each other. Her hands threaded through his hair, loosening his ponytail until his long hair fell across his shoulders.

"This way I want you," he murmured, breaking the kiss with a glance around them. Only one elderly lady was staring at Shay in confusion, and he bent low, kissing her again. "This way I need you, the taste . . . it overcomes me sometimes."

"The street is not the best spot for overcoming . . . or coming undone." She giggled, wiping the back of her hand across her wet lips.

He recomposed himself, assuming soldier mode. "The entrance is on the right, and you'll go in first—then I will follow."

"Tell me again how you plan to circumvent the metal detectors and security check?"

"Simple. You're going in, and I'm *sneaking* in."

She stopped dead in her tracks. "Sneaking how?"

"You're the only one who can see me right now, sweetness." He glanced down at their joined hands, then gave her an innocent grin. "And so I'd guess that anyone passing by wonders who *you're* pretending has hold of your hand."

She stomped the ground, tossing him a mock glare. "Lovely. Now I'm not only that eccentric girl from the demon-hunting family. Now I'm also the pitiful girl with an *imaginary* boyfriend. Thanks a ton for helping out my reputation in what, I should point out, is a very small city."

He gave a shrug. "If it keeps future suitors away, I'm all for it." He'd meant the barb to be funny, but by the way she instantly dropped his hand and set off ahead of him, he knew that reminding her of the reason for this treasure hunt hadn't been a smart move.

He picked up his pace and fell in beside her. She'd stopped in front of the museum's carriage house and was staring up at a sign that stated its hours of operation. "We have plenty of time," she said. "But it's a guided tour only." She sighed, although clearly not about the scheduled museum tours. He felt her sadness pierce his own heart like a wounding arrow.

Wrapping her in his arms, he held her from behind. Bending his mouth low to her ear, he whispered, "I want your happiness when I'm gone. Even if it means that there will be other men in your life."

She was stiff in his grasp, not breathing, it seemed. Then finally she relaxed a little. "I don't want to talk about that right now. I just want to focus on solving the prophecy. We'll work out the details later."

Although her words were brave ones, he didn't miss the jagged pain in her tone.

"Yes," he murmured, nuzzling her, "there is time for all of that later."

Shay looked at her watch. They'd gained five hours during the portal jump, and now she was back on Eastern Standard Time. Confusing, to say the least. "It's three thirty-four p.m. right now. We have to know where to go by seven a.m. tomorrow morning. Can you cloak me, too?" she whispered under her breath. "That way we don't have to fool with the tour."

"Of course." The truth was, he'd already done so the second time he'd moved to kiss her. "Done."

Jax held her tighter and prayed to the Nameless, Highest, Truest God that they would beat Sable in solving the mystery. All of their lives, mortal *and* immortal, were going to depend on that fact.

Chapter 24

They'd done several laps through the carefully restored rooms of the Regency-era museum house,
but so far neither of them had seen anything that revealed a clue about the prophecy. Shay studied every
piece of art, every museum employee, every tourist, but
got nothing.

When they arrived at the top of the staircase and
began walking—for the fourth time—over the unique
wooden bridge that spanned both sides of the house, she
turned to Jax. "You're absolutely certain that Leonidas
said the Oracle emphasized 'Tell thee fair'?" she asked
in a low voice, facing him in the middle of the bridge.

"You don't have to whisper." He took hold of her
hand and drew it to his lips. "Remember, I've got you
under my protection right now, so they can't hear you or
see you either."

She glanced over the bridge railing, her stomach reacting when she saw how far down the first floor was. "I always whisper in museums. My mama raised me right."

"She did indeed—and, yes, I am certain about what
Leonidas said. Perhaps we should try the other museum
location now?"

"That one's not on Oglethorpe Square, though." She
sighed. It was becoming intensely frustrating hashing
out the same clues between them, yet getting no tangible result.

She'd already made Jax recite the prophecy at least

ten times as they'd trailed their way from room to room, dodging unsuspecting museum visitors who couldn't see them. The fact that he'd memorized the scroll after reading it only twice had proved at least one thing—not only was he gorgeous, but his thick skull housed a smart mind as well. Double jeopardy.

A new tour group mounted the stairs beside them, led by a docent whom Shay actually knew. She had to fight the urge to duck and cover right on the little wooden walkway. She did squat down; the natural instinct to hide from the woman was just too powerful.

Jax squatted beside her, threading his hands through the railing bars. "What? Did you see something?" He glanced all around them.

She pointed. "I know that docent. It's Marty ... she's a friend of my mama's."

Jax brushed his knuckles across her cheek and smiled at her. "Sweetness, it's like I said—"

"I know, I know," she finished for him, hovering low against the rail. "Nobody can see me. Check. It's just weird, that's all." She brushed her hands off and rose to her full height once again. "I think you're right. We've probably exhausted any leads here, so we should hit the main museum."

Once downstairs, they stepped outside onto the large portico overlooking the gardens below. "Greek Revival elements," she said in her best art-student voice, pointing at a pair of columns. "You should feel right at home.... Wait." Shay noticed a sign for the gift shop that was in the carriage house straight in front of them. They'd bypassed buying tickets, going Jax's Invisible Man route instead, and the shop gave her an idea.

"I want to run in there." She pointed through the closed garden gate toward the carriage house. "There might be something that we missed."

Shay poked her way through the crowded gift shop, just about ready to call it quits, when something spectacular caught her sight.

"Jax! Check this out!" She'd stopped fooling with the unnecessary whispering, and—bouncing unseen amid the throng of tourists—now tugged him by the hand toward a long display of replicas of the famous *Bird Girl* statue. "Look at these. I can't believe I didn't make this connection before."

He picked one of the small replicas up, turning it in his hand. "Lovely statuary, but what does it mean?"

"It's a replica of the *Bird Girl*. She used to be in Bonaventure and was photographed for the cover of *Midnight in the Garden of Good and Evil*. A true iconic image of this city. Think about the prophecy . . . that part about 'a bird flies east and west . . . ' "

Jax studied the line of replicas on the shelf and seemed to be mentally sorting through the prophecy.

"I want to buy one of these *Bird Girls*." She grabbed the one he'd just set down. "You got any money on you?"

"Love, I'll remind you again of our current situation. Nobody"—he waved about the crowded gift shop—"can see you or me. Or the statue that you are presently holding."

She swatted him on the chest. "Well, I'm not gonna steal it, if that's what you're saying."

"Why not? In the old days we Spartans valued the clever art of theft."

"That's . . . disillusioning."

He shrugged. "It was a means for survival—if you were on a battle campaign, you might need to steal some poor bloke's goat or sheep just to stay alive."

She shook her head. "This is a statue, not a goat. It doesn't bleat; it doesn't moo."

"Fine, then." He grabbed the replica out of her grasp. "*I'm* stealing it." And he swaggered right out the door, clutching it boldly in his hand. Since his cloaking ability extended to the object itself, any observers would have sworn to themselves that a statue had just vanished off the shelf. Not her problem at the moment; unsuspecting "civilians" could just think the shop was haunted. Hey, the museum might even profit by landing on one of the town's celebrated ghost tours.

She followed Jax outside and into the garden below the main house, jogging to catch up with his long strides. The azaleas and dogwoods were in full bloom, their branches dipping beneath the weight of heavy blossoms. She was just opening her mouth to remark on that fact, to draw his attention to the beautiful garden, when all at once he came to a dead stop.

She collided with his solid back like she might a brick wall, all the air whooshing out of her lungs. "What are you . . ." She gasped.

He held both hands at his sides and moved slightly so that he was positioned squarely in front of her. "Stay back, Shay," he growled, sidestepping again in a semicircle. "Don't make a move."

She placed a hand against his back, knowing that whatever had him going all ninja on her couldn't be good. It had to be demonic in origin. Right on cue, the hair along her nape prickled just as she spotted a tall, spindly creature off to Jax's right. Probably eight feet tall with absurdly thin legs and gleaming beetle's wings across his shoulders, the demon tromped across a full bed of daffodils, ruining them.

Jax growled again, deep and snarling this time—a sound she'd never heard from him before that very moment. He swung his head first one direction, then another, sizing up their opponents.

"How many?" Her throat tightened with an anxious spasm. Was it really possible that she'd be murdered by demons in a beautiful Savannah garden bursting with spring? This was tour-of-homes territory, not a supernatural-bloodbath zone.

"No telling, not yet," he said, his voice hawklike.

Great. There could be at least one hundred soulless Djinn descending upon them. She took a deep breath and reminded herself of her destiny and her newfound strength as a huntress. A week ago she wouldn't even have known how to battle demons with a knife or just a praise hymn. She might not be as skilled as she would become, but she wasn't as unprepared as she'd been that first night in the cemetery either.

You're a huntress; this is what God made you to do. Ditch the fear now!

Ajax's hands balled into fists, flexing, and out of the corner of her eye she saw a streak of silver shoot up his left forearm. The muscles of that arm bulked visibly, thickening and enlarging. His height increased, his full body morphing spectacularly right in front of her. The bright afternoon gave her a true, unhindered glimpse of just how powerful her lover truly was, and the sight awed her to the core. He was beautiful, primal . . . terrifying in the extreme—at least, he should be to their enemies. But never to her; Shay's heart soared with an unexpected rush of pride for all that Ajax was in that moment.

Once again that low-pitched, guttural sound emanated from deep inside him, causing chill bumps to race across her arms. "Shay . . . I want you to step back. Carefully." His words were slow and precise.

She clutched the little *Bird Girl* statue in one hand. It would be useful in the fight, but not enough. "I need a weapon." She started for his hip holster, but he held out a staying hand; then they both froze at the sound of a horrifyingly familiar voice.

"Well, well, my old friends. Ajax, you surprise me. I wouldn't have pegged you for the museum type."

Hooves clomped loudly on the stone walkway that bisected the garden, and Shay began to tremble. Sable had nearly killed them both on two other occasions, and she wasn't sure how they'd survive a third encounter.

In a light-speed leap, Jax hurled himself through the air, lunging at the centaur. Shay inched back and sideways toward the garden wall, knowing instinctively that she needed to get her rear flank protected. At least that way she'd be able to see any demon that approached without having to wonder if she was about to be blindsided.

Jax had already transformed, his body now fantastically larger, his darkly gleaming wings spread wide across his back. He used his Spartan shield to deflect blows from Sable's twin swords, and as they battled across the open garden a statue crashed to the brick walkway.

Recovering quicker than his opponent, Jax flew at Sable again, striking a serious blow to the demon's side. They went down together in reaction, falling into a terrible rolling maneuver across the open grass; all at once she saw the bright flash of a silver dagger in Jax's hand.

River! Help him!

She didn't have time to see if Jax was able to slice Sable with the transformed blade; off to her right the spidery, tall demon began to approach her lazily. He ambled toward her as if he were out for a demonic afternoon stroll. She cringed as she got a better look at him. His face wasn't a face, not exactly; it was more black mist than anything defined. Instead of eyes or facial features, there was just a tense black fog, a soullessness that looked like death itself.

In a garbled, raspy voice the creature threatened, "Shay Angel, your brothers and their Shades ... I've met them before."

"And you lived to tell about it?" she shot back at him, thrusting her chest out in defiance.

"You tell your brothers they can bite me."

She started to laugh despite herself, and it took the edge off the fear. "Oh, my God, you are just dumber than a box of rocks, aren't you?" She laughed even harder, a little hysterically, as the thing spindled its way closer.

It snarled at her, the black hole of its face suddenly opening, revealing a snapping set of jaws. "And ugly," she added, doing a frantic mental search for any sort of binding spell or other assistance she could remember from the family lore.

As if in slow motion, first one, then a second and a third arm reached toward her, lengthening across the five yards that still separated them.

"Holy Mother of God!" she shrieked. "Aren't two

hands enough for you people?" She barely dodged the demon's claws as he grabbed for her.

A harsh laugh rumbled from the entity's chest area as it stretched forth yet another arm. "All the better to hold you with, my dear."

Clutching the statue in her right hand, she was thankful that she'd grown up with athletic brothers, and pitched the pewter figurine through the air, hitting the creature hard in the center of its face. Howling, the demon took several staggering steps forward. Although she'd temporarily unbalanced him, she'd still be toast in a matter of seconds if she couldn't get on the offensive.

At that moment innocent tourists approached, blissfully unaware of the battle that waged invisibly among them. The crowd came right between Shay and the demon; perhaps out of some perverse gentlemanly politeness, Scrabble Legs stepped back and allowed them to pass.

"At least his mama raised him right," she muttered under her breath.

Jax seized the quick moment and flew to her side, leaving Sable fallen to the ground and still struggling to rise. In his frantic flight Jax managed to overturn yet another statue, and it broke into shattered pieces on the stone walkway. Shay winced, unable to shake her art background.

At the unexpected crash the crowd of tourists gasped, backing away—God love 'em, they had to be preparing to spread more rumors about the place being haunted.

Jax landed again, right in between her and Spidery Demon, his wings a protective shield. "I'll get this one," he hissed, pointing his heavy Spartan shield at the dark being.

Those familiar, safe wings spread all about her, lengthening and reaching backward to safely encase her.

There was lunging and more hissing; together she and Jax moved as one—she tightly held between his wings, he battling for both their lives. Still she burned to get in the fight, not to cower, and she hated that she couldn't see a thing except Ajax's black wings. Then he stepped forward, releasing her with a dancing sidestep, and in horror she realized that Sable was already back on him—and that the other demon hadn't been fazed by any of Jax's maneuvers. The demon flew at them, screeching, and one of its nasty wings sliced through an azalea bush, sending bright pink blossoms flying into the air all around them.

She wasn't sure what made her do it, but she took off at breakneck speed for the actual museum house, ignoring the sounds of flying hoofbeats and leather wings flapping right on her heels. When she reached the downstairs door—the one that led to the cistern area—she bounded inside, but the demons moved seamlessly through the closed partition and into the old basement right on her heels.

Great, supersmart move, she thought. There was only one way in—and one way out—with this lower level: the main door. For some reason she'd been thinking that a set of stairs would lead to the upper floor.

To the right was the original kitchen, with its antiquated bricks and fixtures; at the back of the hallway stood the old cistern. For lack of a better plan Shay bolted toward the latter, leaping over its containing wall.

Sable trotted near, slow and methodical, his ugly face twisted into a cruel, triumphant sneer. "Bad move, little mortal," he taunted, glancing sideways at his compatriot. "You've made it much too easy for us to take you."

Jax stormed into the small basement area, right on their heels. His breathing came heavily, and his naturally olive-skinned face seemed ashen. Shay gasped when she saw the reason: His right wing had been slashed nearly straight through. It hung awkwardly at his side like deadweight, his black feathers even darker than usual because of his own heavily drenching blood.

"Ajax!"

He raised his right arm in a charging motion, silencing her at the same time. She covered her mouth with her hand, biting back further cries even though she could hardly look anywhere else except at his maimed wing. It dragged the floor, lagging several feet behind him as he approached, his bright red blood streaking the stone floor. Incredibly purposeful and silent, he pursued the demons, seemingly unaware of how critically injured he was.

Sable lunged forward, forelegs braced along the cistern wall, grabbing at her; at the same moment the black-faced demon slid into the small area, ready to take hold of her. Jax attacked before she could breathe, before she could even blink. There was no noise except the flurry of violent wings and the heaving of his hawk's breast, the piercing cries of her dark angel flying at the attackers.

He scooped her into his arms and soared toward the ceiling. She braced, actually covering her head, thinking that somehow he'd forgotten she couldn't pass through walls. But yet again his spectacular magic protected her, and in less than a breath she found herself in the house's upstairs hall once again. He sagged against her slightly, holding to her.

"Your wing, Jax." She spun toward him, reaching for the appendage with both hands. "You have to get us out of here, let me take care of the wound."

He bit down on his lip, shaking his head. "Regenerates. Fast," he ground out between clenched teeth. Then he was already studying the staircase, assessing escape routes. "We don't have long."

From the entry level the pair of demons burst forth, slamming the door behind them so hard that it sent splinters of wood flying. Jax ushered her into the dining room, a large D-shaped room, shoving past terrified tourists and the shouting docent. The group huddled in alarm, clearly confused by all the disaster being created by assailants they couldn't see with their own mortal eyes. Although the tangible evidence of the supernatural struggle was physically happening, the demons—as well as Jax and herself—were fighting in another dimension. The tour guide quickly ushered the tourists out of the room, leaving the dining area an empty battlefield, for all purposes.

Sable circled on one side of the long antique table, Jax and Shay on the other. It was like a standoff in some ridiculous Hollywood bar-fight scene, one where at any moment a cowboy was going to smash a bottle of booze over Jax's head.

As if reading her thoughts, Sable reached for that very object she'd just imagined him using, a rare Wedgwood vase. And, just as she'd imagined, he hurled it straight at Jax's head.

"Watch the art, pal!" she shouted as Jax ducked the hurling projectile, pulling her toward the floor with him.

"None of the patrons can see this battle," Jax answered, his breathing heavy as he urged her up underneath the table, crawling beside her.

"I got that part. But they can see the *damage*!"

"They'll just think the place is haunted." He moved on his elbows as if the Oriental rug were the front lines of the Western Front, covering her whole body with his injured wing . . . which, come to think of it, already seemed fully functional once again. But the scent of his recently spilled blood still hit her nose like an assault, making her fear for his safety.

"It's not the tourists I'm worried about," she hissed back at him, studying Sable's long, horsey legs as he moved about the table. They had him on the agility front; no way could he—nor probably any of his cohorts—climb underneath the table they were now using to shield themselves. Unless they got the bright idea to hurl the polished table down the hallway. Hopefully none of them would be that smart.

She peered out from underneath the table's far edge just in time to see Sable's hindquarters nearly knock over yet another antique vase.

"Demons and warriors!" she shouted in outrage, bounding to her feet. "For the last time! Watch. Out. For. The. *Art!*"

Sable laughed and, using his wide hindquarters, intentionally shoved the antique to the floor.

"You're just egging him on," Jax told her out of the

side of his mouth, thrusting his sword at Spindly Demon. "Besides, what's the big deal?"

Nothing like a lover's quarrel at full throttle. "It's art! It's beautiful!" She breathed heavily, putting her back to the wall. "All right, so you're a Spartan . . . art isn't high on your radar."

Jax eyed Sable, who'd begun stomping the floor. "Not like survival is."

Shay pointed at the centaur, still talking to Jax. "Okay, this guy's fixing to get on my last nerve."

"What shall I do then, my lady?" Jax moved forward, shield raised.

"Go kick his demon ass—and let me kick some, too, while you're at it."

She reached toward his holster, but he'd already anticipated her maneuver. He slid River into her hand, passed him off like a baton in a relay race, and she clasped the hilt of his dagger form gratefully.

"Thanks, River," she whispered. "I'll owe you big-time for this."

With a spinning lunge she ran at the other demon. Perhaps he hadn't expected her to go on the offensive, or perhaps she possessed some heightened huntress's skill that she wasn't aware of—but whatever the case, the demon didn't seem able to resist her assault. Or maybe he tried, but she simply overcame his barriers. She had no idea, really, because the motion happened faster than she could blink. One moment she was lunging, and the next she was already sinking River's dagger form deep into the thing's chest. A hissing sound escaped from the wound like air rushing out of a tire. The long, demonic jaws that had seemed so menacing just a moment before sagged as the creature flapped and sucked at air.

Jerking her arm back and forth, she pried River out of the demon's body, prayed very hard, and then plunged the dagger back into the demon several more times. At last the beast dropped to its knees and collapsed face-first right on the Oriental rug. Not two seconds after that his body turned to black, misty vapor. And then there was just nothing left at all except some mystified and frightened tourists, who had massed in the main foyer and were screeching louder than any demon horde ever could, probably all the more terrified because they couldn't see any cause for all the upheaval and destruction going on around them.

Victory was short-lived, unfortunately. Shay turned to find Jax flat on his back, pinned beneath one of Sable's hooves.

"You won't beat me to the looking glass," he threatened, leaning his massive bulk onto Ajax.

She tensed her own body in reaction, practically feeling the pain that must be weighing on her lover's chest.

Sable leaned even harder on Jax, who barely managed to stifle a cry of pain. The heavy hoof was planted near the center of his chest, directly above his heart.

Sneering down at Jax's prone form, Sable seethed. "I will find the looking glass first . . . and I will then use it for your ultimate punishment. I will win by depriving you of an eternity spent with *her*."

Sable reared wildly, lifted his sword, and sent it singing through the air—aimed right at Shay.

"No!" Ajax roared, rolling out from beneath Sable.

Shay felt frozen to the spot, unable to move, but this time she wasn't letting the demon get the better of her. Words came pouring out of her spirit, over her tongue—ancient words from their sacred texts. Just as the hymn had worked at her mother's funeral, these words seemed to have an impact. Sable gaped at her in horror as the chants continued to roll off her tongue.

The tomes had said they had the power to paralyze a demon—and she hadn't recalled them until this precise moment, right when she needed them to use as an assault against their enemies. She had a feeling that their sudden appearance in her mind had more to do with the powers of righteousness than with any particular recall abilities of her own.

She moved her mouth, amazed as the ancient Greek words strung together, forming a spiritual sword that was rapier sharp. The centaur appeared paralyzed in midleap; the sword hung suspended in the air, still aimed at her chest. Its hilt vibrated, humming slightly from the momentum of being halted so firmly.

The words became far more than mere language—they were becoming something physical, a genuine weapon in the spirit realm. They grew louder as they poured out of her, and she vaguely wondered why the sword hadn't pierced her straight through.

The words stopped bubbling out of her, and an eerie, peaceful silence settled over the entire room. Ajax knelt on the floor, panting, beaming up at her in obvious pride. All around them the dark forces had been bound as if by powerful restraints. Only she and Ajax could move; good thing they weren't demons, she thought, assessing her "damage" with raised eyebrows.

Slowly Shay collapsed against the wall and sank all the way to the floor.

"My little huntress. A power-packing woman if ever I've seen one." Jax shook his head as if in wonder, brushing off his hands as he rose to his feet. With a glowering look at Sable's statuesque form, he asked, "How long will he stay this way?"

"Beats me." Her whole body quivered with tremors. "So we'd better get the hell out of here."

Their gazes locked, they both laughed, and at the exact same time they said, "Bad choice of words."

Chapter 25

They stood on the edge of her family's property, a good fifty yards down the sandy, unpaved driveway that wound to the main house. Jax had flown them from downtown out to the property in what seemed like only thirty seconds. For once she hadn't been frightened as he'd carried her skyward, had been able to appreciate the gleaming golden beauty of the rivers down below them. The sun was setting; russet, gold, and pink tones seemed to have been brushed across the marshes and rivers by God himself.

Jax had been unusually quiet, holding her close in a tender, protective gesture. So much had changed between them since the last time he'd flown with her in his arms. Before, she'd wondered if he could be a demon. Now she knew he was the greatest love of her life.

"I hate that you have to do the brother thing," she told him. Jax didn't seem concerned about her brothers, though. In fact, he appeared far more interested in studying the place where she'd grown up.

"You've already had to put up with my brothers, so it seems only fair." He gazed upward at the branches of the live oaks that formed an archway around the drive. "The Spanish moss is lovely. Is it safe to touch?"

"Absolutely not." She caught his arm as he reached out to gather a piece. "Little critters live in the moss. Things that bite."

A slow, sexy smile appeared on his face. " 'Little critters,' " he mimicked, even doing a good job of copying her accent. "Shayanna, I love the way you talk."

"I love knowing more than you do," she fired back, lifting to her very fullest height as she met his gaze flirtatiously. "At least about a few things."

He slid large palms atop her shoulders. For several long seconds he just looked into her eyes, smiling in an unreadable way.

"What are you doing?" she asked, laughing in embarrassment. Her face burned beneath his close scrutiny.

His smile slipped a little. "Memorizing your face."

She tried to turn away from him, but he kept her moored with his heavy hands. "Shay."

"Please, Jax, can we at least pretend that you're not going to leave me? That if we manage to find the stupid looking glass that it won't mean my losing you?"

He stroked her cheek with his knuckles. "I hate hurting you."

"Big clue, then!" She shoved him hard in the chest, forcing him to release her. "Don't do it. Stay here with me." She took off running, heading toward the house. "By the way, my brothers have always hated most of my boyfriends. They're going to really get on your ass for breaking my heart."

All at once he was in front of her; how he got there, she couldn't say. "I have no other choice, sweetness. You know I'm right."

Tears stung her eyes, and she moved to the right, hoping to sidestep the giant man.

But he blocked her. "I am right. Say it."

She burst into tears, unable to fight them. "Don't do this to me . . . to us."

He pulled her into his arms, cradling her close. "No other choice, love. No other choice. But we will have eternity together. Know that."

She believed she would go to heaven because of her faith in God, but this ancient warrior of hers had tripped the light fantastic through impossible spiritual zones. Where would he go?

"I believe in heaven," she said, pressing her face against his warm chest. The steady, beating heart beneath soothed her. Her tears dampened the cotton of his T-shirt. "That's where I believe I will go when I die. Everything my family believes is in the power of God."

He stroked her hair. "I have always believed in the Highest God. And I saw heaven, Shay, when I died. What we call Elysium. I was heading there, but turned back."

She looked up into his eyes. "What—why would you turn back?"

He gazed past her, his voice very quiet. "Because Ares summoned us, offered us our immortality there on the banks of River Styx. And how could I not sacrifice heaven in order to serve humanity? There was never a question."

As she'd been struck before, she understood what Jax's potential release from his eternal wandering would truly mean. How could she begrudge him his freedom, this warrior who had spent so long protecting all mankind? And his own people even before that?

Wrapping her arms about him, she sighed—a painful, wistful sigh. "Just know how much I hate this . . . hate knowing I won't be with you for such a long time. But know, too, that I'm gonna do whatever I can to help you get free."

"The brother gauntlet," Shay muttered, drawing in a deep breath as they walked up the front steps to her family's home. "It's gonna suck for you, but hopefully they'll be swift and merciful."

Jax just smiled at her. Did she honestly think that a couple of Southern good ol' boys—as she'd described her pair of overprotective siblings—were anything he couldn't handle? That she even worried about his potential discomfort at all charmed him totally.

As they stepped onto the veranda the front door opened like a rifle explosion. The sandy-haired one from the other night—he figured it was Jamie, based on her description—stormed forward, nearly shoving Shay out of the way.

"Jamie, don't!" Shay shouted, but the guy's fist was already halfway toward a brutal impact with Jax's jaw. Jax caught the hand in midair, clasping it in an iron grip that made her brother visibly wince.

"I'm Ajax Petrakos," he said, staring down at the shorter man but not releasing his hold on him. "I generally prefer familial introductions before the brawling starts."

The brother squirmed in Jax's hold. "I generally prefer that bastards like you keep away from my sister."

"Jamie, stop it right now. I mean it. Ajax is good...." She dropped her voice low, as if she were easing a suicidal man back from a ledge. "He's good to me. He's mine."

" 'Mine'? 'Mine'?" Jamie howled, giving his hand another jerk. "Let go of me, you freak of nature."

Ajax couldn't help smiling proudly. "Indeed," he said, the word crisply British, "and your sister is mine as well."

Jamie relaxed in his hold slightly, releasing a weary-sounding breath. Jax felt a little sorry for the guy; he couldn't help himself. If Jamie thought he was tired now—after a full day and night of worrying about Shay, no doubt—the news that his sister was in love with an ancient Spartan was going to drain the living piss out of the man.

"If you'll promise not to punch me, I *will* let you go." Jax gave his would-be brother-in-law a friendly grin. "But for the record, Jamie? It's not a great idea to throw punches at a man like me."

Jamie retracted his other hand, aimed it right at Jax, and once again Jax caught the punch in midair. He now had Jamie captured in a manner that couldn't be doing much for the demon hunter's ego.

"Say we're friends," Jax told him patiently.

"I ain't no friend of a demon who kidnaps my sister." Shay shoved her way into their physical space, grabbing hold of Jamie's arm. "Let him go, Jax. If he tries to beat you again, I'll kick his redneck ass. Geez, James. Fistfighting? What are we, an outtake from *Deliverance*? Thanks a lot for the good first impression. Mama probably just leaped out of her grave at Bonaventure."

She wrangled her brother toward the home's entry and, glancing back over her shoulder at Jax, rolled her eyes. "Welcome to my family, Jax. Despite appearances, we do have nice manners."

"Not for demons," Jamie grumbled. "And not for creatures like him." Shay shoved him hard between the shoulder blades, and he stumbled forward a few steps.

"Big brother, you have no idea what kind of *creature* you just took a shot at." She laughed, waving Jax into the foyer. "But when you do find out, you're going to be mighty embarrassed."

River listened—if you could actually call sensing vibrations of tone and meaning listening—and decided that Jax wasn't in danger. The push and pull of whatever physical confrontation he'd just experienced had been easy, not like earlier, when Shay had used him to stab the demon. The tang of that monster's blood still stung. Neither of them had taken time to clean him properly, either, so the stench of the kill was playing holy havoc with his senses.

As he bumped along in Jax's care, he thought wistfully of the freshly pressed olive oil that they used to apply to their swords back in Sparta, and wished that a jar of it were handy here. Thinking about the old days set his thoughts wandering to places they had no business going. Still, being locked in his altered form left him with little else to do but think; the dark memories and aching longing that he normally worked so hard to ignore pressed hard on his mind.

For all his fighting glory—and he was proud of his special calling as Jax's right-hand blade—the one thing he secretly wished was that he were a true equal with the Spartans. Of course, if he were, he wouldn't have been able to help them earlier today, and he certainly wouldn't be useful against Sable as this battle played out.

For some reason he thought of that fateful day by the Styx, the one when he'd accepted Ares' proposal. He'd been so eager, desperate to join with the Spartans as an immortal protector. There was nothing waiting for him in Elysium, nothing back in Greece herself. But the Spartan warriors, they were his true brothers. He'd leaped forward at the invitation, the first to accept Ares' gift.

The god had taken hold of him underneath his armpits and, with an incongruous laugh, had hurled River right into Styx. Its molten power hadn't burned—yet if he'd known that his acceptance meant he was actually going to take a dip in the monumental fire, he probably never would have accepted the offer. The thought would have been too terrifying, not that the bargain itself wasn't. But by the time River had understood how Ares planned to enact the agreement it had been much too late to argue. Besides, the flowing source of the river had actually soothed him, his battle wounds sealing, transformation moving through his whole body. He'd known he was changing, had accepted it without question as waves of rolling power surged through him, about him . . . as he'd felt himself move from mortal flesh to liquid to gleaming hardness.

Ares had withdrawn him from the river and held him in sword form, turning him appreciatively in his powerful grip. As now with Ajax and Shay, River had sensed more than *heard* what the god said about him there on the banks of the Styx that day. He'd felt the war god's pride in his creation—pride in River himself. He'd known Ares was placing him within Jax's solid grasp. They'd always been joined in life, he'd thought dimly. It made sense.

Only after Ajax had turned River's glinting form within his hands and examined his sword's hilt with murmurs of wonder—only after master and servant had been forged together completely—only then had Ares changed River back into human form again. He'd stood gasping, awed by what the god had made him.

"From now on," Ares drawled slowly, staring him hard in the eyes, "you will be called River. Only that name, no other. For you were forged in the mighty River Styx, the greatest weapon I have ever created."

River's heart slammed in his chest, excitement and quicksilver power speeding through his body. The war god had given him a special calling. He would be crucial to the duty the Spartans would carry out. No longer clamoring or praying that he'd be allowed in the fight, he would be indispensable to the warriors he loved and served. No longer a slave, but a true weapon of vengeance.

Ares continued, clasping River's shoulder: "And I smelted you for Ajax, your fine Spartan master. Only he will brandish you with the glory a fine blade like you is due."

Still a slave? *Master?* He'd referred to Jax as his master, but that couldn't be right.

Jax shook his head. "He goes free," he said firmly. "That helot is my equal, my brother. Our caste system doesn't matter here, not in this world."

Ares glanced between them, amusement sparkling in his eyes. "Are you certain? Am I not a god? Are you not human dust that I've deigned to touch?"

"This man," Ajax insisted, voice rising, "deserves his freedom. To join us as an equal."

River was too overcome by the power thrumming in his body to care as he should—and he had so many questions. "Please," he tried again with Ares. "My lord, am I *only* a sword? Or may I be an arrow also? A spear, perhaps . . . or even a breastplate?"

Ares turned back one last time, his gaze piercing. "You will assume more forms than you can fathom, blessed River. If for warfare, a poison draft, but if for healing . . . the elixir of life. You will serve your master well."

Then, with a quick wave of his golden hand, Ares dismissed him. The god was clothed in the Spartans' crimson cloak, and it swished regally about him, just as all the Spartans' glorious cloaks billowing in the hot wind around them.

At the moment, the difference between the warriors and himself pierced his heart like the silvered weapon he'd become, ripped into his flesh, tore at his soul.

He would never be given a scarlet cloak.

The mighty war god had gazed down on all the gallantry and fearlessness that he'd displayed at the Hot Gates. And he'd approved. Ares had found him worthy! He'd even given him the touch of life and death itself. But he'd denied River the one thing he'd secretly desired ever since boyhood, since the day he'd first accompanied Jax to the Agoge.

He'd refused to let River stand shoulder-to-shoulder with the warriors he loved and admired ... and simply belong.

They sat at the kitchen table, the one where they'd always eaten Sunday brunch and read the newspaper as a family. The same table where their father had explained their family calling to Shay for the very first time so many years ago. Somehow, bizarrely, it felt perfectly natural to her to have Jax sitting there with the three of them. Although Jamie obviously didn't agree. He was working his best imitation of the evil eye every time he looked at Jax. Mason seemed more open and relaxed, a surprise after how reserved and closed off he'd been the past few months. Then again, maybe Jax's strange arrival was enough to shake even Mason out of his withdrawn state. And if that was true, then it was only reason number one thousand why she loved this big Spartan.

"You look like a military man," Ajax observed as he studied Mason. *Oh, boy.* This one was gonna be rich. Mason had admired the Spartans from boyhood and had continued studying them all through his time in the marines.

"USMC," Mason said simply, then released the famous Marine Corps cheer. "Hoo-rah!"

This clearly tickled Jax to no end, although to his credit he did his level best to stifle a laugh. *Bad, bad idea,* she wanted to warn him. Too late—Mason was already halfway out of his chair.

"You're mocking the United States Marines?"

Jax stayed perfectly relaxed and reached to sip from the glass of wine she'd poured him. "No, Mason, friend, I am laughing because of what you'll soon learn of me."

"And what's that?" Mason held his position, poised halfway between sitting and lunging for Jax's throat.

"We share a warrior's bond, you could say."

"Who are your people?" Jamie asked, eyeing Jax like an enemy.

Jax glanced toward Shay, who gave a shrug of acceptance. No time like the present. "Go for it," she said, leaning back in her chair.

Ajax rose to his feet, towering over all of them. Then, tossing back his head, he cried something in ancient Greek and released a slightly different version of the war cry. His own. The Spartan version.

Mason sank into his chair, eyes wide with surprise ... shock. She knew what Jax didn't: Mason was easily conversant in ancient Greek. So whatever he'd just said—and then the confirming shout—had clearly gone a long way toward making Mason a believer. Or at the very least, toward confusing her big brother completely.

"I only caught a passing translation of that," Jamie said, his expression less hostile—and a lot more curious.

Mason shook his head. "It's impossible."

"What did you just tell them?" she asked Ajax.

"I stated my military designation and rank and gave my commanding officer's name, then Leonidas's as commanding general."

"Sweet." She started to laugh. "You're a name-rank-and-serial-number sorta guy. Good to know."

"I will repeat," Mason said, louder this time, "that what you're implying is an impossibility."

Jax took a lazy sip of wine. "You gentlemen are demon hunters. You've seen all manner of creatures and spiritual entities and fought many battles. What's so hard to believe about what I claim to be?"

"For one thing," Jamie said slowly, "you didn't really tell us who and what you are."

"*Neh*, I did indeed. I am Ajax Petrakos, son of ancient Sparta. I perished at Thermopylae, and on the day of my death at that great battle"—he paused, reaching across the table for Shay's hand—"I took a vow of immortality. I agreed to protect mankind. That's the short version."

"And the long one?" Mason asked, and Shay noticed that he'd paled dramatically. She'd been right in how she'd called this little meeting. Of course Mason was the one who would believe most easily—and also be the most stunned. For all they'd seen as a family, living Spartan warriors wasn't even on the hunters' checklist.

"The long one is *too* long for right now," Jax explained. "Suffice it to say that Ares is a meddling war god. He saw fit to protect mankind, but managed to make himself my master in the process."

"Are there others like you?" Mason pressed, leaning forward in his seat now.

"Seven of us, including King Leonidas himself, our eternal commander."

Jamie hit his feet. "That's it; this is ludicrous. Shay, I don't know what you're into here, but you're clearly far more naive than even I've always figured. Somebody's obviously seen *300* too many times and let it go to his head."

Mason stayed perfectly still, his gaze locked on Ajax. "Jamie, remember the book. What it said about seven warriors . . . something about them making a deal by the River Styx."

Jamie slid into his chair, apparently mollified, at least for the moment. "Go on," he said coolly. "Tell us more about how you came to be here with Shay in Savannah."

She ignored both her brothers. "Show them," she urged Jax. "It's the only way they're really gonna get it."

He lifted a silky black eyebrow. "The whole kit?"

"Kit and caboodle," she agreed. "Show them so they'll shut up already."

Jamie slid out of his chair and stepped close to Mason, as if they honestly thought they were about to kick a little ass. Shay had to swallow a laugh. When they finally realized just whom they thought to jump, really believed, they were going to feel pretty ridiculous—and way out of their league.

"Just go on." Shay nodded toward Jax, and he winked back at her.

Jax rose politely to his feet, set down his glass of wine, and, with a gentleman's bow, proceeded to turn full raptor right in her kitchen—complete with Spartan shield, breastplate, greaves, and sword. And, of course, the wings. The fantastically beautiful, otherworldly wings.

As her brothers stood by the table, paralyzed at the image, Jax gave them a brotherly grin. "Want to check out the sword?" He gave the weapon's hilt a loving stroke. "It's the same one I used at the Hot Gates."

And with that she thought both her brothers might faint dead on the spot.

Chapter 26

Shay slumped in her chair and released a loud yawn. It was nearly eleven p.m.—also known as four a.m. back at Leonidas's castle. She'd completely lost track of when she'd last caught any sleep. As for Ajax, she was beginning to realize that his immortal body never needed any significant rest.

"We humans, mere mortals that we are, still need sleep," she announced, annoyed that the three men had been gabbing, semioblivious to her, for the past few hours. Mason hadn't stopped petting Jax's shield, his eyes shining with wonder and admiration.

"But the goat path behind us, as I'm sure you know, was our undoing," Jax said. He'd been explaining the details of Thermopylae for the last few minutes, a momentary break in their discussion about the prophecy. The only thing Ajax hadn't shared was what he planned to use the looking glass for—and she was glad. Her brothers clearly saw how deeply in love she'd already fallen with Ajax. She didn't want to undo that goodwill by explaining that in eight hours' time he planned to break her heart. That was, if they could solve the prophecy. So far they were at a dead end.

"Prophecy," she piped in, even though they weren't listening to her. She whistled for their full attention. "Time limit, Ajax. Seven a.m., remember?"

He straightened in his seat. "Yes, gentlemen, we'll

have to discuss the other specifics another time. We have a serious deadline in the morning."

Mason stood from his squatting position beside Jax's shield and turned back to the table, where a dusty volume sat unopened. "I have a possible lead," he said, dropping into the chair. Flipping pages of the book, he turned to a marked place. "When Shay left with you last night we went digging in the archives, and I found something that seems to describe . . . well, I think you, Ajax."

Mason began reading, translating the ancient Greek text that outlined types of winged entities. When he got to a particular point, he hesitated, his gaze moving from Jax to Shay. "Listen to this bit," he said. " 'These are the mighty warriors, the ones who were born beside the great River Styx. If any vow is taken upon that river's shadowy banks, the vow will stand forever. Seven warriors of unknown caste pledged such a vow there—a vow that placed dread wings upon their backs.' "

Shay grabbed for Jax's hand. "Oh, my God, Ajax, that's the seven of you."

His dark brow furrowed deeply. "Who is the author of this text?"

Mason shook his head. "Author unknown, but obviously Greek. And I'm not sure this tells us anything new."

Jax reached for the book. "May I?"

Mason handed it to him, and Ajax read for several long moments, his brows rising, then knitting together, then rising again. "Ah, but there is more here." His face brightened with excitement, and Shay wondered what he'd found—but she didn't dare interrupt him as he continued reading. Thrusting a hand through his disheveled hair, he announced, "Ah, Shay, love, this is supremely helpful. Mason, good work."

"So what's it say?" Jamie demanded, trying to crane a look over Ajax's shoulder.

Jax began reading in English, " 'These great ones know no reprieve, find no release, save a looking glass forged in Hades . . . this, the key to eternity itself.' "

"But we already know about that," Shay said. They had told her brothers they were seeking that item, just not about the freedom it might bring Ajax.

Ajax continued staring down at the page. "True, but that word *key* seems significant to me," he said. "Perhaps it relates to the rest of our current prophecy."

They sat in silence, each pondering and puzzling. Shay reached for the *Bird Girl* statue that sat between them. "So all we have so far is a theory that the *Bird Girl* relates to the prophecy."

"You two met in Bonaventure, where it used to be before they moved it to the museum. That's probably it."

Shay sighed. "But it's not there anymore, so . . ."

Jamie began to laugh. "I may not be an ancient Spartan, but I do get an idea or two on occasion." He took the statue out of her hand, turning it back and forth. "Anyway, your key undoubtedly lies somewhere in Bonaventure."

"That doesn't give us anything to go on," Shay blurted in exasperation. "Damn it, I am so exhausted I can't think straight, and we're running out of time." She suddenly wanted to cry. If they couldn't solve the mystery, she might still live a so-called normal life with Jax—one where she'd age and grow old and die. Yet if they did solve it, she would lose him, possibly in just a few hours. There was no way to win, and she bit back a sob that threatened to erupt from her chest.

Jax glanced up and frowned in concern. "Sweetness, you go sleep a few hours. We're not getting anywhere right now. Besides, remember that the battle begins at seven a.m. Or the contest, rather; I doubt that Sable has advanced any further in this quest than we have."

She rubbed her tired eyes. "He's not still frozen back at the museum, though. I'm not nearly strong enough to pull off something like that." She waited for her brothers' shock that she'd successfully utilized a fighting prayer spell, but they held silent. "See, you two, I knew I had a calling. I managed to halt an ancient Djinn all by my lonesome this afternoon. Anything to say about that?"

Jamie avoided her eyes. "Not particularly. At least, not at the moment."

"When we're past this little crisis, you're going to tell me the truth." She gave the table a forceful rap. "About who I am, what I am—and about that letter."

"What letter?" Jax asked, curious.

"Doesn't matter, not now." She glared hard at Jamie. "But I will find out the truth. And in the meantime, thank God I've been secretly studying the family books. But I have no idea how long Sable would have held in that frozen form—certainly not long."

Jamie sighed. "Probably an hour. That's how long it would have lasted . . . based on your limited skill development."

"I'm already learning, Jamie—and fighting. I stopped Sable at the museum on my own."

"Still, you're a newbie, Sis."

"Could you sound a little *less* excited? Ya think?" Anger and frustration swamped her hard. "I might be dead now, for all you've helped prepare me for this."

Mason met her blazing stare. "Sis, let's not argue—"

She cut him off, turning back to face Jax. "Let's not," she agreed, happy to be as dismissive with her brothers as they'd always been with her. "The thing about Sable, Ajax, is that he was at the museum," she continued, calmer. "That means he's probably chasing our same lead with the statue."

"Perhaps. Or perhaps he merely scented our arrival when we returned to Savannah." Jax stood and took her by both hands. "You need rest. Let me go tuck you into bed. Gentlemen, if you'll excuse me for a moment?" Jax gave her brothers each a courtly bow, and she loved the respectful smiles they gave in return. They finally liked one of her lovers, and she chalked that one up as reason number thousand and one for loving Jax as much as she did.

Jax wandered about her room, eyes wide and sparkling as he studied every item from her youth. "And you did this one, as well?" He leaned closer to study her framed drawings that hung on the bedroom wall.

She beamed proudly. It was one of her favorite pieces. "Yeah, that's an etching I did in school. I went to Savannah College of Art and Design—SCAD. I haven't done anything much with my training, though . . . at least, not yet. A little bit of graphic design here and there, that's about it."

He glanced at her. "And why not?" He didn't seem disappointed or chastising; no, it was as though he challenged her.

The answer wasn't an easy one, and it was painful to admit. "I'm good—but not great. Passable. I could get more design work, sure, but it's always felt like a waste. Limiting. I've never gotten past the feeling that there's something big I'm supposed to do with my talent, but I just can't seem to figure out what that 'big' thing is. I've sorta been drifting along, not sure how it fits into seeing demons and all that."

He nodded, studying the drawing of their family dock one last time, and she added, "That's down on the river." She lifted back the window curtain, pointing to the creek that wound right by their property. "We used to go crabbing all the time when I was little. Mason and I spent lots of time fishing, too."

Pulling her into his arms, he kissed the top of her head. "I want you to have that life again. A peaceful life, not one burdened by all this relentless darkness."

She leaned into him, and it was strange, but somehow she knew that Jax would find a way to give her that calmer life. Even if it was years from now, in some distant place in the afterlife. "I love you," she murmured, soaking in the warmth of his body, needing him more strongly than she ever had before now. "We're going to figure this stupid prophecy out."

"Yes, we will." He released her and guided her by the hand to the bed. "For right now, though, you rest." He pulled back the comforter on her bed. "I'll come lie beside you in a little bit, after I'm finished talking to your brothers."

She climbed into the bed, collapsing against the pillows, surprised at how wide-awake Jax still seemed. "Do you sleep? I mean, do you have to or need to?"

He settled beside her on the bed, rolling to face her. She'd not even taken time to undress; she was that weary.

He shrugged. "Not much. A few hours each night. Not like I did before I was transformed."

"Then come sleep with me," she said, rubbing her eyes again. They were so heavy, already drifting shut. "I want to feel your body against mine."

I want to know you're with me ... even if it's our very last time together, she thought, and released a prayer that somehow, by some inconceivable miracle, it would be the first of many nights when they would sleep together.

She was already being tugged below the surface of consciousness when she heard a rustling sound beside her. "What's this?" Ajax asked, and she cracked open her eyes to discover him flipping through one of her sketchbooks—one of her visionary ones, filled with the sketches of him and of demons and other winged creatures that flew the night.

"It's nothing." Feeling embarrassed, she tried to take the sketchbook from him, but he studied the drawings intently, scowling as he studied one page in particular. Glancing over his shoulder, she saw that it was of him—an image that she'd drawn several nights ago after they'd first met.

"This is me," he observed softly. "When did you sketch this?"

"We'd already met ... briefly."

"But the details of my wings," he said, gazing in amazement. "You even show my wings electrified, and you hadn't even—"

"Seen them do that yet, no," she agreed, finishing for him.

"Do you sketch this way often? Producing images that you can't possibly understand?"

He started to flip the page, and she shook her head.

"No, please don't. It's ... The things in this book are a little weird. There're some demons and other bizarre stuff."

With his eyes he begged her to continue, even though he held out the book. "I want to see," he told her softly. "I need to see how *you* see the world, Shay, so I can know you better."

Finally she nodded. "I'm just saying ... it's pretty dark, some of that stuff."

He grew quiet as page by page he studied the images. Some were of her first demons that she'd seen. Other pictures were of Bonaventure—she'd always sketched there, ever since childhood. Only now as she gazed at the book's images did she realize that these in particular had been filtered through a spiritual prism, her artist's eye serving as a sort of third eye.

"Shay," he told her finally as he returned the book to her grasp, "you have many gifts. It seems to me that this art of yours, this sketching, goes beyond just drawings. It's tied into your huntress calling, as you said. It relates in some way that hasn't fully blossomed yet."

She smiled, exhaustion pulling at her hard. "Yeah, I keep waiting for the moment when I'll get the Big Vision—the one that somehow matters in the scheme of good versus evil."

Jax bent to kiss her forehead. "It might be coming sooner than you think. For now, sleep, and I'll rest beside you in a little while."

Hours must have passed, Shay thought, jolting awake. The bedside alarm quietly glowed red in the darkness; it was already after three a.m. She'd slept longer than she intended. Sitting up in bed, she became instantly aware of a heavy weight beside her. Lying neatly on his back, one arm thrust across his forehead, Jax slept the rest of angels. She wondered how long he'd been beside her, and bent over him, studying his beautiful, dark face. Not a furrow in his brow, not a crease of concern around his eyes. Moonlight filtered through the nearby window, painting his features as if he were a Greek god; she could hardly breathe for the desire that stirred inside her.

Very gently she bent over him and brushed her lips over his.

In sleep there was a peace to his features that she never saw when he was awake, an almost innocent expression of release. The compact way that he held his body was undoubtedly a testimony to his many years of catching naps while at war. Although relaxed, he still seemed poised for battle, ready to leap to the ready at a moment's notice; no wonder he hadn't been cradling her while they slept.

She sank back down onto her pillow, letting her thoughts run free. She'd been dreaming something significant right before she woke up, and whatever it was niggled at her subconscious. The dreams had all been fitful, populated with demons and monsters . . . and Ajax himself. But there had been several set in Bonaventure, and she pried at her mind, trying to recall exact details.

That last dream finally began to come seeping back, rolling loose inside her mind's eye. She could see the battle, a key . . . a mausoleum. The image grew vivid and colorful; there was a wafting mist surrounding both her and Jax, Spanish moss right beside them, the live oaks. All at once the dream was no memory; it peeled away like gauzy tissue paper until she felt her feet at that spot, smelled the river, and heard the slight gurgling sounds coming off of it.

Guided by what she saw, she felt incredible conviction come over her. So many things —questions and mysteries that had plagued her for the past few years—suddenly came clear in her mind. Her fingers literally burned with what she had to do, and, feeling her way along the wall of her room, she located the items she would need. She couldn't see them because of the unfurling vision before her eyes, so she let her hands and years of living in this house guide her down the hall, all the way along the steps, until she arrived downstairs.

Settling at the kitchen table, she arranged her utensils with both hands. Then, taking a deep breath, she set quickly to work. There wouldn't be much time, not now—not with the duty she now realized she had always been meant to undertake.

Jamie came chokingly awake, shocked to find massive, bear-sized hands wrapped about his throat. He sputtered, gasping for air, as the giant Spartan literally shook him against his pillow.

Jamie cried out. "What the—"

Ajax released him with a growl. "Why didn't you tell Shay about her full calling?" the Spartan demanded. "About the role her artistic expression is meant to play?"

Jamie rubbed his aching throat. "What calling?" His voice was hoarse from being choked; plus he was still only half-awake. "You know she's a huntress."

"Don't pull that bullshit on me. It's bad enough that you've deceived your own sister about what and *who* she really is. The music, the singing, the art . . . all of it is part of how she's meant to fight demons."

Jamie fell back on the standard lie, hoping the Spartan didn't know what he seemed to have figured out. "I'm not sure what you mean."

"Oh, really?" The warrior's voice grew louder. "Then what in bloody hell's name is *this*?" He waved a sketch in Jamie's face with an angry gesture. His big hand had crumpled the paper's edge. "You tell me, and don't pretend you don't know."

Jamie squinted, and even in the darkness he could recognize Shay's detailed work. "Something Shay did, looks like." He coughed some more, rubbing his aching throat. After Jax had left Shay sleeping upstairs, they'd looked at more of the family books, chasing any lead they could find. Finally, no closer to finding any hard solutions, they'd all agreed to take a one-hour power nap, but as tired and muddled as he was, Jamie couldn't figure out what had the other man so upset. "Where'd you get it?" he asked in confusion.

Ajax murmured something at him in Greek, eyes

wide and furious—and fearful. Not something Jamie would have expected in the eyes of one of the most bad-ass breed of soldiers that had ever existed. An uneasy feeling crawled right up Jamie's back. Why would a warrior like Ajax be afraid—unless Shay was in some kind of danger?

Jax bellowed at him, "Yes, it's one of her drawings. A brand-new one that I found on your bloody kitchen table just now. So let me repeat: Why didn't you tell Shay about her special gift? She knows nothing about her other talents, does she?" Jax waved the drawing again, his enormous form looming over Jamie where he lay in his bed. "Nothing about the role her artistic abilities are meant to play?"

A roiling, sick sensation filled Jamie's stomach. It was happening. Shay's opening was going to be complete, her rare gifts fully manifested. Why hadn't they moved faster? Told her sooner? Now, with the stakes raised so high, she was fully open—becoming more so with every passing moment—and she hadn't been equipped for the fact at all.

"Let me see that." Jamie willed his heart back out of his throat, and tried his best to calmly reach for the paper.

Jax kept it in his grip. "It's a sketch of Bonaventure Cemetery. But, oh, trust me," he said in a seething, quiet voice, "there's far more to it than that."

"Go get Shay and we'll ask her about it." Jamie swung his legs off the bed.

"We can't, you bastard. She's gone. She sneaked out of here without any of us!" Jax flung the paper at him, and it floated into his grasp. "That, *friend*, is why I'm so bleeding upset."

"Gone where?" Mason asked from the door, his voice chillingly calm. "I heard the shouting and came to see what's up."

Jax spun to face Mason and jabbed him vehemently in the chest. "The two of you have been keeping quite the secrets, haven't you?" He marched out the door, then

turned back at the threshold. "Maybe you've been trying to protect her, but now she's exposed—even worse
than she was the other night. She's channeled a vision,
an image of herself in Bonaventure."

"So she's solved the prophecy," Jamie said, his mind
a whirlwind of thoughts. "But she's gone on her own."
He leaped off the bed, haunted by the image he'd just
glimpsed in the drawing. Yes, it was of Shay holding the
prophesied looking glass, but he hadn't missed the fact
that Shay was staring into it, captivated, with a look of
abject terror in her eyes. Not only that, but she truly was
all alone.

"Tell me everything you know about Shay's calling,"
Jax insisted, grabbing Jamie by the upper arm. "While
you get dressed. Let's hope for all our sakes that we're not
too late, especially given how the demons were drawn to
her the last time she went to Bonaventure. Imagine how
strongly she'll beckon them now," he added ominously.
"Now that her gifts are fully manifesting."

"You don't know that for a fact." Jamie slid into a discarded pair of jeans that lay on the chair by his bed.

"No," Jax told him, "but you do." He waited for Jamie
to give an answer of any kind, but Jamie let his own silence speak loudest of all.

"Just as I thought." Jax shook his head incredulously.
"She's in the worst possible danger that any hunter or
huntress might face. Because of you. So you'd best be
praying that my wife—and, yes, I intend to make her so
one day—lives past tonight."

Chapter 27

S able watched from the shadows, obscured from the mortal's view by the mausoleum that he hid behind. What he'd been watching unfold was almost too good to be true: Shayanna Angel, here in Bonaventure again, all on her own. With his gnarled hands he silently signaled his gathered team of demons. *Hold and wait,* he conveyed with the prearranged hand gesture.

Sable wanted to be sure that her four-a.m. appearance here on the battlefield wasn't some sort of Spartan trick. For one thing, in his long years of exile he'd developed a healthy respect for Ares and his warnings; for another, he'd learned long ago to beware of Spartans who came bearing gifts. And while this unexpected turn of events seemed quite the prize, he knew better than to take battle events at face value when dealing with potential Spartan trickery.

What a luscious treat the small woman was, he thought. With her long, flowing hair, that compact, yet curvaceous body. Sable licked his parched lips, sudden lust alive in his loins. To drink this one's soul dry might actually satisfy his endless, untamable thirst. Well, the relief would probably not last for very long, but no matter. The taste of a huntress in his gullet would be like nectar for at least a few days. And the pleasure of knowing he'd taken Jax's great love would sustain him even longer.

Holding deathly still, he kept his watch, amazed at how perfectly the plan had already played out. She moved from plot to plot, stepping around the critical target, almost having figured out the mystery. *Just a few more steps, mortal. Almost there.*

She hesitated, sighed heavily, and her thoughts sped into his mind, becoming clear. Listening to her inner voice, he became certain that indeed she knew that the key to the looking glass's location lay right near where she stood.

So close, so close, he whispered into her spirit.

Soon she would find it. Then their dark trap would close tight.

Jamie ran toward the pickup truck, Mason behind him. Jax focused inward, allowing his physical transformation to overtake him even faster than usual. As Jamie gunned the engine, his door still open, he stared at Ajax in surprise.

"You're gonna fly while we drive?"

"I don't have time for mortal means of transportation," Jax explained impatiently. "You meet me there. I can't leave her unprotected for the duration of the drive."

"Then how can I tell you what I know about that drawing?" Jamie waved him closer in exasperation, his gaze traveling the length of Ajax's form uneasily. It was evident that Shay's brothers still didn't totally trust him, Jax thought in annoyance—even though they were the ones who had placed her in this current predicament.

Ajax strode briskly to the truck, his wings pushing at the air in angry frustration. Jamie's eyes widened slightly at the display, but to the hunter's credit he focused only on Jax's eyes as soon as he stood by the truck. "Tell me what I need to know, but be fast." Jax braced his forearm on the door's top frame, peering in at the human.

"I know where that mausoleum is, the one in the drawing," Jamie blurted. "It's behind the plot where the statue used to stand. I can show you. Supposedly the family buried in that rear plot had pirates in their past."

Pirates. It all made perfect sense, Jax thought, remembering Ares' explanation about how the mirror had been lost in the first place.

Jax shook his head. "No need to guide me," he said. "I'll scent her as soon as I'm there."

"But ..." Jamie started to argue, albeit too late, because Jax was already midrun, heading away from the truck.

"Meet us there!" Jax shouted over his shoulder. "I need the fighting support—we both will!" Feeling for the transformed dagger at his belt, he breathed a prayer of gratitude that River had convinced Shay to bring him along. "River, I need you, old friend. Like I never have before. Shay needs you even more."

Behind him he heard the tires of Jamie's truck wheels sputter on sand and gravel.

I'll already be there before you have pulled out this long drive, brother, he thought. *You'd best be fast ... or surely this battle might already be demon-won.*

Then, beating his wings faster than at any other moment in his immortal life, he catapulted himself across time and space—straight toward Shay's side.

Shay stepped her way carefully through dew-dampened leaves and grass, staring up at the mausoleum she'd drawn in the picture. She'd known exactly where the place was located, recognizing it instantly upon completing the sketch. All those trips over the years to the graveyard with Mama had finally paid off. She'd also known in her spirit that she had to come alone—come now—without Ajax or her brothers. The *why* of everything ... well, she hadn't puzzled that through just yet, but she'd promised herself in the midst of the past days that from now on she would trust the strange gifts emerging inside of her. That sketch had been just one more bit of compelling evidence that she should.

And one part of her vision had been crystal clear: She was in the sketch alone, just her, and that meant this mission was hers alone to complete. Reaching for the mausoleum's door, she gave the handle a turn. It didn't open, and she jangled the lock in frustration. Mason had said something about a key when they'd been at the table poring over the prophecy. Shay sighed in frustration. Just one more roadblock, and she didn't need any additional ones right now.

The key has to be here somewhere close by, she thought, remembering the way the vision had filled her mind. She'd seen herself opening the door, which meant that either it wasn't really locked—as it appeared to be—or that the key was hidden around the mausoleum somewhere. Reaching on her tiptoes, she felt along the cobwebbed top of the low roof. It wasn't a large building, and to enter it she would have to duck her head.

"Looking for this?" a smooth, purring male voice asked. She stiffened, lowering onto the balls of her feet.

Feeling in her pocket, she didn't turn at all. She'd been sure she'd brought River's dagger-self in her pocket, but as she patted her side she was horrified to realize that she was unarmed. It must've been the effects of the trancelike state she'd been in after receiving her vision, but somehow she'd managed to leave her one sure protection behind.

She heard hooves crunching gravel just a few yards behind her. "Shayanna Angel," the demon drawled. "Your search is complete. I've got what you're seeking, here in my hand." She heard the rusty jangle of old keys.

Slowly she pivoted to face the demon. "Sable, I'm pretty sure I don't want any of whatever you're selling tonight."

"Tonight?" He laughed, rubbing one horn as if polishing it. "It's now morning, little huntress. Speaking of which—the meeting time was established for three hours from now."

Her heart slammed like a backbeat, her throat clenched tight. "I'm not here on official business. Not yet."

"And yet you come seeking the sacred object?" he asked, his voice velvet smooth.

"You're here, aren't you?"

"I always believe in a healthy headstart."

"So do I." She did a subtle search of her other pocket, wishing that she hadn't been so careless as to leave River behind. Hopefully Jax and her brothers would wake up very soon and realize that she was gone; maybe they already had.

But you saw yourself alone in that drawing. You're here now for some purpose that just doesn't make sense yet.

"The reason you are here alone"—Sable trotted closer—"is so that I have plenty of time to devour you. To steal you away from the greatest enemy I've ever had." Sable stomped the ground with first one hoof, then another, as if preparing to charge her. In the far distance a high-pitched series of cackling taunts rang through the trees. Even the Spanish moss about them swayed as if in reaction, a light wind suddenly filling the cemetery.

Shay's hair blew across her face, becoming tangled against her mouth. When she lifted a hand to dislodge it, Sable captured her by the arm, twisting it cruelly behind her back. "Where is he now?" the demon lord hissed. "Your beloved? I do not know the Spartan to leave any avenue unprotected. Are you bait, sweet Shayanna?"

She gave her head a slight shake. *He doesn't know,* she almost answered, but knew enough to bite back the words.

Sable rose to his full height, looming above her, and tossed back his head with delighted laughter. "He does not know! How perfect for all of us." With a magnanimous gesture he indicated the treetops and surrounding darkness. "Boys, the Spartan is unaware that his wench has trespassed here in our territory. Perfection."

"I came alone, unarmed," she attempted weakly. "You have to fight fair in exchange."

His clawed hand swept through her hair, tearing and ripping so hard that pained tears filled her eyes. "I don't have to do anything, my dear. Except taste my revenge . . . and make Ajax pay for what he stole from me."

"He took your wings." She folded arms over her chest, aiming for a tough-bitch persona. "Get over it."

A red gleam filled Sable's eyes, and at once the same shade hovered about him like an evil, smoky halo. He gave a snort, bending down toward her face; she took two retreating steps, her back pressing flat against the stone mausoleum.

One clawed finger stroked beneath her chin, slicing her flesh. She bit back a cry as the smell of her own blood filled her nostrils.

"If you'd ever been winged, my dear, you wouldn't treat my maiming in such a cavalier manner."

Trembling, feeling another and yet another claw scrape along her throat, Shay said, "Why didn't they grow back? Heal? That's what Jax's do."

The beady red eyes bored into hers, and she fought the urge to glance away. This was a battle for strength, a true show of wills between the huntress and the hunted. After a long moment Sable released a heated breath against her cheek and lifted to his full height.

"My demon wings were part of me, seeded into me by my demon father. Irreplaceable! Unlike your lover's raptor's feathers, those filthy vulture's appendages. Mine gleamed every color known to immortalkind, hues you've never even thought might exist. And *he*"— the centaur's voice became enraged—"took them from me."

"You tore his family away from him. You cost him everything that ever mattered to him. Of course he cut off your wings!"

Sable grabbed a handful of her hair and forced her head back harshly, exposing her bare neck. He bent his mouth to the flesh, sniffing and baring gleaming, sharp teeth.

"Cut my wings off? Is that the tale you heard?" he snarled, panting hot against her throat. She held her breath, waiting for him to sink those teeth into her flesh, to drain her dry, as Jax had said the demon would crave doing.

But he lifted himself taller, continuing: "Your lover— your brave warrior whom you think so honorable . . . he should have been so kind to me," he seethed. "No, nothing so simple as slicing my wings off, no quick justice for him. First, Ajax staked me through the right wing with his own sword, like this." He used his free hand to pin her shoulder against the cold crypt. "And then he used his brother Aristos's sword to pinion me through the other wing—like *this*!"

Harshly he held her, riveting her against the cool stone by both shoulders, forcing her back to arch at an unnatural angle. The only sound in her ears was the rushing of her own blood, which had begun to roar so loudly she could hear almost nothing else.

"You deserved . . . it," she managed to choke out. "For robbing him of his wife and sons. You . . . were wrong."

The demon's hold upon her tightened, the claws of his hands digging into her shoulders, cutting her. Again, she caught the metallic smell of her own blood as he sliced into her flesh, cut through her shirt.

"And next," he continued with a hot snort and an exhalation, "Ajax left me there, against the mountain, without another glance. The vultures came, circling me like carrion. My wings bled, then dried, the pain like being staked over and over through my beating heart. And on the fifth day—the last day, when I watched the vultures draw ever closer—*I* had to consume myself in my own demon fire. *I* had to burn my own cursed wings off! That's the reason I'm so horribly scarred, so hideous now—and the reason I'm no longer gloriously winged."

A powerful rush of wind blew Shay's hair, causing Sable to glance sideways in surprise. "Why don't you finish the tale? You might as well tell Shay the rest."

Sable hissed at Ajax, who had landed just a few yards to the left of the crypt. "She should know the beast that you truly are," the demon cried.

Jax walked closer, still talking. "All three of us know that this battle was initiated by you, Sable." Shay had the sense that he was intentionally distracting Sable as he edged closer. "You, on that ancient day so long ago. You can't fault a Spartan for merely fighting back."

Sable clutched Shay tighter in his grasp. "You killed more Persians at the great battle than any other warrior," Sable argued. "I was sold by my own god into Ares' hands because of the shame. You brought that shame upon my head!"

Jax stepped over the small gate, taking a position beside Sable and very close to Shay. All the while he kept his gaze fixed on the demon, moving with the subtle grace of a cat. "That didn't give you the right to steal my family."

The Djinn growled low, flashing his wicked teeth at Ajax, then turned slowly back to Shay. "After my wings were gone, Ares punished me further, my greatest humiliation of all. He made me into this"—he slapped his own withers in disgusted illustration—"and set me to the desert places, made me roam the earth. Jax's doing. And now," Sable announced with a whistle toward a pair of burly demons, "Jax's crime to pay for. Finally."

The demons appeared obediently at Shay's sides, their grotesque, leathery bodies covered in tangled hair. "Put her on sword point," Sable hissed, rotating his head so that his glowing red eyes locked with Jax's. "Don't let her make a move. If she so much as breathes, slice her to bits. Just make sure *he*"—Sable nodded toward Ajax with a snarl—"witnesses every stroke of your blades."

Shay could hear the demons breathing, the mocking sounds they made. It was more than the nasty pair who held her, their twin swords precariously close beneath both of her arms. The circling sounds of demons, their laughter uproarious, seemed to come from every direction, from some even more wretched realm than there types usually inhabited. Shay shivered, biting down on her lip. Ajax would save her; he had to have a plan—of course he did! He'd been fighting these things for more than two thousand years, and he'd bested Sable before. That was the only reassurance she could give herself as she felt the demons' harsh blades pierce her T-shirt, prick into her very human skin. *Ajax!* she cried inside. *You have to do something . . . for you and for me.*

Jax took a step toward her, and a swift motion of the demons' swords ripped her shirt to shreds. Oh, their point had been made all right. Shay's stomach spasmed with terror and she struggled to tamp down the roiling urge to be ill.

"No," Jax said firmly, spreading his wings wide behind him. He kept deathly still, his gaze never leaving Shay's, and told Sable firmly, "She's not part of the battle."

Sable trotted close to her again, his wretched stench enough to finish the job with her upset stomach. He bent his marred lips toward her forehead. "Ah, but Ares made her a player in this little gambit, and if for no other reason, that makes her fair game. Perhaps when my warriors are finished with you, Spartan, I'll keep her as a trophy." He flicked his tongue against her skin, licking her forehead, and she cried out. "Or take her as a mate. You'll be dead, so why should it matter, anyway? She'll be mine for the choosing . . . won't you, lovely one? Oh, the magic we might have together, you astride my back, the two of us riding the mists of Hades together."

She spit right in his face, but this only pleased the demon. "Oh, sweet Shayanna, I like it rough. But save all that for after I've finished Ajax."

If he'd wanted to terrify her, the images of him taking her as some sort of victory-prize lover was certainly doing the job. Shay's teeth were nearly chattering together, her body breaking out in a cold sweat despite the slight chill in the cemetery. And all the while, those demons' swords seemed to edge a little closer toward her exposed sides. Oh, yes, Sable's message was obvious— he was the one in control here. Not Ajax and certainly not her.

Just then she noticed that Ajax was making use of Sable's interest in her and one small step at a time was getting closer. The demons around her continued to cackle and gloat like a bunch of drunks in the pub past closing time. So drunk, it seemed, on the sheer pleasure of the fun, they weren't warning Sable about Ajax's approach. Then again, maybe it was all part of the game for them—the chance to see their own master fail.

Fair enough, she thought, and lifting her chin in the air, determined to help Ajax by further distracting Sable. "Let me go, or I will work my huntress's spell on you. Maybe you'd like to be frozen for thousands of years in your centaur's form," she threatened, trying to summon a last bit of courage. "You want to make me into a statue, pal? Yeah, well I'm betting you'd fit right in here in Bonaventure."

Sable bared his fangs in reaction and fondled her hair with unsettling gentleness. She wondered if he'd taken her threat as a come-on, if violence and aggression were actually some sort of aphrodisiac for the freak. "Sweet mortal's flesh," he murmured like a psychotic lover, "how I long to taste of thee." Then, before she could blink, a glowing dagger appeared in his grip. He pressed it against her throat, and for an infinitesimal moment she actually thought the dagger was River himself, somehow in the Djinn's grasp.

Sable hissed, casting a glance at Ajax. "Spartan, if you value her life," he ordered, "back up. And drop the dagger that you hold in your right hand. *Now!*"

Ajax held up both hands.

Sable motioned to her captors. "Keep her steady there with the swords." He trotted toward Ajax. "The dagger, too, Petrakos."

"I'm not bearing a dagger," Ajax lied, and Shay shuddered. How did Sable know that he had River in his possession?

"I sense your servant here. I smell his metallic aggression. I've been pierced by his blade and recognize his Spartan stench."

Shay pleaded with Ajax visually, their gazes locking. *Leave River out of this,* she wanted to say. *At least he might be saved.* Ajax suddenly rushed toward them, River extended in one hand, a long sword in the other. Everything happened preternaturally fast. One moment she was still in the demons' clutches, the next tucked safely behind Jax's widely spread wings.

"You won't have her," Ajax said in a seething tone. "She is mine."

But the momentary victory was lost as quickly as it came; all at once a host of demons surrounded them, swords drawn at Ajax's chest.

She stroked the long, sleek feathers of Jax's wing, transmitted all the love she felt for him—and stepped out from behind his protection. Jax whirled to stop her, but was a heartbeat too late; Sable's underlings already had her by both arms, moving her out of Jax's reach. They pointed matching swords at the center of her back, making it impossible for the Spartan to intervene. She heard him curse in frustration, Greek accusations hurtling at the demons like flaming daggers.

"Ajax stays out of this," she told the centaur. "I've seen what happens here, and it's just me who's gonna stare into that looking glass."

Sable smiled in reply, suddenly dangling the keys to the crypt temptingly in front of her eyes.

He gave a bow. "But of course."

Jax released a screeching war cry, sweeping toward them, but somehow Sable's minions leaped in between.

"Go open the mausoleum," the centaur ordered her, pointing the way. "Now, Shayanna."

With shaking hands she took the keys and went to do as he commanded.

The mirror, Shay discovered, was prominently displayed along the door to one of the crypts. Not ornate, not very special-looking at all, in fact; it was simply a piece of aged, slightly broken reflective glass. Prying it loose was shockingly easy, and she stood there in the dimness, watching little bits of moonlight glimmer off its ancient surface. *So much commotion over something that looks so insignificant,* she thought as she took it within her hands.

"Bring it out," Sable ordered through the open doorway. "Bring it to me now."

She heard Jax telling Sable that Ares' offer didn't begin for several more hours. She shivered when Sable replied, "I'm on my own time right now. I have a new set of plans."

"He'll send you back to the desert prison if you defy him—or worse," Jax argued as Shay emerged from the crypt's interior.

"But I'll have taken my own vengeance by then."

The swords were pointed against her back once again, and one of the sharp blades sliced into her skin, forcing her to cry out. With shaking hands she released the looking glass into Sable's waiting grasp.

He turned it in his hands, examining it. "How plain it is. How unadorned! Who'd have guessed it possesses such a grand importance?"

Shay eyed him warily, not yet sure exactly how the demon planned to use the mirror, not without Ares also here to guide him.

"It's not gonna work for you, not now." She looked him right in the red-hot center of his demon eyes. "Ares isn't here to help you."

"You think I've gone to so much trouble so I can use it?" He laughed, a sinister sound that echoed off the mausoleum walls. "I don't care about myself. It's *him* I'm interested in." Sable crooked a clawlike finger toward Jax, motioning him closer. "Step closer, Petrakos."

When Ajax didn't budge, several of Sable's minions wrestled him to a kneeling position before the centaur. Ajax met her gaze then, and his thoughts carried to her like a whisper on the wind—he was letting the demons overpower him. Because if he didn't, she would likely be killed. Even though he had the strength to battle them all, risking her life was not worth it for him. Not worth a thousand of his own deaths. She shook her head, trying to get through to him, to will him to fight their attackers.

With a terrible look of sadness, he stared away from her.

"You're going to look into this mirror, Spartan," Sable

threatened. "Right here, right now. You do it, or your love dies by my own sword. Yes, you will gaze into the surface of the looking glass."

What? If Jax did that he'd step into eternity, leave his immortal life behind! Shay stared at her kneeling lover, panicked. *You can't do it, not yet,* she wanted to cry, but forced herself to swallow the words. Still, what possible reason would Sable have for wanting to help Ajax cross over?

Jax settled his wings down his back, the motion sending several demons forward. One of them pressed hard on Jax's shoulders, pinning him to the ground. "Stay down," the stocky creature barked.

"No. I want him standing, actually. I want to see the expression in his eyes the moment my goal is reached." The demon forced Jax to his feet, although Shay was certain that no being could move the Spartan unless he wanted to be moved. Except for her . . . she was the only person who could compel him to act so obediently. *Don't do it!* She cried to him in her mind. If he somehow heard her through that powerful thread that joined them, or by his own immortal's gifts, he gave no indication.

"Get those claws off of me." Jax glowered at one of the demons, who took a rather timid step back.

"Ajax Petrakos, you will gaze into this glass at my command," Sable repeated, his voice low and harsh.

Jax laughed. "You want to free me from my eternal duties? You know that's the very thing I want. Why would you give that to me?"

"This glass is special. Very special, in fact, because it possesses yet another property, one that Ares didn't take the . . . well, the time to explain." Sable snickered, stroking the edge of the mirror's surface in a loving gesture. "You see, if any immortal gazes into the glass—any creature like you, Ajax—and he doesn't have the assistance of one of the gods themselves— someone like Ares, for instance—then that immortal will be extinguished the moment he glimpses his own reflection. Not sent to Elysium, but dead. Blotted out. Made into nothing." Sable grasped Jax's chin in a rough gesture, forcing him to look up. "Now do you see why I'd offer you this sweet passage?"

Ajax's breathing became heavier, and he jerked a glance in Shay's direction, but his captors took hold of him by both elbows.

Sable held the mirror out. "Bring him closer, lads," he ordered the demons that held Jax. "Force him to gaze into its surface."

"No! Wait!" Shay cried out, and was immediately punished, a sword blade piercing the skin along her side.

Jax beseeched her with his eyes. "Love, what's begun here must now be finished."

"Don't try to protect me!" She searched her lover's face, desperate to see any hint that he was bluffing, but saw nothing to indicate that.

Sable drew his sword tip across Shay's throat. "You'll obey me, Ajax, or she dies, too."

"What will you do to her when I'm gone?" Jax asked, his eyes shining and locked with Shay's. "She's innocent. Say you'll leave her unharmed."

"I make no promises, not for you." Sable tightened the sword against her throat. "But if you go easily, quietly, I think mercy can be shown."

"Jax, please. Please," she begged frantically. "Just look at me." He met her eyes, his face ashen with visible pain. Shay's shoulders began heaving uncontrollably with the force of her sobs. She'd found him—he'd found her—and to end like this? Surely he had to be bluffing somehow; it had to be part of a plan to free them both. But the look she saw in his eyes gave her no such reassurance.

She was the one in the drawing, the one looking into the mirror. That was what destiny had decreed. If she could only gaze down fast enough, before Ajax did, then whatever fate meant for them would be enacted. *Yes, that was it, was what had to happen here,* she thought, resolving it in her mind.

"I love you," she cried, her throat tight with tears. "I love you. Somehow we'll see each other again; I know it.

Somehow we'll be together." But if his soul were going to be extinguished, there would be no eternity together. She gasped with the force of her sobs, the tears blinding her to anything but the truth of what was being done to Ajax—the demons were literally murdering him, soul and spirit.

I must be the one to gaze into the mirror. It has to be me . . .

"I promise you," she vowed, her mind racing for any strategy. "We'll find each other."

"Yes, sweetest love." The tears in his eyes brightened. "The Highest will have mercy on us . . . somehow."

Jax took a breath, studying Shay one last time. Just then she caught a small flash of River in Ajax's grasp; apparently she was the only one who saw. Still, she knew what she'd seen in the prophetic drawing—knew what she herself had to do. She prayed that her action would buy him enough time to use River to free himself. "I'm ready," Ajax said finally, and slowly lowered his gaze to the mirror's surface.

At precisely the same moment that Shay did.

Jax removed River from where he had hidden him. He slid River's slicing dagger into Sable's side with a shout, averting his gaze from the mirror at the last possible moment, just as he'd planned to do. The centaur roared and bucked; the mirror crashed to the ground with a sharp clattering sound, but didn't break.

At the exact same moment there was another sound of falling, and Ajax whipped around to find Shay had dropped like deadweight to the earth. "What have you done to her?" he bellowed in alarm, grasping Shay as she crumpled lifelessly in his arms. "What did you do to Shay?"

Her eyes remained open, but they were empty of any spark of animation, and her body felt as if all the life had gone out of it; she was totally limp in his grasp.

Rubbing at his wounded side, Sable sneered down at him. "Didn't you lose this?" he taunted, holding River's dagger form high overhead. He had withdrawn it easily.

"Give that back to me," Ajax said coldly, still clutching Shay close. River had to turn now, had to transform. There'd be no other way out of Sable's greedy grasp if River didn't return to human form, and *now*.

Now, River Kassandros, now, Ajax urged in anguish, but nothing happened. Not both of them! Not Shay and River.

Sable slowly lowered the blade, turning it in his hand. "What a prize dagger this one is, made of Styx's finest silver. *River*," the demon whispered in an almost loving tone, drawing the hilt close to his twisted lips.

"Ah, the intricate carving of wings. Hawk's wings, they look to be." Sable met Jax's gaze with menacing delight, then pointed the dagger tip in Jax's direction. "For that, I'm afraid I'll be forced to punish this one."

"River!" Ajax shouted, straining against his captives' hands, but he couldn't break free, not without letting Shay's body fall to the ground. Even in death he would protect her to the end.

"Call to him again," Sable cautioned Jax, "and I'll use this blade to slice open your dead lover's body—from head to toe I'll gut her. You know I'll do it, too, so don't push me on this."

Nothing happened at all. It was obvious that River had maintained his weapon form for too long, just as Jax had feared would happen; he was trapped in the silver blade's prison, unable to transform.

Sable smiled cruelly and passed the blade to one of his leather-winged servants. "Go toss this vile blade in the river, please. Make sure it hits the deepest part, the very center of the river, where the tides will wash it out to the Atlantic Ocean."

His friend was gone. Shay was gone from his arms and his heart and life . . . forever.

"Shayanna!" Jax screamed his beloved's name over and over. Not both of them! Oh, gods, not Shay and River, not at the same time. He watched in horror as the demon took the precious dagger and hurled it far out into the flowing water.

"It's fitting that River should die at the bottom of the *river*, don't you think? He will drown, no doubt, if he attempts to change form. And that Shayanna Angel should die here"—Sable pointed at a graceful, half-broken statue of an angel right near them—"by a ruined, fallen angel. I must say, I orchestrate my dramas well."

"You bastard!" Ajax roared. "You robbed me of my wife, my sons . . . and now you've murdered Shay and my best friend. I will cut those horse's balls off and feed them to you—I will make you pay."

Lost to him . . . both lost forever. The despair in his soul was almost more than he could withstand.

Sable trotted closer and bent over Jax where he knelt, cradling Shay's lifeless body in his arms. Dimly aware that his face was wet with tears, Ajax screeched his most pained hawk's cry right in Sable's face.

Sable winced slightly at the sound, but pushed his face right up against Jax's, nose-to-nose, his sulfur breath and his manure scent nearly making Jax retch.

"There's one more property to this miraculous artifact." Sable pointed to the looking glass, his voice colder than ever, cruel. Calculating. "If any mortal glances into its surface, desiring to reach the other side, their soul is captured swiftly. Captured and held within the very mirror itself, caught between this world and Elysium."

Jax bent over her, hearing noises of deep anguish that he barely realized were coming from his own tortured soul. He clutched Shay's limp body, his shoulders heaving. It didn't matter what Sable said now; he'd known Shay was gone to him the moment he'd heard her collapse from gazing into the mirror's depths.

"How could you take her . . . her soul? Her spirit?"

"Payback," Sable taunted. "Totally fair."

There was no rage left in Jax for his oldest enemy, not this time. He buried his lips against the top of Shay's head, fully lost.

Dimly he heard Sable issue orders to his horde and knew his life would be taken next, but without Shay there was no life left for him anyway. Greedy, gnarled hands grabbed at her body, but he held her tight, not willing to have her pried from his grasp. A sword pierced his side, and demons wrestled to free her from his arms. At last there were just too many demons for him to resist, too many attacks by fists and knives.

Too grief-stricken to fight on, Jax let go of Shay's body and collapsed face-first upon the ground. The last sounds he heard were those of galloping hoofbeats and cackling demons.

Lifting his head up, Jax reached for the mirror, ready to extinguish his own life—but he discovered that Sable had taken it, along with Shay, as his final, eternal punishment.

Chapter 28

Sable felt the heavy bounce of Shay Angel's lifeless body upon his back as he galloped hard to the farthest side of the cemetery, then beyond the boundary of old Bonaventure and into the adjacent newer graveyard. His side deal with Ares would be complete now—he'd proved his worth once and for all. The god had charged him with destroying Ajax in whatever way he saw fit. Although it hadn't been the bargain Ares had publicly issued, it had been his true intention.

All that bullshit about a treasure race had been an elaborate smoke screen to obscure the true underlying fact: Ares was through with Ajax. Finished with him once and for all, the god had said. His centuries of disrespect had to be paid for, and Ares figured that robbing Jax of Shay Angel was as good a way as any to accomplish that.

Coming to a halt, Sable trotted a few more yards, holding Shay's limp body steady by pressing one hand behind his back. She was a light little thing, disgustingly lovely and pure. It was almost more than he'd dreamed of, having her body in his possession and the soulbinding mirror in his grasp. His vengeance and payback would soon be complete.

He could return the mirror to Ares—who had always known where it was safely hidden—and, if he were truly lucky, then perhaps a thousand years from now Sable would be given his magnificent wings once again. He licked his parched lips in anticipation. Tomorrow, today—time meant nothing to him anyway; all that mattered was being made glorious and beautiful once again. The dark realm's princes would honor him; the dominion's captive females would bow down as they had once done years before. He galloped a few yards in thrilled delight.

Yes, he had completed his mission successfully, and the small mortal on his back was little more than war booty. However Ares chose to dispose of Shay was the god's own business.

Reaching behind his torso, he took hold of her arm and tossed her onto the open grass beside the river. Her lifeless body gave a dull thud, almost as if she were a duffel bag, and the sound made him smile in glee. The sound of victory, he thought, sniffing the dank air of the marshes. Thrusting his chest out, he trotted toward the bank's edge and briefly wondered how far that pitiful Spartan dagger had already floated. Down below the water like that, the man would never regain his previous form.

Maybe he'd show up on some beach somewhere, but more likely not. He'd float like flotsam and jetsam, hither and yon beneath the waters, until he landed in a whale's belly—might even slice the innocent creature open. Perfect ending to the absurdly loyal helot, Sable figured.

Sable turned back to face Shayanna Angel, and was forced to squint as a shimmer of golden energy illuminated the dark swath of ground where she lay. In an eyeblink Ares materialized in the trailing light's wake, kneeling beside Shay's prone body.

The god studied her casually, lifting one of her hands and letting it drop back to her side. "I'll admit I'm surprised you pulled this one off," Ares said after a moment, then rose to his feet again.

Sable rose to his full height, meeting the god's stare eye-to-eye. "You promised freedom for good service, my lord. How could I disappoint?"

The god's mouth twisted into a perverse smile. "Nor shall I."

"I'll have my wings back?" Sable panted, unable to hide his fear that Ares might not keep his bargain, or that there would be a last-minute double cross. There had already been too much evidence that the glowing god was fully capable of that kind of treachery.

"In good time, my Djinn. In good time."

Sable nearly gasped. "But my lord . . ."

"I need to examine her first—and the mirror."

Ares knelt beside her again, brushing a long lock of black hair off of her eyes. "No wonder she ensorcelled him. She's a beautiful one, this Shayanna."

"And then we ensorcelled her in exchange," Sable agreed with a bitter, triumphant laugh. "Fitting, indeed."

Ares bent over, gazing into her eyes, which were staring ahead blankly—then, with alarm, he straightened like a rod. "Her eyes," the god murmured. "Have you seen her eyes?"

Sable hadn't been able to get a clear look at her face, not any of the times he'd encountered her, because it had either been too dark—or, as at the museum, she'd been too far away. He stepped close, lowering his fore legs so he could get a good glance. What he saw sent the very breath out of his lungs with a spasm of shock.

And hit him straight-on with a flashing, terrible jolt of terror.

"My lord . . ." He couldn't finish. Couldn't say it. Ares turned to him, his bronze face having gone slightly pale.

The god hadn't *known.* Sable was sure of it then and there. When Ares had set the plan in motion, he'd had no idea of Shay's true lineage. For once the capricious god was speechless.

"Shay belongs to Apollo. Look into her eyes. Their exact blue hue— it marks her as one of his own."

There were certain things you didn't dabble in, realms where you didn't trespass. Shay Angel's lifeless blue eyes guarded such borderlands. Unique, otherworldly eyes that only one line of humanity had ever possessed—or ever would. Apollo might not be as powerful as Zeus, but he took protecting those of Delphi very seriously, indeed.

"He won't let you do it," Sable said firmly, trembling despite himself. Of course, the Great One kneeling before him already knew that much. Sable wasn't sure it was a risk he was willing to take either, not even if it meant the restoration of his wings. Inwardly, he seethed, Persian expletives bursting in his brain like fireworks. He actually felt the pulsing blood at his temple begin to run white-hot. "The magnitude of what's involved here, my lord, the risk . . ." Sable allowed his words to trail off, pressing a hand to his exploding temple.

Ares shook his head, rising to his feet. "It's already done." He glanced about, angry frustration knitting his golden brow. "She's yours to dispose of; I can't risk staying here a moment longer."

"Apollo will learn about what you've done to Shayanna," Sable argued hotly, unwilling to take the fall if things came to that. "This wasn't my idea, remember."

Ares gave him a shove in the chest, forcing him to back up a few feet. "You dare to defy me, Djinn?" the god stormed. "Forget about the curse; it remains intact. You remain a centaur, and there will be no wings in this bargain for you. But if you go against me now, if you refuse to finish this job, be certain I'll find new methods for extracting my justice. Perhaps you'll pull my chariot for the next thousand years," he suggested.

Ares made a motion with his hand, and behind him his chariot appeared, drawn by four fire-breathing horses. They eyed Sable suspiciously, whinnying in agitation. Ares' further point had been made: Sable would serve the god or be *made* to serve him, perhaps pulling his chariot for the next thousand years.

"My lord, as ever, I serve you." Sable forced the words past his lips, bowing even lower. "I'll finish the job," he hissed between bared teeth.

Ares vanished completely as soon as Sable had made

the promise. But the god wasn't the only fickle one in their midst.

Sable knelt low, gathering Shay's still body into his arms. Brushing her hair back from her eyes, he gazed into them for just one moment more. They were trespassing in a dangerous war zone, a place no demon or lesser god ever dared step. A strong breeze filled the air about them, and Sable didn't even look. It would be Ajax, come for him. So be it.

Sable swallowed hard, preparing to fight Ajax to the final death. Still, he felt the need to make one thing clear, just in case the gods were listening. "If I'd known she was Apollo's own," he confessed to the Spartan standing behind him, "I wouldn't have." Deep inside he hoped that Apollo himself heard the words—if the god had yet become aware of his horrific transgression. But Apollo would know; he always did in such instances.

He was answered by a joyous, musical voice. "Of course you wouldn't have," the owner of the voice told him, falling to her small knees beside Shay. Then she looked up at him and smiled, a warm expression on her face. No being, human or immortal, ever glanced at him with kindness. He scowled back at her, unsettled, but she met his gaze without blinking.

"We have to move quickly to counteract the spell," the woman told him in a bright voice.

Why didn't she curse him? Despise him, as she should? Goodness and light could never coexist with the blackness of his soul.

"Who are you?" he barely managed to ask, noticing by the moonlight that she had sparkling blue stripes in her black hair.

She put a hand on her hip and gave him an impatient look. "You *know*. You know exactly what and who I am." Then she knelt beside Shay, touching her cheek fondly. "I'm the same as she is. We're both the reason you're terrified right now—for once. You should have wise fear more often, but you don't. Time and the Highest will reckon a cost from you for that."

Her words chilled him; he'd lived long enough to recognize a prophetess's announcement. *What would time and the Highest do?* he wondered with a flick of his tail. Suddenly a familiar voice came from behind him.

"Get out of my way, you damned Djinn," Ajax shouted, and between Sable's ribs a shocking pain sliced him. Glancing at his right side, he saw the shiny hilt of a Spartan's sword jutting out, and Sable went down hard, all four legs folding.

"Ajax," he groaned, knowing that he wasn't dead, not close—that he was merely felled for the moment. That didn't make the pain any less intense, he thought, working at the sword, too weak to extract it. "This was your . . . due."

But Ajax was already through with him, moving toward his lover. Sable collapsed face-first against the grass, his mind already muddling through a new revenge, something for later in the day, when his body regenerated.

The last words Sable heard from the despicable warrior were directed toward that Oracle. Jax said, "Whatever we need to do, please, Oracle, tell me."

Jax knelt at Shay's side, gathering her still body into his arms. "What can be done?" He swallowed hard, fighting the tears that threatened again.

His blessed Oracle bent over Shay, murmuring unknown words in her ear. "She's special, Ajax. You know that, don't you? And I don't just mean to you."

He closed his eyes, wanting to slay himself for not having protected her better. "So I've gathered." Then he added in Greek, "*Neh*, she is gifted and anointed by the Highest, I know."

"But she has no idea of her destiny?" the Oracle asked, glancing up at him. He shook his head and then she bent low, her lips pressed to Shay's ear.

He recognized the look on the Oracle's face because it was one he'd glimpsed countless times over the years—she was prophesying, and in this case her living words that always brought direction or power were literally bringing life. Just as Shay used words as a huntress, and the Spartans themselves used words as a weapon in their duty as protectors, the Oracle now wielded her own prophetic utterances to return Shay's soul to her body. To free her.

With a quick glance at Ajax, the Oracle nodded, letting him know that her utterances were having the intended impact; then she bent low again and whispered more of her prophetic, life-giving words in Shay's ear. It took time, and at first Jax almost despaired as he clutched Shay's body close in his lap. But then, right when his heart began to grow heavy, the mirror beside her started to glow white-hot with light. Something beamed from Olympus itself burst into light and filled the looking glass's surface.

In response, Shay began coughing as if she'd been saved from the ocean, as if she'd had life breathed back in her lungs. Sputtering, gasping, she struggled wide-eyed in his grasp.

"Shh," he told her, shaking as he pressed her close to his chest. "You're safe, sweet Shay. Safe."

Shay sagged against Ajax, more than a little confused. The last that she remembered they'd both been looking into that mirror—or she'd been pretending she wasn't going to, and then she'd done it. Now she was held close in Jax's arms, encircled by that fairy woman from the other day—the Oracle, as she'd learned in Cornwall.

"What happened?" she asked vaguely, trying to see where they were. The flowing river ebbed peacefully just beyond where Sable lay.

The small woman leaned forward and stroked a lock of Shay's hair out of her eyes. "Do you know who I am, little one?" Her voice was so gentle, like a summer breeze—it soothed Shay that deeply.

"Their Oracle," she answered obediently. "You guide the Spartans."

"I'm a daughter of Delphi." She announced, smiling down at Shay. "And I have a little bit of news. . . . You are, too."

"What?" Shay asked, wrinkling her brow. "What does that mean?"

"You're a direct descendent of Apollo's oracles, from Mount Olympus itself."

Shay glanced up at Jax, then touched his face when she saw the wet tears still gleaming there. "But ... I don't understand."

Jax drew her close against his breast. "I think your brothers have a lot to share with you."

"In simple terms," the Oracle said quietly, "you have a rare and special bloodline. And it makes us, you and me, cousins of a sort."

The woman bent closer to her ear, whispering in that quiet, magic voice of hers, and said, "It also means I can give you my name. I'm Daphne, but don't tell the others. It's special ... powerful. Plus, not knowing vexes Jax." Daphne giggled right in her ear.

"What?" Ajax stared at them both with a sulky expression.

Shay nestled close in his grasp. "It's girl stuff, dude. Don't worry about it."

He began to laugh, kissing her forehead, her eyes, every inch of her face he could find. "Why do I have the feeling I've just been ganged up on somehow?"

Daphne laughed brightly. "Because you have!" Then, with a little pirouette, she blurted quickly, "Must go! Have to leave! Good-bye!" She halted her spinning gyration and stepped very close to them. Gazing back and forth between the two of them, Daphne announced conspiratorially, "You never needed the looking glass to be together eternally."

"What?" Jax shouted. "What do you—"

Daphne cut him off with a little wave of her fingers. "You marry her, Ajax, and you seal the union with your immortal's kiss. The gift is passed to Shay at that moment."

"I don't get it," Shay said, her thoughts wild with hope. "I can live forever with Ajax? That's what you're saying?"

Daphne nodded slowly, her twinkling blue eyes fixed on Shay as she kneeled to the ground and took hold of the looking glass. "You have to receive his immortal essence at the moment of the wedding union. It will be in his kiss." Suddenly Daphne twirled again. "I like that song. . . ." And in a blur and wavering of the space where she stood, the petite Oracle vanished, the precious mirror along with her.

Shay watched in disbelief. "That was a little abrupt," she said, surprised that Daphne had left almost without warning.

Jax sat up on the grass, cradling her closer. "It's sort of her signature. She tends to do things in a rush and a flurry. Besides, that's not the most important thing. Did you just hear what she said about you becoming immortal?"

Shay beamed. "Yes and yes."

Jax cocked his head sideways. "Explain."

"Yes, I'll marry you and yes, I'll accept the immortality you can give me."

Jax whooped and cradled her close, covering her lips heatedly. His tongue plunged deep inside of her mouth, twirling and twining aggressively with hers. Everything with the warrior was a battle, of sorts—sometimes a playful one, sometimes a sexual one; it was just in his Spartan nature, ingrained there in ancient times.

At last they had to break the kiss, but not before she'd practically climbed up into his lap, her legs about him, and begged for it. He kept telling her that she needed to be careful and rest, that they would make love later, once she'd healed. Shay didn't like the idea of waiting at all. They rose to their feet, and, turning, both stared at the empty spot on the grass where Daphne had stood a moment earlier.

Then Shay remembered Sable and whipped her head in the direction where he lay. "Is he dead? Oh, please tell me he's so totally dead."

Jax eased her off his lap and rose, stalking toward the felled demon who lay on the bank in a large, heavy heap.

Black-red blood covered his dark coat; his human torso lay facedown in the grass. Even fallen as he was, his hands were twisted into balled fists, as if he might gasp a few breaths and lunge forth fighting without warning.

Jax kicked at his horse's side. "Unfortunately, love, this one's as immortal as I am. At least until I find the way to truly fell him once and for all. I would have taken more than his wings that day long ago if I could have."

Shay slowly rose to her feet, brushing off her hands and knees. "You're joking, right? We have him—right here, laid out for dead—and there's not a damned thing we can do to finish the job? Surely we can summon one of your swords and slice off his head. Wouldn't that do it?"

Jax shrugged. "If it makes you feel better, we can try. But he'll only sprout another. He's regenerating now, but the wound was deep, so he'll be out for a bit."

For a moment, she honestly thought about extracting that kind of payback from the unconscious demon. She knew Jax didn't think it would be right to torture him more right now—and she didn't think so either. He was their enemy, but dirty fighting was dirty fighting, and even if Sable would have done the same to them, they weren't going to stoop so low.

She turned from him. "You know what I want?" she murmured softly.

Jax wagged a finger as she stepped toward him. "*Ohi*, Shayanna, you must rest first."

She kept moving closer. "Oh, come on, I just survived a fight with one of your worst enemies. I should've earned a little hide-the-sword time with my big, strong"—she reached out and stroked his chest with her palm, feeling the muscles flex and react to her touch—"Spartan lover."

He roared in lusty reaction, swept her into his arms, and flew her out over the flowing river.

The morning light turned the world below them a glowing golden pink. Shay held Jax's left hand, letting herself fly freer than she ever had with him, her feet dangling behind her. He had a huge grin on his face, one that revealed his dimple and his adorable joy at having her flying at his side.

"I always wanted to share this with you," he shouted, lifting them higher as they passed over the marshes. "It was one of my greatest dreams while I waited for you to come to me!"

She squeezed his hand, then cried out when, for a moment, she feared she would drop out of his grip. He swept her up into his arms, cradling her close as he had the first night. "Sweetness," he promised, nuzzling her seductively, "if ever I drop you, I'll merely swoop and catch you close. Like this."

Suddenly she couldn't breathe. Her bruises and injuries from the battle left her mind, and all that she could focus on, breathe for, was the warrior holding her in his arms. She reached out a hand and stroked his cheek, the softly curling beard—he clearly hadn't shaved in days— feeling prickly and sexy beneath her hands. His defined cheekbones seemed even more graceful by the light of morning. His ponytail whipping lightly in the wind, his chest bare as it had been the first night, his wings gleaming with morning light . . . all of it made him seem epic. Beyond gorgeous.

"Please, Jax." She circled her arms about his neck. "Make love to me. Stroke me with your wings again, like the other day. Or not . . . maybe just your human body."

He growled in pleasure, black eyes fluttering closed. "I like that idea." He hitched one thigh upward, sliding her hip against his groin, and she could feel how hard he was for her. "Just my human body this time, just yours."

"Where?" She slid one hand around his lower back, stroking the hyperwarm flesh that melded with his wings at his spinal base. The feathers tickled and almost seemed to tremble themselves at her light touch. "It should be someplace romantic."

"You tell me," he said, covering her mouth with his. At once his wings beat harder, and she felt a bottomless sensation as he surged much higher on the winds. He was aroused and excited—his wings always gave him away, she thought, returning his full kiss with love. Oh, and how she loved this man who carried her on the breezes of heaven itself this morning.

They devoured each other, focused on nothing more than kisses and caresses, her hands slipping about his waist, cupping his leather-clad ass, he stealing strokes of her nipples. As she worked the muscles of his behind, squeezing and kneading them in first one hand, then the other, she felt the leather that wrapped his loins tighten in reaction. The front was obviously expanding, and that meant less room for his full hips.

"You'd better . . . find someplace . . . pick somewhere," he stammered. "Soon. Like bloody right now, love."

Opening her eyes, she was shocked to see that they were out over the ocean. "Uh, Jax?"

"Umm?" His own eyes were squeezed shut, a look of such abandon and pleasure on his face that she grew even wetter between her legs.

"Ajax, you've flown us out over the ocean. There isn't anywhere we can land."

His almond-shaped silver eyes flew open in shock, and with a downward glance he began to chuckle. "So I have."

"Go to the beach, Jax. We'll find a spot in the dunes."

He gulped hard, his Adam's apple bobbing, and glided a turn back toward land. Only at that moment did she realize it was that sketch she'd drawn of them flying together, the vision she'd seen the first night that she'd met him.

The last of the night faded overhead, but a full moon was still visible, even as the sun began to fully rise. Shay had led Jax to a private beach area, back into the dunes, where hopefully—although who really cared?—no beach-goers would spot them.

With a wink he'd transformed into a naked state, then hungrily stripped Shay out of her clothes. They lay to-

gether on the night-chilled sand, sea oats bobbing overhead. Jax levered himself atop her, wingless, looking
like a mere mortal of a man—and as exhilarating as his
hawk-self was when it came to lovemaking, somehow all
she wanted from him today was his human side.

His cock pushed heavily against her opening, swollen
and already releasing a little dampness. She lifted both
legs, wrapping them in an embrace about his hips, urging him inside of her. There was a slight push as his head
penetrated; then the rest of him slid into her as if it were
where he naturally belonged. She was so heated for him,
so slick and ready, that the joining was easy and sweet.

The sound of morning gulls filled the air; the roaring
give and pull of the waves matched their own bodies'
rolling motions. Into each other, apart, clasping at backs
and shoulders. Neither said a single word. It was silent
and hushed between them, a pure, heightened moment
of joining. Whereas they'd been so frenzied for each
other the first time, this time they were ... worshipful,
aware that even a word between them might break
something precious—or alert anyone walking on the
beach beyond the dunes.

Shay slid her hands along the back of Ajax's thighs,
feeling the soft, tickling hairs. She rubbed the muscles,
then very daringly slid her hands between them, reaching for his sac. He made a soft moan of pleasure when
she took hold of it, squeezing and stroking, and he burrowed his head against her shoulder as the intimate
touch began to make him tremble with need.

Ajax closed his eyes, riding the sensation of Shay's
touch. The sand was rough beneath his elbows, and he
had to be cautious with her. The last thing they needed
was to get too raucous together and wind up with sand
in places where nobody wanted it. Ever.

Still, the way her breasts lifted and pushed into his
chest, that soft, supple feel ... he had to get a better touch
of them. Carefully he levered his weight onto just one
elbow and reached sandy fingertips for her breast. Swirling those fingertips across her right nipple, he watched

it bead and pucker in reaction. The sand, he thought with a wicked grin, was quite a handy thing. Very gently he rubbed the grains against her sensitive nipple, and watched in masculine triumph as she leaned her head backward, a sweet cry of pleasure passing her lips.

Digging his toes into the sand, he began to increase their rocking momentum, and he hitched one of her legs even higher about his hips. Gods, how he loved the feel of those strong, feminine legs—so shapely and provocative—cinched about him like a belt. His eyes drifted shut, the warmth of the early sun stroking his back even as his lover—the woman who would be his wife soon, too—stroked him also.

The sun was a reminder, though, that soon they might be discovered, and so he rocked more feverishly, coming at her with a furious motion that she met thrust for thrust. Those small hips of hers, so delicate and feminine, rose up over and over, practically slapping against his. She was tough even as she was soft, he thought with a hungry, seizing kiss of her mouth. Still, he knew she was bruised and a little cut-up from her earlier fight with Sable, and he tried to be careful. But as he stilled a bit, she slapped him on the buttocks, urging him onward all over again. Who was he not to comply?

Her reaction was a grasping quake, one that seemed to tighten about his cock and wouldn't let go. She cried out, arching in the sand, lifting her legs even higher about his upper back and shoulders. That rearrangement of her limbs gave him the deepest possible access, sent him plumbing far up within her—and made her quaking intensify right with her cries. Finally she grew a bit still, stroking his slick back and sliding her legs off him. Her feet dug into the sand beside his, their toes touching briefly in a sweet little caress of their own.

Mine. She's all mine.

At that very thought he sped his motion all over again, felt the drive of a freight train fill his loins. She moved with him, a little more relaxed than he, but meeting every hip thrust that he gave with her own strong thrusts.

All at once he gave a spasm inside of her, his thick cock jerking until he felt warmth shoot out of him, coating her inside and truly claiming her. *My seed, spilled within her—within Shayanna, my one great love.*

Again and again it shot forth out of him until, in a sleepy, relaxed daze, he lay atop her and curled his head close against her cheek. Who needed the looking glass? he thought, his eyes fluttering shut. She was Elysium.

Leonidas sank back in his desk chair, his gaze wandering from the laptop screen before him to the walls of his study and back again. For hours he'd been like this— unable to focus on a single task, worried about his dearest friend's safety. And not just Ajax, but River as well. The voices that had begun speaking to him of late—the ones that accompanied his uncontrollable gifts of hearing and knowing things that perhaps he shouldn't—were shouting loudly this morning. So loudly, in fact, that a dull headache had begun to throb in the center of his forehead.

However, not even all those distractions had caused his thoughts and feelings for their Oracle to fade by an iota. In short, he was muddled and worried, altogether unlike his usual stoic self. But what he'd been seeing lately about their future, the signs and omens, the dreams, all of it, had him unsettled.

Shaking his head, he stared down at the real estate page he'd been trying to browse on the Internet. He had to believe that his sense about an upcoming move signaled Ajax and Shay's safety; he hoped River's, as well. Savannah. He was to relocate the entire camp to America, to the sleepy city in southeastern Georgia. Unbelievable what fate seemed to be speaking in his ear.

"Is there a picture of me on that screen?" the familiar, joyous voice asked from right beside him. Apparently fate wasn't the only thing whispering in his ear. His entire body stiffened in response to the woman who had appeared next to him. All of him reacted to the warmth of her against his back as she leaned over his shoulder and studied the screen.

"How did Ajax fare in his battle? And River? Tell me they are well," he said, folding both hands across his lap. He hoped, by the gods, that she wouldn't see just how excited she already had him. The joy in her voice had already answered his question—she wouldn't sound so bubbly, like the brook that traced the far edge of his property, if their comrades were still in danger.

"Yes, Sable has been defeated. The last I saw of him he lay on a riverbank, run through with Ajax's sword."

"He's dead?" Leonidas asked in surprise. Sable was a demon lord, and so far they hadn't learned a way to fully execute any of his unholy kind.

"Unfortunately not dead. But defeated in the plans he'd apparently made with Ares." She slipped a warm hand along the nape of his neck, giving it a tender caress that caused a shockwave throughout his entire body. Focus; he had to focus.

Leonidas coughed. "And what were those plans, precisely?"

"Ares knew where that bloody looking glass was all along. He'd hoped to capture Ajax with it, binding him with its power. But all that glitters is not always golden. That mirror has many powers, and I guarantee you Ares won't like how this particular battle turned out."

Leonidas stared up into the Oracle's eyes, and for a moment the facets in them reflected with almost magical radiance. They were beyond human—and beyond any earthly beauty he had ever encountered. "I'm not sure I understand you, Oracle."

She slid her hand down his arm, stroking it tenderly. "Take a look at this, Leo, and you'll understand." Stepping around him, she placed a swathed item on his desk. It was her own robe, glowing white around a large, flat object. "I've brought you a war prize, my dear king."

As she bent over his desk, straightening the object where it lay, her hip grazed his arm. Every part of him wanted to reach out and take hold of her, to pull her onto his lap without giving a damn just how much of him she would feel—or how aroused she made him by simply appearing in the same room.

Clearing his throat, he forced his hands to stay rooted in his lap. "What have you brought me?"

The Oracle turned toward him, sliding up to sit on the edge of his desk. She began to swing her legs lightly, her blue eyes bright with victory and . . . something else. An emotion that his heart could barely hope that she returned.

"I've brought you a few things, actually," she said, tilting up her chin coyly. "First, the Looking Glass of Eternity, the prize that Ares was supposedly after. Obnoxious god—as I said, he knew where it was all along. But I can tell you all about that later on. Right now, just know that I've brought it to you for the safest possible keeping. There is no man, immortal or otherwise, who I would trust with it more than you."

"I don't understand. What is it exactly?" He stared past her at the wrapped object; it was gilded in otherworldly light—perhaps from her robe, perhaps from the item's own power.

"Many have died for it . . . protecting it, seeking it. It contains the power to transport one to Elysium with a simple glance. Or to capture a mortal's soul and bind it eternally. For Ares' purposes, however, there is one sure reason that he won't be glad to have lost hold of it today." She met his gaze, absolutely serious for once, the usual flirtation and brightness narrowed to a laser point of intensity.

He nodded for her to continue, and drawing in a sharp breath, she reached out for his hand. Very cautiously he extended his right hand, a betraying tremor making him curse inwardly. Then, as their fingers wound together and the heat between them intensified by several degrees, she whispered, "It can rob Ares of his power, my lord. He must be stopped and now you—we . . . all of us—have the power to do so. All we need is the right plan."

He couldn't help smiling as she drew his hand to her

lips. "But today," she said, "I've not come to discuss matters of war, not with you, not now. With Ajax safe, and Shay at his side, we must celebrate now. We will strategize together, all of us, in the coming days."

Again his thoughts returned to the safety of his warriors and also of Shay Angel. "So they all survived the battle? River? Ajax? Shayanna?"

Something in the Oracle's gaze darkened, and Leonidas's heart lurched. "Tell me," he commanded, all softness gone from his tone.

"Ajax and Shay are fine. River is ... missing just now."

" 'Missing' how? In what way?"

"Sable tossed him, in dagger form, into the river. I wasn't there, not precisely, but I saw it nonetheless." She frowned, chewing on her lip, a disturbed expression on her face. Then she shook her head, as if clearing away some vision. "We will speak of it later. I will seek the Highest God for counsel on that matter ... but not right now."

The king inside him needed to know battle plans now—the man, however, had much lustier thoughts in mind.

"Then what have you come for?" he nearly growled, reaching for her with his free hand. Without asking any sort of permission, he slid her easily onto his lap. Instantly his cock leaped at the contact, at the fact that they were separated by only the thinnest membrane of fabric. "Oracle, tell me what you want." He growled the words, tired of the waiting and the long dance that their duties always imposed on them.

With a radiant smile she pressed her face close to his and whispered, "I've come to give you that kiss. A long, uninterrupted kiss, sweet king."

Stroking her thumb across his beard, she wrapped the other arm about his neck. He froze. Upon his lap was a woman of legendary beauty and power; what she was fully capable of, none of them knew. It wasn't like he hadn't already kissed her twice, yet he felt hesitant, as if kissing her now would be more assertive act, as if it would begin something real between the two of them. Truly, what right did a battle-hardened war hound like himself have even touching someone of her grace, her perfection?

"To Hades with that," he murmured to himself. He wanted this woman in a way that he'd never thought he would want any woman in his immortal life. And so, without another regret or second thought, he lowered his head and pulled her mouth to his. The kiss was long and slow, the heat in their bodies twining, the fever in their blood singing a low, ancient love song.

As she broke the kiss he knew she would vanish from his arms in the space of a few heartbeats, and he felt a fleeting but nearly desperate need to cry, *My lady, to truly love you, I must know your name.*

And she was gone in the very next breath.

"The letter was faked by Mama." Jamie placed the ancient document they'd spent so long guarding on Shay's bedside table. Although she'd gone rough-and-tumble with Ajax on the beach, she was exhausted and a bit beaten up. Rest was the order from all the men gathered in her room.

"But why would Mama do something like that to me?" Shay really couldn't believe her mother would have willingly hurt her so badly.

Jamie gave her a bittersweet smile. "You were her baby girl, Sissy. She would have done anything to protect you, would have moved the stars and moon—even if it meant hurting you a little bit, to her it was a necessary cost."

"But I wanted my destiny," Shay argued, for a moment imagining that it was her mother standing beside her bed, not Jamie. She argued and grew teary-eyed, as if that were the fact. "Mama, I wanted to be all that I am," she said, tears filling both her eyes.

Jamie stepped closer. "Sweetheart, think about it from her perspective—as a mother, one who loved you so damned much. When Daddy died and she didn't have him to go to for advice ... well, I think she wanted to protect you all the more."

"She should've told me." Shay shook her head. "I have a thousand questions for her, and now she's gone. I'll never get to ask them."

"I know, I feel the same way. Like, I keep thinking of all the things I never said. But try to remember this: She loved you very much, Shay. Somehow, along the way, she became convinced that if you just never *knew* the truth, then you wouldn't open, or at least not completely."

Mason stepped forward, leaning against the end of her four-poster bed. "Yeah, I always told her that was a piss-poor idea." Mace laughed wistfully. "But you know how Mama was. Once she had an idea in mind, you couldn't do much to sway her."

Now it was Jamie's turn to laugh, and he slugged his brother. "Nobody in this family's like that. Come on, man, who're you fooling?"

Shay looked up at them, and for the first time since entering the room Jamie could see the dark blotches beneath her eyes. Yes, there was peace in her expression— and genuine love as she turned briefly to smile at Ajax, who stood on the bed's other side—but there was also extreme exhaustion. What if the morning's earlier battle had gone much differently and they'd lost her?

Jamie coughed uncomfortably, feeling like a heel that he'd never given her the document before. She didn't seem bothered, smiling up at him as she reached for the rolled parchment he'd placed on her table, an ancestral tracing of every female throughout their bloodline who had passed Shay's special anointing on to her.

Shay sat up against the pillows Ajax had fluffed for her and glanced over at the Spartan uncertainly. "Did *you* know about what I am?"

Ajax shook his head. "Not until this morning." The warrior pushed off the wall he'd been propped against for the past several hours while Shay rested. Jamie had decided that not only was Ajax a first-rate demon hunter, but he was going to make a fine husband for his sister, too.

Jax continued, "When you drew the prophetic sketch, it all became clear to me: how you'd been able to see our Oracle, your sense that something more important was intended by your art, your ability to see the demons. The only people who can see our Oracle are other oracles—or their descendants . . . well, or me and Leonidas at this point. But for you as a mortal woman to see her? That meant you had to be descended from the Delphic oracles, and also meant you were one of Apollo's blessed ones. He never lets anyone touch one of his oracles, you know, not without severe retribution."

"So let me get this straight: I'm a huntress and a seer? By the combination of both sides of my bloodline because of Daddy's heritage as a hunter and because Mama was descended from the ancient oracles?"

"That's your question?" Jamie blurted. "I was hoping you'd aim for, 'So Apollo is real?'"

Ajax gave him a brotherly clap on the shoulder. "One day, brother, I will explain precisely what the gods of Olympus are—how they fit into the spiritual framework of the universe. There is much I can tell you, but not today. We focus on Shay and her questions right now."

"Yeah, James!" She gave him a mock scowl. "For once I get all the attention as a demon fighter; how 'bout them apples?"

"Fair enough, Sissy Cat. Fair enough." Jamie smiled despite himself. "So here's the truth. We never knew for sure if you'd see the demons like we do . . . well, until you did. And before you ask, yes, I had a pretty good notion that was going on, even before you told me. We all figured it was the oracle lineage that overrode the male-only inheritance on the Angel side of the family."

Shay sank into the pillow and began unfurling the scroll, her brow creasing with curiosity. Hell, yeah, she had to be curious—as many times as Jamie had studied the thing, it still boggled his mind. "That's a full lineage detailing of the female ancestors who passed your oracle heritage to you," he told her. "Dating all the way back to ancient Greece and the first of them who were ordained by—yes, I'm sure he is real—Apollo."

She peeked at the document, then let it snap back into a tight roll. "Later on that one. The sprawling ink makes me nauseous."

"There's this, too." It was now Mason's turn to step forward; he handed her a dusty bound volume that they'd been hiding in their father's files. The fragile book was literally the font of all they'd kept from her.

She cracked the spine, slowly opening to the first page. "And what's in here?"

Jamie couldn't look her in the eye, not with this revelation. "You were foretold to the family. Three hundred years ago."

"What?" Shay practically screeched, closing the book. "What's the deal, like the whole world was waiting for me to pop out of Mama's belly? Ajax with his prophecy . . . now you and this book."

Jamie settled on the edge of her bed and took her hand in his. "Sissy Cat, you're going to be a key warrior, a prophetic warrior in this spiritually dangerous time. They called you the Eye, because of what you see, what you draw . . . the way that you'll be trained to fight."

Shay sighed heavily, her eyes fluttering shut. "That's just way too much to think about right now."

Jamie scuffed his shoe against the Oriental rug on her floor. "Yeah, probably so. Probably so. But looks to me like you've got a pretty good guide—that big lug there by your bedside." Jamie and Jax exchanged a brotherly smile. They both loved Shay now; it wouldn't always be Jamie's job to watch over her so much. It was a strange thought, imagining letting her go into the other man's care. "But, you know, I think he'd stand down thousands of Persian Djinn to keep you safe."

His sister stared up at Jax, adoration in her eyes. "Are you kidding? From now on he'll have to shove me out of the way if a good battle is on. All I need is a handy weapon."

Then she and Jax grew much more serious, some shared sadness passing between them. Something that Jamie figured he'd learn about in the coming days.

"Yeah," he agreed. "A good weapon is key."

Shay let her eyes drift shut. "I'm going to sleep now. Sleep and dream that I find a precious dagger I'm going to be looking for."

Epilogue

"You've never been back? Not one single time?" Shay pressed him as they hiked up the rocky hillside. Down below, the Eurotas River wound its way through the valley, marking and feeding the land—and not looking so different from Jax's last time on this same hillside years before.

"I mean," she continued, "I know you told me that, but it's just so hard to believe. You love this place. I can feel your love for Sparta and Greece vibrating in my own veins."

He dropped down on the hillside, pulling her with him, and they practically tumbled together onto their backs. "It hurt too much," he said softly after a moment. "I'd lost everything here. But now . . . I can see it with new eyes because you're with me. It's alive to me again, and I want to share it with you."

"Now that we're here, any big plans for us?" she asked, rolling to face him.

"I think so." He grinned at her, thinking how this place that had once represented such heartbreak to him now spelled new life. Slipping fingers into his hip pocket, he retrieved the silver band that he'd wanted to give Shay here in Sparta.

With an irrepressible smile, he took hold of her hand. "If you'd call this 'big plans.' " Carefully he pressed the engraved band into the center of her palm. She stared down at it, mysterious blue eyes wide and wondrous. "It says only one simple thing in Greek," he explained, staring down at it along with her. " 'Eternity.' "

Still holding the ring tight, she flung both arms about his neck, squealing and starting to cry. "You know I'm yours for that long," she promised.

"Not until we seal our wedding vows—you remember what the Oracle told us."

The amazing prophetess had come to them during Shay's brief recovery, explaining more about Shay's destiny. How the mixed bloodline of her heritage gave her an even more heightened ability with prophetic words and images—particularly the visual manifestations. She had also offered to train Shayanna and help her learn the ways of her unique gift.

The Highest One has his hand on you, Shay, she'd said, joining her hand with Jax's. *His hand is on both of you.*

"We're going to walk through eternity together," Shay said, repeating the words from that day. "As soon as we seal our marriage with a binding kiss."

"You're sure?" he asked, a wave of uncertainty crashing over him. The doubts still came sometimes—that feeling that he wasn't worthy of such love, such pure acceptance. "It's a lot for me to ask, to expect you to endure . . . living an immortal life with me."

"I'll be sad about some things," she told him, becoming serious. "I can't imagine seeing my brothers grow old . . . knowing I'll be left without them."

"We think," he added. "Of course, with the way things are going . . ."

"I know. I know; anything can happen," she agreed with a sigh. Leaning onto her back, she stared up at the sky, sliding his ring onto her finger. "And I'm not going to doubt, not about you . . . or about my decision."

"I don't even know what to say," he admitted, curling beside her on the grass. Shoulder-to-shoulder they lay, staring at the clouds gliding past in the sky overhead. "I'm humbled."

"Wow, I really do have a rare and special ability if I can bring you to your knees."

He stared into her oracle's eyes. "I'm powerless when it comes to you."

She smiled, but then the expression faded. "My heart still breaks about River. I can't help but totally blame myself."

Jax glanced away, the instant pain he felt almost more than he could bear. "I know. I'm heartbroken, too, but I don't blame you. . . . River wanted in on our fight."

"Is there some way he could've survived? I mean, being tossed in the water like that, untransformed back to his human body?"

Jax shook his head; truly, he had no idea what fate his dear friend was currently suffering—or had suffered, perhaps. "I pray for his soul," he said softly. "I pray for my own, that I might be truly worthy of you."

Suddenly all the warmth between them seemed to slip away as one thought entered Shay's mind: Sable. Knowing her thoughts in the way he had already come to do, Ajax drew her even closer against him, protecting her.

"We have the looking glass now. It's safe with our Oracle, and that's at least one trick Sable can't try again."

"But he's not dead . . . and he's still carrying a serious vendetta against you. And me now, too, I guess, huh?"

A deep frown creased Ajax's brow. "I won't ever let him harm you again, sweetest love. Of that, you can be sure."

"But we've only won this battle."

"I have a fear," he said softly, looking past her at some unseen thought, "that our war with Ares has only just begun. But the time has come for it. He called the battle down and now the fire of it must rain. He may be a god, but there's just one of him and seven of us . . . and now you and your brothers and the Oracle, too, bless her divine soul."

"I'm praying for you, too, Ajax," she said softly, feeling her heart warm again. The thought that such great evil and forces of such magnitude still waited on the horizon should have frightened her, but in some odd way it only made her feel closer to the immortal warrior who held her in his arms.

"Like I said"—he grinned at her, that disarmingly handsome smile with the dimple—"I pray that I will one day be worthy of your pure love."

She leaned forward and planted a luscious, sweet kiss on his lips. "Ajax Petrakos, you're the best gift, the purest gift that God could ever have given me. Yeah, it's a little scary, but I know I've got a huge calling, same as you. Besides, just think." She giggled in his ear, her breath warm and tantalizing. "There are lots and lots of ways we can come up with for passing all that time."

He rolled her beneath his heavy body, careful to support his weight on both elbows. With one glance over his shoulder, he ensured that they were all alone in the warm meadow.

"How about I show you an ancient sex secret, my lady? The mysteries of the Greeks?" Licking her earlobe, he suckled it gently until she began to arch in pleasure.

"Sure," she half groaned. "I love sexual mysteries. What not-so-good girl doesn't?"

One by one he began popping open the buttons along the front of her blouse. "Why don't you try guessing what I'm thinking of."

"Umm . . . rubbing oil?" She glided open palms up underneath his soft cotton shirt. "Nah, that's not Spartan. I know—we're doing it on a bed of porcupine quills or something."

"You think you're being funny." He reached between them for the final button of her shirt and unfastened it. "I once spent most of a winter barefoot, fighting to survive, just so I could earn a ranking place in our military."

"In honor of that, you want to give me a foot massage?"

He slid her shirt off her shoulders, then deftly unsnapped her bra. Her gorgeous breasts swelled free right there in the sunshine, the nipples a rich, dark pink.

"No, sweetness," he promised, lowering his mouth to cover hers. "I want to show you the pure pleasure of making love outdoors, in the light of day . . . your back warmed by the sun, your body prickled by wildflowers. I want to show you, Shayanna, what it's going to be like spending eternity with me."

"Ooh, Spartan, I like the sound of that idea."

"*Neh, neh*, sweet lass of mine, so do I. So do I."

Before either of them could say more, he took decisive action and sealed their words with the deepest, most erotic kiss he could offer his almost-wife.

On a side street that almost no mortal frequented, an old café served drinks all afternoon. Only die-hard locals knew of the place, and that was undoubtedly the reason why her "host" had chosen the meeting spot.

"They're married now. Not a thing in the universe you can do to stop it." Daphne smiled broadly at the obnoxious god who sat across from her. "And she's immortal—again, totally out of your control."

Ares grumbled something that she couldn't quite make out and took another sip of his ouzo. "Nasty drink," he said through pursed lips. "I blame Dionysus for having discovered the concoction."

"Stop changing the subject. You overstepped this time, and you know it."

Ares stared haughtily back at her. "If I'd known her true heritage I wouldn't have touched her. That's why Apollo hasn't punished me yet."

"You know he has a soft spot for each of us who are oracles." She smiled slowly. "And that wouldn't be you."

Ares jerked forward in the chair, grabbing her hand harshly. "You may be one of his treasures, but don't think to threaten me, little Oracle."

She met him head-to-head, suddenly furious—and she rarely ever got mad at anyone. "If you so much as touch a hair on Shay's head ever again—or even so much as think about having anyone else harm her—I'll make it my personal mission to torture you for the rest of eternity." She stared at him, wanting him to see the fury in her Oracle's eyes. "Do you understand, *my lord*?" she practically spat.

"You dare to talk to me—a god—in this manner?" He began to rise to his feet, but she caught his arm, squeezing it roughly. Slowly he sank back into the seat.

"You're not within your rights in harming her at all. You have no legal ground for touching any daughter of Delphi, one of Apollo's very own. Not Shay, not me. Not any of us. If you try it again, you can be very sure I will go to Him and explain exactly what you've been up to."

"If not for our special relationship . . ." He let the words dangle with dark intent, then reached for an olive and popped it in his mouth. "Ah, to be back in Greece is such a glorious thing."

She felt the blood run hot to her cheeks. How could he toy with her so easily, pretend to be unmoved by her show of force?

"There is no relationship between us, special or otherwise."

Another olive in hand, he held it poised in the air between them. "Oh, now, now. How can you insult our family name that way?"

"I share no blood with you."

"Because yours isn't pure? Please, Oracle, talk more of that fancifulness. I have nothing else better to amuse me this afternoon."

She scooted back from the table and rose to her feet. With her diminutive size and Arcs' massive frame, she practically stared him in the eyes, even though he remained seated. "Not a hair on her head. Not any daughter will you touch. Never again."

Without waiting for an answer, she turned and walked down the side alley, hurrying to the church where Jax and Shay had sealed their vows only moments before. If she was in time, she could kiss them both; if not, she'd find them easily enough.

But somewhere in her mind, her Oracle's perception

heard Ares' smooth voice. The sound of it chilled her whole body, despite the brilliant afternoon sun in the sky.

She heard him laugh, too. She pushed the words out of her spirit, tried to tell herself they meant nothing, just more idle entertainment for a bored and malicious god.

But the words followed her, trailing her like a hungry demon. *But, my dear Daphne,* his voice had threatened, *you said nothing about not harming the Spartans.*

Read on for a special preview of the next
Gods of Midnight novel by Deidre Knight,

RED KISS

Coming from Signet Eclipse in June 2008

It had been a bumpy ride; that was the best River could say for the timeless languishing he'd done ever since the day he'd been tossed into the Wilmington River, cast there by their most vile and ancient enemy, Elblas Djiannas. He was the Persian Djinn who possessed one of the darkest souls ever encountered by River and his fellow Spartan immortals. This recent maneuver was just one of countless dark deeds, typical of his demonic handiwork.

At the time of the battle, River had been in dagger form, serving his Spartan master, Ajax Petrakos. They had a unique fighting relationship: River was capable of shape-shifting into a weapon in Ajax's hand, and a strange symbiosis existed between the two fighters. For that particular battle in Savannah's Bonaventure Cemetery, River had been transformed for too long—returning to human form had already proven impossible, even without any additional challenges.

For that demon centaur, it had been nothing to fling River into the fast-flowing waters near where they fought that day. Just one less immortal soldier with which the entity had to deal. And Elblas had undoubtedly guessed the truth, too, which was that River was incapable of shape-shifting once submerged, at least not without drowning in the process. Worse than that, the longer he remained unreturned to human form, the more impossible a reversal would become.

Since that day, eternity had become even more burdensome for the immortal warrior. He remained shackled inside the same thin wedge of a dagger, a silver blade engraved with the intricate, masculine wings that he sometimes bore upon his back. Hawk's wings, the glorious other half of his immortal nature, which afforded him flight and the independence his soul craved. Or at least they had. Now he could only yearn for such past freedoms, beg for his silver-black wings to once again grace his human form, his bare shoulders and strong back.

It was difficult to say precisely how long River had been bound in his prison, this dagger form he'd chosen to assume. The gift of being a shape-shifting warrior—the ability to assume whatever weapon the battle required— was both his blessing and his curse, granted to him by the war god, Ares himself, more than two thousand years earlier. Time became murky enough when you lived forever, but when you were trapped in inanimate form, the minutes bled together, a slow build toward insanity. Especially if you were locked in the form of an object whose main purpose was violence.

He was growing mad with his cravings for terror and bloodshed, just like the dagger he'd become. His darkest nature had become relentless, demanding an outlet—any release whatsoever—while day after day no reprieve could be found.

If he ever did manage to find freedom again—and how that would occur, he no longer knew—one fact was certain: There would be blood spilled. Probably the blood of an unsuspecting innocent, given his current descent into near-insanity. If only he could keep the sex-lust out of the event this time, maybe then, somehow, it wouldn't be as horrific as his imagination had begun to promise.

Inside his prison, River's very soul shook with need; how was it going to be possible for whoever happened to free him, that poor human innocent, to escape the punishment of his darkest nature? Perhaps he was no better than Elblas after all, he decided with yet another failed attempt to tamp down his bloodlust, which was a losing proposition.

And as if his own true nature weren't enough, lately others had begun whispering in his ear. All of them males, others who were trapped in voids of their own, that in-between place that the restless dead sometimes occupied, a realm between Hades and Earth. One voice in particular, the one with the American accent, stayed persistent and demanding, for some reason eager that River break free of his captivity. These others seemed perfectly content for him to stagnate in the void right along with them, but not American, as he'd started calling the nameless, faceless man. It seemed that was what the poor fellow wanted to be called, although his distant voice was so difficult to hear, River couldn't be certain.

The ghostly male constantly pressed River toward escape, whipping his trapped soul into a frenzy even as he apologized for doing so, explaining that he was depending upon River. For what, he never said, although clearly there was something American wanted from him. Still, the man did one hell of a job when it came to inciting a riot inside River's mind and spirit. Even now, he felt the burning escalation begin all over again.

With a mental curse, he shook off this latest swarm of impulses and tried to understand where he'd found himself. For weeks nothing had changed, not after he'd been passed from human hand to human hand. After that there had only been darkness and quiet.

He surveyed the clues about him at the present moment. He could taste the steel of his own blade, felt it brushing against something soft like velvet, sensed the careful folds of paper about his weapon-body, too. Whoever had sealed him away had treated him kindly—much *too* kindly for a bloodletting, sex-driven warrior like himself. He just hoped such gentleness wasn't present when, gods willing, he burst free at last.

That was the very best for which he could hope. The worst? The worst was beyond imagining, a horrific mingling of murder and sex that he refused to contemplate.

Still, he felt that burn grow in his steely core, day after numberless day, his sinister urges growing less controllable the longer he remained trapped.

Someone, he begged within his soul, *please, someone find a way to free me. But if you value your life, your innocent body, don't stick around once the deed is done.*

JESSICA ANDERSEN

NIGHTKEEPERS:
A NOVEL OF
THE FINAL PROPHECY

*First in the brand new series that
combines Mayan astronomy and lore with
modern, sexy characters for a
gripping read.*

In the first century A.D., Mayan astronomers predicted
the world would end on December 21, 2012. In these
final years before the End Times, demon creatures of
the Mayan underworld—The Makols—have come to
earth to trigger the apocalypse. But the descendants of
the Mayan warrior-priests have decided to fight back.

**"Raw passion, dark romance, and seat-of-
your-pants suspense, all set in an
astounding paranormal world."**
—J.R. Ward, #1 *New York Times* bestselling author

**Available wherever books are sold or at
penguin.com**